THE CORNELIUS
BOOK

Michael Moorcock was editor of *New Worlds* from 1964 until 1971, and again in 1978. Born in London in 1939, he was contributing to and editing juvenile magazines such as *Tarzan Adventures* while still in his teens. As a writer of science fiction and fantasy he has achieved an international reputation: *Behold the Man*, the Cornelius Chronicles (*The Final Programme*, *A Cure for Cancer*, *The English Assassin* and *The Condition of Muzak*) and the novels in the Elric, Dancers at the End of Time, Hawkmoon and Corum series are classics of their kind. In recent years he has moved steadily away from this field and is now recognized as a major contemporary novelist, through such novels as *Gloriana*, *The Brothel in Rosenstrasse*, and *Byzantium Endures* and *The Laughter of Carthage*, the first two volumes of a long and ambitious work entitled *Between the Wars*. His most recent novel is *Mother London*.

'A myth-maker, an epic fantasist'
The Times

Michael Moorcock

THE CORNELIUS CHRONICLES
BOOK TWO

The English Assassin

The Condition of Muzak

FONTANA/Collins

The English Assassin first published in Great Britain by
Allison and Busby Ltd 1972
Revised edition first published by Fontana Paperbacks 1979

The Condition of Muzak first published in Great Britain by
Allison and Busby Ltd 1978
First issued in Fontana 1978

This edition first published in Great Britain by
Fontana Paperbacks 1988

Printed and bound in Great Britain by
William Collins Sons & Co. Ltd, Glasgow

THE ENGLISH
ASSASSIN

A Romance of Entropy

For Arthur and Max Moorcock

DEDICATED to the memories of Peregrine Worsthorne, Malcolm Muggeridge, Dennis Hopper, Shirley Temple, George Steiner, Angus Maude, Robert Conquest, Bernard Braden, Spiro Agnew, Christiaan Barnard, Norman St John Stevas, Colin Wilson, Lord Longford, Rap Brown, John Wayne, Jerry Rubin, Chris Booker, Robert Heinlein, Sam Peckinpah, Miroslav Moc, Kingsley Amis, Sir Arthur Bryant, Richard Neville and all men of good will and Jolly Englishmen everywhere.

The English Assassin is the third novel in a tetralogy about Jerry Cornelius and his times. It has been slightly revised for this Fontana edition. The two previous books are *The Final Programme* and *A Cure for Cancer*. The last book is called *The Condition of Muzak*.

Many of the newspaper quotations used here might cause further distress to parents and relatives of the deceased if they read them. Therefore I have in some cases changed the names. No other part of the quotation has been altered.

CONTENTS

SHOT THREE

SHOT FOUR

PROLOGUE (*Commencement*)

As a child I lived in that well-kept back garden of London, the county of Surrey. In this century, at least, Surrey achieved vitality only once. That was during the World War when the incendiaries fell, and the Messerschmidts blew up, and the V-bombs dropped suddenly from the silent sky. Night flames, droning planes, banging ack-ack, shrapnel and bombed buildings are the happiest impressions from my childhood. I long to find them again. The pylon, the hoarding, the ruined street and the factory are images which to this day most satisfy and pacify my psyche. I was very happy then, while the world fought its war and my own parents quarrelled, suppressed quarrels and finally parted. The War was won, the Family lost, and I remained, as far as I knew, content. But now, with great effort, I recall the nightmares, rages, weeping fits and traumas, the schools which came and went, and I know that, after the war, I was only happy when alone and then chiefly when I was able to create a complicated fantasy or, in a book, enter someone else's. I was happy but, I suppose, I was not healthy. Few of my illnesses were not psychosomatic and I became fat. Poor child.

. . . I suspect that many people experience this nostalgia and would dearly love to recreate the horrifying circumstances of their own childhood. But this is not possible. At best they produce reasonable alternatives.

MAURICE LESCOQ, *Leavetaking* 1961

Addict was Dead with Syringe in His Arm

A young North Kensington addict who had made an attempt to give up drugs was killed by his addiction, the Westminster Coroner decided last week. Anthony William Leroy (sometimes known as Anthony Gray) died at St Charles Hospital in the early hours of August 29, after taking two shots of heroin in his arm when he was found, the coroner was told. Leroy was a boutique manager ... Professor Donald Teare, pathologist, said that there were two recent injection marks on Leroy's right arm. Cause of death was inhalation of vomit due to drug addiction.

Kensington Post, September 26 1969

A Bundle

South of Bude and its neighbour, Widemouth Bay, you come to the quaint little harbour of Boscastle, with its grey stone, slate roofed cottages and background of sheltering hills, and thence to Tintagel, home of the legendary King Arthur and the famous cliff-top ruins of his mediaeval castle. Although other counties in the West may dispute Cornwall's claim to be the sole possessor of the original authentic stronghold of the Knights of the Round Table, Cornishmen stick as closely to their time-honoured contention as the limpets to the rocky, sea-washed walls of Merlin's mysterious cave at the foot of the great granite cliff. It is the blood split by the magic sword Excalibur, they insist, that keeps a small lawn of turf within the precincts of the castle forever emerald green, as if constantly fed by spring water where none exists. And what else, they ask, was Camelot if it were not the old name for Camelford, the little inland town on the River Camel not half a day's horse-trot away? . . .

Cornwall: A Tourist's Guide

Some time ago, possibly in the winter of 1975, the following events took place at Tintagel Bay on the north coast of Cornwall:

Tintagel's bay is small and walled by high, bleak cliffs, a natural subject for romantic painters and poets of the past two centuries. Most of the castle ruins stand on the inland cliff, but some are on the west cliff, which is a narrow promontory now crumbling dramatically into the sea and carrying the ruins with it.

Though, in the summer, Tintagel is a great tourist attraction, at other seasons it is virtually deserted, save for a few local inhabitants who remain in the village some

16

distance inland. One dull December morning two of these residents, a butcher and a retired chemist, who had been born and brought up in the area, were taking their regular stroll along the cliffs when they paused, as usual, among the ruins and rested on a wooden bench provided for people like themselves who wished to enjoy the view of the bay in comfort.

The view on this particular day was not really up to much. The water in the bay was flat, sluggish and black. On its surface drifted grey scum and dark green weed. The sea resembled a worn-out blackboard upon which an inspired idiot had scrawled equations and then tried to erase them. The sky was clammy and the air was thick with too much brine. From the small patch of shingle on the beach below there came a strong and unpleasant odour of rotting sea-weed. It was as if the whole place – castle, cliffs, sea and beach – were in a process of sudden decay. The butcher and the chemist were both old men, bearded and grey, but the butcher was tall and straight, while the chemist was small and bent. The wind tugged at their beards and hair as they huddled on the bench and massaged their legs and hands. Their skins were cracked, wrinkled, weather-beaten and, in colour and condition, very little different from the leather jerkins they wore to protect themselves against the weather. They chatted for about ten minutes and were ready to continue their walk when the tall butcher narrowed his eyes and pointed at the gap between the cliffs where the sea entered the bay.

'What d'you make of that, then?' he asked. He had one of those unfortunate voices which is naturally aggressive in tone and liable to misinterpretation by those who did not know him well.

The chemist frowned. He reached into his jerkin and found his spectacle case. He put the spectacles on and peered out over the water. A large, shapeless object floated in the bay. It was drifting with the tide towards the shore. It might have been the remains of a shark, covered in

17

rotting algae; a tangle of dead eels, or just a mass of seaweed.

'It could be anything, really,' said the chemist mildly.

They watched as the bundle drifted closer. It came to rest on the shingle below. It was vaguely cylindrical in shape but just a little too small to be any kind of wrecked boat. The weed which wrapped it seemed to have decayed.

'Bloody unsanitary looking, whatever it is,' said the chemist. 'The council should do something about this beach.'

But the beach itself was unwilling to accept the bundle. The next wave that came in was forced to withdraw it. The bundle bobbed about twenty yards offshore: the sea wished to be rid of it, could think of nowhere else to deposit it, but refused to swallow it.

The chemist, a morbid man by nature, suggested that the object might be a corpse. It was the right size.

'What? You mean a drowned man?' The butcher smiled.

The chemist understood that his suggestion had been too sensational. 'Or a seal, I thought,' he said. 'You don't know, do you? I've seen nothing like it before. Have you?'

The tall butcher hadn't any inclination to follow this line of thought. He got up: he rubbed his beard. 'Well, she'll probably be gone by tomorrow. It's getting a bit nippy. Shall we – ?'

The chemist took one last, frowning look at the bundle before he nodded agreement. They walked slowly inland, towards the almost deserted village.

After they had vanished, the tide began to turn. It hissed. It whispered. It sighed. As it receded, a lip of a cave was revealed in the west headland, a black gap flaked with foam. The sea pushed the bundle towards the cave; it forced the thing into the mouth which gurgled reluctantly, but swallowed. The tide fled, leaving behind it the weed-smothered beach, the salty stink, the foam-flecked entrance to the cave. The wind blew stronger, whining and moaning about the castle ruins like a dog at its master's grave, pawing a tuft of coarse grass here, sniffing a clump of shrubs there. And then the wind went away, too.

By now completely exposed to the air, the gloomy cavern contained a comprehensive collection of debris: rusty cans, pieces of drowned wood, glass shards worn smooth by the action of the ocean, plastic bottles, the torso of a child's doll, and the twisted corpses of about twenty deformed, oversized crabs; the creations of an effluent only recently introduced to this coast. On a shelf of rock about half-way up the slimy far wall, well out of the faint light from the entrance, lay the bundle where the sea had lodged it.

A gull flew in from the grey outside and perched on the bundle before fluttering down to peck at the soft shells and the hard flesh of the mutant crabs.

When the texture of the day had grown a little less disgusting, a cumbersome skiff, powered by an outboard motor imperfectly mounted in the stern so that its screw often lifted completely clear of the water and caused it to progress in a series of spluttering jolts, rounded Tintagel Head and made for the small patch of shingle leading up to the cave. There was only one person in the skiff. She wore yellow PVC oil-skins, a yellow sou'wester and white plastic trousers tucked into red rubber seaboots. The sou'wester shaded her face. The tiller was tucked firmly under one arm as she directed the skiff at the beach. The engine coughed, screeched and spat. The bottom of the skiff rasped on the pebbles and the motor cut out. Awkwardly, the girl clambered from the stationary boat and pulled it completely clear of the sea; she sniffed the wind, then she reached over the side to remove a big blue Eveready flashlight, an old-fashioned gasmask and a coil of white nylon rope. She sniffed again, by way of confirmation, and seemed satisfied. She looped the rope over her shoulder and trudged in the direction of the cave. When she reached the entrance she hesitated, switching on her electric torch before going in. Her clean, protective clothing gleamed in the reflected glare. Her booted feet crunched on the corpses of the crabs; a beam of light illuminated the awful walls, disturbed the carrion gulls. They squawked and flapped nervously past her head to the open air. She directed the beam over all the filthy flotsam before focusing on the shelf of rock from which came a smell partly of brine and partly like cat's urine. She put the torch in her pocket and used both hands to ease the gasmask under her sou'wester and over her hair and face. Her breathing became a loud, rhythmic hiss. Adjusting the rope on her shoulder she again took out the flashlight and looked the bundle over. The thing was predominantly black and green and had resumed its earlier, roughly cylindrical, shape. There were small grey rocks imbedded in it, some yellow grit, a few supine starfish, seahorses and shrimps, a fair number of mussels and limpets and pieces of what looked like tropical coral. The black and green areas were unidentifiable; they were possibly organic; they might have been made of mud which had started to solidify. It was as if the bundle had been rolled along the bottoms of the deepest oceans, gathering to it a detritus which was completely alien to the surface.

The girl bent down and wedged the flashlight between two large stones so that the beam stayed on the shelf. Then she crossed to the wall and began to climb skilfully and rapidly until she stood with her legs spread wide, balancing carefully on the ledge beside the bundle while she pulled on a pair of rubber gloves. Steadying herself with her left hand against an outcrop of granite, she bent and felt over the bundle with her right hand. At last she found what she was looking for and withdrew it with a squelch from a tangle of weed.

It was a transparent polythene bag dripping with green algae. She wiped the plastic against her thigh until it was as clean as she could get it, then she held it in the torch's beam so that she could see the contents. There was a single sheet of white paper inside, covered with doodles in black ink:

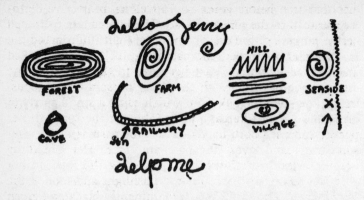

She was satisfied. She stuffed the message into an inside pocket and unslung the rope from her shoulder, winding it round and round the slippery bundle until it was thoroughly tied up. With considerable difficulty she managed to brace her back against the wall and with her booted feet shove the bundle to the edge of the shelf. Taking a coil or two of rope around her right arm she was able to lower the bundle to the cavern floor. Then she let the end of the rope drop and climbed down after it. She rested for a moment, retrieved her torch, switched it off and put it away. Working in the faint light from the entrance, she picked up the rope and wound it twice on each hand. She turned so that the rope was now braced on her shoulder. She strained forward, hauling the bundle after her. Broken corpses of crabs scattered in its path as the girl slowly pulled it from the cave and dragged it bumping down the beach to the waiting skiff. Panting painfully into her gasmask she heaved with the last of her strength and got the thing into the boat, putting her whole weight against the bow so that the skiff slid back into the sea. Standing knee-deep in the seedy water she pulled the painter until the bow was pointing away from the beach, then she carefully got in and resumed her place at the tiller, lowering the screw into the sea and tugging at the motor's cord.

After a number of false starts she brought the outboard to

life and the screw began to turn. The boat moved into deeper water, going back the way it had come. It still made jerky progress, so that at times the girl in the yellow sou'wester, gasmask and oilskins was lifted completely from her seat. At last she disappeared round Tintagel Head, bouncing out to sea.

As if commissioned to wash away from the bay all traces of these events, the sky let loose its rain.

Major Nye

'Another age will see all this in quite a different perspective.'

It was not certain what he meant as he stared about him at the little white laboratory, at the Formica-topped benches, the racks of test-tubes, the specimen jars and the aquarium which occupied one whole wall.

'So you say, general.' The young Japanese marine biologist sounded sceptical as he held a bottle of sea-water up to the light from the plate glass window which offered a view of the Atlantic.

'M . . .' Major Nye put his hands in the pockets of his threadbare blazer and drew out a crushed wooden matchbox. He held it with the tips of his fingers, in both hands, as if afraid to damage it further. Part of the tray was still inside the box, but all the matches were gone. The label was predominantly blue, white and brown and the picture showed three dark skinned men in blue loincloths and red caps trying to launch a sampan into the sea. Along the right edge the label was torn a little but most of the trademark was visible: a diamond with the word *WIMCO* printed inside it. In the top left quarter of the box was the slogan: **SEA-FISHER**. At the bottom centre: 'SAFETY MATCHES Made in India.' On the reverse side of the box it said: *These matches are made in India by the celebrated WIMCO works at Bombay. They are specially imported by* THE CORNISH MATCH COMPANY *Av. contents 45.*

Major Nye was a stringy man in his late sixties with a scrubby grey moustache and pale, introspective blue eyes. He was just above average height. The veins in his hands and wrists were prominent and purple and matched the ink-stains on his fingertips. The badge of his old regiment was stitched on to the breast pocket of his blazer and the badge was as faded and frayed as the blazer itself. He put the

23

matchbox carefully back in his pocket. He cleared his throat and went to his seat behind the green steel desk which had been effected for him at the far end of the lab. There was nothing on the desk. He opened a drawer and took out a Rizla tin. He began to roll himself a thin cigarette.

'I only agreed to do all this because my daughter was keen on it.' He seemed to be trying to explain his embarrassment and apologize for it. Not so long ago he had loved India and sworn loyalty to the Empire. Now he had only his children to love and only his wife demanded his loyalty. This was something of a come-down after a sub-continent.

He lit his cigarette with a Swan Vesta, cupping his hand against a non-existent wind. He puffed hard and began to hum a tune – always his unconscious response to small pleasures like smoking. Through the window of the little square marine biology lab Major Nye could see the rocks and the grey, roaring sea. He was puzzled by this coast. Cornwall was alien to him; it depressed him. He could not understand the Celtic point of view. These people seemed to enjoy burrowing into the ground for no particular reason. Why else had they built their fougous? He had noticed, too, how they had turned quite naturally from wrecking to tourism without, apparently, any change of spirit. His right hand went to his thinning grey hair and smoothed it, descended to the grey eyebrows and smoothed them, came finally to the grey moustache and smoothed that. With both hands he tightened the small knot of his regimental tie and tugged at the frayed collar of his shirt, which was white with thin blue and red stripes which had almost faded to invisibility. There was a khaki handkerchief protruding from his left sleeve. The cigarette was now unnoticed and unappreciated in the corner of his grey mouth.

A surly looking laboratory technician, with long, black hair falling over the shoulders of his white coat, came in, hovered over a bench, picked up a rack of test-tubes, nodded moodily at the Japanese and the Englishman. Then he left.

Major Nye got up and went to look at the bound and

spread-eagled assassin who lay on the slab just under the window-sill. The wrists and ankles were in steel clamps.

'How are you feeling, old son?'

He had spoken awkwardly and gruffly. He cleared his throat again as if he wished he had been able to use a more natural tone.

Jerry Cornelius snarled. A high-pitched screech broke from his writhing lips. He began, pathetically, to struggle on the slab.

'Eeeeeee! Eeeeeee!'

Gently, Major Nye frowned. 'Damned shame. Poor old chap.' He turned his pale eyes upon the Japanese biologist who had been attracted by the screech and now stood beside him. 'How long was he down there?'

The biologist shrugged and scratched behind his left ear with his right hand. 'A year? The brain has been flushed. The flesh, however, is surprisingly fresh. Like a baby's, general.'

Major Nye plucked at his heavily veined nose and rubbed the under edge of it with his right forefinger. 'Poor old chap. Young, too, eh?'

'Who can say? It is a strange physiology. Hard to guess the age without the proper instruments. We should have been warned. Then maybe we could have had some equipment sent down from London. As it was, he was just dumped on us. Like a baby on a doorstep.'

Major Nye's ulcer bit suddenly and he straightened his shoulders and firmed his jaw to take the pain. 'Sorry about that,' he said. He removed the cigarette from his lips and dropped it to the floor. 'There wasn't very much time, as I understand it. It was "goodbye Dolly I must leave you" and then "tramp, tramp, tramp the boys are marching".'

'I realize that. I was not complaining about your organization, general. I was merely explaining our inability to do more than superficial tests.'

'Naturally. You've done jolly well, anyway. Splendid show.' The major looked at his watch. It seemed to be losing again. 'First class,' he muttered absently. 'Not my organiza-

25

tion though, you know. Nothing to do with me. Friend of my daughter's . . . Well, we'd better get off before dark. It's a goodish run from here up to Sussex.'

'You're taking the truck?'

'The old lorry. Yes, I thought so, unless – ?'

'No. No. By all means take it.'

'Splendid. Good, well, shall we um?'

Jerry Cornelius was all but insensate. His eyes glowed, his lips curled back from his stained teeth, his fingers curved like claws and he still stank of brine and tar. Even after they had cleaned him up (using for the most part methylated spirits and linseed oil) he had continued to glare at them silently, like a mad gull.

Major Nye and the Japanese biologist wheeled the slab from the lab and out on to the concrete which had replaced the turf. Parked close to the cliff was a run-down 1947 Bedford two-ton military lorry with a khaki canvas canopy. Major Nye untied the canopy flaps, got into the back and let down the tailboard. He pushed two planks from the lorry to the ground so that they made a ramp up which they could roll the slab with Cornelius on it. They wheeled the slab to the far end of the lorry, nearest the cab, and secured it there using chains. Major Nye turned the key in the padlock and put it in his pocket. He straightened up and crossed back towards the tailboard. As he did so his foot struck a rusty spanner on the floor of the lorry. The spanner skidded and clanged against a greasy jack pedestal. Major Nye winced. He jumped down, slid the planks into the lorry, bolted the flap up and fastened the canvas. He shook hands with the Japanese, walked round to the cab, opened the door and climbed on to the tattered bench seat. He rolled himself another smoke in his Rizla machine before giving his attention to the controls. He had some difficulty starting the engine and getting into gear but at last with a wave he drove off down the bumpy mud track towards the tarmac road which led to the A30 and thence to the M5.

The sky changed from cold white to cold, dark grey and a cold rain was falling by the time Major Nye left the lane and headed north between flat, grey fields.

He shivered. Keeping his left hand on the steering wheel, he buttoned up his threadbare blazer.

The lorry rattled and whined. It snarled with every gear shift. The noise did much to drown the occasional screech from the back. The fumes from the engine helped cover the smell of brine.

It was nearly dark when they reached the A30. Major Nye rolled himself another cigarette as he waited to get on to the road. The rain was bearing down on the black tarmac. The Bedford's single windscreen wiper clacked erratically. Moving out, Major Nye began to sing to keep himself awake. He sang *Hold Your Hand Out (Naughty Boy)*, *My Old Dutch*, *I love a Lassie*, *It's a Long Way to Tipperary*, *Pack Up Your Troubles*, *The Army of Today's All Right*, *Burlington Bertie from Bow*, *If It Wasn't For the Houses in Between*, *Are We to Part Like This, Bill?*, *The Honeysuckle and the Bee*, *You're the Cream in My Coffee*, *Dolly Gray*, *On the Road to Mandalay*, *Rio Rita*, *Maxim's*, *Only a Rose*, *Moonlight Becomes You*, *Jolly Good Luck to the Girl who Loves a Sailor*, *Am I Blue?*, *Change Partners*, *Fanlight Fannie*, *Auld Lang Syne*, *White Christmas*, *The Riff Song*, *My Little Wooden Hut*, *We're Here Because We're Here*, *The Cornish Floral Dance*, *Mairi's Wedding*, *Phil the Fluter's Ball*, *My Old Man*, *Mammy*, *The Eton Boating Song*, *Yesterday (*half*)*, *A Whiter Shade of Pale (*part*)*, *What Shall We Do With the Drunken Sailor?*, *The Dying Aviator*, *When This Bloody War is Over*, *Sonny Boy*, *Sally*, *Maybe It's Because I'm a Londoner*, *I Belong to Glasgow*, *Molly Malone*, *Land of My Fathers*, *Underneath the Arches*, *Run, Rabbit, Run*, *Rose O'Day*, *I'll Be Seeing You*, *Coming in on a Wing and a Prayer*, *That Lovely Weekend*, *Lucky Jim*, *September Song*, *The Man Who Broke the Bank at Monte Carlo*, *Mr Tambourine Man (*part*)*, *The Physician*, until at last he reached Ironmaster House in Sussex croaking the last few bars of *Has Anybody Here Seen Kelly?* and stopped the lorry by the brook.

Una Persson

'The peak was reached in 1808 and civilization has been in decline ever since, thanks, in particular, to the Saxon race – many of whom happened to share my view. Here's to Beethoven!'

Prinz Lobkowitz saluted with his stein, lowered it to his lips, tilted his leonine head and swallowed a litre of Bil beer. His voice had been drowned almost entirely by the first movement of the 'Pastoral' played by the Berlin Philharmonic Orchestra conducted by Eugene Jochum which came from the two great Vox speakers on either side of the bay window. Wiping the foam from his moustache he went to the ornate Victorian mantelpiece on which stood the newish Garrard deck with its Sony amplifier and turned a knob to reduce the volume slightly, adding: 'Open the window. It stinks of disinfectant in here.' The first movement ended and the second began.

From a gilded chair upholstered in stained red and white Regency stripe, his mistress Eva Knecht efficiently rose and with long strides crossed the wide eighteenth-century room which was full of half-emptied packing cases, a grand piano with roses painted on its light walnut wood, scattered dustsheets and piles of objets trouvées. Reaching the diamond-paned windows she raised her hands to the catch but paused as the huge bulk of a Zeppelin filled her entire field of vision; it was flying low over the ruins to the south east of the city. It coursed towards the sunset. She smiled quietly and pushed open the double windows. The distant mumble of the Zeppelin's engines reached her. She took a deep breath as if to inhale the sound rather than the stink which blew from the Koenigstrasse gravepit. She looked back enquiringly at the Prinz who waved his hand. 'I suppose so. Though I don't know which I prefer – that or the DDT. It's about time something was done for Berlin.'

There came a faint vibration and a faraway thump as the Zeppelin began to distribute its first incendiaries of the evening. Prinz Lobkowitz lit a Jamaican corona and burnt his thumbnail with the match when the beginning of the third movement (*Merry Gathering of Peasants*) struck up. 'Fuck,' he said, and then: 'What's German for fuck?'

'I haven't got that far yet.' She started towards the shelf of dictionaries in the far alcove.

'Don't bother. Nobody else does. What's the point of trying to revive a dead language? Who wants a "national identity" any longer? Politics has come down to rather more fundamental issues.'

'Who wants to *talk* about it?' Eva smoothed her skirt. 'That newspaper soon went back to English.'

'The bloody language is always at the root of it.' He coughed and put his cigar in the Directoire chafing dish he used as an ashtray. 'Do you still want to go to the waxworks tonight?'

'Suits me.'

'I bet it does!'

He roared with laughter, frowned, and turned off the stereo.

The house, most of which was still intact, had been restored in 1850 and was huge with lavish appointments. It had all the tatty grandeur of a Versailles, with the same fading gilt, fly-specked mirrors and chipped, painted terracotta.

A gentle knock on the great oaken double door.

'Come,' said Lobkowitz.

The doors opened and a small black and white cat walked in, its tail erect. It stopped in the middle of the dusty Persian carpet. It sat down and looked up at them.

It was followed by a beautiful girl in a black military topcoat and patent leather boots with gold buckles (from *Elliotts*). Her brown hair was cut relatively short and her face was heart-shaped, amused, controlled. She held a heavy Smith and Wesson .45 revolver in her right hand and her left hand was still resting on the door knob as she paused and surveyed the room.

Eva Knecht scowled. 'Sebastian Auchinek's sidekick,' she muttered. 'Una Persson. What an actress!'

Eva, only slightly beautiful, with the same kind of brown hair, felt herself fade. She wished that she were wearing something other than the fawn Jaeger twinset and green spikeheels as she hissed: 'Proper little heroine of the revolution, isn't she.'

Prinz Lobkowitz ignored his mistress. He flattened one palm against his waistcoated diaphragm and made his dignified way towards the door, the other palm extended. He was wearing a black frock coat and pinstripe trousers. In the lapel of his coat was the tiny button of the Legion de Liberté. Under the trousers were the outlines of his brown riding boots. He had forgotten to take off the silver spur attached to his right heel. He smirked (though he thought the expression one of friendly dignity) and as a consequence ruined the handsome lines of his face. He rumbled some pleasantry, of which his smirk made ingratiating nonsense, and introduce himself to the newcomer. 'Prinz Lobkowitz.'

'Una Persson,' she replied contemptuously. 'Auchinek said you would take delivery.'

'I thought it was tomorrow.' Lobkowitz looked vaguely about him. 'Tomorrow.' Slowly the smirk dissolved.

'I saved time by coming through Czechoslovakia.' Una Persson put the gun into her deep pocket. She turned and snapped her fingers. Four unhealthy Slavs stumbled in. There was a pine coffin on their shoulders. The coffin was stamped *VAKUUM REINIGER (ENGLISCH-PRODUKT)*. The Slavs put it down on the Persian carpet. They trotted off.

Una Persson reached inside her maxicoat and withdrew a document and a blue ballpoint. 'Sign both copies, please,' she said. Lobkowitz put the papers on the lid of the walnut grand piano and signed without reading. He handed them back to her. 'And how is Auchinek?'

'Very well. Shall I open the box for you?'

'If you would.'

She slipped out her Smith and Wesson and accurately shot off the bolts on the coffin's four corners. One of the spent bullets narrowly missed Eva Knecht. With the barrel of the gun Una Persson plucked away a blanket, revealing the glaring countenance of Jerry Cornelius, still stinking of the sea.

Lobkowitz backed off and went to put the Mozart Clarinet Quintet in A on the deck.

'Mein Gott!' said Eva self-consciously. 'What caused that?'

Una Persson shrugged. 'Some form of hydrophilia, I gather. A disease with symptoms similar to enteritis in cats.'

'I mourn the Age of Steam,' said Lobkowitz returning with a box of *Rising Sun* matches. They were made by the Western India Match Co. Ltd.

'A peculiar diagnosis.' Eva Knecht bent to look more closely at the creature. 'Where was it found?'

'On the coast of North Cornwall, eventually, but he'd been seen once or twice earlier. They think he went in somewhere around the Bay of Bengal. I was to take delivery of five cases of M16s?'

'Yes, yes, of course.' Lobkowitz indicated the crates laid out under the grand piano. 'With ammunition. Shall I get someone to load them for you, or . . . ?

'Thank you very much.'

Lobkowitz pulled a frayed velvet bell-rope near the mantelpiece. 'This is the old Bismarck mansion,' he told her.

'I gathered.' With a battered brass Dunhill Una Persson lit a long brown Sherman cigarettello. 'I should like to wash my hair before I leave.'

As best she could, Eva Knecht flounced from the room. 'I'll check if the water's on.'

Four ex-POWs with shaven heads and wearing stained blue dungarees, came in and began to take the crates of M16s outside to Una Persson's SD Kfz 233 armoured truck.

The ornate ormolu 'Empire' style telephone commenced to ring. Lobkowitz ignored it. 'They all do that. It means nothing.'

'Well, I think I'll just . . .' Una Persson strode across and lifted the receiver to her head. 'Hello.'

She listened for a moment and then replaced the receiver. 'A sort of rushing noise.'

'That's right.' Lobkowitz moved rapidly towards her, his spur jingling. 'Jesus Christ, I'd like to . . .'

She placed a small hand against his chest and kissed him on the chin.

Eva Knecht stood in the doorway, one hand clutching her Jaeger cardigan round her shoulders. 'I'm afraid there'll be no more water today.'

Una Persson stepped away from Prinz Lobkowitz and nodded gravely at Eva. 'I'll be off, then.'

Lobkowitz coughed behind his hand. His eyes fell on his right boot and for the first time he noticed that he was still wearing one spur. He bent to unstrap it. 'Don't leave, yet . . .' He glanced up at Eva and added briskly: 'Well, cheerio, my dear.'

'Cheerio,' said Una Persson. Decisively, she left the room.

Eva Knecht glared at Lobkowitz as he straightened to his feet, holding the spur in his hand. 'Mozart!' she said. 'I should have . . .'

'Don't be corny, sweet.' Lobkowitz put the spur on a pearl inlay table.

'Corny!'

Picking up an Erma 9mm machine pistol from the Jacobean sideboard, she offered him a round in the hip. He pursed his lips as if objecting to the noise rather than the pain, and went down on one knee as the dark stains dilated on his jacket and pinstripes. He clutched the ruined hip.

She spent the rest of the clip on his face. He fell. Smashed.

Una Persson came back at the sound. She raised her S&W and shot Eva Knecht once below the left shoulder blade. The bullet entered Eva's jealous heart and she toppled forward. Murdered.

Eva Knecht's murderess took a black beret from the pocket of her maxicoat and adjusted it on her head, glancing once into the mirror above the mantel. For a moment she looked thoughtfully from the coffin to the corpses. She replaced the S&W in her other pocket. She opened her mouth a quarter of an inch and then closed it. She took off the Mozart and flicked through the pile of albums on the floor until she found a Bach Brandenburg Concerto. She put the record on the deck, glanced down at the contents of the coffin, hovered undecidedly by the door, and then she left as quickly as her coat would let her.

The Brandenburg was an inferior performance, spoiled further by a persistent screeching from the box.

From below there came the noise of an SD Kfz 233 starting up, backing out and roaring off down the emergency track through the rubble.

The screeching assumed a melancholy note and then ceased. Night fell. From time to time the room was illuminated by incendiary explosions from the East. Later there was darkness relieved by a little moonlight and the sound of the Zeppelin returning to its shed. Then there remained only a rustle of atmospherics from the speakers.

The small black and white cat, forgotten by Una Persson, woke up. It stretched and began to walk towards Lobkowitz. It lapped at the congealed blood on the face, then moved off in disgust. It washed itself beside Eva's corpse and then sprang into the coffin to curl on Jerry's chest, heedless of the insensate, agonized eyes which, wide open, continued to stare at the terracotta ceiling, before slowly filling with tears.

Sebastian Auchinek

The long, gentle hands came down to reveal a sensitive Jewish face. The large, red lips moved, emitting softly-accented English: 'Perhaps you should have brought him back, Una?' He was a thin, pale intellectual. He sat on a camp chair with its back against the far wall of a dry, limestone cave. He was dressed in standard guerilla gear; it hung on his thin body like a wet flag.

The cave was full of crates; it was lit by a tin oil-lamp which cast black shadows. On one of the crates stood a half-eaten Stilton cheese, an almost full bottle of Vichy water and a number of East German and Polish military maps in leather cases.

She was undoing the top button of her black maxicoat. 'That would have been theft, Sebastian.'

'True. But these are pragmatic times.'

'And we agreed we wanted no part of them.'

'True.' He sucked his upper lip into his mouth, his large lids slowly falling to cover his eyes.

She said defiantly: 'The M16s are as good as new. There's plenty of ammunition. He kept his side of it. Many new Germans are very straight in that respect.' She shrugged. 'But her violence upset me.' She lit another Sherman's with a match from a box on the nearby crate. 'I've still got a feeling I've forgotten something.' She reached into her pocket and pulled out her gun, turning it this way and that. 'What else could I do? If saving her would have brought him back to life . . .'

'True.'

'Well, I know if I'd thought about it for a moment I might not have done it. But so many people waste time thinking about things and when they act it's too late. I didn't want to hurt anybody.'

Sebastian Auchinek got up from the camp chair and

walked to the cave entrance, drawing back the camouflage net. Outside, the drizzle fluttered like a tattered curtain in the wind and Auchinek peered through it, hoping to get a sight of the tiny Macedonian village in the rocky valley below. A herd of goats emerged from the thin rain. They bleated their discomfort as they trotted down the mountainside and disappeared. The water swished on the rocks and it smelled faintly of benzine. At least the air was reasonably warm.

'Sebastian.'

His inclination was to leave the cave, for he hated any form of homecoming ceremony, but he turned.

She was kneeling by the chair wearing a gold and brown puff-sleeved shirt with a long black waistcoat and matching black trousers. Her coat was folded neatly beside her.

With a sigh he returned to his place and spread his spider legs. She reached forward and undid his fly. He gritted his teeth and his hand stroked her head once or twice before falling back at his side. He squeezed his eyes shut. Her face was grave as she moved it towards his crotch, as if she were considering different and more pleasant things while conscientiously performing a distasteful but necessary task.

Auchinek wondered if she did it because she thought he liked it. She had done it regularly for the past few months; at first he had pretended to be pleased and now he could never tell her the truth.

When she had finished, the fellatrix looked up at him, smiled, wiped her lips, swiftly closed his zip. He gave her a strained, bewildered smile in return, then he began to cough. She offered him one of her cigarettellos but he waved his hand towards the bottle on the upturned crate. She did not notice the gesture as she lit and then drew upon the long, brown Sherman's staring pensively at her own shifting shadow on the floor. Her eyes were blue and private.

'Perhaps I should go back for Cornelius. We might need him if things get any tougher. On the other hand he might be dead by the time I got there. Is that my fault, I wonder?

35

And the Cossacks are supposed to be moving in, too. Did you say you wanted a cigarette?'

His pale face was puzzled, his gesture nervous as he lifted an exhausted hand to point again at the bottle.

'No,' he said. 'Water.'

Mrs C. and Colonel P.

'Yerst.' Folding her hands together on her great stomach, the fat old bag got her forearms under her unruly breasts and jostled them in her dress until they were hanging more comfortably. "S'im, orl right.' Her three sly chins shivered. Her round, red stupid head cocked itself on one side. Her tiny eyes narrowed and her thick mouth opened. 'Pore littel bleeder. Wot they dun to 'em?'

'We do not know, Mrs Cornelius.' Colonel Pyat stepped away from the coffin which lay where Una Persson's Slavs had left it. The other bodies were no longer visible, though the small black and white cat was still hanging around. 'But now that you have positively identified him . . .' He drew off his white kid gauntlets. They were a perfect match to his well-cut, gold-trimmed uniform, to his kid boots, his dashing cap. '. . . we can try to find out. I almost caught up with him in Afghanistan. But the express was delayed as usual. This could have been avoided.'

"E always wos a bit've a pansy, I s'pose,' Mrs C. said reflectively.

Colonel Pyat went to the grand piano where his vodka things had been arranged by an orderly. 'May I offer you a drink, madame?'

'Where's all them balloons gorn? I 'eard . . .'

'The Zeppelins have left the city. They belonged to the Nieu Deutchlanders whom we routed yesterday.'

'Well, I'll 'ave a small one. Did anyone ever tell yer – yer look jest like Ronal' Colman.'

'But I feel just like Jesse James,' Colonel Pyat smiled and gestured towards the record player on the mantelpiece. Faintly, from the Vox speakers, came the muffled sounds of a Bob Dylan record. The colonel poured an ounce of Petersburg vodka into a long-stemmed Bohemian glass, poured

37

the same amount for himself, crossed back and handed Mrs
C. her drink.

She drained it. 'Ta.' Then, with a fat, knowing chuckle,
she flung back the monstrous arm and hurled the glass at
the mantelpiece. 'Sköl! Eh? Har, har!'

Colonel Pyat took an interest in his white knuckles. Then
he straightened his shoulders and quietly sipped his drink.

Mrs C. ran a grimy finger round the neck of her cheap, red
and white print dress. ''Ot enough fer yer?'

'Indeed?' Pyat put a finger to his lips and raised his
eyebrows intelligently. 'Aha.'

'Wouldna thort it. Not in bleedin' *Germany* – innit?'

'No?'

She turned, digging at a rotting back tooth with her
thumbnail so that her voice was strangled. 'Will 'e get
better, Kernewl?'

'That's up to the boffins, madame.'

'Courst, 'is *bruvver* – Frankie – was allus th' nicest of
'em. I did me best after 'is dad run orft, but . . .'

'These are unsettled times, Mrs Cornelius.'

Mrs C. looked at him with mock gravity for a moment, a
little smile turning up the corners of her crimson mouth.
She opened the lips. She belched. Then she burst into
laughter. 'Yer not kiddin' – ter-her-ka-ka – ooh – give us
anovver, there's a pet . . . nkk-nkk.'

'I beg your pardon?'

'Nar – sawright – I'll 'elp meself, won' I?' She waddled to
the grand piano. Grunting contentedly, she poured half the
remaining contents of the bottle into another long-stemmed
glass. She rounded on him, raising her glass with a leer and
tossing off the best part of the contents. ''Ere's ter yer!' The
drink warmed her further and large beads of sweat sprang
out on her happy face. She sidled up to Colonel Pyat,
nudging him with her lumpy elbow. She winked and nodded
a streaky orange head at the vodka. 'Not bad.' She belched
again. 'Not 'alf! He, he he!'

Colonel Pyat clicked his heels and saluted. 'I thank – '

A piercing screech came from the coffin. They both turned their heads. 'Gawd,' said Mrs C.

Cautiously, Colonel Pyat went to peer in. 'I wonder if they've been feeding him.'

''E never wos much of an eater.' Mrs C.'s bosom heaved as she joined the colonel and stared sentimentally down at her son. 'I never knew where 'e got 'is energy from. Proper little fucker you wos, woncha, Jer?'

The head rolled. The stink of brine was nauseating. The screech came again. The hands, thin and knotted, with broken nails and bruised knuckles, were rubbed raw at the wrists by the twisted nylon cords holding them in the coffin. The mouth opened and closed, opened and closed; only the whites of the eyes were visible.

With a decisive and slightly censorious gesture Mrs C. looked away from her child, finishing her vodka. She glanced almost thoughtfully at the colonel before putting her glass on the Jacobean sideboard. She wriggled her massive shoulders, rubbed her left eye with the index finger of her left hand, gave the colonel a quick smirk of encouragement and said: 'Well . . .'

Colonel Pyat bowed. 'Some of my men will escort you back to London.'

'Ah,' she said. 'That wos it . . .'

'Madame?'

'I wos thinkin'v seein' some o' th' sights whilst I wos 'ere. Y'know.' Another wink.

'I will instruct my men to make a tour of the city. Though there are very few sights left.'

'Oo! All them soljers all to meself! Oo-er!'

'And thank you so much for your help, Mrs Cornelius. We'll get your boy back to normal. Never fear.'

'Normal! That'sa good 'un!' Her entire body quivered with laughter. 'You'll do, Kernewl! Eh? Har, har, har!'

She shambled cheerfully from the room. 'You'll do!'

The Bohemian glass fell off the Jacobean sideboard and landed unbroken on the Persian carpet.

The sounds from the coffin became pensive. Colonel Pyat was filled with sadness. He picked up the fallen glass and took it to the grand piano where he poured himself the last of his vodka.

Reminiscence (A)

Beautiful love.
Beautiful love.

Terence Green, 9, and Martin Harper, 8, died last night when overcome by fumes from water heater while having bath in house in Estagon Road, Norwich.

Sunday Times, April 5 1970

At least 90 Vietnamese men, women and children, held behind barbed wire in a compound at the Cambodian town of Prasot, were killed by machine gun and automatic rifle fire early yesterday, as a Vietcong force launched an attack in the area.

The events surrounding the killings were not clear.

The Times, April 11 1970

A French woman, aged 37, stabbed three of her children, killing one of them, before committing suicide in Luneville yesterday, police said. Mme Marie-Madeleine Amet stabbed Joanne, aged 14, and Philippe, aged 11, who managed to escape. But Catherine, aged 10, was killed.

Guardian, April 14 1970

It's a shame, really, said Major Nye as they stood on the flat roof of the looted dispensary and watched the barbarian migration cross the swaying remains of Tower Bridge. The sky began to lighten and to some degree improve the appearance of the horde's filthy silks, satins and velvets. A few were mounted on horses, motorbikes and bicycles, but the majority trudged along with their bundles on their backs. Some were playing loud, primitive music on stolen Gibsons, Yamahas, Framus twelve-strings, Martins and even Hofners. It's a shame, really. Who can blame them?

Jerry fingered his new gloves.

You and they have more in common than I, major.

Major Nye gave him a sympathetic glance. Aren't you lonely, Mr Cornelius?

For a moment self-pity flooded all Jerry's systems. His eyes gleamed with water. Oh, fuck.

Major Nye knew how to get through.

When half the barbarians were on the South Bank, the bridge, shaken by a hundred different twelve-bar blues and a thousand moccasins and calf-length suede boots, fell slowly over into the grease of the Thames. Large stones broke away from the main towers as they toppled; pieces of asphalt cracked like toffee struck by a hammer. The whole mock-Gothic edifice, every inch of grimy granite, was falling down.

Their long hair fluttering behind them, those babies not in slings and packs falling from their arms, their guitars and bundles scattering around them, their beads and furs and laces flapping, the barbarians sank through the air, struck, and were absorbed by, the river. For a moment a cassette tape recorder could be heard playing *You can't always get what you want* by the Rolling Stones and then that, too, was logged by the water.

Arriving too late, a Panther patrol lowered its .280 EM1s as if in salute to the dying. Standing in single file along the North Bank they watched the children drown.

The Panthers were led by a tall aristocrat in a finely tailored white suit, a neatly trimmed Imperial beard and moustache and short hair cut close to the nape of his black neck. He carried an elegant single-shot Remington XP-100. The bolt-action pistol was borne more for aesthetic effect than anything else. He held it in his right hand and his arms were folded across his chest so that the long barrel rested in the crook of his left elbow. The Panthers in their own well-cut cream uniforms, looked enquiringly at their Head. It was unquestionably a problem of taste. The Panthers lived for taste and beauty, which was why they had been the most virulent force against the barbarians. The war between the two had been a war of styles and the Panthers, under their American leaders, had won all the way down the line.

At last the Panthers on the North Bank reached a decision. Lining the embankment, they turned their tall backs, dropped their chins to their chests and lounged against the balustrade, listening to the fading cries of the dying until there was silence in the river again. Then they climbed back into their open Mercedes and Bentley tourers and rolled away from there.

A few barbarians stood on the far bank, twisting themselves joints, hesitating before rejoining the exodus as it ploughed on towards the Borough High Street, heading for the suburbs of Surrey and Kent and what was left of the pickings.

And those, said the major, indicating the disappearing Panthers, do you identify, perhaps, with them?

Jerry shrugged. Maybe a little more. No – no, there's nobody left at all, major, let's face it. I'm on my own in this one and I can't say I like it. My fault, perhaps.

Possibly you lost sight of your targets, Mr Cornelius.

I've hit all the targets, Major Nye. That's the trouble. He

took out his needler and turned it this way and that to catch the light on its polished chrome. Is there anything sadder, I wonder, than an assassin with nobody left to kill?

I shouldn't think so. Major Nye's voice was now more than sympathetic. I know exactly what you mean, my dear chap. And I suppose that's why we're both standing here watching. Our sun has set, I'm afraid.

Keep moving towards the sun and it will never set, said Jerry. That's positive thinking, major. It will never happen. It's a matter of finding the right place. The correct speed for forward momentum.

Major Nye said nothing as he shook his grey head.

It will never fucking happen! Jerry shouted.

The masonry had blocked the flow of the river and was making it flood over the embankment. A few corpses were washed up and there was other, fouler, flotsam, too.

Jerry went back to the skylight and put his feet on the scarred wooden steps. He was going inside. Coming, major?

No, I'll stop here for a while, old son. And keep your chin up, eh?

Thanks, major. Same to you.

Jerry climbed down into the ruined bedroom and stood staring at the dreadful corpse of the girl in the fourposter. The rats ignored him and went on eating. He aimed the gun but, after a minute or two, replaced it in his holster without shooting. Even the rats couldn't last much longer.

Smoothly, with mock-apologetic smiles, they nailed him to the lowest yard of the mizzen. They were standing off the Kent coast, near Romney, out of sight of land. The three-masted schooner-rigged yacht rocked in the heavy sea. The sea tugged at the anchors, hurled its weight against the white sides. Waiting for the waters to subside, they paused in the hammering. Almost expectantly they looked up at him. The two women, who had nailed his hands, were Karen von Krupp and Mitzi Beesley. They were dressed in deck pyjamas and chic little sailormen's hats. The man who had nailed his feet was his brother Frank. Frank wore grey flannels, a white open-necked shirt and a fairisle pullover. He was kneeling beside the mizzen, the hammer in both hands.

Jerry spoke with great control. I made no claims.

But many were made *for* you, said Bishop Beesley through a mouthful of beige fudge. He stood by the rail, his bottom wedged against it. You didn't deny them.

I deny nothing. Have I disagreed with your opinion?

No. But, then, I'm not sure . . .

We have that in common, at least.

The sea grew calm. Bishop Beesley made an impatient gesture, withdrawing a Mars Bar from under his surplice. The three resumed their hammering.

Together with the nails in his palms there were ropes supporting his wrists so that the weight of his hanging body would not rip the impaled flesh too quickly, for they wanted him to die of asphyxiation, not of pain or loss of blood alone. He breathed hard. The sharp pressure increased in his chest. The last blows fell. The three stood back to inspect their work. The corpulent Bishop Beesley licked his lips, sniffed the odour of the stale sea.

Dead fish, said the bishop. Dead fish.

Alan Stuart, aged four, who sprayed his mouth with what is believed to have been a pressurized oven cleaner at his home in Benhillwood Road, Sutton, Surrey, has died in hospital.

The Sun, September 28 1971

A boy aged 14 died after being stabbed in the chest in the playground of Wandsworth School, South London, yesterday. He died in Queen Mary's Hospital, Roehampton, soon after the stabbing, which happened during the morning break at the boys' comprehensive school. Last night another boy, also aged 14, was accused of the murder. He will appear at Southwark North juvenile court today.

Guardian, November 19 1971

Shirley Wilkinson, aged 16, daughter of the train robber Jack Wilkinson, died last night in the South London hospital where she had been detained after being injured in a car crash.

Guardian, November 20 1971

Scores of rush-hour cars flashed by as a 10-year-old girl fled naked and terrified from a sex maniac. But not one driver stopped. And motorists took no notice of the girl's frantic cries for help as the man dragged her into his car. Later the man raped and strangled her. The body of little Jane Hanley was found at the weekend in a field outside Rochester, New York. 'At least 100 people must have seen her,' said a policeman. 'She had apparently been kidnapped but jumped from the man's car and pleaded with passing motorists to help. The kidnapper grabbed her and drove off again.' Now rewards totalling £2,500 have been offered by newspapers and citizens' organizations for information leading to the killer. Three drivers have now admitted they saw the drama on Highway 400 – 10 miles from where Jane disappeared while on a shopping errand. One said: 'I went by so fast I couldn't believe what I saw.'

The Sun, November 22 1971

Reminiscence (B)

Save us.

From the basement in Talbot Road. From mother's breath and mother's saliva. From cold chips. From dirty hand-me-downs. From stained mattresses. From old beer bottles. From the smell of urine. From damp squalor.

From the poverty trance.

Mrs C. and Frankie C.

'So we fetched up 'ere again 'ave we?' Mrs Cornelius said sullenly as her lean son guided her off the decrepit street and down the foul basement steps. 'Yore doin' okay fer yerself, incha? Yer ole mum'd never know it.'

'You prefer it here, mother,' said Frank patiently. 'When we got you that council flat you complained.'

'It wasn't the bleedin' flat it was the arrangements. Orl them stairs. I can't get inter a lift it makes me sick. And them neighbours reckonin' theirselves . . .'

'Well. There it is.' Frank took the door handle in both hands and lifted it so that the damp wood just cleared the step. 'I'll get you some more batteries for your wireless.'

They entered the stinking gloom.

'I could do wiv a drink.'

Frank took a half-bottle of Gordon's gin from the pocket of his sheepskin coat. She accepted it with dignity and placed it on the warped and littered sideboard, near the primitive television which had stopped working, well before the electricity had been cut off. 'I'd make yer a cuppa tea,' she said, 'but . . .'

'I've paid the gas bill. They're coming round to turn you on tomorrow.'

She waded through the litter of old newspapers and broken furniture. She lit the two stumps of candles on the rotting draining board. She moved a pile of old, damp Christmas cards. 'Wot yer fink Jerry's chances are, Frankie?'

'Ask the experts.' Frank shrugged and rubbed at his pale face. 'It's probably nothing more than exhaustion. He's been overdoing it recently.'

'Workin'!' said Mrs Cornelius derisively.

'Even Jerry has to graft sometimes, mum.'

'Lazy sod. 'Ow's yer antique business doin'?'

Frank became wary. 'So so.'

'Well, at least yer 'elp out sometimes. I don't see 'im one year ter the next.' She sighed and lowered herself into the discoloured armchair. 'Oooch! Them fuckin' springs. Damp as Brighton Beach, too.' The complaints were uttered in a tone of comfortable approval. She had been too long out of her natural environment. She reached up for the gin and began to unscrew the cap. Frank handed her a dirty glass from the sink.

'I must be off,' he said. 'Got everything you need?'

'Couldn't lend us a coupla quid couldya, Frankie?'

Frank reached into the right pocket of his cavalry twill trousers and removed a mixed handful of notes. He hesitated, then extracted a fiver. He showed it to her and put it on the sideboard. 'You'll have to go down to the Assistance on Monday. That should do you for the weekend. I won't be around for a while.'

'Be up in yer flat in 'Olland Park wiv yer nobby mates, eh?'

'No. Out of town.'

'Wot abart the shop?'

'Mo's looking after that. I'm off to Scotland to see what's still going in the big houses there. Everybody's running out of antiques. There's nothing left in England – even the sixties have gone dry. We're catching up on ourselves. It's funny.' He smiled as she stared uncomprehendingly at him. 'Don't worry, mum. You enjoy your drink.'

Her features flowed back into their normal lines of stupid complacency. 'Thanks, Frankie.'

'And give Cathy my love if you see her.'

'That slut! Wors'n Jerry if yer ask me! I 'eard she was on the game. Shacked up wiv a black feller.'

'I doubt if she's on the game.'

'I disown 'er,' Mrs Cornelius said grandly, raising the bottle to her lips, 'as any daughter o' mine.'

Frank buttoned up his suede car coat and pulled the lambswool collar around his dark face. He smoothed his Brylcreemed hair with the palm of his hand then slipped the hand into a suede-backed motoring glove. 'Mo said he'd come and clean this place out – give you some better furniture.'

'Yeah?'

'When shall I tell him to come?'

She looked nervously around her. 'Later,' she said. 'I'll 'ave ter fink abart wot I do and don' wanna keep. We'll discuss it later, eh?' She hadn't thrown a thing out since well before the war.

'You'll have that bloke from the council round again,' he warned.

'Don't worry abart *that!* I can deal with the fuckin' council!'

'They might find you alternative accommodation.'

Her heavy face was full of apprehension. 'Abart time, too,' she moaned.

He left, pulling the creaking door shut behind him.

She leaned the gin bottle on the arm of the mephitic chair and looked tenderly around at her home. It had been condemned in 1934, was scheduled for redevelopment by 1990, which meant any time after the turn of the century. It would last her out. The first candle guttered and threw peculiar shadows on the mildewed walls. The gin began to warm her chest and belly. She peered at the cracked mantel-piece on the far side of the room, locating the faded pictures of the fathers of her children. There was Frank's father in his GI uniform. There was Cathy's father in his best suit. There was the father of the dead twins, of the three abortions – the one who had married her. Only Jerry's father was missing. She didn't remember him, for all she'd borrowed his name. Through all her marriages she'd always been known as Mrs Cornelius. She'd only been about sixteen, hadn't she? Or even younger? Or was that something else? Was he the Jewish feller? Her eyelids closed.

Soon she was dreaming her nice dream as opposed to her nasty dream. She was kneeling on a big white woolly carpet. She was completely naked and there was blood dripping from her mangled nipples as she was buggered by a huge, black, shapeless animal. In her sleep her hands fell to her lap and she dug at herself with her nails and stirred and snorted, waking herself up. She smiled and drank down the rest of the gin and was soon fast asleep again.

Auchinek

'Poverty,' said Auchinek to Lyons, the Israeli colonel, 'increased markedly in Europe last year. This, in itself, would not have threatened the status quo had not a group of liberal politicians persistently offered the people hope without, of course, any immediate prospect of improving their lot. Naturally they moved swiftly from apathy to anger. Without their anger I doubt if I should have been anything like as successful.' He smiled. 'I owe at least some of my success to the human condition.'

'You're modest.' The colonel stared approvingly at his troops as they joined with their Arab allies and began, systematically, to lay dynamite charges throughout what was left of the city of Athens. 'Besides, wasn't the collapse to some extent cultural?'

'It was a culture without flexibility, I agree. I must admit I share the view that Western civilization – European civilization, if you like – was out of tempo with the rest of the world. It imposed itself for a short time – largely because of the vitality, stupidity and priggishness of those who supported it. We shall never be entirely cleansed of its influence, I'm afraid.'

'You aren't suggesting that the only values worth keeping are those of the Orient?' Lyons' murmur was sardonic.

'Basically – emotionally – I do think that. I know the question's arguable.'

'I detect a strong whiff of anti-aryanism. You support the pogroms?'

'Of course not. I am not a racialist. I speak only of education. I would like to see a vast re-education programme started throughout Europe. Within a couple of generations we could completely eradicate their portentous and witless philosophies.'

'But haven't our own thoughts been irrevocably influenced by them? I can't echo your idealism, personally, General Auchinek. Moreover, I think our destiny is with Africa . . .'

'The chimera of vitality appears again,' Auchinek sighed. 'I wish we could stop moving altogether.'

'And become like Cornelius? I saw him in Berlin, you know.'

'There is a difference between tranquillity and exhaustion. I had a guru, colonel, for some time, with whom I would correspond. He lived in Calcutta before the collapse. He convinced me of the need for meditation as the only solution to our ills.'

'Is that why you became a guerilla?'

'There is no paradox. One must work in the world according to one's temperament.'

The hillside, covered in tents, shook as the white ruins of Athens began to powder under the impact of the dynamite explosions.

Dust clouds rose slowly into the blue air and began to form peculiar configurations: ideograms from an alien alphabet. Auchinek studied them. They were vaguely familiar. If he studied them long enough, they might reveal their message. He changed the angle of his head, he narrowed his eyes. He folded his thin arms across his spare chest.

'How beautiful,' said Colonel Lyons, and he seemed to be speaking of Auchinek rather than of the explosions. He placed his brawny hand on Auchinek's bony shoulder. His large digital wristwatch shone beneath the tangle of black hairs, the coat of dust. 'We must get . . .' He removed his hand. 'How is Una?'

'In excellent health.' Auchinek coughed on the dust. 'She's leading our mission in Siberia at present.'

'So you are serious about your loyalty to the Oriental idea. Have you forgotten the Chinese?'

'Far from it.'

'Would they agree to an alliance? And what about the Japanese? How deep is their reverence for occidental thought?'

'A few generations deep in both cases. You've seen their comic books. All China wants, in international terms, is her old Empire restored.'

'There could be complications.'

'True. But not the confusion created artificially by Western interference since the fifteenth century.'

'*Their* fifteenth century,' smiled Colonel Lyons.

Auchinek missed the reference.

Persson

Una Persson watched the military ambulance bouncing away over the yellow steppe towards the wooden bridge which spanned the Dnieper. The sky was large, livid, on the move, but it could not dwarf the Cossack sech with its ten thousand yurts of painted leather and its many corrals full of shaggy ponies. Compared with the sky's swift activity the sech was almost static.

The ambulance reached the bridge and shrieked across it, taking the Cossack wounded back to their special encampment. A dark eddy swept through the sky for a hundred miles. The Dnieper danced.

In the strange light, Una Persson left her Range-Rover and strode towards the sech. Cool and just a trifle prim, with her big coat completely open to show her long, beautiful legs, the short multicoloured kaftan, the holstered S&W pistol on the ammunition belt around her small waist, the knee-length black boots, she paused again on the edge of the camp, allowing her blue-grey eyes to reveal the admiration she felt for the Cossack host's picturesque style.

These were not the Westernized Cossacks who had taken Berlin with their sophisticated artillery and mechanized transport. These were the atavists; they had resorted to the ancient ways of the Cossacks who had followed Stenka Razin in the people's revolt three hundred years before. They wore the topknots and long flowing moustachios copied from the Tartars who had been their ancient enemies but who now rode with them. All who presently dressed in Cossack silk and leather had been recruited east of the Volga and most of them looked Mongolian.

Their leader, wearing a heavy burka, blue silk trousers and yellow leather boots typical of the Zaporozhian Cossack, rode to where she stood. A Russian SKS carbine jostled on his back as he dismounted from his pony and wiped a large hand over his huge, hard face.

His voice was deep, humorous and resonant. 'I am Karinin, the Ataman of this Sech.' His oval eyes were equally admiring as he studied her, putting one foot in his pony's stirrup, hooking his arm around his saddle pommel and lighting his curved, black pipe with a match which he struck on the sole of his boot. 'You come from Auchinek, they tell me. You wish to make an alliance. Yet you know we are Christians, that we hate Jews worse than we hate Moslems and Muscovites.' He removed his floppy grey and black sheepskin shako to expose his shaven head, the gold rings in his ears, to wipe his dark brow and thick moustache. A calculated set of gestures, thought Una Persson, but well accomplished.

'The alliance Auchinek suggests is an alliance of the Orient against the west.' She spoke precisely, as if unimpressed by his style, his strength, his good looks.

'But you are – what? – a Russ? A Scandinavian, uh? A traitor? Or just a romantic like Cornelius?'

'What are you but that?'

He laughed. 'All right.'

The wind began to bluster, carrying with it the overriding smell of horse manure. The sky seemed to decide its direction and streamed rapidly eastward.

Karinin took his foot from the stirrup and slid the slim, scabbarded sabre around his waist until it rested on his left hip. He knocked out the pipe on his silver boot heel. 'You had better come to my yurt,' he said, 'to tell me the details. There's no one much left for us to fight in these parts.' He pointed into the centre of the sech, where the circles of yurts were tightest. His yurt was no larger than the others, for the Zaporozhians were touchily democratic, but a tall horsehair standard stood outside its flap.

Una Persson began to see the farcical side of her situation. She grinned. Then she noticed the gibbet which had been erected near Karinin's yurt. A group of old Kuban Cossacks were methodically putting a noose about the neck of a young

58

European dressed in a yellow frock coat, lilac cravat, yellow shirt and a blue, wide-brimmed hat. The European's expression was amused as he let them tie his hands behind him.

'What are they doing?' Una Persson asked.

The ataman spoke almost regretfully. 'They are hanging a dandy. There aren't so many as there were.'

'He seems brave.'

'Surely courage is a characteristic of the dandy?'

'And yet those old men plainly hate him. I thought Cossacks admired courage?'

'They are also very prudish. And a little jealous.'

The tightening rope knocked the blue hat from the fair hair; it covered the face for a moment before falling to the mud. The dandy gave his captors a chiding glance. The Kubans slapped at the rumps of the two horses on the other end of the rope. Slowly the dandy was raised into the air, his body twisting, his legs kicking, his face turning red, then blue, then black. Some noises came out of his distorted mouth.

'Sartor Resartus.' Karinin guided Una Persson past the gallows and ducked to push back the flap of his yurt and allow her to precede him. The yurt was illuminated by a lamp on a chest – a bowl of fat with a wick burning in it. The little round room was tidily furnished with a wooden bed and a table, as well as the chest.

Karinin came in and began to lace up the flap from the inside.

Una Persson removed her coat and put it on the chest. She unbuckled her ammunition belt with its holstered Smith and Wesson .45 and placed it on top of the coat.

Karinin's slanting eyes were tender and passionate. He stepped forward and took her to him. His breath smelled of fresh milk.

'We of the steppe have not lost the secret of affection,' he told her. They lay down in the narrow bed. He began to tug at his belt. 'It comes between love and lust. We believe in moderation, you see.'

'It sounds attractive.' Much against her better judgement she responded to his caress.

Nye

Ironmaster House was built of grey stones. It was Jacobean, with the conventional small square-leaded windows, three floors, five chimneys, a grey slate roof. Around its walls, particularly over the portico, climbed roses, wistaria and evergreens. Its gardens were divided by tall, ornamental privet hedges; there was a small lawn at the front and a larger lawn at the back. The back lawn ran down to a brook which fed a pool in which water-lilies were blooming. In the middle of the lawn, a water-spray swept back and forth like a metronome, for it was June and the temperature was 96°F.

From the open windows of the timbered sitting room it was possible to see both gardens, which were full of fuchsia, hydrangeas, gladioli and roses all sweetening the heavy air with their scent. And among these flowers, as if drugged, groggily flew some bees, butterflies, wasps and bluebottles.

Inside the shadowy house and seated on mock-Jacobean armchairs near a real Jacobean table, sat Major Nye in his shirt-sleeves; two girls, one fair and one dark; and Major Nye's wife, Mrs Nye, a rather strong-looking, weather-beaten woman with a contemptuous manner, a stoop and unpleasant hands.

Mrs Nye was serving a sparse tea. She poured from a mock Georgian, mock silver teapot into real Japanese porcelain cups. She sliced up a seed cake and slid the slices onto matching plates.

Major Nye had not bought Ironmaster House. His wife had inherited it. He had, however, worked hard to support the place; it was expensive to run. Since leaving the army and becoming Company Secretary to the Mercantile Charitable Association, he had lost his sense of personal authority. Many of his anxieties were new; he had previously never experienced anything like them and consequently was at a loss to know how to cope with them. This had earned him the contempt of his wife, who no longer loved him, but continued to command his loyalty. One of the girls in the room was Elizabeth, his daughter. He had another daughter, Isobel, who was a dancer in a company which worked principally on ocean-going liners, and he had a small son who had won a chorister's scholarship to St James' School, Southwark, a school reputed to be unnecessarily brutal but, as Major Nye would explain, it had been the only chance 'the poor little chap had to get into a public school', since the major could not afford to pay the kind of fees expected by Eton, Harrow or Winchester (his own school). In the army Major Nye had rarely had to make a choice; but in civilian life he had been given only a few choices and most of his decisions had been inevitable, for he had his duty to do to his wife, her house and his children. During the summer they usually took a couple of paying guests and they also sold some of the produce of their market garden at the roadside. Mrs Nye was seriously considering selling teas on the lawn to passing motorists.

Major Nye had to work solidly from six in the morning until nine or ten o'clock at night all through the week and the weekend. His wife also worked like a martyr to help keep the garden and the house going. Her heart was weak and his ulcer problems were growing worse. He had sold all his shares and there was a double mortgage on the house. Because he was insured, he hoped that he would die as soon as his son went up to Oxford in ten years' time. There were no paying guests at the moment. Those who did turn up never came for a second year; the atmosphere of the big house was sad and tense and hopeless.

Elizabeth, the dark-haired girl, was large-boned and inclined to fatness. She had a loud, cheerful voice which was patronizing when she addressed her father, accusing when she spoke to her mother and almost conciliatory when she talked to the fair-haired girl with whom, for the past nine months, she had been having a romantic love affair. This affair had never once faltered in its intensity.

61

The fair-haired girl was being very polite to Elizabeth's parents whom she was meeting for the first time. She had a low, calm, unaffected voice. Her name was Catherine Cornelius and she had turned from incest to lesbianism with a certain sense of relief. Elizabeth Nye was the third girl she had seduced but the only one with whom she had been able to sustain a relationship for very long.

It was Catherine who had asked Elizabeth to get Major Nye to collect Jerry Cornelius from Cornwall and deliver him to Ironmaster House where her brother had been picked up by Sebastian Auchinek's agents and transported to Dubrovnik. Catherine had come to know Sebastian Auchinek through Una Persson who had introduced Catherine to her first lover, Mary Greasby. Una Persson had convinced Catherine that Prinz Lobkowitz in Berlin would be able to cure Jerry of his hydrophilia and so Catherine had been deceived into providing the collateral (her brother) for the guns which had helped reduce Athens. She had also been instrumental in delivering Jerry into the hands of his old regimental commander, Colonel Pyat of the 'Razin' 11th Don Cossack Cavalry, who, for some time, had been obsessed with discovering the reason for Cornelius's desertion. He desperately wanted, once he had proved Jerry authentic, to revive the assassin and question him.

Catherine was only gradually becoming aware of her mistake. She had still not voiced the suspicion, even to herself, that Una Persson might have deceived her.

'And how is the poor blighter?' asked Major Nye, dolefully watching the water fall through the overheated air and rolling himself a thin cigarette. 'Hypothermia, wasn't it?'

'I'm not sure, major. I haven't heard from Berlin yet. It's confused, as you know.'

'It beats me,' said Mrs Nye harshly, rising to collect the tea paraphernalia, 'how your brother managed to get himself into that state. But then I suppose I'm behind the times.' Her wide, cruel mouth hardened. 'Even the diseases have changed since I was a girl.' She gave her husband a sharp,

62

accusing glare. She hated him for his ulcers. 'You haven't eaten your scone, dear.'

'Old tummy . . .' he mumbled. 'I'd better see to that weeding.' His wife knew how to whip him on.

'The heat . . .' said Catherine Cornelius, and her bosom heaved. 'Isn't it a bit . . . ?'

'Used to the heat, my girl.' He squared his shoulders. A funny little smile appeared beneath his grey moustache. There was considerable pride in his stance. 'Drilled in full dress uniform. India. Much worse than this. Like the heat.' He lit the cigarette he had rolled. 'You're the cream in my coffee, I'm the milk in your tea, pom-te-pomm-pom-pom-pom.' He smiled shyly and affectionately at her as he opened the door which led into the back garden. He gave her a comic, swaggering salute. 'See you later, I hope.'

Left alone, Elizabeth and Catherine looked longingly at each other across the real Jacobean table.

'We should be getting back to Ladbroke Grove soon if we're not to get caught in the traffic,' said Catherine glancing at the door through which Mrs Nye has passed with the tea things.

'Yes,' said Elizabeth. 'We shouldn't leave it too late, should we?'

J.C.

Jerry's coffin was being rocked about quite a lot. The train carrying it stopped suddenly once again. It was about a mile outside Coventry. The awful smell always increased when the train was stationary. Was it the steam?

Colonel Pyat got up from the dirty floor to peer through the little hole in the armour plating of his truck. The light was fading but he could see a grimy grey-green field and a pylon. On the horizon were rows of red brick houses. He looked at his watch. It was nine o'clock in the evening; it had been exactly three days since the train had left Edinburgh. Pyat brushed at his torn and grubby uniform. He had nothing else to wear, yet it was now far too dangerous to be seen in military uniform outside London. He munched the last half of his stale sandwich and sipped a drop of vodka from his hip flask. There had been no change in Cornelius and Pyat had had no time to revive and question him. The colonel had given up his original ambition, anyway; now he hoped he might use the contents of the coffin as his safe-conduct, his guarantee of asylum, when he reached Ladbroke Grove and contacted one of the Cornelius relatives. Matters had not gone well in Berlin after Auchinek and his Zaporozhian allies had arrived. Somebody had told Pyat that no one could hold Berlin for more than a month and he hadn't believed them. Now this knowledge was his consolation – even the Jew would not last long before someone else took over what was left of the city.

From within the coffin came a further succession of muffled shrieks and cries. Pyat heard a querulous shout from further up the train. Another voice replied in a strong Wolverhampton accent.

'Electricity failure, they think. The two other trains can't run. No signals, see.'

Again the distant shout and the Wolverhampton voice

replying: 'We'll be moving shortly. We can't go until the signal says we can.'

Pyat lit a cigarette. Sourly he paced the carriage, wishing he had thought of a better plan. A week ago England had seemed the safest state in Europe. Now it was in chaos. He should have guessed what would happen. Everything broke down so rapidly nowadays. But then, on the other hand, things came together quickly, too. It was the price you paid for swift communications.

The light faded and the single electric bulb in the roof glowed and then dimmed until only the element shone with a dull orange colour. Pyat had become used to this. He settled down to try to sleep, convinced that the sharp pain which had returned to his chest could only be lung cancer. He wished he had some cocaine.

He began to nod off. But then the sounds from the coffin filled his head. They had changed in tone so that this time they seemed to be warning him of something. They had become more urgent. He stretched out his boot and kicked at the coffin. 'Shut up. I don't need any more of that.'

But the urgency of the cries did not abate.

Pyat climbed to his feet and stumbled forward with the intention of unstrapping the lid and putting a gag of some kind into Cornelius's mouth. But then the truck lurched. He fell. The big Pacific-class loco was moving again. He hugged his bruised body. His eyes were tightly shut.

It was dawn.

A green Morgan of the decadent Plus 8 period droned swiftly along the platform, passing the train as it pulled at last into an almost deserted King's Cross station. The car followed the train for a moment, then turned off the platform into the main ticket office and drove through the outer doors and down the steps into the street. Through his peep-hole Colonel Pyat watched blearily, certain that the Morgan had some connection with himself. A strong smell, like that of a fair quantity of hard-boiled eggs, reached his

65

nostrils. He spat on the boards and jammed his eyes once again to the spy-hole.

Expecting a large crowd at King's Cross, he had planned to lose himself in it. But there were no crowds. There was no one. It was as if all the people had been cleared from the station. Could it be an ambush? Or merely an air-riad?

The locomotive released a huge sigh of hot steam and halted.

Pyat remembered that he was unarmed.

If he emerged from the carriage now, would he be shot down? Where were the marksmen hiding?

He unbolted the sliding doors of the wagon and slid them back. He waited for the other passengers to disembark. After a few seconds it became clear that there were no other passengers. A few small, innocent sounds came from various parts of the station. A clatter. A cheerful whistling. A thump. Then silence. He saw the fireman and the driver and the guard leave the train and swagger through the barrier towards the main exit, carrying their gear. They wore dirty BR uniforms; their caps were pushed back as far as possible on their heads. They were all three middle-aged, stocky and plain. They walked slowly, chatting easily to each other. They turned a corner and were gone. Pyat felt abandoned. Steam still clung to the lower parts of the train and drifted over the platform. Pyat sniffed the smoky air as a hound might sniff for a fox. The high, sooty arches of the station were silent and the glass dome admitted only a little dirty sunlight.

Because it was dawn, a bird or two began to twitter in the steel beams near the roof.

Pyat shivered and got down. Walking to the far side of the platform he took hold of a large porter's trolley. The wheels squeaked and grated. He dragged it alongside the armoured carriage. He felt faint. He looked warily about him. Silent, untended trains stood at every platform. Huge black and green steam engines with dirty brasswork faced worn steel bumpers and the blank brick walls beyond. They were like monsters shocked into catatonia by a sudden understand-

66

ing: this had been their last journey. They had been lured into involuntary hibernation, perhaps to remain here until they rusted and rotted to dust.

Pyat manhandled the heavy coffin on to the trolley. It bumped down and a somewhat pettish mewling escaped from it. Pyat took the handles of the trolley with both hands. He strained backwards and got it moving. He hauled it with some difficulty along the asphalt. The wheels squeaked and groaned. In his filthy white uniform he might have been mistaken for a porter who had been mysteriously transferred from some more tropical station, perhaps in India. He was not really as conspicuous as he felt.

He trudged through the ticket barrier, crossed the grey expanse of the enclave and reached the pavement outside. The streets and buildings all seemed uninhabited. Wasn't this the heart of London? And a Thursday morning? Pyat looked up at the bland sky. There were no aircraft to be seen. No dirigibles. No flying bombs. The bright early sunshine was already quite warm. It dulled his shivers.

A tattered horse-drawn lavender cab stood untended by the kerb outside the main entrance. Now that the Morgan had disappeared, it was the only form of transport in sight. The driver, however, was nowhere to be seen. Pyat decided that he did not care about the driver. With almost the last of his strength, Pyat got the coffin into the hansom and climbed up to the box. He shook the reins and the bony mare raised her head. He flicked her rump with the frayed whip and shouted at her. She began to walk.

Slowly the hansom moved away, the horse refusing to go faster than a walk. It was as if the hansom were the only visible portion of an otherwise invisible funeral procession. The horse's feet clopped mournfully through the deserted street. It reached Euston Road and began to head due west for Ladbroke Grove.

. . . and perhaps the greatest loss I still feel is the loss of my unborn son. I was certain it would have been a son and I had even named it, my subconscious coming up with a name I would never have chosen otherwise: Andrew. I had not realized what would happen to me. The abortion seemed so necessary at the time if she were not to suffer in several ways. But it was an abortion of convenience, scarcely of desperation. For a long while I did not admit that it had affected me at all. If I had ever had a son after that, I feel it would have banished the sense of loss, but as it is it will go with me to my grave.

MAURICE LESCOQ, *Leavetaking*

SHOT TWO

Thunder Brings Coma Boy Back to Life

Only a miracle could save nine-year-old Lawrence Mantle,
said doctors. For four months he had been in a deep coma.
Twice he 'died' when his heart stopped beating. There was
no sign of life from his brain, surgeons told his parents.
Then, in the middle of a thunderstorm, it happened. A flash
of lightning and a loud thunderclap made nurses in the
children's ward at Ashford hospital, Middlesex, jump . . .
and Lawrence, still in a coma, screamed.

London Evening News, December 3 1969

The Observers

Colonel Pyat had first met Colonel Cornelius in Guatemala City, in the early days of the 1900–75 War, before the monorails, the electric carriages, the giant airships, the domed cities and the utopian republics had been smashed, never to be restored. They met at some time during what is now called the Phoney War period of 1901–13. They were both representing the military establishments of two great and mutually suspicious European governments. They had been sent to observe the trials of the Guatemalans' latest Land Ironclad (the invention of the Chilean wizard, O'Bean). Their two governments had been interested in purchasing a number of the machines should the trials prove successful. As it happened, both Pyat and Cornelius had decided that the 'clad was still too primitive to be of much practical use, though the French, German and Turkish governments, who also had observers at the trials, had each ordered a small quantity.

Their duty done, the two men relaxed together in the bar of the Conquistador Hotel, where they were both staying. Next day they would catch the aerial clipper *Light of Dresden* to Hamburg. Once there, they would go their separate ways, Cornelius to the West and Pyat to the East.

Through the tall, slightly frosted Charles Rennie Mackintosh windows they could see Guatemala City's bright marble streets and elegant mosaic towers with shopfronts by Mucha, Moulins and Marnez. Sometimes an ornate electric brougham would hum past, or there would be the anachronistic jingle of harness as a landau, drawn by high-stepping Arab stallions, rattled by; sometimes a steam car would come and go, the hiss from its engines barely audible, the sun catching its brasswork and making its stainless steel body shine like silver. The steam car was now in use all over the world. Like the mechanical farming equipment which had turned South and Central America into such a paradise, it was the creation of O'Bean.

Colonel Pyat, leaning back in his black plush chair, signalled for the waiter to bring fresh drinks. Jerry admired his grace. The Russian had been wearing his white uniform for the best part of the afternoon and there was not a smudge of dust to be seen on it. Even his belts, his holster and his boots were of white kid, the only colour being the gold insignia on his collar and a touch of gold on his epaulettes. Jerry's dark green uniform was fussy in comparison, with a smear of oil evident on the right cuff. Some of the gold braid frogging on his sleeves, shoulders and chest was badly snagged, too. His belts, holster and boots were black. They were not quite as brightly polished as they might have been. Like Pyat's, his was a cavalry uniform, that of some Indian regiment by the cut of the long-skirted coat, but worn without a sash. (Pyat, who had seen some service on the frontier – largely courier work of an unofficial nature – could not place the uniform at all. He wondered if Cornelius might be a civilian given military rank for the sake of this assignment. Certainly Cornelius did not look much like an English cavalryman. The way he had undone his coat at the first opportunity suggested that Cornelius found military dress uncomfortable.)

The drinks were brought by a haughty waiter who refused to respond to Pyat's friendly and condescending smile and left the proffered tip on the Husson silver salver he placed on the table. 'Democracy gone mad!' said Pyat with a movement of his eyebrows and leaned forward to see what they had. There were Tiffany glasses. A bottle of Malvern water. A Glen Grant malt whisky and a Polish Starka vodka. Jerry looked at them all resting on the Dufrêne inlay.

'They think we are barbarians,' said Pyat, filling Jerry's glass with whisky and letting Jerry add his own Malvern water, 'but they do not mind selling us weapons and war machines. Where would their economy be without us?'

Jerry reached his hand half-way to his drink. 'They'd like us to get it over with, though. We disturb them by our continued existence. We've been staving off the apocalypse for so long. Suppose we turned on them? They have no army.'

'Then they are fools. How long can this *Traumrepublik* last? A few more years?'

'Months, more likely. Keep your voice down. They don't have to know . . .'

Pyat's ironic glance gave way to a look of introspection. 'You speak like a priest. Not a soldier.' It was a statement which hoped for a reply, but Jerry merely smiled and picked up his glass.

'To which regiment do you belong, Colonel?' Pyat decided on a direct approach.

Jerry looked curiously at his uniform as if he himself hoped to find some clue to the answer there. 'The 30th Deccan Horse, I think.'

'You have been seconded, then?'

'Quite likely. No.'

'You are a civilian!'

Jerry laughed. 'Well, I'm not sure, you know.' He shook his head. There were tears in his eyes now as his whole body trembled with mirth. 'I'm simply not sure.'

Pyat laughed too, because he enjoyed laughing. 'Let's get a bottle each, shall we? I have a suite upstairs. And perhaps someone can find us a couple of girls? Or perhaps two girls will volunteer their services! Everyone is emancipated in Guatemala City!'

'Fine!'

When they had risen. Pyat flung his arm around Jerry's slender shoulders. 'Do you feel like a girl, Colonel Cornelius?'

The Performers

Dressed as a gentleman, Una Persson stalked the stage behind the green velvet curtain.

From the other side of the curtain came the noise of the crowd: shouts, laughter, screams, ironic cheers, groans, the clink of glasses and bottles, the rustle of heavy clothing. In the pit the orchestra was tuning up for the overture.

His paleness emphasized by the astrakhan collar of his chesterfield, Sebastian Auchinek raised a gold-tipped Unfiadis to his curved lips and coughed. He sat on a prop – an imitation rock – and looked through hooded eyes at the ballet girls in their frothy costumes as they took their places for the opening divertissement. Behind the girls was a backdrop showing Windsor Castle. The girls were dressed to represent *Rose*, *Shamrock*, *Thistle* and *Wales* (in a tall black hat and a pinafore because a leek had been thought too indelicate a plant). The divertissement was entitled 'Under One Flag'. In the wings, waiting to go on, stood Sailors, Highlanders and Beefeaters. Una Persson was not appearing in the first of the two tableaux. She would feature in the second, 'Honour to the Queen', and lead the chorus in the closing cantata.

'You will be a success, Una!' Auchinek got up and caught her by the arm. 'You are bound to be! Come, the curtain!' The gas flared brightly above the stage, the electrical spotlights began to come on. 'It is going up!'

She walked swiftly into the wings. Auchinek hurried behind her. She pushed her way nervously past Mr Clement Scott, author of the opening Patriotic Ode. The orchestra began to play a rousing chorus of the satirical *Oh, What a Happy Land is England*:

We shall soon be buying Consols, at the rate of half-a-crown,
For like the Russian battleships, they're always going down!

75

We have lately built an Airship and the only thing it lacks
Is the power to go on rising like the British Income Tax!
      Hip-hip-hooray!
    Oh! what a happy land is England!
    Envied by all Nations near and far!
    Where the wretched Alien
    Robs the British working men!
    Oh! what a lucky race we are!
    O! what a happy land is England!
    Envied by all Nations near and far!
    All Foreigners have found
    This a happy dumping ground!
    Oh! what a lucky race we are!

sang the audience and then began to cheer. The curtain rose.

Una reached the dressing room. Though she shared it with Marguerite Cornille, the comedienne, it was the best equipped dressing room she had ever used. This was her first time at the Empire, Leicester Square. It was one of the most respected of the newer, better class of music halls: a Theatre of Varieties. But it was the very reputation and respectability of the Empire which distressed Una so much. She was used to the friendlier, less ostentatious halls of Stepney, Brixton and Shepherd's Bush.

'The atmosphere's a bit frosty.' She entered the dressing room and nodded to Mlle Cornille who was making up already, with one eye on the mirror and the other on a magazine she held in her left hand, even though she was tenth on the programme.

'You get used to it, love. The crowd's all right. Same as anywhere.' The pert-faced girl was re-reading a short photographic feature about herself in *Nash's Magazine* which had just come out. 'The rules and the snobs is the price you pay for regular work. It's my last week here. It'll be back to three different halls a night for me if I'm lucky and no halls at all if it's really bad. So my two weeks at the Alhambra over Christmas'll be like a holiday.' She was boasting a bit, for a feature in *Nash's* usually meant a few good bookings

76

at very least. Una wondered if *she* would ever go so far as showing her legs for a *Nash's* photographer.

Auchinek came in, closing the door softly behind him. 'A good audience, by the sound of it.'

'What I was saying,' said Mlle Cornille.

Auchinek offered them Unfiadis Egyptian cigarettes from his gold Liberty's case. Mlle Cornille shook her head, but Una accepted one. As she lit it herself she looked closely at Auchinek, wondering what his real thoughts were.

'It's a step up, Una.' He was her agent and in love with what he saw as her perfection, but he was embarrassed by the fact that he found Mlle Cornille's brown curls and buxom charms more physically attractive. He was hoping that Una had not noticed. That Mlle Cornille had noticed was evident in the attitude of friendly contempt she took towards him.

Una picked up her music and read over the lines of her songs as she finished the cigarette. There was a knock on the door. 'Overture and beginners second tab.'

Una felt her stomach muscles tighten. She spread her fingers wide as she ran her palms down the front of her thighs, over her trousers. Auchinek stepped forward and adjusted her bow tie. He handed her the cane and the silk opera hat, he flicked a speck of glitter from her tailcoat. 'All right?'

She smiled. If she had had her own way she would have remained out of the West End, but she knew that he desperately wanted her to get to the top; and that was what performing at the Empire meant.

'Good luck, love,' said Mlle Cornille, both eyes now on her article.

'Stay here,' said Una to Auchinek.

'I'd rather . . .' He glanced guiltily away from the comedienne. 'Give you moral support.'

'Stay here.' She straightened her coat and put on her silk hat. 'You can come to the wings and watch as soon as I'm on.'

'Very well.'

She walked down the corridor. Against a tide of returning Highlanders, Sailors, Beefeaters, Roses, Shamrocks, Thistles and Welsh girls, she made her way towards the wings. In the wings she saw that the chorus was already arranging itself on stage. There were eight girls, each dressed as a colony. There was India, Canada, Australia, Cape Colony, the West Indies, Malta, Gibraltar and New Zealand, each with her own verse to sing. In the opposite wings waited Art, Science, Commerce, Industry and a splendid Britannia, whose carriage they were to draw on stage. That was when Una would come on.

The curtain rose and the orchestra began a rousing accompaniment as the chorus sang together:

We, the children of the Empire, pay homage to our Queen!
And we know she can be counted on where e'er her flag is seen!
She's good, she's just, she's mighty and we know you will agree
She's loved, admired and envied through all the seven seas!

Una felt calm now. The music was jolly enough and the audience applauded loudly at the end of every verse and joined in each chorus. They weren't anything like as stuffy as she'd thought they'd be.

Art, Science, Commerce and Industry began to pull at Britannia's carriage. The float moved forward with a slight lurch. India, Canada, Australia, Cape Colony, the West Indies, Malta, Gibraltar and New Zealand fell back on two sides of the stage. The orchestra struck up with the opening bars of Una's introduction. Una cleared her throat, took a deep breath and poised herself.

The gaslight dimmed.

At first Una thought it had been done for deliberate dramatic effect. But then the lights went out altogether, including the electrics, and the clapping faded, matches were struck, an anxious murmur began to fill the theatre.

Something exploded in the gallery. Someone shouted loudly. Women screamed. Una Persson was thrown backwards into the curtains and fell down. Feet struck her face and a body fell across her legs. The curtain collapsed over her. She heard muffled exclamations.

'Anarchists!'

'An air-raid!'

'Una? Una?' Auchinek's voice.

She tried to get up but could not fight free of the velvet folds.

'Sebastian!'

'Una!' His soft hands began to tear away the curtains.

She saw his face. It was bright red. There were flames leaping in the stalls. The crowd was a confused mass of flapping coat-tails, bustles and feather hats. It was climbing on to the stage, unable to use the ordinary exits.

Auchinek helped her to her feet. The heat from the flames was horrible. They were almost pushed into the orchestra pit by the panic-stricken audience. He held her tightly.

'What happened?' She let him guide her back to the wings. They were carried with the crowd towards the stage door. The fire roared behind them. Smoke made their eyes water and stung their throats. Props crashed down. Individual voices blended into one terrified wail.

'Incendiary bomb. Dropped from the gallery, I think. Why did it have to be tonight, Una? Your most important chance. The theatre will be closed for a week at least.'

They reached the alley which ran beside the theatre. It was clogged with bewildered entertainers in flimsy, polychrome costumes, the frightened audience in heavy serge and scarlet and green velvet. At the end of the alley stood a tall, bearded policeman trying to calm the crowd and stop it from rushing headlong over the edge of the street and into the forty-foot-deep crater which, until the air-raids had begun a month ago, had been Leicester Square.

By the time the fire engines arrived at the front of the theatre, many of the people had been allowed to pass through the police cordon and the press had thinned. It was cold and there was a trace of fog in the air. The gas must have been turned off at a main, for none of the nearby street lamps was alight. The only illumination came from the policemen's bullseyes and the fire itself. She felt full of relief. 'Back to Brixton,' she said. 'What's bad luck for some is good luck for others, Seb, my boy.'

He directed at her a mixed look of misery and malice. 'Don't count on Brixton, Una. At this rate they'll be closing down all the halls.' He regretted his spite. 'I'm sorry.' He took off his coat and placed it round her shoulders over the man's jacket she still wore.

More fire engines arrived – steamers this time – and the police let a substantial number of people through the cordon.

A sensation of being watched made her glance back at the theatre. She saw a young man leaning against the open stage door looking for all the world like a masher waiting casually for the appearance of his favourite chorus girl. He wore a dark yellow frock-coat with an exaggerated waist and flair, with brown braid at collar and cuff. He had a matching bowler with its brim tightly curled, a light brown cravat, and bell bottomed trousers cut very tight at the knee. The trousers were in a mustard check some would have considered vulgar. His gold-topped stick was in his left hand and an empty amber cigar-holder in his right. On the third finger of his right hand was a heavy gold signet ring. He seemed either unaware of the confusion around him or careless of it.

Una Persson regarded him with interest. His black, soft hair hung straight to his shoulders in the style of the aesthetes of some years earlier. His long, lean face bore an ambiguous expression which might have been amusement or satisfaction or suprise. His black eyes were large, deep-set, unreadable. Suddenly, with a nod to her, he stepped sideways and entered the burning theatre. Impulsively she made to follow him. Then she felt Auchinek's hand on her shoulder.

'Don't worry,' he said. 'This can't last forever.'

She looked again at the stage door. The dark smoky interior of the theatre was now alive with red flame. She saw the young man's silhouette against the firelight before it disappeared, apparently marching without hesitation in the heart of the inferno.

'He'll die!' Una said softly. 'The heat!'

Auchinek said anxiously: 'Are you sure you're yourself, Una?'

The Seducers

Mrs Cornelius settled her pink feather boa around her broad shoulders and patted it down over the green and white fabric flowers decorating her fine big bosom. She wasn't doing too badly for thirty, she thought, giving her image a wink and dabbing at the rouge on her right cheek with a damp finger which protruded from the *broderie anglaise* cuff.

"And up me 'at, love.'

The mean-faced boy of fifteen wiped his nose on the sleeve of his tattered Norfolk jacket and reached to the mock Georgian mahogany chiffonier for the extravagant pile of artificial roses, peonies and sweet Williams topped off by a yard or two of pink gauze, some wax grapes and a pair of pheasant's wings, which rested amongst her nick-nacks. In both hands he carried the hat to where she stood before the full-length fly-specked wardrobe mirror in its gilded cast-iron frame.

'And the pins, love,' she reproved, donning the hat as if it were the Crown of England.

He took the three long pins with their blue, red and gold enamelled butterfly wings and presented them in the flat of his unhealthy hand, his expression cool, like a nurse proffering a surgeon his instruments. One by one she picked them from his palm and slid them like a conjurer expertly into her hat, her hair and, apparently, her head.

'Cream!' She was satisfied. She tilted the brim just a fraction to the right. She flicked at a pheasant feather.

'Shall I be in this evening?' asked the boy. His accent while by no means educated was definably in contrast to the woman's. 'Or not?'

'Better stay at Sammy's, love. I think I'll be entertaining tonight.' She smiled comfortably at herself and admired her large, well-corseted figure for a while, hands on hips. 'You're looking prime, girlie.' She gathered her pale green satin skirts and pirouetted on her matching patent leather boots. 'You'll do, you will.'

The boy put his hands in his pockets and swaggered about the untidy, over-furnished bedroom whistling, without irony, *I'm Gilbert, the Filbert, the Colonel of the Knuts.* He marched through the open door into the gaslit parlour. The parlour was a dark jungle of aspidistra and mahogany. Opening the front door of the flat he spread his arms, running and leaping down the lodging house's uncarpeted stairs and making a high-pitched whining sound as he pretended he was a fighting aeroplane making a death dive on its enemies. He rushed panting into Blenheim Crescent and was almost knocked over by the baker's motor van which hooted at him as it puffed past in the twilight. On the corner of the dowdy street, where it met Ladbroke Grove, under the unlit lamp and by the wall of the Convent of the Poor Clares, stood a group of younger urchins. They spotted him at once. They yelled at him, jeering insults which were more than familiar to him. He veered and began to walk in the opposite direction, pretending not to have noticed them, and went up towards Kensington Park Road and Sammy's pie shop on the corner. Some people thought Sammy might be the boy's dad, the way he favoured him. The boy always got first chance at shooting the rats in the cellar. Sammy kept a .22 pistol for the purpose. But, when pressed, the boy's mother usually claimed the Prince of Wales for the honour. There was, however, a rumour concerning a Russian.

A thick, tasty smell of grease billowed from the warm shop and steam boiled in the yellow light from the street door and from the grating in the pavement under the window where, on gas burners, sat enamel trays of pies, sausages, bacon, faggots, saveloys and baked potatoes, heavy with shining, dancing fat. At his stoves behind the wooden counter stood warm, greasy Sammy. With his thin assistant beside him he gave his attention to a score of long-handled frying pans, each of which contained a different kind of food. The shop having just opened for the evening, the only customer was little frightened Mrs Fitzgerald, from round the corner in Portobello Road, getting her husband's dinner. Her shawl was drawn close to her face, but Sammy had noticed what she was hoping to hide. 'That's a lovely shiner!' He grinned sympathetically as he wrapped the pies but Mrs Fitzgerald looked as if he had caught her in the act of some mortal sin. Her right eye was swollen green, blue and purple. She gave a barely audible but evidently embarrassed cough. The boy stared neutrally at her bruise. Sammy saw the boy. 'Hellow, there, nipper!' The colour of his own sausages, his fat, Jewish face ran with sweat. His striped shirt sleeves were rolled to his elbows and he wore a big white grease-spotted apron. 'You come to give me a hand have you?' The boy nodded, stepping aside from Mrs Fitzgerald who seized her pies, left the correct number of pennies on the counter, and, like a mouse making for its hole, scuttled from the shop. 'Mum says can I stay the night?'

Sammy's expression became serious and he said in a different tone, attending suddenly to his frying pans, 'Yes, that's all right. But you gotta work for your keep. Get yourself an apron off the hook, son. We'll be busy in a minute.'

The boy removed his threadbare Norfolk and hung it on the hook at the back of the shop. Taking down a sacking apron he pulled it over his head and tied the strings round his waist. He began to roll up his sleeves. Sammy's assistant was a young man of eighteen or so, his face gleaming with large, scarlet pimples. He said, 'Go on up the other end. I'll do this end.' The boy squeezed past Sammy's great bottom and went to stand near the window where the sizzling trays filled his nostrils full of the stink of frying onions. His eyes wandered past the trays and through the misted glass where they fixed on the street.

It was now dark and populated. Men, women, and children came from all sides, bearing down on the pie shop, because it was Friday. They all had the glazed look of the really poor – the poverty trance had overtaken them, robbed them of their wills and their intelligence, enabling them to continue life only in terms of a few simple rituals. There was little animation on even the faces of the children and their tired, heavy movements, their set expressions, their dull eyes made it seem that they all belonged to the same family, so strongly did they resemble one another. The boy felt a shudder of fear and for no reason that he could tell he suddenly thought, with some tenderness, of his mother. He turned to look at the pub on the opposite corner to Sammy's, the Blenheim Arms. The gas was being lit. The large crowd of out-of-work Irishmen and local loafers which had gathered outside its doors gave a ragged cheer. It was opening time.

Again the boy shivered.

'What's the matter, son?' said Sammy noticing. 'You catching something?'

The Interpreters

Captain Nye received an order to report to his barracks, the Royal Alberts in Southwark, where his CO, Colonel Collier, informed him that the Black Flag had been raised in Argyll and that an anarchist army of some 8000 men was camped in Glen Coe where it would shortly be joined by a force of French Zouaves (about a thousand) which had landed at Oban a week earlier, claiming to be independent volunteers. It was no secret that the French had territorial ambitions in Scotland, but this was the most blatant act of support to the rebel clans they had yet given. It was putting a distinct strain on the fiction of the Entente Cordiale.

'We do not want a direct confrontation with France for all sorts of reasons at the moment.' Colonel Collier fingered his buttons and the cuffs of his tunic. 'So this must be handled damned delicately, Nye. Neither, it seems, does the present government want any military action against the hill tribes if we can help it. You've had dealings with these people before, I gather?'

'I've some experience of the Highland clans, sir.'

'I want you to go and talk to Gareth-mac Mahon, their chief. He's a sly old devil, by all accounts. Used to serve with one of our native regiments. Learned all our tricks, needless to say, and took 'em back to the hills with him. I'm sure he knows he can't beat us. Probably be satisfied with a few concessions. So find out what he wants and let us know as soon as possible. This is more in the nature of a diplomatic mission than a military one.'

'I understand, sir.'

'They're plucky blighters, but it looks as if their virtues have turned into vices.' Collier stood up behind his desk. 'It's the same with their pride. They're prepared to sacrifice all that they've gained under British rule in order to chase this chimera of "independence". Even if they should have some success, the French would move in at once. Mahon must realize this. They call him the Red Fox, I gather. Because of his cunning. Well, he's certainly no fool. Try to talk him round.'

Captain Nye refused the offer of a squadron of motor escorted cavalry and instead asked for a single small dirigible flying machine which might be loaned by the Royal Airship Corps. 'Let us impress them,' he said, 'with our science rather than our sabres.'

Glen Coe was glorious in her autumn colours. Her bronze hills shivered with white streams which fell from scores of sources high up near the crest of the range. The dirigible hovered over the valley and Captain Nye peered through the observation ports in the large aluminium gondola and noticed, with some satisfaction, the consternation of the Zouaves in their blue tarbooshes, blue tunics and baggy red trousers as they became aware of the green and khaki camouflaged monster over their heads. The shadow of the ship moved implacably across the camp, its steam turbines purring as a hungry leopard might purr while stalking a herd of unsuspecting and succulent antelope. Down the glen sailed the aerial frigate, just a few feet above the tops of the tallest hills, following the boisterous river upstream to the falls at the far end of the valley. The bravest of the French mercenaries (if mercenaries they were) took a few pot-shots at the airship, but either they missed, fell short, or their bullets failed to penetrate the tough boron-fibre shell of the vessel.

Then the Zouaves were left behind and Captain Nye signalled to the captain to cut his engines to half-speed, for they were almost at their destination. The main camp lay ahead, a collection of semi-ruined crofts, hide tents, and peat or bracken shelters. They were clustered on the tawny hillside which shone like beaten gold as the sunlight struck it. Horses, tracked vehicles, Bofors guns and Banning cannon, as well as cooking and medical equipment, had been scattered apparently at random amongst the other

87

paraphernalia of the camp. Broadswords, dirks and lances glittered beside pyramids of stacked rifles with fixed bayonets. Kilted clansmen sat talking in groups, passing bottles and cigarettes, or else wandered drunkenly about with no apparent purpose. Over this savage encampment fluttered the sinister black banner of Anarchy – Mahon's adopted standard. Gareth-mac Mahon's own tent was easily spotted. It was a huge expanse of intricately woven blue, yellow, green and scarlet plaid. The scarlet was predominant. The folds of this great pavilion undulated slightly in a wind which blew through the hills from the west.

'Break out the flag now, sir?' The smart young second officer saluted Nye and the airship's captain, a man named Bastable. Bastable looked enquiringly at Nye. Nye nodded. They watched as the white parley flag billowed over the side, suspended from a line attached to the stern of the control gondola.

'Take her down a couple of degrees height, coxswain,' said Captain Bastable.

'Two degrees down, sir.'

The ship dropped lower. Its engines reversed to keep it steady against the wind. As it fell, a number of the savages dived for cover while their braver (or drunker) comrades ran forward waving their broadswords and howling like devils. They calmed down when they recognized the white flag, but they did not sheathe their words. They watched with glowering suspicion as the ship steadied less than fifteen feet over the Mahon's own tent. Captain Nye brushed his fine brown moustache with the back of his hand, waited a few moments and then stepped on to the outer gallery and stood with one hand on the rail, the other in a dignified salute of peace, speaking clearly in their own language. 'I come to offer peace to the Mahon. To you all.' There was a pause while the savages continued to glower and then the flap of the pavilion was pushed back and a heavy Scotlander emerged. For all his barbaric finery, the Mahon was an impressive man. He was clad in the traditional costume of the hill chieftain: the philabeg kilt, the huge, hairy sporran;

the elaborately worked (if rather grubby) lace shirt, the plentitude of little leather straps and buttons and buckles and pins of bronze and silver, the big woollen bonnet secured by a hawk-feather badge; the green coatee with silver epaulettes; the black, buckled shoes; the clan plaid flung over his shoulder – the regalia befitting a great clan leader. All the cloth he wore, save for the coat and shirt, including the decorative tops of his green cross-gartered stockings, was of the same tartan as the tent. Nye recognized it as the red Mahon Fighting sett. The Mahon himself was short and broad-shouldered, with a red, belligerent face. He had a hooked nose, pale, piercing blue eyes and a monstrous grey-streaked red beard. With one hand on the hilt of his heavy, basket-hilted broadsword and the other on his hip he raised his head slowly, calling out in a proud growl.

'The Mahon acknowledges your truce flag. Do you come to parley?'

Although the Red Fox revealed nothing, by his expression, Captain Nye was sure he was properly impressed by the aerial frigate. 'My government wants to preserve peace, O Mahon,' he said in English. 'May I descend to the ground?'

'If ye wish.' Gareth-mac Mahon replied in the same language.

At Captain Nye's request, the rail was broken and a rope ladder rolled through the gap. Nye went down the ladder with as much dignity as was possible until he stood confronting the wily old hill fox. This was a man who had discovered the creed of anarchism while serving as a soldier in the capitals of the civilized world. He had brought the creed back to his native land, adapted it and turned it into a philosophy capable of bringing together all the previously disunited tribes. Nye was by no means deceived by the Mahon's appearance. He was well aware that he was not addressing a simple savage. If he had known nothing at all about the Mahon, he would still have recognized the look of profound cunning which glinted even now in those pale eyes.

'O Chieftain,' began the captain in Scottish as soon as he had recovered his breath, 'you have made the great Chief-of-us-All sad. I come to tell you this. He wonders why his children gather all these weapons to themselves.' He spread his arms to indicate the camp. 'And give hospitality to soldiers from other shores.'

In the distance the autumn river roared down the narrow gorge, its flow altering constantly as it was fed by a thousand tiny streams which streaked the hills; white veins in yellow marble. Throughout the half-mile radius of the camp the savage warriors stood and looked as their leader talked with the soldier who had come from the sky. Each of the men had a naked sword in his hand and Nye knew that if he made one mistake he would never be able to reach the airship before he was slaughtered beneath those shining blades.

The Red Fox's smile was grim and his eyes were like polished granite. 'His Majesty will be sadder still, O Emissary, when he learns we intend to make war on those of our own folk who are foolish enough to side with the soldiers. We have already razed Fort William IV.'

'The Chief-of-us-All should punish you for that,' said the captain, 'but he is slow to anger. He understands that his children have been misled by the honeyed tongues of men from across the seas. Men who would make his children fight their battles for them.'

The Mahon rubbed his nose with a large hand and looked amused. 'Tell His Majesty that we are not his children. We are mountain warriors. We shall preserve our ancient ways. We would rather die than become the subject race of any foreigner.'

'But what of your women? Your sons and your daughters? Do they wish to see their menfolk die? Will they be happy if the schools, the doctors, the medicines – aye and the merchants who buy their wares – disappear from this land?'

'We'll provide our own schools and doctors – and we'll have no more merchants ever again in the mountains of Argyll!'

Captain Nye smiled at the idea and was about to reply

when he noticed a movement of the tent flap behind the Mahon.

A tall figure emerged to stand at the chief's side. He wore a suit of heather-mixture tweeds. A shooting hat was pulled down to shade his face, a monocle gleamed in his right eye. From his mouth jutted a black cheroot. 'I'm afraid you'll have no luck with that argument, captain. The chief here has already decided that the advantages of British rule are outweighed by the disadvantages.'

For all the evidence of his eyes and ears, Captain Nye could hardly believe that this was an Englishman. A renegade. He tried to hide his astonishment. 'Who the devil are you, sir?'

'Just an observer, old chap. And an adviser, of sorts, I suppose.' The man paused, his attention given to the faint humming which filled the air, drowning, eventually, the sound of the water. He smiled.

'This is Mr Cornelius,' said the Mahon. 'He has helped us with our fleet. Here it comes now.' The hill chieftain pointed behind Nye. The captain turned to look.

Over the brow of the farthest hills came swimming upwards of a hundred massive aerial men-o'-war. They were airships of a type far in advance of anything Nye had seen before. They bristled with artillery gondoli. Their slender cigar-shaped hulls were like the bodies of gigantic sharks. On each silver-grey side, on each elevator fin was painted a livery which combined the black flag of Anarchy and the blue cross of Scotland.

'Cornelius . . . ?' Nye looked back towards the tent but the tall man had gone inside. The Red Fox chuckled. 'An engineer, I believe,' he said, 'of some experience.' He broke into English. 'Perhaps we shall meet again in Whitehall, will we not, Master Emissary?'

'I'll be damned!'

Nye turned again to look at the massive battle fleet cramming the sky, to notice the power of the guns, to speculate upon the destruction they and the aerial torpedoes could accomplish. 'I'm dreaming.'

'D'ye think so?'

The Explorers

Catherine Cornelius left her brother's lodgings in Powys Square. She hurried back through the dark streets to her own house where she had heard Prinz Lobkowitz and his friends awaited her. One or two gaslamps glowed through the clinging fog but cast little light. There were a few muffled sounds, but she could identify none of them. It was with relief that she entered Elgin Crescent with its big overgrown trees and its tall comfortable houses; perhaps because the street was so familiar the fog did not seem so thick though she still had to walk with some care until she reached Number 61. Shivering, she unlatched the gate and at last mounted her own steps, searching in her Dorothy bag for her key. She found it, unlocked the door and went inside. Fog drifted in with her. It filled the cold and gloomy hall like ectoplasm. Without taking off her coat she crossed the hall and opened the door to the drawing room. The drawing room was painted in a mixture of yellow and pale brown. She noticed that the fire was almost out. Removing her gloves she reached down and put several pieces of coal on top of the red cinders, then she turned and acknowledged the company. There were two others beside Prinz Lobkowitz; a man and a woman.

'These are the guests I mentioned,' explained the Prinz softly. 'I'm sorry about the fire.' He indicated the woman. 'Miss Brunner' – and the man – 'Mr Smiles' – and sat down in the horseshoe armchair nearest the grate, one booted foot on the brass rail.

Catherine Cornelius looked shyly at Miss Brunner and then became wary. Foxy, she thought. Miss Brunner had neat red hair and sharp, beautiful features. She wore a well-cut grey travelling cape and a small pill-box hat perched over her right eye, decorated with a green feather, a tiny veil. Her clothes were buttoned as tightly as the black boots she revealed when seating herself on the arm of Prinz Lobkowitz's chair. Mr Smiles, bald-headed and large in a dark brown ulster, a long scarf wound several times round his neck, cleared his throat, fingered his mutton-chop whiskers as if they were not his own, unbuttoned the ulster and felt in the watch-pocket of his waistcoat, producing a gold half-hunter. He peered at it for a while before he began to wind it. 'What's the time? My watch has stopped.'

'Time?' Catherine Cornelius stared around the room in search of a clock that was going. There was a black marble one on the mantle, a grandfather in the corner.

'Nine twenty-six,' said Miss Brunner, referring to the plain silver pendant watch she wore about her neck. 'Where are our rooms, my dear? And when shall we expect supper?'

Catherine passed her hand over her forehead and said vaguely, 'Soon. I must apologize. My brother gave me very little warning, I'm afraid. The preparations. Excuse me. I'm sorry.' And she left the room, hearing Miss Brunner say, 'Well, it's a change from Calcutta.'

Catherine found Mary Greasby, the maid-of-all work, in the kitchen enjoying a glass of madeira with cook. Catherine gave instructions for beds and supper to be prepared. These instructions were received with poor grace by the servants. She returned to the drawing room with a tray on which were glasses and decanters of whisky, sherry and what remained of the madeira.

Mr Smiles stood with his back to the grate. The fire now blazed merrily. 'Ah, splendid,' he said, stepping forward and taking the tray from her. 'You must forgive our manners, dear lady. We have been travelling in a rough and ready way in some rather remote parts of the world. Just the thing. We were reluctant to impose, but – well fugitives, you know, fugitives. Ha ha!' He poured whiskies for all save Catherine who raised her hand to decline.

'How is your dear brother, Miss Cornelius?' The red-headed woman's tone was patronizing. 'We have missed him so much while we have been abroad.'

'He is well, I think,' replied Catherine. 'I thank you.'

'You are very alike. Are they not, Mr Smiles?'

'Very.'

'So I believe,' said Catherine.

'Very alike.' Reflectively Miss Brunner lowered her eyelids and sipped her drink. Catherine shivered and sat down on a hard chair near the piano.

'And how is old Frank?' said Mr Smiles. 'Eh? We've had some exciting times together, he and I. How is he?'

'I am sorry to say I have not seen him recently, Mr Smiles. He writes to Mother. The occasional postcard, you know.'

'Like me, young Frank. Bit of a globe-trotter.'

'Yes.'

Prinz Lobkowitz rose. 'I must be going, Catherine. It isn't very wise for me to stay here, considering the opinion the police hold of me at the moment. Perhaps we'll meet at the conference.'

'Shall you find a cab at this time of night? If you would care to stay – '

'I dare say I'll find one. It's a long way back to Stepney. But I thank you for the offer.' He bowed to Miss Brunner and kissed her hand. He shook hands with Mr Smiles. 'Goodbye. I hope your stay is peaceful.' He laughed. 'For you if not for them!' Catherine helped him on with his old-fashioned Armenian cloak and saw him to the front door. He bent down and kissed her on the cheek.

'Keep your spirits up, *petite Katerina*. We are sorry to make use of your house like this, but there wasn't much choice. Your brother – give him my regards. We'll probably meet soon, tell him. In Berlin, perhaps. Or at the conference?'

'I think not the conference.' Catherine hugged him. 'Be careful, my dear, my own dear Prinz Lobkowitz.'

He opened the door and drew his muffler about his mouth and chin as the fog surged in. He fitted his tall hat on his head. There came the sound of horses' hoofs on the road outside. 'A cab.' Gently he squeezed her arm and then ran into the cold darkness. Catherine closed the door and started as the maid spoke from where she stood half-way up the stairs.

'Is it just the three of you now, mum?'

Miss Brunner appeared in the drawing room doorway. Her face seemed flushed, perhaps by the alcohol. She offered Catherine a look of considerable intimacy. 'Oh, I think so,' she said, 'don't you?' She smoothed her red hair back, then she smoothed her straight flannel skirt over her thighs and pelvis. She stretched out and took Catherine's hand, leading her back into the room. Mr Smiles stood by the piano glancing through a Mozart Sonata.

'Do you play, Miss Cornelius?'

Reminiscence (C)

Someone singing.

Two young boys who disappeared from Ballinkinrain approved school near Balfron, Stirlingshire, a month ago were found dead last night at the bottom of a gorge in the Fintry Hills, two miles from the school. The bodies of John Mulver, aged 10, of Balornock, Glasgow, and Ian Finlay, aged 9, of Raploch, Stirling, were found by a search party of police and civilians who have been combing the area for the past month.

Guardian, April 13 1970

Two boys aged 15 and 9 were killed in Dacca today in the latest of a series of bombing incidents. A home-made bomb buried under rubbish in front of Pakistan's council building exploded. A man who was injured was seen riding frantically from the scene on his bicycle.

Guardian, May 12 1970

A three-year-old boy found dead in a disused refrigerator in the garden of his home in Somerset was yesterday named as Peter Wilson, of Hillside Gardens, Yatton. It is understood the refrigerator was self-locking. Eight weeks ago three-year-old twins, Lynn and Caroline Woods, died of suffocation in a disused refrigerator in their home at Farley, near Thames Ditton.

Guardian, June 2 1970

Paul Monks, aged 14, was found dead yesterday after an explosion in a wood near his home at High Street, Dawick, near Buckingham. The boy was seen on Sunday night with what appeared to be an unexploded mortar bomb.

Guardian, June 2 1970

Four people were killed and six injured when a van and two cars collided at Wroot, Lincolnshire, yesterday. Two of the dead were children.

Guardian, June 29 1970

An inquest was opened yesterday into the death at Eton of Martin Earnshaw, aged 14, son of Lady Tyneford and Mr Christopher Earnshaw. The boy was found hanging in his room at the school in the morning ... Mr Anthony Chenevix-Trench, headmaster of Eton, had said earlier that Martin was extremely popular. 'During the last few days he had been sent three times to me to be commended for his good efforts. We cannot account for this tragedy.'

Guardian, December 6 1969

Jerry turned the corner from Elgin Crescent into Ladbroke Grove. He saw that the rag-pickers were still out. They had been working through the night, using stolen hurricane lamps, shuffling in and out of the huge banks of garbage lining both sides of the street. Here and there among the plastic bags and the piles of cans a discreet fire was smouldering.

Jerry made his way down the centre of the road, listening to the sly sounds, the secret scufflings of the people of the heaps, until at last he reached the corner of Blenheim Crescent and realized with a shock that the Convent of the Poor Clares was down. His headquarters lay in ruins. The walls had been demolished, as had most of the buildings. Bricks and rubble had been cleared neatly into piles, but for some reason a few of the trees had been preserved, protected by new white fences – an oak and two black, twisted, stunted elms. The rest of the trees had been sawn down and stacked in a pile in the centre of the site. The best part of the original chapel and the administration wing attached to it, on the Westbourne Park Road side, were still standing. The machinery of demolition was parked here and there: trucks and earth-movers cloaked in dark canvas glistening with drizzle. Jerry climbed over the rubble and plodded through the thick mud until he stood under the nearest elm. He reached up and touched the lowest of the gnarled branches; he kicked at the stake fence. It quivered. He stumbled up a pile of bricks and masonry and got through a gap in the chapel wall. Fragments of stained glass clung to lead frames. The pews had been torn up and scattered, the altar had had been ripped out, the electrical wiring had been pulled down and everything was covered with plaster and white dust. High up, the light fell through the ruined roof onto a crude painting of the Resurrection, its lurid greens, yellows and reds already faded by the action of the rain and the wind. On all the walls were patches the size and shape of the devotional pictures which had hung there. He walked into the administration wing; the first two floors of this had hardly been touched as yet. He noticed small piles of human shit in some of the empty rooms. In the Mother Superior's office, which had been his office, too, he saw the white outline of the big cross which had hung there when he had last visited the convent. All furnishings, with the exception of two sodden mattresses in one room, had been carried off; his friends, his employees, his pets had gone.

As the light improved he moved through the wreckage, picking up small things. A triangle of green stained glass, a fragment of wood from a pew, the bulb holder from a light fixture, a hook on which the nuns had once hung their habits, a key from a cupboard, a 1959 penny left on the floor of the chapel, a nail which had secured part of the large cross to the wall. He put them in the pockets of his black car coat. A few relics.

Then he climbed out the way he had come, trudging back to the road and noticing that his heavy Frye boots were coated with mud and shit.

On the other side of the garbage heap he heard the note of a taxi's engine. He clambered quickly over the refuse, waving urgently at the cab. Rather reluctantly it stopped and let him get in.

'The airport,' he said.

As he had often suspected, the end had come quietly and the breakdown had been by slow degrees. In fact the breakdown was still going on. Superficially there was nothing urgent about it. As the weeks passed and communications and services slowly worsened, there always seemed to be a chance that things might improve. He knew they could not improve.

He remembered his old friend Professor Hira (who now sometimes called himself Hythloday) escorting him through the chaos of Calcutta and saying, 'There *is* order in all this, though it's not as detailed as we're used to, I suppose. All

100

human affairs can be seen as following certain basic patterns. The breakdown of a previous kind of social order does not mean that society itself has broken down – it is merely following different forms of order. The ritual remains.'

The cab-driver glanced nervously at the rag-pickers. Some of them seemed to be eyeing the taxi as though it were an especially fine piece of carrion. The driver speeded up as much as he dared, for there was only room for a single line of traffic on what was still, officially, a two-way road.

Jerry stared reflectively at the shit on his boots.

You got to believe in something. You can't get excited about nothing, Colonel Cornelius, said Shakey Mo.

The four of them were squeezed into the cabin of a 1917 Austin-Putilov half-tracked armoured car. Beesley was driving while Cornelius, Shakey Mo Collier and Karen von Krupp manned the machine guns. The car was travelling slowly over the stony countryside of West Cornwall. In the distance a farmhouse was burning. They were trying to reach St Michael's Mount, a fortified islet about ten miles down the South Coast, opposite the town of Marazion. Beesley believed he would find friends there.

Cornelius tried to make himself more comfortable on the pressed steel saddle seat, but failed. They went over a bump and everyone clung on to the hand-grips. It was very hot inside the half-track, even though they had lifted up the lid of the conning tower for ventilation. The original crews had worn gasmasks.

You're probably right, said Cornelius.

He saw a few figures, armed with rifles, move along the crest of the hill where the farmhouse burned. They didn't seem to offer a threat, but he kept his eye on them. His machine-gun was inclined to jam. He took out his Smith and Wesson .45 revolver, retrieved, like the rest of their equipment, from the Imperial War Museum, and checked it over. There was nothing wrong with that.

He was worrying about his wife and children. It was years since he had last remembered them: There was a list in his mind:

One Woman
One Boy
One Girl

A woman had recently slashed her wrists in Ladbroke Grove after gassing her little boy and girl. All were dead.

There was no reason why it should be his particular relatives. But there had been something about a Nöel Coward and Gertrude Lawrence record on the gramophone and it seemed to him to be a clue to something even more familiar. He wiped the grime and the sweat from his face and glanced across the cabin to the opposite position. Karen von Krupp, her skirt hitched up, straddled her seat looking at him, her back to her gun. She was so old. He admired her stamina.

Whoever suggested the Highlands as a safe retreat was a fool, said Bishop Beesley, not for the first time. Those Scotchmen are barbarians. I said the Scilly Isles was a better bet and now we've wasted three months and nearly lost our lives a dozen times over.

The half-track droned on.

I think I can see the sea, said Karen von Krupp.

Jerry wondered how he had come to throw in with these three.

It's getting dark, said Mo Collier. He climbed out of his seat and stretched, making the stick-bombs at his belt rattle. What about making camp?

Let's wait until we reach the coast road, if it's still there, said Bishop Beesley. He looked over his shoulder, straight into Jerry's eyes. He smirked. Now what's wrong with you? Can guilt be anything more than a literary conceit, Mr Cornelius? He uttered a suggestive chuckle. What truly evil person ever feels guilty? You might almost argue that evil-doing is an honest reaction against that sham we call 'guilt'. Repentance is, of course, a rather different kettle of fish. He returned his attention to his steering.

Jerry considered shooting him and then seeing what happened to the half-track without a driver. The bishop was always transferring his own problems on to others and Jerry seemed his favourite target.

Speak for yourself, he said. I've never understood you, Bishop Beesley.

Mo sniffed. You sound as bored as me, colonel. I could do with some action, I don't know about you.

It's freezing. Karen von Krupp drew up the collar of her

103

dirty sheepskin jacket. Could we have the tower closed now?

No, said Bishop Beesley. It would be suicide with our exhaust in the condition it is.

Karen von Krupp said sulkily: I'm not sure I believe you.

Anyway, it's still quite warm. Shakey Mo was conciliatory. Chin up, Frau Doktor. He grinned to himself and began to move his machine-gun about in its slit. Brrrrr. Brrrrr. We might just as well've come on bikes, the chances we've had to use these.

Portsmouth wasn't enough for you, eh? said Karen von Krupp bitterly.

Mine was the only bloody gun working, Collier pointed out. I maintain my equipment. All the others jammed after a couple of bursts.

We were nearly killed, she said. She glanced accusingly at Jerry. I thought that Field-Marshal Nye was a friend of yours.

Jerry shrugged. He's got his duty to do just like me.

Law and Order freak, explained Collier, lighting a Players. Groovy. I wish we had some music.

An explosion rocked the car and the engine whined miserably.

Bloody hell! yelled Collier in relief. Mines!

Late News

A 14-year-old boy died after falling 60ft from the roof of a block of shops near his home in Liverpool on Saturday night. He was William Brown of Shamrock Road, Port Sunlight.

Guardian, December 29 1969

A boy of 13 was remanded in custody until February 16 at Ormskirk, Lancashire, yesterday accused of the murder of Julie Mary Bradshaw, aged 10, of Skelmersdale. The girl's body was found on Monday night in the loft of a house.

Guardian, February 11 1969

A boy aged 12 found murdered on a golf course at Bristol yesterday was killed by four or five savage blows on the head it was said after a post mortem last night. The blows could have been made with a tree branch, said police. Martin Thorpe, of Rye Road, Fulton, had gone to Shirehampton golf course to search for golf balls.

Guardian, April 2 1970

A schoolgirl was killed and five other children and three adults wounded when Arab guerillas fired Russian-made Katyusha rockets into the Northern Israeli town of Beison yesterday. Three of the rockets fell in the playground of the school. Two of the injured children were in a serious condition.

Guardian, April 2 1970

Schoolboy Michael Kenan, aged 12 was drowned in a reservoir at Durford, near Chelmsford, Essex, yesterday while bird nesting with friends.

Daily Express, June 8 1970

Police tightened security in Warsaw yesterday as a curfew was again clamped on the port of Szezecin, the scene of violent street fighting on Thursday ... A Swedish radio reporter, Mr Anders Tunborg, said, 'The tanks repeatedly charged the crowds who sprang out of the way to avoid being run down. A mother and her young daughter did not get out of the way in time and an onrushing tank hit them both. A young soldier stood watching nearby and crying.'

The Scotsman, December 19 1970

Reminiscence (D)

You are killing your children.

The Lovers

With her chemise pulled up to her navel, Una Persson pressed her slim self to Catherine Cornelius who lay beneath her. Catherine's clothes were neatly folded on the stool near the dressing table. Una Persson's summer shirt-waist frock, stockings, drawers and corsets were scattered on the carpet. The bedroom needed painting. It was a bright summer afternoon. Sunlight crept through the tattered net and the dusty glass of the windows.

With passion Una said:

'My own dear love. My darling sweet.'

And Catherine replied:

'Dear, dear Una.'

She arched her perfect back, quivering. Grasping her buttocks, Una kissed her roundly in the mouth.

'Love!'

Una gave a long, delicious grunt.

'Oh!'

Later the door rattled.

In stepped Miss Brunner, trim and prim.

'All girls together.' She laughed harshly. She made no apology because it was obvious she relished interrupting and embarrassing them. 'We must be about our business soon. This place needs a tidy.'

Una rolled clear, directing a muted glare at Miss Brunner who was crisp in linen and lace, like an ultra-fashionable bicyclette.

'The new chambermaid's arrived,' said Miss Brunner. She began to fold Una Persson's dress. 'She wants to clean in here.'

Catherine was puzzled. 'There's no need . . .'

'Come now,' said Miss Brunner, flinging open the door, 'we mustn't let ourselves go.' She revealed the maid, a huge, red figure in a green baize overall and a sloppy cap, a bucket in one hand, a mop in the other. Her hair hung down her face. 'This is Mrs "Vaizey".'

Una pulled up the sheets.

'Oh, my gawd!' said the cleaner, recognizing her daughter. Catherine turned over.

Mrs 'Vaisey' gestured with the mop and bucket. She was miserably upset. She looked ashamed of herself. 'This is on'y temp'ry, Caff,' she said. She looked wretchedly at Miss Brunner, who was smiling privately. 'Could I – ?' Then she realized that Miss Brunner had known all along that her name hadn't been Vaizey and, moreover, that Miss Brunner had known Catherine was her daughter.

Mrs Cornelius sighed. 'You bloody cow,' she said to Miss Brunner. She glanced at the pair in the bed. 'Wot yer up ter?' She remembered how she had looked like Catherine once. She recalled the money she might have had if she had not been so generous, so soft. Her heart went out to her daughter then. She dumped the mop into the bucket of water, pointing the handle at Miss Brunner. 'You watch this one, love,' she said to Una Persson, since only Una Persson was now visible above the bedclothes. 'She'll 'ave yer fer sure if she gets a chance.'

'You're not being paid for cheek, you know,' Miss Brunner replied somewhat feebly, striding towards the door, 'but to clean the rooms. Your type, Mrs "Vaizey", are ten a penny, as I'm sure you know. If you're not happy with the position . . .'

'Don't come it wiv me, love.' Mrs Cornelius began to splash about the linoleum with her mop. 'Not everybody'll work in a third-rate whorehouse, neither!' Her anger grew and she became proud. 'Fuck it.' She picked up the bucket and threw the contents over Miss Brunner. As the starch ran out, the linen and the lace sagged and the Lily Langtry wave fell apart over her forehead.

Una grinned, sitting up with interest.

Miss Brunner hissed, clenched her hands, began to move with staring eyes upon Mrs Cornelius, who returned the stare with dignity so that Miss Brunner paused dripping.

'Yore nuffink, yer silly little tart. I've 'ad too much. Caff!'

Catherine peered out from the bed.

'You comin', Caff?'

Catherine shook her head. 'I can't, mum.'

'Jest as yer like.'

Una Persson said: 'I'll look after her, Mrs Cornelius.'

Mrs Cornelius removed her cap and apron and threw them at Miss Brunner's feet. 'I'm sure yer'll do yer best, love,' she said softly. 'Don't let Modom 'ere shove yer abaht!'

Miss Brunner seemed paralysed. Hands on fat hips, Mrs Cornelius appeared to grow in stature as she waltzed around the drenched figure. 'I know yer! I know yer!' she chanted. 'I know yer! I know yer! Ya ya ya!'

'Everything all right at home, mum?' said Catherine desperately.

'Not bad.' Mrs Cornelius was pleased with herself, although later she might regret this action. She'd taken the job because of the boy, after she and Sammy had had words. But tonight it would be feathers and frills again and a trip to the Cremorne Gardens. Her right hand swept down on Miss Brunner's sodden and corseted rump. There was a loud bang as flesh struck whalebone. Still Miss Brunner did not move. Mrs Cornelius giggled. 'Don't let 'er wear yer aht.' She circled Miss Brunner once more and then waved at her from the door. 'Ta, ta, Lady Muck.'

In terror, Catherine murmured to her mother, 'See you soon.'

'Keep yourself clean and yer can't go wrong,' advised Mrs Cornelius as she closed the door. The last Catherine saw was her leering wink.

Miss Brunner came alive with a snort. 'Dreadful woman. I was forced to sack her. I'll get changed. Can you two be ready by the time I've finished?'

Una was amused by Miss Brunner's attitude. 'This is a farce. Whom are we to entertain this evening?'

'Prinz Lobkowitz and his friends will arrive at six.'

'Oh,' said Catherine, reminiscently.

'Silly creatures,' said Miss Brunner.

Una Persson raised her lovely eyebrows. 'Aha.'

'Our success depends on tonight's meeting,' Miss Brunner said as she left. The door slammed.

Una stroked Catherine's thigh beneath the sheet. 'I wonder if this is the "big meeting"?'

Catherine shook her golden head. 'That's not for a while.'

'For all we know it's already happened. And what comes after the meeting? This identity's getting me down. Not enough information. Do you ever think about the nature of Time?'

'Of course.' Catherine twisted so that she could place her delicate lips on Una Persson's flat stomach and at the same time her hand rose lightly to touch her friend's clitoris, Una sighed with pleasure. From where she lay she could see the abandoned mop, the fallen bucket, the apron and the cap. 'Your mother has spirit. I hadn't expected that.'

'Neither had I.' Catherine's tongue fluttered like a trapped butterfly, the pressure of her hand increased. Una made a noise.

'I was terrified of them both,' said Catherine. 'I still am.'

'Forget it.'

Una gave a coarse, satisfied grunt.

'Good?' whispered Catherine Cornelius.

The Businessmen

Molly O'Morgan with her little organ
Was dressed up in colours so gay,
Out in the street every day,
Playing too-ra-la-oor-a-li-oor-a-li-ay.
Fellows who met her will never forget her,
She set all their heads in a whirl.
Molly O'Morgan with her little organ
The Irish-Aye-talian girl!'

sang Major Nye, twirling his splendid moustache and swirling his huge, tartan ulster as he strode over the moor with Sebastian Auchinek in tow. Auchinek was miserable and sought desperately about him for some sign of human habitation, preferably an inn. But there was none; just grass and gorse and boulders, the occasional bird and a few shy sheep. If Major Nye had not been the largest shareholder in a chain of well-appointed provincial halls, Auchinek would have complained. But he had to get Una a good year's bookings, at least thirty weeks, outside London (for as he predicted they had closed the London halls), if he was going to make it up to her for the disappointment she must feel at losing the Empire.

'One of Ella Retford's,' explained Major Nye, pausing in his stride and looking with relish at the dark green Exmoor heather.

'Has your girlie got anything like that?'

'Better,' said Auchinek automatically, staring at the vast moor with disgust and resignation. 'She has the real quality, major.' He whistled a complicated melody. 'That's one of hers. *Waiters get me going.*'

'It will mean a trip to London for me,' Major Nye said, stalking on. 'And London's not the safest place in the world these days, is it?'

'No really exciting place is, major.'

'I heartily dislike London, Mr Auchinek.'

'Oh, well – yes, I suppose so.' Uncertainly, Auchinek watched a large bird flap in the sky. Major Nye lifted his ashplant and pretended to sight down it at the bird.

'Bang!' said the major.

'Well,' he continued, 'I have, as a matter of fact, got to be in London on some pretty important business fairly shortly. Not quite certain of the date, but ask my office. They'll keep you posted.'

'And you'll give her an audition.'

'That was the idea, old boy. If I've time. By the way, what is the time?'

Auchinek stared at him in surprise.

Major Nye shrugged. The sky was deep blue, bland and warm. 'I'm kept pretty busy,' he said. 'What with one thing and another.'

'You have many interests,' Auchinek said admiringly.

'Oh, many. I play,' the major laughed, 'a wide variety of parts, you might say.' He put a hand to the knot of his Ascot cravat. 'But then we all do, really . . .' His moustache tilted upwards on the right side as he gave a mysterious smile. Auchinek determined to get himself a suit of solid tweed, like the major's, and a good ulster, and aim towards the acquisition of a small estate somewhere in Somerset or Devon. He hated the country, but these days there was hardly any choice. They came to a hill overlooking the winding white road to Porlock. Beyond the road lay the sparkling sea. On the dusty, unpaved road a carriage, drawn by two pairs of bays, was struggling, making poor time. The carriage was old and much in need of an overhaul.

Major Nye leaned on his ashplant and stared in amusement as the carriage slowly climbed the hill. 'Could this be the vicar on his way to see me? He travels in style, our vicar. Used to ride. One of the best hunting men in these parts. He fell off his horse, though. Ha, ha.'

A white head appeared at the window and a pale hand hailed the couple. 'Major! Major!'

'Vicar! Top o' the morning to ye!'

'Your son, major, have you heard?'

'What about the young rip?' Major Nye smiled at Auchinek. 'He's in the army, you know.'

'Captured, major. A prisoner of war.'

'What? The eldest boy?'

'Yes, major. I have the telegram here. I was in town when it arrived. I told them I'd deliver it.'

Auchinek knew that his luck hadn't changed yet. He sighed. He had picked a bad time to see Major Nye.

'Armoured steamrollers of some kind,' continued the vicar, growing hoarse, 'broke their lines and cut them off. Almost all were killed. He fought bravely. It will be in tomorrow's press.'

'The devil!'

'He's wound-ay-ed!' The vicar's voice cracked completely as the carriage hit a rock and bounced. His coachman shouted at the horses.

'You'll be returning to London on the seven-twenty, won't you, Mr Auchinek?' said Major Nye.

'Well . . .' Auchinek had hoped to be invited for the night. 'If that's the most convenient train.'

'I'll come with you. Quickly, get a hold on those leading horses and make 'em move. We'll take the vicar's carriage back to the house and I'll just have time to pack a bag.'

'In what engagement was your son captured?' Auchinek asked as they clambered down the hill towards the road.

'Damn!' said Major Nye, catching his sock on a piece of gorse and stopping to free himself. 'Regiment? 18th Lancers, of course.'

'Engagement?'

'What? My boy? Never!'

The Envoys

Prinz Lobkowitz was almost sure that he had been followed all afternoon by a police agent. He hoped that he was wrong. He glanced at his watch, waiting outside the remaining gate to Buckingham Palace. He looked out of the corners of his eyes to see if he could recognize the agent; surreptitiously he inspected each of the passers-by (there were few) but none was familiar. He turned to inspect the palace. It had been boarded up for a year now, but there were still redcoated and bearskinned Guardsmen standing in sentry boxes at various points. This had seemed as good a place as any to meet the other envoy. And surely it must be some of the most neutral soil in the world at the present moment. The watch, a Swiss hunter with an alpine scene decorating the inner case, was a gift from Miss Brunner. He had never been able to find the catch. As soon as the big meeting was over, he thought, he'd buy himself a twenty-four-hour digital wrist-watch of the kind the French were now making. He loved gadgets. It was what had led him into politics, after all.

The other envoy was late.

Prinz Lobkowitz took a rolled copy of *The Humorist* ('Typically British, but not old-fashioned') from his Prince Albert frock-coat pocket and began to study it intently, displaying the cover which sported a Bonzo dog cartoon. This had been arranged earlier and the specific issue of the specific magazine agreed upon. Prinz Lobkowitz was fond of *The Humorist*. Already he was becoming absorbed in it, smiling involuntarily at the jokes.

A few moments later a distinguished middle-aged man of military bearing bumped into Lobkowitz and pretended to recognize him. In slightly accented English he cried with delight: 'Good heavens! Why, it's old Henry, isn't it?'

115

For a second or two Lobkowitz feigned puzzlement. Then he said: 'Could you be George?'

'That's right! Spiffin', seeing you again!'

Lobkowitz frowned as he tried to recall his lines. A little reluctantly he rolled up his magazine and replaced it in his pocket where it made a noticeable bulge in the line of the overcoat. 'Come and have a drink, old boy.' Lobkowitz clapped the man on the shoulder. 'We've a lot to talk about.'

'Yes, indeed!'

As they crossed the road and entered St James's Park, which was filled with the noise of a dozen different calliopes from the nearby fairground, a man said softly: 'I am Colonel Pyat, our Embassy sent me.'

'And I'm Prinz Lobkowitz, representing the exiles. I hope this will be a fruitful meeting at long last.'

'I think it might be.'

They had reached the fairground which occupied both sides of the ornamental lake. Bunting and banners and candy-striped canvas, brass and steel and luridly painted wood, moved round and round and up and down as the people screamed or giggled or laughed aloud.

Pyat stopped at a stall on which sat a miserable monkey tended by an old Italian in a stovepipe hat. The Italian grinned and offered to sell Pyat an ice cream. Pyat reached out his hand and stroked the monkey as if looking for fleas, yet the touch was tender. He shook his head and moved on. 'Ice cream!' shouted the Italian, as if Pyat had forgotten something. 'Ice cream!'

In his frock-coat and top hat, Pyat moved with dignity away.

'Ice cream?' said the Italian to Lobkowitz who was a few paces behind Pyat. Lobkowitz shook his head. Pyat spoke over his shoulder. 'Any news of Cornelius?'

'Jeremiah, you mean?'

'Yes.'

'None. He seems to have vanished completely.'

'Perhaps it's for the best. Yes?'

'His insight's useful.'

116

'But he could foul things up. And we don't need that at present, with the big meeting coming along.'

'No.'

Under the low-hanging willows, where young prostitutes showed off their soft, painted flesh, they went, through the happy crowds, between the merry-go-rounds, the swinging boats and the helter-skelters.

'How jolly the peasants are,' said Pyat in an attempt at irony which somehow failed. 'Alas! Regardless of their doom, the little victims play.'

'Were you at Eton? So was I,' said Lobkowitz grinning back at a cheeky girl. 'Don't you enjoy fairs?'

'I've hardly ever seen one of this kind. In Finland once. With the gypsies, you know. Yes. Near Rouveniemi, I think. In Spring. I didn't attend. But I remember seeing the gypsy women by the river, breaking the Spring ice to wash their clothes. The sideshows were very similar, though there was more wood and less metal. Bright colours.' Colonel Pyat smiled.

'When were you last in Finland?' Lobkowitz avoided the guy rope of a sideshow tent. He took a deep breath of the air which was heavy with motor oil, candy floss and animal manure.

Colonel Pyat shrugged and waved his hands. 'When there was last a Finland.' He smiled again, more openly. 'I used to like Finland. Such a simple nation.'

An old woman selling lavender appeared. She wore a bright red shawl which clashed with her flowers. She whined pathetically at them, holding out her sprigs. 'Please, sir. Please, sir.' She nodded her head as if she hoped, by sympathetic magic, to make them nod back. 'Lucky, sir. Sweet lavender, sir. Please buy some, sir.'

Pyat was the first to reach into his trouser pocket and pull out a half-crown. He handed it to her, receiving the sprig in return. Its stem was wrapped in silver paper. Lobkowitz gave her two shillings and received a similar piece. The woman tucked the money away in the folds of her thick, dirty skirt. 'Thank you, gentlemen.'

The lavender forgotten in their right hands, they walked on.

'But you people had to take Finland out,' said Lobkowitz.

'Yes.' Pyat raised his hand to his face and noticed the lavender there. He began to adjust it in his buttonhole. 'It was a question of widening the available coasts.'

'Expediency.' Lobkowitz frowned.

'Does anyone act for another reason? Come now, Prinz Lobkowitz. Shall we confine ourselves to schoolboy moralizing? Or shall we discuss the real business at hand?'

'Perhaps that, too, involves schoolboy morals?' Lobkowitz flung his lavender from him. It fell into the mud near the water's edge.

Colonal Pyat said sympathetically, 'Forgive me. I know . . . I know – ' He gave up. 'Jews . . .'

A crowd of urchins ran past them shouting. One of the urchins gave Lobkowitz a brief, piercing glance before running on. Lobkowitz frowned and felt over his pockets to see if he had been robbed. But everything was there, including *The Humorist.*

They mounted a boardwalk which led through the mud to the jetty which stretched out into the lake. There were two couples on the jetty. They stopped.

'The sides change,' said Prinz Lobkowitz. They stood side by side watching the ducks and flamingoes. On the opposite bank promenaded a score of belles in pretty dresses, arms linked with a score of beaux, dressed to the nines, their curly-brimmed bowlers tilted at exaggerated angles. A barrel organ played sentimental tunes. A bear danced. A punt passed.

They could see the shell of Buckingham Palace outlined against the evening sky in the west and, to the east, the shell of the Treasury Garrison, bristling with big naval guns.

'It's growing colder,' said Colonel Pyat, adjusting the collar of his elegant coat. Prinz Lobkowitz saw that Pyat had a silk handkerchief tucked into his left sleeve. Clouds of red-tinged grey streaked the sky and streamed north.

'Everyone's leaving now.' Pyat stopped and picked up a

pebble. He threw it into the dank water. Sluggish ripples appeared for a few seconds. A fish put its lips to the surface and then submerged. 'There are hardly any of our old friends left. Dead singers.'

The Gatherers

'It's nice ter go away, but it's nicer ter come 'ome, innit?' said Mrs Cornelius as she sharpened the carving knife against the steel and looked with loving pride upon her roast pork.

The table had been laid with a red plush cloth. There were big blue tassels on the cloth. Over this had been laid a white linen cloth, its edges stitched with *broderie anglaise*. On the linen rested the vegetables in their monstrous china serving dishes with roses painted on the sides. There were large knives with weathered bone handles, solid forks, big spoons, napkins in rings of yellowed ivory, a silver salt cellar, a silver mustard pot, a silver pepper pot. Around the table sat Mrs Cornelius's children and their guests. They had all come for one of Mrs Cornelius's 'special' Sunday luncheons. Sammy, who always stood in as 'man of the house' on these occasions, sat in his tight best black serge suit beside her, sweltering as ever, but this time the quality of his swelter was different; the swelter of fear had replaced the swelter of work. The boy, pinch-faced and hungry, sat next to Sammy, his mouth watering as he waited for his share. His mother's huge red lips rounded as she scraped metal against metal. She had her hair done in a pompadour coiffure with a marcel wave and she was wearing the purple princess gown with the yellow imitation Valenciennes lace on it. The padded shoulders added to her already impressive size.

'Pass yer plates along,' she said, preparing to cut.

There was a clatter as the plates were picked up and passed. Catherine, seated on the other side of her mother, stacked her brother Frank's plate on top of her own. Frank took his friend Miss Brunner's plate and passed it to Catherine. Frank and Miss Brunner were dressed in rather similar suits of severe grey. Frank, however, wore a rose. His ravaged face was set in a smirk which showed he was on his best party manners. Miss Brunner, too, was doing her best to be affable.

'It's a loverly bit o' pork,' said Mrs Cornelius as she sliced.

'It looks nice and juicy,' said Miss Brunner. She winked across the table at Mr Smiles, who was dressed as the vicar he had once been.

'Shall I be barman?' asked Mr Smiles, indicating the beer barrel on the sideboard and gesturing at the same time towards their glass mugs. He grinned nervously through a black beard.

'Good idea,' said Mrs C.

'Light?' said Mr Smiles.

'Suits me,' said Sammy.

Mr Smiles got up and put the first mug under the spigot.

For all that it was lunchtime, the heavy velvet curtains were drawn and the gas lamps were full on at either side of the littered mantelpiece. Mrs Cornelius was suspicious of the neighbours who overlooked her rooms at the back. She suspected they might be burglars. If they saw a spread like this, they could easily guess there'd be money in the house. As there was, at this moment.

The air was close. The smell of the meat filled the room. The vegetable dishes steamed.

Slice by slice the pork and the crackling and the stuffing was heaped on the plates. Mrs Cornelius was a generous hostess, if an indifferent cook.

The noise increased as vegetables were ladled out.

'Gravy?' Miss Brunner passed the gravy boat to Frank.

'Apple sauce?' Sammy passed the sauce dish to the boy who helped himself to a large portion. He loved apple sauce.

'There's more spuds in the oven,' said Mrs Cornelius as Mr Smiles considered the almost empty bowl. 'Go an' get 'em, love,' she told the boy. He sprang up, anxious to get the job over with so that he could tuck in.

'Greens?' said Catherine to Frank.

'Swedes?' said Miss Brunner to Mr Smiles.

'Parsnips?' Sammy held the bowl enquiringly.

'Marrer?' Mrs C. asked, looking for it.

'All the marrow's gone, mum,' said Catherine in a small voice.

Mrs Cornelius loved marrow. But she contained her fury and lifted her glass of light ale, toasting them all. ''Ere's ter the lot o' yer, then!' She drained the glass, spluttered thickly behind her red hand, and delicately picked up her knife and fork. 'Ah, this is ther life!'

Her son came back with the extra potatoes and put them on the table. Hurriedly he clambered into his place and began to wolf the food. Miss Brunner, eating rapidly but discreetly, eyed him as he ate. She dabbed at her thin mouth with a napkin. He did not notice her.

'It's a pity your friend couldn't come,' said Mrs Cornelius to her daughter, 'Ill, wos she?'

'Yes, mum.'

'Shame.'

Save for the noise of the cutlery, they ate in silence for a while until Frank said, 'I heard there were some people looking for Jerry, mum.'

'Don't talk ter me about 'im!' she said.

The boy, who had almost devoured his whole meal, looked up in interest. 'What's 'e done, then?'

'We won't go into that, will we?' said Mr Smiles laughing. He glanced at Mrs Cornelius. 'No offence.'

'None taken,' said Mrs Cornelius grimly. 'Yore quite right. We won't go inter it.'

'They'll never find 'im,' said the boy.

'It's unlikely.' Catherine looked tenderly and with some admiration at her little brother.

'Who were they?' said the boy. 'These people that was looking for 'im.'

'Foreigners,' said Frank, 'mainly.'

Miss Brunner tapped his sleeve with her fork and left four tiny points of grease there, like little teeth-marks. 'Maybe they want to give him a job?'

'And maybe they don't,' said Frank.

'Seconds?' said Mrs Cornelius.

Everyone, except the boy and Miss Brunner, refused.

'Yer get ter miss good 'ome cookin', I shouldn't wonder,' said Mrs C. to Miss Brunner. She laid two small slices of meat on Miss Brunner's plate.

'Tasty,' said Miss Brunner. She offered Mrs Cornelius a secretive smile, as if she referred to some shared experience about which only they knew.

Mrs Cornelius gave the boy what was left of the joint and then, without reference to him, piled the cooled vegetables on to his plate.

Miss Brunner quickly finished and leaned back with a contented grunt.

Catherine began to take the dirty plates into the kitchen.

'See 'ow the duff's doin', luv, will yer?' requested her mother. She confided to Miss Brunner: 'It's a loverly duff.'

'I'm certain of that.'

After the plum duff and the cheese and the port, the family and its friends, with the exception of the boy, who had gone to sleep, smoked their cigarettes, pipes and cigars.

'Well, that was a bit of all right,' said Sammy. 'Makes a change from meat pies, I can tell you.'

Mrs Cornelius smiled complacently. 'Not arf, yer cuddly ole fat pig.' She bent from where she was helping herself to a pint from the barrel on the sideboard. She kissed his bald head. He snorted and blushed.

Mr Smiles, who had hated the meal, stroked his gravy-stained beard and said, with some strain, 'You are a splendid cook, dear lady.'

'A plain cook,' Mrs Cornelius replied, by way of confirmation and amplification of the compliment. 'Oh fuck.' The beer mug had overfilled. She dabbed at the sides with her fingers, raising the finger to her mouth and sucking it. 'Sorry, vicar.'

Sammy had taken out his spectacles and was polishing them. He inspected one side carefully.

'Lens,' he said. 'Cracked.'

''Ave yer seen the rest o' the 'ahse?' Mrs Cornelius

enquired of Miss Brunner. 'Not,' she laughed raucously, 'that there's a lot ter show.'

'I'd love to see it.'

'Come on then.' The two women left the room.

'Any news from America at all?' Mr Smiles packed tobacco into his pipe.

Frank was staring at the door through which Miss Brunner and his mother had passed. He looked worried. 'Do what?' he said.

'America? What's going on over there? Much doing?'

'No, nothing much.' Frank got up, glancing absently at Mr Smiles. He leant against the mantelpiece. 'How's business?'

'Which business?' Mr Smiles winked at him. It was a sad old wink. Frank, staring again at the brown door, didn't notice. He began to move towards the door.

Catherine put her hand on his arm. 'Cheer up, Frank. It's not the end of the world.'

This idea seemed to frighten him. She said quickly, 'A shilling for your thoughts.'

'Cheap at arf the price!' desperately guffawed Sammy from the easy chair in which he now sat. He was feeling very lonely. As he had expected, nobody responded.

Mr Smiles felt sick. 'Ah, where's the you-know-what?' he asked Sammy.

Sammy pointed at the brown door. 'Through there and on yer left,' he said. He picked up an old copy of *The Illustrated London News* which had a coloured supplement on the Jubilee headed *The Glory that is England*. Sammy smiled. It was such a short time ago. He wondered what would have happened if the old queen had lived on.

On the landing Mr Smiles turned right by mistake and found himself outside the bedroom door. There were peculiar sounds coming from inside. He stopped to listen.

'At least yer don't run ther risk o' 'avin' babies', he heard Mrs Cornelius say.

'Don't count on it, dearie,' said Miss Brunner.

Mr Smiles remembered about the bathroom.

In the dining room Frank was saying, 'If she doesn't hurry up soon, I'm off without her.'

'Calm down, Frank,' said Catherine.

But Frank was glaring now. 'Why does she always have to spoil everything? The fat old bag.'

'Oh, don't, Frank.'

His head among the used dishes on the table, the boy stirred. He groaned.

They all looked at him.

'Poor little sod,' said Sammy. 'Let's not have a row, eh?'

'Well . . .' said Frank, reluctant to stop before his climax. 'I mean . . .' He felt nothing for the boy, but he did not wish to offend his sister at that moment, particularly since there was a likelihood that she knew where Jerry was.

Catherine's perfect features bore an expression of infinite sympathy as she went to stroke the sleeping child's hair.

'He's having a nightmare, I expect.'

The Rowers

Considering that he was a prisoner of war, Captain Nye was having quite a good time. It was almost like a holiday. His captors had proved to be courteous and allowed him considerable freedom within the reservation. Even now he was boating on Grasmere Lake with a very pretty girl. Save for the basic facts of his circumstances, he couldn't have imagined a more perfect situation. The sky was a beautiful deep blue and the surrounding hills were a rich, varied green. The lake was absolutely still, reflecting in impressive detail the oaks and willows on its banks.

Captain Nye pulled vigorously on the oars and the boat shot away from the little landing stage at the end of the tea-gardens with their comforting wrought-iron balconies overlooking the water. All the iron was painted green, to blend in with the hills and the trees.

The girl was called Catherine. She made a lovely picture as she sat in the stern with a Japanese silk parasol over her shoulder, a wide-brimmed Gainsborough straw hat on her golden curls, her filmy summer frock cut low at the neck and high on the ankle. With touching lack of expertise she gingerly held the rudder rope and pulled it to left or right when Captain Nye directed.

Soon they were alone in the middle of the lake. Far away on the other side there were one or two more boats. Captain Nye rowed towards a little island, eager to get a better look at the rather picturesque ruined bell-tower which stood on it. A system of these towers had once covered the area, the work of an eccentric clergyman who had erected them so that travellers or boatmen would hear them through the fog and thus be able to find their bearings. Unfortunately there were a number of tragic accidents and the flaws in the system became more than obvious when the clergyman had himself drowned on Derwent Water under the impression he had reached the sanctuary of his own churchyard. Now the towers were merely romantic and a source of speculation amongst those who knew little of the local history of the Fell country.

'What mysteries shall we discover, I wonder, in Merlin's castle?' asked Catherine, in a fanciful mood.

Captain Nye looked back over his shoulder at the remains of the building. 'Perhaps we'll find Arthur's sword and with it bring peace where today there is nought but strife.' She alone could elicit these fantasies from him. He wished very much that they were on the same side. He knew that essentially Catherine was his gaoler and that therefore she must be highly trusted by his enemies. It was a damned shame.

'Nearly there,' he said. 'Standby for landing!' He shipped the oars as the bottom scraped on the tiny beach. Leaping into the shallow water, careless of wetting his white flannels, he took the painter and hauled the boat up to the point where Catherine, gathering her skirts about her, could reach the prow and take his hand, descending prettily to the land. She twirled her parasol and smiled at him.

'But if we find the sword,' she said, 'will you be able to pull it from the stone?'

'And if I could, what would you think then?'

She frowned. 'I don't know. People play such awful tricks on one, these days.'

He laughed. 'I know that.' He held out his hand. 'Come. To the castle!'

They climbed the grassy slope to the tower but were less than half-way there before the smell struck them.

'Ugh!' Captain Nye wrinkled his nose.

'What could it be?' she asked. 'Sheep droppings?'

He was a little shocked by her outspokenness. 'Maybe. Or a dead animal, even?'

'Shall we look?' Her face became concerned. 'In case it isn't a sheep or something?'

'What . . . ?'

'I mean – '

127

He understood what she meant now. Reluctantly he said, 'You stay. I'll go.'

She stood, heels together, holding her parasol, while he forced himself to the top of the hill and disappeared behind the wall of the ruin. She was puzzled by the peculiar briny aspect of the smell. They were a good forty miles from the coast, surely?

She knew that she should have stayed with the captain. It was her job. But the smell disturbed her more than physically. She felt extremely nervous and depression was swiftly creeping in. The perfect day was over.

When Captain Nye returned he was pale and he could hardly look at her. He had a handkerchief over his mouth. Wordlessly, he took her arm and guided her back to the boat.

She climbed in and he shoved off. All his movements were disorganized, hasty. The boat almost turned over as he got aboard and swung the oars into the water, rowing back towards the tea-gardens. But he had only gone a few strokes when he was forced to abandon the oars and lean over the side, vomiting, as discreetly as he could, into the water.

Catherine came forward and took the oars before they could slip from the rowlocks. She did her best to keep the boat on course.

Captain Nye wiped his lips, then dipped his handkerchief into the water, wiping his whole face. 'I must apologize.'

'Good heavens! Why? What was it you saw?' With a steady, accomplished stroke, she began to row for the shore.

'I must report it to the pol – to your authorities. A man, I think. Or something that had been a man. Or – I'm not sure . . .'

'Murdered?'

'I don't know.'

The really awful thing about the dead creature was that it had had a certain ape-like cast of features and yet at the same time the remains of the face had reminded him unmistakably of the girl who now rowed so smoothly away from the island. Every time he looked at her frank, blue

128

eyes, her full, pink lips, her well-shaped nose, he saw the ape face of the rotting creature which had lain amongst the debris and sheep-dung in the gloomy interior of the tower.

He began to wonder if the whole thing had been deliberately arranged for him. Perhaps his captors had other reasons than kindness for allowing him so much freedom. But what could they possibly want from him, anyway? He knew no secrets.

'Do you – ? Did you expect to find anything like that in the tower?' he asked her.

Her body moved rhythmically back and forth as she rowed. She shook her head.

'Intimations,' she said. 'I couldn't explain.'

THE PEACE TALKS
Preliminary Speech

In his speech to the Court of Appeal, shortly before his exile, Prinz Lobkowitz said:

'In our houses, our villages, our towns, our cities, our nations, time passes. Each individual will be involved, directly or indirectly, in some 150 years of history – before birth, during life, and after his death. Part of this experience will be received from parents or other adults, from old men; part will be received from his own life, and his experience will, in time, become part of his children's experience. Thus a generation is 150 years. That is how long we live. Our behaviour, our prejudices, our opinions, our preferences are the produce of the fifty or sixty years before we were born and in the same way do we influence the fifty following our deaths. Such knowledge is apt to make a man like me feel that it is useless to try to alter the nature of his society. It would be pleasant, I think, if we could somehow produce a completely blank generation – a generation which has not acquired the habits of the previous generation and will pass no habits on to the next. Ah, well, I thank you, gentlemen, for listening to this nonsense with patience. I bid you Au Revoir.'

AT THE PEACE TALKS
The Ball

The major social event during the Peace Talks was the Gala Ball at San Simeon. Hearst's monstrous white castle had been bought for the nation by an unknown benefactor some years before and re-erected on the site of the old Convent of the Poor Clares at Ladbroke Grove, where it was now a familiar local landmark and a favourite tourist attraction, more impressive, in the opinion of many, than the buildings of Versailles, Canberra or Washington.

Everyone had been invited. Commentators said that it was equal in magnificence to the Great Exhibition, the Diamond Jubilee, the New York World's Fair or the Berlin Olympics. In a mood of immense optimism (the Peace Talks could be said to be going splendidly) the castle was prepared for the Ball. Illumination of every sort was used. There were tall Berlage candelabra of silver and gold in which were fitted slender white and yellow candles; Schellenbühel crystal chandeliers holding thousands of red candles; Horta flambeaux in brackets along the walls; huge globular gas mantels, electric lights of a hundred different shades of colour, neon of the subtlest and brightest, antique oil lamps the height of a man, and little faceted glass globes containing fireflies and glow-worms, strung on threads through the grounds of the various 'casas' which made up the whole of the original Hearst complex. Hearst himself had always called his castle The Enchanted Hill. Now, of course, it was, if anything, an Enchanted Dale. The Casa Grande, with its twin Hispano-Moresque towers containing thirty-six carillon bells, its hundred rooms and its ornate bas-reliefs carved from white Utah limestone, dominated the other three 'guest castles' arranged before it, north, south and west – Casa del Monte, Casa del Sol and Casa del Mar. Tall cypresses, willows, poplars and firs had been planted thickly among the buildings, replacing the Californian palms which had once grown there. Within the branches of the trees and the privet hedges had been buried more tiny lights to make the gardens sparkle like fairyland. Rhododendrons, poinsettias, orchids, chrysanthemums, roses and azaleas grew in well-ordered profusion and the overall appearance reminded at least one visitor of the old roof garden at Derry and Toms blown up to an enormous scale ('and none the worse for that'). Bas-reliefs decorated the Spanish walls of the gardens and there were copies of famous statues from all over the world, in marble and granite or cast in terracotta or bronze, one of the grandest being Boyar's copy of Canova's 'The Graces' in St Petersburg. This statue, in the classical manner, was permanently illuminated and showed Joy, Brilliance and Bloom, representing, in the words of the guide book, 'all that was beautiful in Nature and that which was gracious and charming in Mankind.' *The Times*, in its leader for the day of the ball, had written: 'It is to be hoped that this lovely statue will symbolize to the guests the rewards which they can win if their talents are devoted to the pursuit of peaceful endeavour, rather than to Strife and her attendants, Greed and Envy.' Many newspapers had echoed these sentiments in one form and another and even the weather, which had been singularly delightful for several weeks, seemed to make a special effort for the occasion. All through that day hundreds of footmen, housemaids, cooks, butlers, kitchen-maids and pages had hurried to and fro among the lavish rooms preparing them for the ball. There was to be available every kind of culinary delight. In the ballrooms (or those rooms which had been turned into ballrooms for the occasion) musicians practised many styles of music. The flags of all nations, embroidered in threads of precious metal on the finest silks, glittered from the walls. Tapestries in rich brocades proclaimed the glories of those nations' histories and the set pieces of the buffet tables were the great national dishes of the world. In the grounds were mixed forces of soldiers, arranged there both for ceremonial and for security reasons, their dress uniforms dazzling in the variety of their colourings, their swords, pikes and lances shining like silver. Through rooms lush with mosaics, murals, carvings and bas-reliefs, with gilt and silver and enamelling, with paintings and sculpture from Egypt, Greece, Rome, Byzantium, China and India, from Renaissance Spain, Italy and Holland, from eighteenth-century France and Russia, from nineteenth-century England and America, with tiled floors and inlaid floors set with mother-of-pearl and platinum, with wall-hangings and curtains from Persia, with carpets from Afghanistan, with carved wooden ceilings from sixteenth-century Italy and seventeenth-century Portugal, all polished so that they shone with a deep, warm glow, crept the smells of roasting ox and sheep and pigs and calves, of delicious curries and dhansaks, of Chinese soups and fowl, of paellas, strudels and bouillabaisses, of succulent vegetables and subtly spiced salad dressings, of pies and cakes and pâtés, of glazes and sauces and gravies, of bombes surprises, of lemon, orange, pineapple, and strawberry water-ices, of peacocks and quails, grouse, pigeons, ortolans, chickens, turkeys, wild ducks, turning on spits or stewing in pots, of rotkraut and kalter fisch, of syllabubs, of sausages and baked ham, of tongue and salt beef, of fruits and savour roots, of carp and haddock and halibut and sole, of mushrooms and cucumbers, of peppers and bamboo shoots, of syrups, creams and crêpes, soups and consommés, of herbs and fats, of venison and haggis, of whitebait, mussels and shrimps, of hares and rabbits and caviar, of livers and tripes and kidneys. There were wines and spirits and beers from every province of the world. There were glasses and steins and goblets of the clearest crystal and the most exquisite china. Cups and plates and dishes of gold, pewter, silver and porcelain stood ready to receive the food; pretty girls and handsome men in national costumes stood ready to serve it. Only one tradition would not be kept tonight; there would be no host or hostess to receive the guests. The first guests to arrive would make it their business to receive the others and introduce them after the Master of Ceremonies had announced them in the main ballroom. This peculiar arrangement had been considered the most diplomatic. And now the sun was setting. The ball was about to begin.

'I do hope,' said Miss Brunner, curling her ermine robe over her arm as Prinz Lobkowitz helped her from the carriage, 'that we are not the *first*.' Up the marble staircase they went, between rows of rigid soldiers, holding flickering candelabra, to where, from behind colonnades, two footmen appeared and took their invitations, bearing them through the great gold doors into the anteroom of lapis lazuli where they were handed to a head footman, in scarlet and white with a tall, many-waved white wig which curved outwards over his head, who gave them to the Master of Ceremonies who bowed, read the cards, bowed again and ushered them through doors of crystal and filigree into the blazing splendour of the great ballroom.

'Prinz Lobkowitz and Miss Brunner!'

'But we *are*.' Miss Brunner glowered furiously as her name and his echoed through the empty expanse. She smoothed her green velvet gown and fingered the pearl collar at her throat.

'Is it my fault, dear lady,' Prinz Lobkowitz was equally put out, 'if you are obsessed with time? We are always too early.'

'And, consequently, always too late,' she sighed, making the best of it. They walked slowly towards the far end of the hall. They inspected the servants; they went to the sideboards and tasted a morsel or two while glancing rather disdainfully about them at all the opulence. 'What a lot of gilt.'

He turned solicitously to listen, his many orders dazzling her for a moment. 'Mm?'

'Gilt.'

'Ah.' He nodded thoughtfully, his patent leather toe tracing whorls of mother of pearl on the floor. 'Quite so. A great deal of it. Still, perhaps we'll be able to do something about that now. We mustn't quarrel. That would not be in the spirit of the occasion.'

'I'm reconciled to that,' she said.

Footsteps sounded in the distance. They looked towards the doors. They saw the Master of Ceremonies raise a scarlet sleeve and read the card before him:

'The Right Reverend, Father in God, Denis, by Divine permission Lord Bishop of North Kensington!' intoned the MC.

'He's overdoing it a bit, isn't he?' Miss Brunner prepared to receive Bishop Beesley. The corpulent priest had dressed himself in his cloth-of-gold cloak, his most ornate mitre and held a crook so rich in engravings and curlicues that it out-did anything San Simeon could offer. The bishop's pale face broke into a smile as he saw his old friends. He waddled slowly forward, his eyes wandering over the cakes and trifles on the buffet tables. At last he reached the pair and, with his attention still on the food, held out a beringed hand, either to be kissed or to be shaken. He did not seem offended when they did neither. 'My dear Miss Brunner. My dear Prinz Lobkowitz. What a scrumptious feed they've laid on for us! Oh!'

From the gallery, musicians began to play selections from Coward's *Private Lives*.

'How charming,' said Bishop Beesley, leaning foward and scooping up a handful of syllabub in his palm and sliding it gracefully into his maw, licking each of his little fat fingers and then both his little fat lips. 'How nice.'

Again the great voice echoed:

'My Lady Susan Sunday and the Honourable Miss Helen Sweet!'

'Well!' whispered Miss Brunner. 'The SS. I hadn't expected *her*. Her friend looks worn out.'

'Captain Bruce Maxwell!'

'And I thought he was dead,' said Bishop Beesley.

'His Excellency the President of the United States.'

'And he looks it,' said Miss Brunner. She smiled as Lady Sue and Helen approached. 'How delightful.'

Prince Lobkowitz noticed how alike the two older women were. Miss Brunner had been right about Helen Sweet. The girl had faded. Even her ball gown was a faded blue in comparison with the royal blue of Lady Sue's.

'My dear!' Lady Sue was saying. She embraced Miss Brunner. A slim, well-corseted woman in a dress by Balenciaga, she wore six strands of blue diamonds at her powdered throat, with matching pendant earrings and tiara. It was to be an evening of ostentation, it seemed. 'Good evening,' said Helen Sweet mildly.

The band was now playing an instrumental version of *Little Red Rooster*.

Captain Maxwell was shaking hands with Prinz Lobkowitz. The captain's hands were cool and damp. There was sweat on his brutish forehead. His great backside, much heavier than any other part of him, seemed to waggle in sympathy. 'Good to see you, old boy,' he said in a military accent (though in fact he was a Salvationist).

'Professor Hira!'

In impeccable Indian dress the small professor crossed the floor, nervously fingering his white turban. His coat was of deep pink silk with little round panels of a lighter pink stitched into it. The trousers matched the panels. The buttons were perfect pearls.

'Professor Hira!' Miss Brunner was genuinely pleased to see the physicist. 'How long has it been?' she scowled. 'Will it be?' She smiled. 'Well, how are you, anyway?'

'So so, thank you.' He did not seem to share her pleasure at the meeting.'

'Mr Cyril Tome.' Thin, pale, with white hair but with lips so red they seemed rouged, his hornrims glittering, the critic and would-be politician stood in his monkish evening dress for a second or two beside the Master of Ceremonies before braving the floor. Nobody greeted him.

'Mrs Honoria Cornelius and Miss Catherine Cornelius.'

'Good God!' said Captain Maxwell, chewing a stick of celery. 'Who d'you think put her on the list?' Largely because it was what they had all been wondering about him, nobody answered. 'Honoria, eh? I bet!'

'Major Nye and Captain Nye.'

'They do look alike, don't they?' murmured Lady Sue to Miss Brunner. It was true. Save for the obvious difference in ages, father and son might have been the same man. The impression was sharpened by the fact that they wore the uniform of the same regiment.

The guests began to spread themselves a little more evenly around the perimeters of the room.

'The Right Honourable Mr M. Hope-Dempsey.'

'He's drunk!' murmured Prinz Lobkowitz as the young Prime Minister looked vaguely around him, then weaved genially in the general direction of the others, his long hair waving beyhind him. He seemed to have a live animal of some sort hidden under his coat.

'It's a cat,' said Miss Brunner. 'Where on earth did he get hold of it?'

The guests were now arriving thick and fast. Vladimir Ilyitch Ulianov, resident in China and extremely old and bad-tempered now, wearing a baggy black suit, hobbled in. Following him was his friend and protector the Eurasian warlord General O. T. Shaw, ruler of North China. Beside Shaw was Marshal Oswald Bastable, renegade Englishman and chief of Shaw's airforce. After them came Karl Glogauer the Revivalist, small, shifty, intense; a tall, moody albino, whose name nobody caught; the ex-Literary Editor of the *Oxford Mail*; a score or so of assorted conference delegates; Hans Smith of Hampstead, Last of the Left-Wing Intellectuals; the Governor-General of Scotland; the Viceroy of India, the King of North Ireland, the recently abdicated Queen of England; Mr Roy Hudd, the entertainer; Mr Frank Cornelius and his companion Mr Gordon 'Flash' Gavin; Mr Lionel Himmler, the theatre impresario; Mr S. M. Collier, the demolition expert; Mr John Truck, the transport expert and Minister of Controls; the Israeli Governor of Central Europe; Admiral Korzeniowski, President of Poland; General Crossman (Crossman of Moscow) and Lady Crossman; Miss Mitzi Beesley and Dr Karen von Krupp; Miss Joyce Churchill, the romantic novelist; the cathedral correspondent of *Bible Story Weekly* and his son and daughters; the

Paris correspondent of *Gentleman's Quarterly* and his friend Sneaky John Slade, the blues singer; Miss Una Persson and Mr Sebastian Auchinek, her agent; a Lapp parson called Herr Marek; Colonel Pyat and Miss Sylvia Landon, Présidente of the Académie Française; more than a hundred of the finest male and female film stars; a round thousand politicians from all over the world; thirty American deserters; five fat field-marshals; eighty-six ex-nuns from the original Convent of the Poor Clares; some Arabs and a German; Spiro Koutrouboussis, the Greek tycoon, with a group of other Greek millionaires; a bank manager and a television script writer; a Dutch soldier, the King of Denmark and the King of Sweden; the Royal Canadian Mounted Police rugby team; Mr Jack Trevor Story, the jazz band leader, and Miss Maggie Macdonald, his star singer; the Queen of Norway and the ex-Emperor of Japan; the Governor of England and his chief advisor General K. G. Westmoreland; Mr Francis Howerd, the comedian; a number of dons who wrote children's novels at Oxford; the most corrupt and feeble-minded paperback publisher in America; Mr Max Miller, the comedian; a number of television producers; Nik Turner, Dave Brock, Del Dettmar, Robert Calvert, Dik Mik, Terry Ollis: members of the Hawkwind orchestra; some advertising executives, pop music critics, newspaper correspondents, art critics, editors and recording artists and show biz personalities including Mr Cliff Richard, Mr Kingsley Amis, Mr Engelbert Humperdinck and Mr Peter O'Toole; the Dalai Lama; some Trades Union officials; thirteen schoolmasters; Mr Robert D. Feet, the pedant (who had thought it was a Fancy Dress Ball and had come as G. K. Chesterton); Miss Mai Zetterling and Mr David Hughes; Mr Simon Vaizey, the society wit, and a host of others. They ate, they conversed, they danced. The mood became gay and the worst of enemies became conciliatory, claiming with sincerity and passion that they had never really disliked one another. Peace was just around the corner.

'We could all be said to be prisoners, Mr Cornelius,'

Bishop Beesley was saying as he munched a piece of short-bread, 'and these revolutionists are perhaps the most hopeless of all prisoners. They're prisoners of their own ideas.'

'I'll drink to that, bishop.' Frank Cornelius raised his champagne glass. 'Still, abolish war and you abolish revolution, eh?'

'Quite so.'

'I'm all for the good old status quo.'

Miss Brunner was laughing. Gordon Gavin, for all he was dressed in evening clothes, still managed to give the impression that he was clad from neck to knee in an old gaberdine raincoat. The seamed and seedy face, the hot, guilty eyes, the hands that rarely left the pockets of his trousers or else hovered helplessly near his flies, all contributed to the impression. 'I'm flattered,' said Miss Brunner, 'but I'm afraid all my dances are spoken for.' Flash looked relieved.

The musicians were playing Alkan's *Symphony for the Piano on the theme 'Five'* to waltz-time. Mrs Cornelius was having marvellous fun. All the boys were after her! She clutched the little Lapp parson, Herr Marek, to her and raced him round the floor. He was scarcely visible, buried, as he was, in her bulk, but he seemed to be enjoying himself. He had an evil glint in his eye as his muffled, heavily accented English came from the region of Mrs Cornelius's bosom. 'Morality, my dear lady, what is that? If it feels good, do it. That's my philosophy. What do you say?'

'Yore naughty, that's wot I say!' She laughed comfortably, completing a pirouette which took him off his feet. He giggled. They just missed colliding with Colonel Pyat and one of the most beautiful of the ex-nuns, Sister Sheila.

The dance ended and the laughter and the conversation swelled. Not only the main ballroom was packed, now. All the subsidiary ballrooms and many of the guest rooms were crowded. As Dick Lupoff was to report to the *L.A. Free Press* 'the world's finest were letting their hair down that night'.

The band struck up with *A Bird in a Gilded Cage* and many of the guests began to sing the words as they took

142

their partners for the dance. The babble of voices grew gayer and gayer. Champagne corks popped and glasses clinked.

'Prinz Lobkowitz was commiserating with the ex-Queen of England as they waltzed discreetly in the shadows beneath the musicians' gallery. 'My dear Eva, it is a situation one can never really get used to. Training, you know, and background. Not, of course, that you were expecting anything, I suppose, at the beginning.'

'The epidemic . . .'

'Exactly. At least Lady Jane was executed. Poor girl.'

'It's a bit warm in here, isn't it?' Frank Cornelius was saying on the other side of the ballroom as he danced expertly with Helen Sweet. 'You look thoroughly washed out.'

'Oh, it's all right.' Helen Sweet glanced timidly into the gap between his chest and her breasts.

Lady Sue swept past in a flash of crystalline blue. 'Don't overdo it, Helen!' Lady Sue was dancing with her friend the ex-emperor of Japan. Dressed in traditional Japanese costume, the old man was finding the waltz steps a bit difficult.

Catherine Cornelius, feeling a trifle dizzy, leaned against a buffet table. She was a picture of beauty and well-supplied with beaux. They crowded round her. She brushed a lock of fair hair from her forehead, laughing as Captain Nye, who had brought her another drink, said: 'I'm afraid they've nothing non-alcoholic left. Will champagne do?' She accepted the glass, but put it down on the table. All of a sudden she began to shiver. 'Are you cold?' asked three Austrian hussars solicitously and simultaneously.

'I shouldn't,' she said. 'Is anything speeding up?'

Captain Nye was filled with forboding.

They started to play *The Wind Cries Mary* as a foxtrot. Captain Nye held out his hand to her and smiled kindly. 'This must surely be mine.' She gave him her hand. It was ice cold. He could barely hold on to it. With an enormous effort of self-discipline he drew her freezing body close to his. She had turned very pale.

143

'If you are not well,' he said, 'perhaps I might have the honour of escorting you to your door.'

'You're kind,' she said. Then she almost whispered: 'But it is not kindness I need.'

Major Nye had already had three dances with Miss Brunner. This was the fourth. Major Nye asked Miss Brunner if she knew anything of the theatre.

'Only what I see,' she said.

'You must let me take you backstage sometime, at one of my theatres. You'll like it.'

'I'm sure.'

'You're a very lovely woman.'

'And you're a very handsome man.'

They stared into each other's eyes as they danced.

In the third bedroom of the Casa del Monte, seated on a black walnut panelled Lombardy bed, covered in seventeenth-century carvings, the most corrupt and feeble-minded paperback publisher in America sipped his vodka and tonic and stared sourly at his tennis shoes while one of the Oxford dons bored him with a long and enthusiastic description of the joys and difficulties involved in doing *Now We Are Six* into Assyrian. It was what they both deserved. Of all those at the ball, only the publisher was not enjoying himself.

Colonel Pyat and Prinz Lobkowitz smoked their cigars and strolled in the gardens, stopping on the terrace of the Casa del Monte. 'Peace at last,' said Colonel Pyat, breathing in the richly-scented air. 'Peace. It will be such a relief, don't you think?'

'I, for one, will be happy,' the Prinz agreed.

'It will give us so much more time to enjoy our lives.'

'Quite.'

Miss Brunner and Major Nye found themselves by the Venetian fountain outside the Casa del Sol. Most of the security guards had gone, withdrawn discreetly as the ball progressed. The house itself glowed with light and the waters of the fountain, topped by a copy of Donatello's David, were illuminated with a dozen different soft colours.

Miss Brunner put her hand into the water and watched it run up her three-quarter-length evening glove and drip from her elbow. Major Nye gently stroked his moustache. 'Lovely,' he said.

'But imagine the expenditure.' Miss Brunner smiled to show that she was not being vulgar. 'And no one knows who paid for it. What a splendid piece of tact. Who do you think it is?'

'It's hard to guess who's got that kind of money in England today,' he said without much interest.

Miss Brunner's eyes became alert. 'That's true,' she said. And she was thoughtful. 'Oh, dear.' She removed her hand from the fountain and placed it lightly against Major Nye's hip. 'What a kind man you are.'

'What kind? Oh, I don't know?'

The night was full of music, laughter, witty conversation. It came at her from all sides. 'It's a magic night! I need someone, I think,' she murmured to herself. She decided she would be wise to stick with the material at hand. 'I want you so much,' she breathed, propelling herself into the major's arms. He was astonished and took a little while responding.

'By God! By God! You beauty!'

The German band on the nearby terrace struck up with a selection of Buddy Holly favourites.

Miss Brunner looked round Major Nye's shoulder, scanning suspiciously the privet hedges. It was just a feeling, but it was getting stronger all the time.

'My dear!' Bishop Beesley lay on a yellow bedspread in the yellow-draped Yellow Room of the Casa del Sol. The room was furnished largely in early Jacobean style and the bed-posts were topped by carved eagle finials. On the Bishop's right was a Giovanni Salvi *Madonna and Child*. Lying on the Bishop's left, and facing him, was the beautiful ex-nun with whom Colonel Pyat had lately been dancing. She had turned out to be an Australian. Now she had no clothes on. Bishop Beesley's mitre had fallen to the pillow and his hands were completely covered in chocolate. He had

145

brought the girl and the chocolate mousse up here together and was intently covering her body with the stuff. 'Oh, delicious!' The girl seemed uncomfortable. She put her hand between her legs, frowning. 'I think I'm feeling a little crook.'

Dr Karen von Krupp was dancing in the main ballroom with Professor Hira. Professor Hira had an erection because he could feel Dr Karen von Krupp's girdle and garter-belt through her gown. He hadn't had an erection since Sweden (and then it had proved his downfall). 'The rhythm of the quasars, doctor,' he said, 'is, essentially, a lack of rhythm.' He pressed his erection tentatively against her thigh. Her hand slipped from around his waist and patted him tenderly. His breathing grew more rapid.

'Quasars,' said Dr von Krupp romantically, closing her eyes, 'what are they, compared with the texture of human passion?'

'They are the same! That's it! The same! Everything is the same. My argument exactly.'

'The same? Are we the same?'

'Essentially, yes.'

The music finished and they wandered out into the garden.

Everyone was smiling, shaking hands, patting one another on the back exchanging addresses, laughing uproariously at one another's jokes, making love, resolving to be more generous, more tolerant and to learn humility. The Peace Talks and the Gala Ball would not be forgotten by most of them for a long time. The whole spirit of the talks had been crystallized here. Nothing but improvement lay ahead. Strife would be abolished and heaven on earth would be established.

Only Miss Brunner, Catherine Cornelius and Captain Nye were beginning to wonder if there wasn't a snag. Bishop Beesley and Frank Cornelius, who would normally have been swift to spot the signs, were both too absorbed in their own activities to notice anything.

Frank Cornelius had locked the door of the movie theatre

146

(done in gold and crimson, with silk damask wall hangings and copies of Babylonian statues holding electric lights made to look like lilies) and sat in the back row with Helen Sweet with his hand up her skirt as they watched one of the prints of *Yankee Doodle Dandy* with James Cagney as George M. Cohan and Walter Huston as his father Jerry Cohan. Frank loved the feel of Helen's lukewarm, clammy thigh; it made him nostalgic for the childhood he'd never had. Shakey Mo Collier, operating the projectors, tried to peer through his little window and get a good look at what Frank was doing.

Bishop Beesley and his ex-nun were now completely covered in chocolate and were prancing around the Yellow Room in an obscene version of the Cake Walk.

Lady Sue Sunday, still in the ballroom, was doing the tango with Cyril Tome who had just proposed marriage to her. She was considering his offer seriously, particularly since he showed an unexpected aptitude for the tango. 'We could probably both live on Sunday's money, I suppose,' mused Lady Sue. 'I have a certain income from my writing, moreover,' said Cyril Tome. 'And there would be so much we could clean up together.'

'Flash' Gordon was in the garden taking a happy interest in the azaleas. Nearby, Mrs Cornelius was wandering hand in hand with Professor Hira while Herr Marek hovered jealously in the background, planning to murder the Indian. In the Games Room, where billiard and pool tables rested on travertine floors and where the walls were decorated with rare Gothic tapestries and antique Persian tiles, with its sixteenth-century Spanish ceiling showing scenes of bullfights, Dr von Krupp and Una Persson were playing billiards while Sebastian Auchinek and Simon Vaizey looked on. 'I used to be rather good at this,' said Dr von Krupp, making an awkward shot awkwardly. The spot ball struck the red with a click. 'Isn't that a foul?' asked Una Persson politely. 'I mean, I thought I had the spot.' Dr von Krupp smiled kindly at her. 'No you didn't, dear.' Simon

Vaizey was seized by a fit of hysterical giggling. 'I shouldn't really be here, you know. I think I'm a gatecrasher.'

The President of the United States and the Prime Minister of England were completely and happily drunk and were dancing round and round the otherwise deserted marble Morning Room together, making the huge silver sanctuary lamps on the ceiling jingle and shake with their merriment. A small black and white cat sat on the window sill, licking its paws.

'You look much nicer without your make-up,' said the President. 'I'm glad it's you who's the Prime Minister now.'

Holding a rather grotesque Tiffany lamp above her head Mitzi Beesley, the bishop's daughter, was trying to limbo with Lionel Himmler, who had learned the dance in Nassau during his brief stay there. They were getting on well together. 'I've never enjoyed myself so much,' Mitzi told him. 'I love you.'

'And I love you,' he said. His normally morose features were beaming. 'I love *love!*'

Spiro Koutrouboussis had just shaken hands on a satisfactory business deal with his fellow Greek millionaires when he saw Catherine Cornelius standing in a dark corner of the Main Library, looking through a rare copy of *Paradise Lost*. He crossed the huge Meshed carpet and presented himself. 'Are you free for the next dance, Mademoiselle Cornelius?' he asked in careful French.

'I'm afraid I'm feeling a trifle unwell, m'sieu.' She tried to smile. 'My escort has gone to find my cloak.'

'May I put my landau at your disposal?'

'Thank you. You are very kind, M Koutrouboussis. I was sorry to hear of the unfortunate collapse of your – ' she shivered uncontrollably – 'project.'

'No matter. A new one is developing. That's business. *On mourra seul*, after all.' His own smile was full and charming.

'*Il n'y a pas de morts, M Koutrouboussis!*' She closed her eyes.

'Could I offer you my coat?'

148

'I – thank you.' Gratefully Catherine accepted his heavy jacket, pulling it around her. 'I'm sorry to . . .'

'Please.' He raised a gentle hand.

One of the carved cabinets swung out from the wall and nearly struck Spiro Koutrouboussis on the shoulder. He leapt back.

From the space behind the bookcase emerged a tall figure with long, straight black hair, a pale, voluptuous face. He was wearing a short black overcoat with wide military lapels. His black trousers had a slight flare. His shirt was of the purest white silk and there was a broad, crimson tie at his throat. One long-fingered hand held an oddly shaped gun. 'Hello, Cathy. I see you were expecting me.'

'Oh, Jerry! I'm cold.'

'Don't worry. I'll deal with all that. What are these people doing in my house?'

'Dancing.'

'You might have dressed for the occasion,' said Koutrouboussis, eyeing the gun. Jerry put the gun in his big pocket.

'It took some time getting warm, myself,' he said, by way of apology. 'How's tricks, Koutrouboussis?'

'The tricks are over. I am back in legitimate business now.'

'Just as well. God, you go away for a little while and you come back to find the place crammed with guests. Is this my party, then?'

'I suspect so.'

Jerry laughed. 'Oho! You know me of old, don't you? But this isn't Holland Park. It's Ladbroke Grove. I'm reformed. I lead a very quiet life, these days.'

'Jerry!' Catherine had turned quite blue and seemed on the point of collapse. 'Jerry!'

He wrapped his arms around her. 'There. Is that better?'

'A bit.'

'I can see I'm going to have to take steps.' Jerry poured himself a large whisky from the decanter on the ebony and marble table. 'I suppose Frank's about?'

'And mum.'

'Fuck.'

'She's all right, Jerry. Tonight.'

'I haven't got a lot of time, either,' said Jerry to himself. 'Still . . .'

'How long are you staying for, Jerry?'

'Not long. Don't worry.' He smiled at her, full of misery. 'This is like the old days. I'm sorry.'

'It's not your fault.'

Miss Brunner came into the Games Room. 'I knew it. You'd better not try anything, Mr Cornelius.'

'Oh, I don't know. This is my place, after all.'

'Sod you. You set it up.'

Jerry shrugged.

'Christ!' She spat on the rug.

In the Morning Room, the Prime Minister of England and the President of the United States were sitting side by side in the same big chair. 'Culturally, of course,' said the President, 'we have always been exceptionally close. That must stand for something.'

The Prime Minister laughed happily. 'Me? I'll stand for anything. What's the score?'

The lights went out. The President giggled.

In the main ballroom the music went on for some time, until the candles and the flambeaux began to dim, to gutter and finally extinguish themselves. Everyone murmured with delight, expecting a surprise. Laughter filled the great hall as men and women speculated on the nature of the treat.

At the entrance, the gold doors swung back; the glass doors swung back. A cold wind blew.

In the gardens the glow-worms and the fireflies were still, but there was one light, from the beam of a large flashlight held in the hand of a shadowy figure who swung up the steps into the Casa Grande. The figure wore a short top-coat with its wide lapels turned up to frame a long, pale face. The eyes gleamed in the reflected glare from the flashlight. The figure entered the ballroom and pushed its way through the silent throng until it stood beneath the musicians' gallery.

The voice was cool: 'There's been a mistake. It's time to call it a day, I'm afraid. You are all on private property and I advise you to leave at once. Anyone still here in half an hour will be shot!'

'Good God!' Prinz Lobkowitz stepped forward. 'Who on earth?'

'This is difficult for me,' said the figure. It directed the flashlight upwards. 'It's to do with the third law of thermo-dynamics, I suppose.' The musicians had replaced their instruments with a variety of submachine-guns and auto-matic pistols. 'But I won't bore you with a speech.'

'Do you realize what you are doing?' Prinz Lobkowitz swept his hands to indicate the crowd. 'You could wreck everything.'

'Perhaps. But things have to keep moving, don't they? Now you must leave.'

A machine-gun sounded. Bullets struck the chandeliers and glass flew. The guests began to scream and mill about. The ex-Queen of England went down, her shoulders cut by several shards. Mr Robert D. Feet, the pedant, clutched a bleeding eye. Others sustained less important injuries. The scramble for the exit began. It was almost dignified.

As the guests flooded from the Casa Grande, others began to arrive from the various guest castles. They wanted to know why the lights had gone out. Car engines started up. Horses stamped and snorted. Wheels churned in gravel. There was a smell of May.

In the cinema, Frank Cornelius began to guess that something was up. Abandoning Helen Sweet, he crept to the doors and gingerly unlocked them. 'Jerry?'

In the Yellow Room Bishop Beesley was strugling to get his surplice on over the hardening chocolate, leaving the half-eaten ex-nun on the floor where she lay. He adjusted his mitre, picked up his crook, stooped for one last lick and then hurried out.

151

In the Morning Room the President of the United States and the Prime Minister of England had already left. Only the cat remained, sleeping peacefully in a warm chair.

Captain Nye found the library and opened the door. 'Are you there, Miss Cornelius?'

'Yes, thank you. I'm feeling awfully better.'

'We must go.'

'I'm afraid we must.'

'This will be the ruin of the talks.'

'Quite a good ruin, though.'

Laughing, they left the library.

Mrs Cornelius, Professor Hira and Herr Marek were already in Ladbroke Grove. 'It'll be nice to get back.' Mrs C. felt in her reticule for her key. 'It's only round the corner, luckily.' The three of them were unaware that anything had happened to mar the ball.

'Can you smell valerian?' asked Flash Gordon as Helen Sweet, weeping, stumbled into his hedge. 'You're a little darling, aren't you?' He gathered her up. 'Come and see Holland Park with me.'

She sniffed. 'All right.'

'What's bad news for some is good news for others,' said Lady Sue as her carriage raced past the couple. She had lost her tiara but had gained Bishop Beesley. She didn't know at that point that he wasn't a Negro.

Slumped in the far corner of the brougham, the bishop groaned. He had horrible indigestion.

Cars and carriages erupted into Ladbroke Grove, scattering in all directions, some colliding in the gloom (for the gas lamps had also been extinguished). A small boy was run over by Colonel Pyat's Lamborghini.

In the third bedroom of the Casa del Monte, several Oxford dons and the most corrupt and feeble-minded paperback publisher in America were blown to bits by explosive shells from the big Schmeisser in the hands of the second cellist. The publisher, for one, was almost grateful for this change of pace.

Some, mostly those who had walked to the gates and

were now strolling up Westbourne Park Road towards the Portobello Road looking for taxis, had taken the events with a certain amount of amused relish. They chattered and laughed as they walked along, listening to the distant sounds of machine-gun fire.

'Well,' said Dr von Krupp, who was of this party, 'it's back to square one, I suppose.'

'Do you live in London?' asked Una Persson, her arm around Sebastian Auchinek's neck.

'Oh, I think I'll want to now.' The doctor grinned.

In Spiro Koutrouboussis' landau, which had been the first carriage to get away, Captain Nye and Catherine Cornelius embraced in a long and tender kiss. They were already halfway to the Surrey border, heading for Ironmaster House.

Spiro Koutrouboussis was still in the Casa, having survived the massacre of his colleagues. He had a gun and was looking for his host. He bumped into Frank on the stairs, mistook him for Jerry, and shot him. Frank, thinking that he had been shot by Jerry, returned the fire. The two bodies tumbled down the stairs together.

Miss Brunner and Major Nye gave up any thoughts of revenge and clambered into the major's camouflaged Humber Snipe. As they roared away, one of the violinists emerged on the steps and lifted his Tommy gun to his shoulder, firing after them, but the bullets bounced off the car's armour and then they had turned a corner and were safe.

Easing the car into Ladbroke Grove, Major Nye asked Miss Brunner: 'Well, what did you make of all that?'

'Now that I look back,' she said, 'I suppose it seems inevitable. But not to worry.'

'I must say you know how to make the best of things,' he said admiringly.

Slowly the great house grew still until the only sound that could be heard anywhere was the purring of the small black and white cat as it stretched itself, licked its whiskers, then settled back to sleep again.

THE PEACE TALKS
Concluding Remarks

Upon his return from exile at the request of the new revolutionary junta, Prinz Lobkowitz made a short speech as he stepped off the airship. The speech was addressed to Colonel Pyat and an ecstatic crowd. He said:

'The war, my friends, is ceaseless. The most we can expect in our lives are a few pauses in the struggle, a few moments of tranquillity. We must appreciate those moments while we have them.'

... the ghosts of the unborn. And the ghosts of the unknown: the war dead and those who died in the concentration camps. Dying in anonymity, without witnesses, they are never decently brought to rest. It's hard to explain. And yet the birth of every new child is a kind of resurrection. Every child welcomed into the world helps to lay a ghost to rest. But it takes so long. And these days, it's hardly a lasting solution. Perhaps we should simply stop killing people.

MAURICE LESCOQ, *Leavetaking*

'Miracle Cure' of Frances, 6

The Pope has been asked to declare that six-year-old Frances Burns is a miracle girl. Three years ago, she was dying of cancer. Surgeons who had been fighting for her life gave her only a few days to live. Now she is a happy, laughing tomboy of a girl. And the consultant who treated her admits: 'A miracle is not too strong a term for her recovery.' The astonishing cure of Frances Burns began when her mother, Mrs Deirdre Burns, took her pain-racked daughter from Dennistoun, Glasgow, to the Roman Catholic shrine of Lourdes in Southern France. Frances was bathed in the waters of the mountain spring where thousands of invalids have sought a cure. Back in Glasgow, after two days in the Sick Children's Hospital, Frances sat up and asked for food. A week later the tumours on her face had disappeared. She was on the road to an amazing recovery. The panel of 31 specialists who make up the Lourdes Medical Bureau have asked the Pope to consider pronouncing Frances's cure a miracle.

The Sun, August 23 1971

The Theatre

Una Persson was on stage. She was playing Sue Orph, latest of Simon Vaizey's sophisticated heroines, in Vaizey's most successful musical comedy to date – *Bright Autumn* – at the Prince of Wales' Theatre. The house was full and Una noticed her old agent, Sebastian Auchinek, occupying one of the front stalls. Auchinek was in politics now and writing thousands of articles and pamphlets. His latest production was called 'A New Deal for Britain's Jews'.

Draped in a light pink silk Chanel pyjama suit, Una leaned against a grand piano and confronted her leading man, Douglas Crawford, as he said:

'I never guessed you kept a diary, darling.'

Una held the book insouciantly in one long hand and said lightly: 'Oh, darling, it's hardly a *real* diary.'

The line had become a catch-phrase everywhere now. Comedians imitated it on the wireless. It might have been written especially for her rich Rs.

'But it *is* secret, I suppose,' Douglas continued. 'Is it awfully secret?'

'It is rather.'

'I thought we weren't to have secrets, you and I. I thought we had agreed it wouldn't be that kind of marriage.' He was offended.

She was eager to reassure him. 'Darling, it *isn't* – it's just that – '

Icily remote, he said: 'Yes?'

'Oh, darling don't be a *bear*!' She turned away from him, looking down at the keys of the piano.

'A prig, you mean, don't you?' He folded his arms and stalked to the cocktail cabinet at the far end of the stage. 'Well, what if I am a prig? What if I love you so horribly I can't stand to think of you keeping secrets from me? You know, people who keep diaries are usually afraid of something. Isn't that what they say? What are *you* frightened of, Susan? What have you written about that man you saw last night – you know – that man? What's his name?' He pretended he didn't care, but it was obvious to the audience that he was barely in control of his passions.

Una replied in a high, offended tone, speaking rapidly: 'You know perfectly *well* what his name is. It's Vivian Gantry.' She paused, becoming reminiscent. 'We were lovers – years ago . . .'

'And you still love him? Is that what you're frightened to tell me? Is that what you've written in your damned diary?' Douglas wheeled round, his face tortured with emotion.

Una dropped the diary and swept towards him. 'Oh, you fool, you fool, you sweet, precious fool! How could I love anybody but *you*?'

'Tell me!'

She stopped suddenly, lowering her head. Then she turned to point at the fallen diary. 'Very well, read it if you like.'

He hesitated. He started to mix himself a drink at the cabinet. 'What does it say?'

'That I love you in so many ways I can't even say it to your face.'

'Oh?' It was possible to see now that he wanted to believe her but was still cautious.

Her voice was almost a whisper and yet it reached the back of the theatre. 'Yes, Charles. I suppose I'm too much in love with you, really . . .'

He put the drink down and seized her shoulders. Her face remained averted. 'Swear it?' he said, almost savagely. 'Do you swear it, Sue?'

She recovered her composure and stared him directly in the eyes. Mockingly, spreading her fingers over her heart, she said lightly, but with something of an edge to her voice, 'Very well, if you think it necessary. There! I swear it.' Her tone softened. She took his hand. 'Now stop all this – this *silly* jealousy.'

By now he was completely miserable for having doubted her. 'Oh, darling I'm sorry.' He folded her in his arms. Softly the orchestra started the introduction to the most popular song of the show. 'I *am* a bear! An utterly boorish bear! And a prig! How could I possibly, possibly doubt you. Forgive me?'

Her voice was warm and soft when she breathed:

'Forgive you.'

'Oh darling!'

He began to sing:

> *'You know I'd be blue, dear,*
> *With someone new, dear.*
> *I'll never weary – of you.*
> *Heartbreak and sorrow*
> *Will never spoil tomorrow,*
> *And I'll never be blue, dear, again . . .'*

As the curtain fell on the act, Sebastian Auchinek, his eyes full of tears, clapped and clapped until a hand fell on his shoulder and he looked into the grave, polite faces of two plain-clothes policemen. 'Sorry to interrupt your evening out, sir. But we wonder if you wouldn't mind coming with us to answer one or two questions.'

It was like a bad detective story compared with the fantasy he had just been watching. He said almost pathetically and with an attempt at levity:

'Can't I answer them here?'

'I'm afraid not, sir. We've a warrant, you see.'

'What are you arresting me for?'

'Wouldn't it be less embarrassing if we answered that when we're in the street, sir?'

'I suppose so. Can I get my coat?'

'That's waiting for you in the lobby, sir.' The policeman scratched his little moustache. 'We took the liberty.'

Sebastian Auchinek looked around at the other people in the stalls, but they were all involved in getting to the bar, studying their programmes or chatting amongst themselves.

'I see,' he said. 'Well . . .' He got up, shrugging. 'I am Miss

162

Persson's manager, you know. The papers will know you've arrested me.'

'Not an arrest, as such, sir. A request for help. That's all.'

'Then surely I can see the play through?'

'It's urgent, sir.'

Auchinek sighed. He darted one last look at the curtain, drew one last breath of the atmosphere, and then left by a side exit.

The Flying Boat

The great grey flying boat manoeuvred on her two outer forward-facing propellers, slewing round in the shallows until she faced the main expanse of the blue lake. Save for the ripples which spread from the flying boat's massive angular floats, the lake was flat, shining and still. In the early morning air the growling Curtiss Conqueror engines drowned every other sound. The boat was a Dornier DoX with twelve 600 hp liquid-cooled back-to-back engines mounted on her 160ft wing.

There was space on the ship for a hundred and fifty, but, with the exception of Captain Nye, who was piloting the plane, there were only three people aboard.

Even the snow-capped grandeur of the Swiss Alps failed to dwarf the monoplane as she coursed over tranquil Lake Geneva, all twelve props twirling when Captain Nye flicked the toggle-switches which brought them to life.

'We're flying light. We'll make time, everything else being equal.' He chatted casually to Frank Cornelius who lounged seedily in the roomy co-pilot's chair and stared through the glass at the glare from the rising sun, a ball of pulsing brass whose rays pierced the morning mist.

The boat surged across the deserted lake and headed towards the ruins of the city on the far shore. Captain Nye waited until the very last minute before taking her up, flying playfully low over the collection of shanties near the lakeside. A few children scattered in fright: then the Dornier was climbing steeply, banking into the sun, going East.

'She's an ugly bitch, but she's fast.' Captian Nye levelled out. They were doing at least 130 mph. 'Go and check if the ladies are all right, would you, old man?' They were now well clear of all but the highest mountains.

Frank unstrapped himself and slid the cabin door open. He crossed Joubert and Petit's 60ft Art Deco ballroom and descended the angular staircase to the first-class deck where Miss Brunner and his sister Catherine were already seated on high bar-stools having Pimms Number Ones prepared for them by Professor Hira. The physicist was to be their guide on this expedition.

'Everything okay?' said Frank. 'Isn't it smooth?'

'Beautiful,' said Miss Brunner, dabbing at her Eton crop and winking. Catherine looked away. Through the observation ports she could see the clean, shimmering peaks. 'It's a lovely day,' she said.

'We'll make Rowe Island by Monday easily,' said Frank. 'Six thousand miles, just like that. It's incredible!'

'Aren't you flinging yourself rather too hard into the part, Frankie, dear?' Miss Brunner fingered her lip-rouge.

'Dear Miss B. You've no enthusiasm left at all. I think I'll stroll back to the pilot's cabin.' Frank blew a kiss to his sister and another to Professor Hira. Pointedly he ignored Miss Brunner. They were always quarrelling; even the Indian physicist paid no attention, placing the tall slab-side Vuitton glasses with a click on the zig-zag black and white inlay of the Kroll bar. He didn't drink himself, but he was a wizard at mixing things up.

'It'll be nice to visit the island again,' said Catherine. 'So warm. People go there for their health, I hear.'

'Just as we are, dear, really.' Miss Brunner adjusted her white cardigan over the blue and black silk day dress, offering Catherine a Gold Flake from her thin silver cigarette case. Catherine accepted. Professor Hira leaned over the bar and lit the cigarettes with the big table lighter which had been built to resemble a heavy Egyptian sarcophagus, but which was really made of aluminium and, like so much of the flying boat's equipment, a spin-off from the airship industry. Miss Brunner found airships not sufficiently *chic* for her taste; indeed, even Catherine thought them a trifle gross. Still, they did enable ordinary members of the public to travel from country to country for comparatively little money, if that was a good idea. She was disturbed, however, by the prediction that they would one day take the place of the flying boat. Progress was progress, but she was sure that people of taste would always prefer the elegance of an aircraft like the Dornier, with her lovely Joubert and Petit and Josef Hoffman interiors. Catherine leaned her elbow on the bar, her hand curving back at the wrist, the jade cigarette holder gripped loosely between her forefinger and middle finger perfectly matching the plain jade bangle on her slim arm. She wore the minimum of make-up, the minimum of clothing on her torso. Miss Brunner gave her an admiring once-over. 'Frank is vulgar, but you, dear, are more than perfect.'

Catherine smiled a private smile, her foot tapping to the rhythm of the Ipana Troubadours record Professor Hira had just placed on the Victorphone. The muffled sound of the Curtis Conquerors seemed to be beating to the same time. 'I'll get by – as long as I have you,' sang Catherine with the record.

'But Frank, I think, is more in tune, eh?' said Professor Hira, breaking both their moods.

Miss Brunner was frosty. 'Should that be a compliment, I wonder?' She slid from her stool. 'I'm going to the powder room. I feel a mess.'

Catherine watched her go through the door marked *Damen*. Sometimes Miss Brunner could be a real stickler for form.

Left alone with Catherine, Profesor Hira was ill at ease. He cleared his throat, he beamed, he played with the cocktail shakers, he looked vaguely up at the roof. Once, when they struck some mild disturbance, he made a move to help her steady herself, then became embarrassed, changing his mind half-way through the motion.

Catherine decided to check the cargo. With a pleasant nod to the professor, she gathered up her Worth skirts and walked aft. The companionway led down to the second-class lower deck, which Hoffman had redesigned as a galley and dining cabin. She went through the galley and into the cool forward cargo hold. Aside from their yellow and black pigskin luggage, there was only one piece of cargo. A cream-coloured box about five feet long, three feet wide and three feet deep. The lid of the box was padlocked. Catherine took a key from the side pocket of the little gold Delaunay bag and inserted it into the lock, turning it twice. Then she opened the lid. Inside was the shiny white skeleton of a child, aged between ten and twelve. The skull was damaged. In the bone of the forehead, just above and between the eye sockets, was a large, regularly-shaped hole.

As a mother might move a sleeping child before drawing the covers over it for the night, Catherine rearranged the skeleton on its red and white leather cushions. She leant with a fond smile into the box, kissing the skull just above its injury; then tenderly she closed the lid and padlocked it up, murmuring: 'Don't worry.'

She sighed, pressing her palms together in front of her lips. 'The Indian Ocean is the friendliest in the world, Profesor Hira says. And Rowe Island is the friendliest island in the Indian Ocean. We'll all be able to rest there.' She staggered as the plane hit more turbulence, banking steeply. She managed to grasp the yellow and green silk safety rope secured to the bulkhead. The Dornier righted herself almost immediately. Catherine checked that the box hadn't shifted in its moorings and then carefully she began to make her way back to the bar.

The Pier

'It's the 'ottest summer in years,' Mrs Cornelius was saying as she waded back to the shore, her jazzy print dress hitched above her red, dumpy knees. She was sweating like a sow, but she was happy, out of breath, having a high old time at Brighton. She'd been to the races, been on the sea-front miniature railway, had two sticks of rock, some winkles, five pints of Guinness, a bit of skate and chips and a sing-song in the pub just before she'd been sick. Being sick had cleared her system and now she felt like a million dollars. It did you good. Colonel Pyat, in perfect civilian summer dress, a white linen suit, a panama hat, two-tone shoes and a malacca cane over his arm, stood on the pebbles holding Tiddles, Mrs Cornelius's small black and white cat, which, of late, she had taken to carrying everywhere she went, even to the shops, the pictures or, like today, on their honeymoon day excursion to the seaside.

'Wot abart th' pier?' Mrs Cornelius panted. She cocked her thumb over her damp shoulder at the East Pier, an affair of rusty scaffolding holding a dance hall, a theatre, a penny arcade and a fun fair. From where she stood on the bank she could hear the dodgems clattering and crashing. Every so often, there came a high-pitched giggle, an excited yell.

Colonel Pyat shrugged his acquiescence. It was his duty. He would do it.

''Ere, give us th' cat.' She seized the limp beast from his arms. 'Looks daft, a man carrying a cat. They'll reckon yore a fairy or somefink if you ain't careful!' She laughed raucously, nudging him playfully in the ribs. 'Not that there aren't a few o' *them* darn 'ere. Brighton! I should think so!' She cast an eye over the jolly crowd which covered the beach, as if vetting them for signs of sexual deviation. Deckchairs, newspapers, raincoats, fairisle pullovers, jackets, towels, were scattered everywhere and on them lay or squatted mums and dads and adolescent boys and girls, the sun shining on their Brylcreemed crops and their permanent waves. The younger kids wandered around eating ice-cream bricks from the Walls Stop-me-and-buy-one man who pedalled his refrigerated bin up and down the front. Other children, clutching their scratched metal buckets and chipped wooden spades, sought wistfully for some sand. The noise of a barrel-organ came closer. Far away, on the promenade overlooking the beach, open top double-decker buses sailed slowly along, crammed with men in white Oxford bags and open-neck shirts, or girls in snazzy summer frocks, their hair tightly curled or waved, their lips blossoming with scarlet and cerise. The smell of brine, of grease, of chips and jellied eels drifted languidly on the still air.

'Phew!' She wriggled her toes into her emerald-green sling-back sandals and led the way through her fellow holidaymakers and up the shingle towards the pier. 'It could get yer darn, too much o' this, eh? The 'eat, I mean.'

On the pier, having paid twopence each to go through the turnstile, Colonel Pyat found to his relief that the wind had changed direction and was blowing all the smells, save that of the sea, back towards the town where the Chinoiserie Pavlion's green domes could be seen among the more down to earth Regency terraces. It certainly was hot and the sun hurt his eyes, making him wish he had brought his tinted spectacles. The cat struggled for a moment in his coat and then was still again.

'Wot a marf, wot a marf, wor a norf an' sarf,' sang Mrs Cornelius. 'Lumme, wot a marf 'e's got. When 'e was a nipper, Cor Lord Lovel, 'is pore ol' muvver use ter feed 'im wiv a shovel! Wot a gap (pore chap), 'e's never bin known to larf — 'cos if 'e did it's a penny ter a quid, 'is face ud fall in arf!'

Colonel Pyat looked apprehensively at Mrs C. The last time she'd sung that particular song, it was just before she'd been violently sick in the gutter outside The Ship.

'This is wot I *corl* a Bank 'oliday Monday,' continued Mrs

Cornelius, taking the cat from him, raising it close to her face and stroking it. 'Let's go on the ghost train now, eh?'

'You don't want to overdo it, you know,' said Colonel Pyat

'Wot? Me?' She shook with mirth. 'You must be joking!'

They went on the ghost train. Colonel Pyat was frightened by the monsters and witches and skeletons which sprang at him from all sides, the screechings, the howls, the cackling laughter, the clammy stuff that touched his smooth-shaven cheeks, the spider-webs, the flashing lights, the rush of cold air, the mirrors, the awful darkness through which they passed, but Mrs Cornelius – although she yelled and shrieked incessantly – had a lovely time.

They took a cup of tea and a bun each in the pier cafeteria, looking out over the sparkling sea. All the waitresses gathered round to stroke Mrs Cornelius's cat. 'Innit *tame*?' said one. Another offered it a bit of biscuit, which it refused. Another girl, with a scrawny face and a wretched body, brought it a saucer of milk. ''Ere, pussy. Pussy? Pussy?' The cat lapped the milk and the girl felt grateful all day.

They got on the dodgems. Mrs C. went in one car, with the cat stuffed down her bosom with only its little head sticking out, looking really comical, and Colonel Pyat went in another. Mrs Cornelius's car was bright red and gold with a number 77 on it. Colonel Pyat's car was green and white with a number 55 on it. The power arms cracked and flashed and sparks flew as the cars started up. Mrs C. leaned forward, driving her car head-on at Colonel P. who resigned himself to the thump which shook his bones and grazed his knees. Through the loudspeakers came the distorted voice of Nat Gonella singing *If I had a talking picture of you.* 'Yer too effin' slow!' screamed Mrs C. delightedly, and off she went to deal damage to other unsuspecting drivers. Even the cat seemed to be enjoying himself on the dodgems. 'Oo! Muvver!' shouted Mrs Cornelius as she flung back her turbanned head and took another victim.

Colonel Pyat began to feel queasy. As soon as the cars stopped moving, he got out and stood on the side while Mrs

Cornelius had another turn. He was amazed that so much violent activity could take place on such an apparently flimsy structure as the pier. It must be considerably stronger than he thought. He lit a cigarette and strolled towards the rail, looking down through the gaps in the planks at the sea swishing below, listening to the distinctive noises of the woman he had married, wondering if after the destruction of the town, this pier would still survive.

The cars had stopped again and Mrs Cornelius was clambering out and waddling across the floor to the boardwalk which ran round the outside of the dodgem arena. She was sweating and grinning when she joined him and she had picked up some of the oily aroma of the cars.

'Come on,' she said, seizing him by the arm and leading him further up the pier, 'we still got time fer a dance.'

The Hills

A smoky Indian rain fell through the hills and woods outside Simla and the high roads were slippery. Major Nye drove his Phantom V down twisting lanes flanked by white fences. The car's violet body was splashed with mud and it was difficult to see through the haze that softened the landscape. In rain, thought the major, the world became timeless.

Turning into the drive outside his big wooden bungalow, he brought the limousine to a stop. A Sikh servant gave him an umbrella before taking over the car.

Major Nye walked through the rain to the veranda, folding the umbrella and listening to the sound of water on the leaves of the trees. It was like the ticking of a thousand watches. It smelled so fresh. Simla hadn't changed much. That was something.

His wife and two little girls were still in Delhi. They had been reluctant to make this journey of return with him. But there had been people he wanted to see. He had felt the need to reassure the servants that he was still in the land of the living.

Inside, the house was cold; all the furniture was draped in white dust-covers. There were no smells and, save for the rain, no sounds. The place was dead. He felt tired, borne down by responsibility, by the sudden understanding that all his dedication had been pointless. How much longer could the Raj last, with the Chinese, the Russians and the Americans hammering at the gates?

He saw that a fire had been lit in the grate. Someone had been burning books. He picked up the poker and turned over the covers, which were only partially burned. *How Michael Found Jesus* was one title, and there were others: *Ragnarok and the Third Law of Thermodynamics*, *Time Search Through the Declining West*, *Bible Stories for Little*

Folk, A Cure for Cancer, How to Avoid Heat Death. All religious and medical stuff, plainly. Who on earth could have bothered to set fire to them? He was crossing to the bell-pull when he was distracted by a sound from outside. On the veranda servants were shouting. He went to the window and opened it.

'What is it, Jenab Shah?' he asked the big Afghan butler.

The man shrugged and grinned in his thick beard. 'Nothing, sahib. A mongoose killing a cobra. See.' He held up the limp body of the snake.

Major Nye nodded and closed the window. He went to the door and into the shady hallway. He walked up the uncarpeted stairs. He entered the bedroom which he and his wife had once shared. The bed and the rest of the furniture was also draped in white sheets. He grabbed the edge of a sheet covering a massive teak wardrobe and yanked it down. Dust filled the room. He coughed. He pulled a bunch of keys from his pocket and selected one, putting it into the lock of the wardrobe. The door creaked open, revealing a mirror in which, for a second, he regarded himself with surprise. He had aged. There was no doubt of it. But he had kept his figure. He reached into the wardrobe and selected an Indian coat of silk brocade. It was blue, with circular panels of slightly lighter blue stitched at intervals all over it. The buttons were diamonds and the cloth was lined with buckram. The high, stiff collar was fixed at the throat by two hidden brass buckles. There was also a scarlet sash. Major Nye took off his own jacket and drew the Indian coat over his white silk shirt. Carefully he did up all the buttons and then clipped the collar together. Finally he tied the sash about his waist. With his greying hair and white moustache, his clear blue eyes and his tan he could still look impressive; as impressive as when he had received the coat. It had been a present from his defeated enemy Sharan Khang, the old hill fox. Was Sharan Khang still perpetuating the fiction that his Himalayan Kingdom was independent? Major Nye smiled.

Wearing the coat, he went downstairs to the gunroom.

With another key he unlocked the door. Lying on the table was the Mauser FG42 where he had left it last. Closing the door behind him, he went over to the gun and picked it up, brushing away the dust which had settled on the barrel. He slotted the telescope sight into its mount, checked the magazine and cradled the gun in his left arm. A small drop of oil now stained his silken sleeve. He opened a drawer and found a box of cartridges. He put these into his left hand and then went out, locking the door again.

He looked at his wrist-watch, checking the time. The rain had stopped for a moment. He began to smell the grass, the rhododendrons, the trees. He went outside and walked acorss the lawn which still had croquet hoops sticking in it from the last game, years before. On the far side of the lawn and partly obscured by foliage was the white ruin of the mansion he had built when he had first come to Simla.

Major Nye had always had a superstitious reluctance to visit the ruin, the result of a single Tibetan bomb dropped from a Caproni Ca 90 BB during the brief Italian crisis some years earlier. It had been the only plane ever to get as far as Simla.

The mansion's roof had collapsed completely now and part of the front wall bulged outwards. All the windows were smashed and the double door at the front had been thrust out by the force of the blast. The only occupants of the house had been an ayah and Major Nye's small son. They had both been killed.

Major Nye took a firmer grip on his rifle. He fitted shells into the magazine and then continued to stalk forward, but it was becoming harder to move at all. He mounted the first two broken steps, making himself look at the door. He was sweating.

Until this moment, he had never considered himself a coward, but he stopped dead before he reached the last step to the doorway. He shuddered at what his imagination made him see behind the doors. Trembling, he lifted the Mauser to his shoulder and, without bothering to sight, fired the whole magazine into the timber. Then he dropped the gun and ran, his face twisting in terror.

He shouted for his car. The Phantom V was ready. He got into it and drove away from Simla, his eyes wide with self-hatred.

In Delhi he booked a passage on a ship leaving Bombay a few days later. He didn't see his wife or children, but stayed at his club. Next morning he took the train to Bombay and, even when his ship, the SS *Kao An*, was well out into the Arabian Sea, he was still weeping.

The Statue

Prinz Lobkowitz straightened his uniform and stood shakily up in the open staffcar as it rolled into Wenzslaslas Square in the early afternoon. The troops, in smart black and gold uniforms, stood in their ranks, straight and tall and ready for review. On all sides of the square the watching crowd was eight and ten people deep. The Mercedes reached the rostrum erected below the statue of the martyr-king. The crowd cheered, the soldiers presented arms. A whistle sounded and the staute blew up. A chunk of stone rushed past Prinz Lobkowitz's head and he flung himself down into the car. General Josef, his aide, seated opposite the Prinz, drew his revolver and shouted for the driver to accelerate quickly, but the driver's nerve was gone and he was having trouble getting the Mercedes back into gear.

Save for the dead and wounded, the troops remained in reasonably good order, but the crowd had panicked. The air was filled with its screams as it tried to escape from the square. Two or three shots sounded. This increased the tension. People ran in all directions.

The smoke and dust was clearing now. Lobkowitz saw that the entire statue had been destroyed. Hardly a stump of the pedestal had survived the blast. The temporary rostrum had become a heap of shattered wood and twisted metal. Prinz Lobkowitz's standard lay half-buried in the rubble near a smashed, bloody corpse which he couldn't identify.

General Josef, the aide, began shouting hoarse orders to his troops. Rifles ready, squads of soldiers broke from the square and drove their way through the terrified civilians, pouring into the surrounding buildings, occupying them, and searching for the assassins. Suddenly something cracked above Lobkowitz's head. A banner had unfurled itself from a bouncing telephone wire. The banner bore a singe word:

176

Lobkowitz pursed his lips. Terrorists. And it wasn't as if he'd taken the country by force. He felt let down.

The Mercedes was in gear now, reversing towards the street by which it had entered the square. Lobkowitz tried to straighten up and see what was happening. Old General Josef pushed him down again. On the roof of a house on the far side of the square some figures appeared. They wore civilian dress but they had bandoliers of cartridges criss-crossed on their chests and there were rifles in their hands. They looked a bit like Slovak brigands. The men and women on the roof began to fire indiscriminately into the square. Some soldiers fell; some ran for cover.

'There'll be hell to pay,' General Josef kept muttering. Lobkowitz wasn't sure whether his aide was frightened of losing his job; whether Josef intended to sack his security officers; or whether he was vowing to take reprisals on the terrorists, whoever they were. Lobkowitz knew the terrorists could be anyone. They could be the disguised 'volunteer' soldiers of half-a-dozen different foreign armies; they could be anarchists; or mercenaries in the pay of some extreme right-wing group; they might be communards; they could even be Czech nationals. Time would tell.

Now the driver had swung the Mercedes round in a circle and headed down the broad, treelined Avenue Mozart, making for the Presidential Palace where they might still find safety. General Josef let the Prinz sit up. Josef put his revolver away, buttoning the holster.

'That's the last time we use an open car,' he growled as he tidied his white hair and re-adjusted his cap. 'It'll be an armoured half-track next. The devil with public relations!'

'They didn't do much damage.' Lobkowitz spoke mildly. He was unhappy in his uniform. It was too severe. He preferred the more comfortable and colourful uniforms of his native land. How much longer should he go on listening to these advisers?

'Freiheit!' muttered the aide bitterly. 'What do they know

of freedom? They think it means license – self-expression. A little freedom is bought at great cost. I know. I was in the original Corps which made this damned city safe. You should have been here, Prinz, before we sent for you. The stink alone would have knocked you out. It wasn't a city of liberty: it was a city of libertines.'

A feeling of intense boredom swept over Lobkowitz. He had heard this remark made by a score of men in a score of different cities.

'That's finished, at least,' Josef went on. 'But it could all be ruined again. We must work fast.'

'Do you know what the terrorists are?' Lobkowitz asked. 'Do you know what movement they support?'

'Not yet. That's the least of our worries.' The aide tapped his teeth with his cane and became reflective. Prinz Lobkowitz asked him no further questions.

Back in the Presidential Palace, Prinz Lobkowitz felt lonely. He sat in his huge, impressive office and looked at no one and nothing. At his back were the crossed flags of both their nations, hanging over the eighteenth-century fireplace. From a window which opened on to the balcony he contemplated the street. In the middle of the avenue, waving a sword and mounted on a horse, stood a granite statue of some other antique hero. Even as Lobkowitz looked, it blew up. It was as if every statue he glanced at immediately burst into fragments. The noble stone head rose towards him and then, as he covered his eyes, burst through the window, taking both glass and frame into the room and bouncing, chipped but unbroken, into the empty fireplace.

For a second Prinz Lobkowitz thought it was his own head. Then he smiled. He crouched down behind his massive desk, keeping it between him and the window in case there were further explosions. After all, he thought, he had no axe to grind. If they didn't want him, fair enough. He'd be glad to get home.

The telephone began to ring. Lobkowitz felt for it on top of the desk and found it. 'Lobkowitz.'

'Are you hurt, sir?' It was General Josef's voice.

'No, not at all, but the firedog's a bit bent.'

'I'll be up right away.'

As he waited for Josef's arrival, Lobkowitz sat on the edge of the desk and lit the last of his Black Cat cigarettes. Before he crumpled the packet and threw it into his wastepaper bin, he took the brightly coloured card (one of a series of 50 given away free with the cigarettes) and tucked it into the top breast pocket of the civilian waistcoat he had always worn under his uniform. It was a picture of a Triceratops, number eighteen in a series of dinosaurs.

The red and black packet was the only piece of scrap in the otherwise clean steel wastepaper basket. He felt for it.

The gilded doors swung open. Una Persson stood there, dressed all in black, a rifle slung over her back, a beret on her shining curls. She opened her arms to him, smiling.

'Darling! I have defeated you again!'

In the early hours of a summer morning a cat kills a mouse in the kitchen, letting it run a little way and then stopping it again. Outside in the garden large black slugs crawl over the iron furniture. There is movement in the toolshed. There is a whisper from beyond the trees.

Late News

A crowd of about 200 attacked two Army scout cars and a
Land-Rover in Belfast last night after one of them ran over
and killed a five-year-old girl. Cars, vans and lorries were
set on fire and there were bursts of machine-gun fire which
injured four young children. The girl was one of a crowd of
children playing on the street corner. An Army spokesman
said she jumped under the wheels of the leading scout car.

Morning Star, February 9 1971

A widow, her five children and an uncle died in a fire at a
cottage in Pontypool yesterday. Firemen found the bodies of
Mrs Patricia Evans, aged 34, Jacqueline, 13, Garry, 11,
Joanne, eight, Martin, six, and Catherine, two, in a bedroom.
On the stairs was the body of Mr John Edwards, aged 63, the
uncle who came to rescue them.

Guardian, February 9 1971

George Laksy, aged four, was drowned when he fell into an
ice-covered pond in a field at Slough yesterday. He had gone
on the ice to pick up a ball.

Guardian, March 2 1971

Murder squad detectives set up headquarters in a holiday
beach café in Cornwall yesterday after the badly-battered
body of a 17-year-old high school girl had been found near
the entrance to a cliff-top camp site.

Guardian, March 15 1971

A three-year-old boy was found dead in a disused refrigerator
last night.

Guardian, June 29 1971

Lynn Andrews, aged 10, was stripped almost naked and punched and kicked to death while her mother looked on helpless, it was said in court at Woolwich yesterday. Raymond John Day (31), unemployed, was sent for trial charged with murdering the girl.

Guardian, June 30 1971

Jerry Cornelius was in Sandakan when the news came of the resumption of hostilities. The news was brought by Dassim Shan, Jerry's major domo, while Jerry swam in the cool waters of the palace pool, all pink and blue marble and tinkling fountains.

Rajah? Dassim, feet together, stood uncertainly on the edge of the pool, one hand against a jade pillar. Jerry was some distance out in the middle of the pool, hidden in the shade. Milky light filtered down from the semi-transparent dome in the roof. Dassim's voice echoed a little.

They are fighting again, rajah.

Oh? A splash.

Does it not concern you, rajah?

Dassim peered into the water, searching every inch of it for his master, but he could see only goldfish.

Bishop Beesley, Mitzi Beesley, Shakey Mo Collier and Jerry Cornelius stood on the footbridge staring down at the railway as the train passed beneath their feet. Through the steam they could see the open trucks piled high with stiffening corpses. Dead troops.

Jerry pushed his helmet back from his forehead and eased the strap of his pack. Well, he said, our luck's still holding.

The smell! Mitzi Beesley, dressed in a complete ARP uniform, circa 1943, held her nose.

Her father sorted through his tin of emergency rations to see if there was any chocolate he'd overlooked. That's not the half of it, he said. He wore khaki battle dress with his dog-collar rather ostentatiously displayed at the throat.

I remember a train like that when I was a kid, said Mo Collier nostalgically. On'y in that case the soldiers on it was alive.

Same difference, said Mitzi with a wink. She rubbed busily at her blue flannel thigh as the last truck went under the bridge.

Jerry looked at his left watch. Well, back to work. Not far to Grasmere now.

They all climbed on to the lightweight Jungle Bug, with its motorbike saddle seats and its canvas windshield. Jerry settled himself in front of the driving gear and started the engine. For a moment the machine reared, its front wheels spinning, and then they were off down the narrow lane as a thin cloud of rain drifted from the fells to the west and the green hills turned suddenly black.

We've never fully been able to reproduce World War Two conditions, Bishop Beesley yelled over the screech of the engine and the slap of the wind. I sometimes consider it a personal failure.

Your moral dilemmas always resolve themselves sooner

or later, dad, Mitzi comforted. She reached over from where she sat alongside him on the pillion behind Jerry and straightened his M60 on his shoulder for him. Is that better?

He nodded gratefully, munching a piece of Nut Crunch he had found in the breast-pocket of his battledress. They bounced on towards Grasmere and, as the rain passed, glimpsed the lake on the far side of a hill lying almost directly ahead of them. They had heard that what was left of an enemy division was hiding out in Wordsworth's cottage. It was a long shot, but it was something to do.

The road went through a pine wood and then bent along the eastern shore of the lake, leading directly into the town of Grasmere. The town was a ruin of looted gift shops and tea rooms. In one or two places they were forced to steer round small craters in the road. Elsewhere a sack had burst and been abandoned, leaving a litter of plaster Wordsworth busts, oven gloves and daffodil vases.

They headed for the main road with its cracked and weedgrown concrete and at last sighted Dove Cottage and, a few doors away, another cottage that was the Wordsworth Museum. There were signs of fighting in the stone, half-timbered buildings. One or two cottages had been destroyed completely, but Dove Cottage, with its roses round the door, was intact. They climbed off the Jungle Bug and readied their weapons, approaching cautiously.

Dove Cottage seemed deserted, but Jerry didn't take any chances. He ordered Bishop Beesley forward. The bishop lay down behind a hedge and raked the windows. There was a musical tinkle as the glass broke. Bishop Beesley waited for a while and then stood up, munching a Mars Bar.

A Webley .45 sounded from an upstairs window and the bullet went past him, hitting the ground. He turned, his Mars Bar half-raised, and darted an enquiring glance at Jerry, who shrugged.

There was another shot. Bishop Beesley eased his bulk to the ground again, put a new clip in his M60 and fired at the window.

When there was no further answering fire, the four of

them spread out and approached the cottage. Jerry noticed that the plaque on the door reading 'Wordsworth's Cottage' had been holed a few times by shells larger than Bishop Beesley's. The door opened easily for the lock had already been blown off. They went in. An American teenage girl, with long black hair and a red mou-mou pulled up around her waist, lay on the polished timber floor. Her blood had dried on her face and her left hand was missing. Apart from the girl, the downstairs rooms, with their glass cabinets of Wordsworth and Lake Poets trophies, were empty. Pictures of Southey, Coleridge, De Quincey and the Lambs smiled down at them. Shakey Mo broke one of the cabinets with the butt of his Sten and lifted out an oddly shaped object of carved ivory. He squinted at the label. Look at this! De Quincey's drug balance. Look at the size! What a head! He put the balance into the gamebag he had slung over one shoulder and rummaged through the rest of the cabinet's contents. He found nothing else of interest. More glass broke in the next room and the three of them trooped in to see what Mitzi was doing. She had smashed the glass partition behind which had been arranged a typical sitting room of Wordsworth's time. She had stripped off her ARP uniform and was draping herself in the dead poet's clothes, his hat, his jacket, his shawl and one of his waistcoats. She held his umbrella in one hand. With her Remington tucked under her arm, she tried to open the umbrella. They all laughed as she paraded round the room pretending to read from one of Dorothy Wordsworth's diaries.

Jerry heard a footfall upstairs and raised his Schmidt Rubin 5.56 to rake the ceiling. The footfall stopped.

I suppose we'd better get upstairs, said Shakey Mo.

Jerry led the way.

The upstairs rooms were much the same as the downstairs rooms, with more cabinets and more trophies, some of which had been smashed by Bishop Beesley's M60 bullets coming through the windows. In the front room sat a woman of about sixty. She was tall, dressed in a plain blue dress and her hair was grey. The empty Webley was still in her hand. She was evidently upset. There are guided tours, you know, she said. You only had to ask.

Bishop Beesley grinned with relish as he advanced on her. I'm going to fuck the life out of you, he said.

Jerry and the rest made a tactful retreat.

Bishop Beesley joined them later in the Wordsworth Museum where Shakey Mo was inspecting an old shotgun labelled 'Wordsworth's Gun'.

My God, said Beesley in disgust, even this place has a tinge of vitality. Bishop Beesley argued that since too much life had led to their present difficulties (overcrowding and so forth), then life meant death and was therefore evil. Therefore it was his duty to wipe out the evil by destroying life wherever he found it. He was a wizard at that sort of thing. Jerry had his eye on him.

Are we all finished here? Jerry asked.

They padded away, turning only to watch when Shakey Mo lobbed a couple of Mills bombs into the cottage and the museum.

Damn! said Mitzi as the buildings went up. I left my uniform behind.

She wrapped Wordsworth's shawl more tightly around her, pursing her lips in rage as she tripped, on Cuban heels, back to the Jungle Bug. Bishop Beesley, Shakey Mo and Jerry Cornelius took the opportunity to piss against a hedge; then the rain came on again.

In improved spirits, they mounted the Bug and headed towards Rydal and the big green hills beyond.

Late News

Lt William Calley, charged with massacring 102 South Vietnamese men, women and children at My Lai hamlet, testified at his court-martial at Fort Benning, California, yesterday, that the army taught him children were even more dangerous than adults. He was taught that 'men and women were equally dangerous, and children, because of their unsuspectingness were even more dangerous'. The army also taught him that men and women fought side by side and women for some reason were better shots. He was told that 'children can be used in a multiple of facets. For example, give a child a hand grenade and he can throw it at an American unit. They were used for planting mines. Basically they were very dangerous.'

Morning Star, February 23 1971

Three boys died when a house caught fire in Cemetery Road, Telford, Salop. They were Keith William Troop, aged five, Peter John Green, aged three, and Matthew Percival Green, aged two. They were the sons of Mrs Joan Green, aged 22.

Guardian, May 3 1971

Mrs Valerie Ridyard, aged 25, pleaded guilty to the manslaughter of Darren, aged five months, Michael, aged three, and Barbara, aged four, on the grounds of diminished responsibility. Her pleas of not guilty to murder were accepted. The children died in separate incidents between October 1970 and January 1971. Mr Arthur Prescot, QC, prosecuting, said the facts were short and tragic. There had been a history of conduct by Mrs Ridyard resulting in illness to the children through partial suffocation and poisoning.

Guardian, June 10 1971

The West Indian immigrant parents of seven children admitted at Berkshire assizes, Reading, yesterday to killing one of their sons in a ritual sacrifice. Olton Goring (40), of Waylen Street, Reading, was committed to Broadmoor after the prosecution accepted his plea of not guilty to murdering the boy, Keith, aged 16, but guilty to manslaughter on grounds of diminished responsibility. Goring's wife, Eileen (44), pleaded guilty to manslaughter and was ordered to be sent for treatment in a mental hospital. It was said the Gorings were members of a Pentecostal mission in Reading – a revival sect widely supported in the West Indies. Followers believed themselves possessed by the Holy Spirit while in a trance and felt they were in direct communication with God.

Guardian, August 23 1971

A boy aged 14 will appear in court at Tamworth, Staffordshire, today in connection with the death of a man aged 19 whose body was found in a house on Saturday.

Guardian, August 23 1971

A girl aged 14 was charged on Saturday with the murder of Roisin McIlone, aged five, whose body was found beside an overgrown bridle path near her home in Brook Farm Walk, Celmsley Wood, near Birmingham. A blood-stained stick was found nearby.

Guardian, August 23 1971

The black, burning warehouses of Newcastle.

The Airship

During the First Night Dance on board the LS *Light of Dresden*, bound for India via Aden, Mrs Cornelius went out on to the semi-open observation deck to get some air. She felt a little queasy; it was her maiden trip on a Zeppelin, but she was determined to enjoy herself, come what may. All she had to do was clear her head and let herself get used to a feeling that was like being permanently in a slightly swaying descending lift that was also moving horizontally. She stood outside the big hall where the spotlights played beams of red, blue, yellow and green on the dancers. The band was called The Little Chocolate Dandies. Their saxophones wailing, they launched themselves into their next number, *Royal Garden Blues*. Mrs Cornelius wasn't too sure she was that keen on jazz, after all. At present she felt like hearing something just a teeny bit more restful. But the only thing she could think of was *Rock-a-bye-baby*: in fact, she couldn't get it out of her head. She looked down at the lights of Paris (she thought it was Paris) and imagined the drop. Though she had been assured that it was completely rigid and part of the main frame containing the helium bags, she was sure she could feel the catwalk swaying below her. The music from the dance floor now seemed much more friendly. She reeled back in again.

Everyone was really jazzing it up tonight. She was nearly knocked down twice by couples as she moved towards the bar. She grinned. Ah, well! She felt a hand on her shoulder.

'Are you perfectly well, dear lady?'

It was that bishop she'd met earlier. She'd liked him from the start, with his nice, jolly fat face, though she hadn't taken to his wife in the baggy pink evening dress, frizzy hair, with her thin, pale, nervous head constantly grinning in a way Mrs C. personally found offensive. If you asked Mrs C., the bishop's wife fancied herself a bit. Lady Muck.

191

The bishop, on the other hand, was a real gentleman, he could mix with anyone at any level. Mrs C. could go for him in a big way. She smiled to herself at the thought, wondering what it would be like with a bishop.

'Quaite well, thank yew, bishop, love,' she said. 'Jist gittin' me air-legs, thet's hall.'

'Would you care to dance?'

'Oh, charmed Ai'm shewer!' She put her left arm round his ample, black-clad waist and folded her dumpy right hand in his. They began to fox-trot. 'Yore a lovely dancer, bishop.' She giggled. Over the bishop's shoulder she saw his wife looking on, nodding to her with that same set, patronizing smile, though you could tell she wasn't pleased. Mrs C. defiantly pushed her bosom against the bishop's chest. The bishop's red lips smiled slightly and his little eyes twinkled. She knew he fancied her. She went all warm and funny inside as his hand tightened on her corset. What a turn up.

'Are you travelling alone, Mrs Cornelius?'

'Well, Ai've got me littel boy wiv me, but 'e's no trouble. Got a cabin to 'imself.'

'And – Mr Cornelius?'

'Gorn, unforchunatly.'

'You mean?'

'Quaite. RIP.'

'I'm sorry to hear it.'

'Well, it was a long time ago, you see.'

'Aha.' The bishop looked upwards, towards the gigantic gas-bags hidden behind the dance hall's aluminium ceiling. 'He's in a happier state than we, all in all.'

'Quaite.'

Well, thought Mrs C., he's not slow. Maybe he was the original bishop in the jokes, eh? Again she couldn't stop herself from smiling. Her queasiness had completely disappeared, to be replaced by that old feeling.

'And how are you travelling? First class, I assume?'

'Ai should fink so!' She roared with laughter. 'No such luck, Ai'm afraid. It's second class for me. It's not cheap, the fare to Calcutta.'

'I agree. I, too – that is to say my wife and I – am forced to travel second. But I must say I've no complaints, as yet, though it is only our first night aloft. We are in cabin 46 . . .'

'Oh, reahlly? Wot a coincidence. Ai'm in number 38. Just deown the passage from you. Mai littel boy's in 30, sharin' wiv a couple of other littel boys.'

'You have a good relationship with your son?'

'Oh yes! 'E's devoted!'

'I envy you.'

'Wot, me?'

'I wish I had a good relationship with my – my sole relative. Mrs Beesley, I regret, is not the easiest woman with whom to be joined in holy matrimony.'

'She seems a naice sort o' woman, if a bit, you know, out of things, as you might say.'

'She does not take pleasure, as I do, in making new friends. Normally I travel alone, and Mrs Beesley remains at the rectory, but she has a sister in Delhi and so she decided, this time, to accompany me.' Now the bishop's stomach pressed against her stomach. It was so cosy, it made her legs feel like jelly.

'P'raps she should rest more,' said Mrs C. 'Ai mean she could take the chance to relax before we get to India, couldn't she? It would probably do 'er good.' She hoped the bishop hadn't noticed the rather savage delivery of that last sentence. He certainly seemed unaware of the change in her tone and only smiled vaguely. The music stopped and, reluctantly, they broke their embrace and clapped politely at the coloured men in tuxedos on the bandstand. One of the musicians stepped forward, his black hands running up and down the keys of his saxophone as he spoke.

'And now, ladies and gentlemen, we'd like to give you my own *That's How I Feel Today*. Thank you.'

Tuba, banjo, three saxophones, drums, piano, trumpet and trombone all started up at once and, oblivious to the other dancers, Mrs Cornelius and Bishop Beesley began to Charleston, still holding each other very close. When Mrs Cornelius next noticed Mrs Beesley, the bishop's wife was quietly leaving through the exit on to the main corridor. Mrs C. felt triumphant. Po-faced bitch! Didn't she believe in a feller enjoying himself?

'Ai'm afraid yore waife 'as decided to leave us,' she said into his plump, red ear.

'Oh dear. Perhaps she's gone to lie down. I wonder if I shouldn't . . . ?'

'Oh, come on, bishop! Finish the dance!'

'Yes, indeed. Why not?'

The lights dimmed, the tone of the music sweetened and Mrs C. and Bishop B. began to fox-trot again. It was very romantic. Everyone on the floor sensed the mood and got smoochy. Mrs Cornelius's bosom began to heave and she wriggled her bulk against Bishop Beesley's, who responded by moving his hand over her bottom.

She murmured, as the music subsided, 'You feel like it, don't you?'

He nodded eagerly, smiling and clapping. 'I do, dear lady. I do, indeed.'

'Would you like to escort me to mai cabin door?'

'I should like nothing better.' The old dog was almost panting with lust. She winked at him and put her arm in his.

'Come on, then.'

This was what she called a ship-board romance.

They went into the passage and turned left, searching for the right cabin number in the dim, blue light.

They slipped surreptitiously past number 46 and Mrs Cornelius searched hastily for her key as they approached number 38. She produced it with a flourish and inserted it delicately into the lock, turning the levers with a soft double click. She stood there coquettishly, a hand on her hip. 'Would you care for a nip of something to keep out the cold?'

He snorted.

He darted a quick look up and down the corridor, and dived into the cabin, his mouth closing on hers, his hands caressing her huge breasts. His breath was oddly sweet, almost sickly, but she quite liked it.

She hitched up her skirt and lay down on the bunk. He pulled down his gaiters and flung his sticky body on top of her. Soon they were bouncing up and down in the narrow bunk, all the aluminium work creaking. They were shouting and grunting in unison as orgasms shook their combined thirty-eight stones of flesh when the door opened and blue light filtered in from the corridor. A spotty youth stood there, peering in. Evidently he couldn't see clearly. 'Mum?'

'Oh, fuck me! It's orlright, son. Git along will yer? I'm busy at the minute.'

The boy, who was probably in his mid-teens, continued to stand there, his mean, ratlike features those of an idiot, his large eyes dull and uncomprehending.

'Mum?'

'Bugger off!'

'Oh,' he said, as his eyes got used to the dark, 'sorry.'

The door closed.

Mrs Cornelius clambered from the bunk, scratching her pelvis. 'Sorry abart that, bishop. Fergot ter lock it.' She pulled the bolt into the socket, then stumbled back, her knickers still around one ankle. She unbuckled her corsets and let them drop and was about to remove her dress when the bishop seized her by the hair and pulled her head down towards his penis which rolled back and forth like the mast of a storm-tossed ship. His eyes continued to stare thoughtfully at the door.

In the passage the boy grinned at his mum's antics and, dressed only in his raincoat, boots and socks, continued to search for a vacant lavatory. He listened to the vibrations from the vessel's great engines, listened to the faint sound of the wind as it slid over the monstrous silver hull, listened to the distant music of the jazz band. He ran his hand through his long, greasy hair and wished that he had a monkey suit he could wear. Then *he'd* go to the dance and the janeys had better look out for their virginity! He shuffled down a side-passage and then slid open the door onto the

195

observation deck. The lights of the city were past now and the airship seemed to be flying over open countryside. Here and there were a few flickering lights from small villages or farmhouses. Even from this height he didn't much fancy the country. It made him nervous.

He looked up at the blackness above. There were hardly any stars out at all and a thin rain seemed to be falling. Well, at least the weather would be better in Calcutta.

The ship shivered as it turned a degree or two, correcting its course. The distant music wavered and then altered. There was something almost hesitant about the way the ship moved. The youth stared forward and thought he saw in the distance the white-topped waves of the Mediterranean. Or was it the Bay of Biscay? Whatever the name of the sea, the sight of it meant something to him. For no reason he could understand, the sight filled him with a sense of relief. They were leaving Europe behind.

The youth watched eagerly as they began to move out above the water. He grinned as he saw the land fall away. Apart from the water, he was the only one to notice this change.

The Locomotive

Wondering how he had come to be involved in this revolution in the first place, Colonel Pyat swayed forward to have a word with the driver of the armoured train. Dirty steam struck his face and he coughed painfully, his eyes watering. He tried to rub at his eyes with his free hand, but the train snaked round a bend and forced him to reach out and grab the other steel hand-rail on the observation platform. The train travelled over a vast plain of burned wheat. In all directions the landscape was flat and black, with the occasional patch of green, white or yellow which had somehow escaped the flames. Colonel Pyat would be glad to get into the hills which he could just see on the horizon ahead. He opened the plate-armoured door of the next compartment and found that it was deserted of soldiers. Here there were only boxes of ammunition and light machine-guns. He made his way cautiously between the stacks. Perhaps military responsibilities were the simplest a right-thinking man could shoulder without feeling feeble. Certainly, the responsibility of commanding an armoured train was preferable to the responsibility he had left at home. On the other hand, he could have been helping the sick in some relatively safe hospital behind the lines, not heading willy-nilly towards the Ukraine and the worst fighting of the whole damned civil war. 193 – had not been a good year for Colonel Pyat

He tried to brush the soot off his uniform and succeeded only in smearing more of the stuff over the white buckskin. He sat down with a thump on an ammunition box and, scraping his match on the barrel of a machine-gun, lit a small cheroot. He could do with a drink. He felt for the flask in his hip-pocket. It was there, all slim brass and silver. He unscrewed the top and raised the lip to his mouth. A single drop of brandy fell on to his tongue. He sighed and put the flask back. If they ever got to Kiev, the first thing he would do would be to requisition a bottle of Cognac. If such a thing still existed.

The thin strains of a piano accordion drifted down the length of the train from behind him. The vibrant, gloomy voices of his troops began to sing. He got up, the cheroot held tightly in his teeth, and continued on his way.

'I should have stayed in the diplomatic corps,' he was thinking as he opened a door and saw the huge log tender looming over him, its chipped black enamel smeared with streaks of green and yellow paint where someone had tried to obscure the previous owner's insignia. There was a door in the tender, leading to a low passage through which he had to pass to get to the engine footplate itself. He heard the logs thumping and rattling over his head and then he had emerged to find the fireman hurling half a tree into the yellow, roaring furnace. The driver, his hand on the acceleration wheel, had his head sticking out of the observation port on the left of the loco. Two guards sat behind him, their rifles crooked in their arms, their legs dangling over the edge of the footplate. They were half asleep, their fur shakos tipped down over their foreheads, and they didn't notice Colonel Pyat's arrival. The footplate smelled strongly of the cedar wood which was now their main fuel. Overlaying this was the well-defined odour of human sweat. Colonel Pyat leant against the tender and finished his cheroot. Only the fireman knew he was there and the fireman was too busy to acknowledge his presence.

Throwing the butt of his cheroot at the blasted fields, he stepped forward and tapped the driver on his naked shoulder. The thickset man turned reluctantly, showing a face covered in dirty fair hair; his red-rimmed eyes glared through the black mask of soot. He grunted when he saw that it was Pyat and tried to look respectful. 'Sir?'

'What sort of time are we making?'

'Not bad, sir, considering everything.'

'And Kiev? When should we get there now?'

'Less than another eight hours, all things being equal.'

'So we're not much more than a half a day behind

schedule. Splendid. You and your crew are working wonders, I'm very pleased.'

The driver was wondering why they were bothering to go to Kiev in the first place, but wearily he responded to his commander's attempt at morale-building. 'Thank you, sir.'

Colonel Pyat noticed that, having tried for a second to look alert after they had noticed him, the guards had resumed their earlier slumped postures. 'Mind if I stay on the footplate for a little while?' he asked the driver.

'You're the commander, sir.' This time the driver couldn't stop the sardonic, edgy note in his voice.

'Ah, well.' Pyat turned. 'I won't bother you, then.'

He ducked into the passage under the tender and stumbled through to the other side. As he tried to get the door open, he heard a faint cry from behind him. A rifle shot sounded. He went back through the passage. Now both guards were on their feet, shooting into the air.

'Look sir!' One of them pointed ahead.

They were almost upon the lowest of the foothills and something was moving just behind the nearest ridge.

'Better take it easy, driver.' Pyat grabbed for the cord to ring the alarm bell through the rest of the train. 'What do you think they are?'

The soldier answered. 'Land 'clads, sir. At least a score of them. I saw them better a moment ago.'

Pyat tugged the alarm cord. The driver began to slow the train which was now about half-a-mile from a tunnel running under a high, green hill. Even as they watched, a pair of racing metal caterpillar tracks appeared on the roof of the tunnel, pointing directly at them. Then they saw a gun-turret above the tracks as they descended. The long 85mm cannon swung round until it pointed directly at the engine. Pyat and the rest threw themselves flat as the gun flashed. There was an expolsion nearby, but the locomotive was undamaged. The driver looked to Pyat for his orders. Pyat was inclined to stop, but then he decided to risk a race for what might be the safety of the tunnel (if it hadn't been mined). There was a chance. The tank barbarians rarely left their vessels. Some hadn't seen direct sunlight for months. 'Maximum speed,' he said. The fireman stood up and dragged more logs off the tender. Pyat yanked open the firedoor. The driver pulled his acceleration wheel all the way around. The train hissed and bucked and lurched forward. Another 85mm explosive shell hit the ground, this time on the other side of the train. The tunnel was very close now. On either side of it there emerged a motley collection of land ironclads, half-tracks and armoured cars, mobile guns, all armed to the teeth. The vehicles were painted with streaks of bright, primitive colour and decorated with shells, bits of silk and velvet. Strings of beads, strips of ermine and mink, bones and severed human heads. Pyat's suspicions were confirmed. This was the roving Makhnovik horde which, months before, had swept down from beyond the Volga, bringing terror and nihilism. The horde was virtually invulnerable. It would be pointless, now, to stop.

The train entered the darkness of the tunnel. Already Pyat could see daylight at the other end. Then, from behind, came a massive explosion and the locomotive was hurled forward at an incredible speed. They came out of the tunnel with wheels squealing, with the whole loco rocking, and in a few seconds had left the tank barbarians far behind.

It was only later, as the driver began to slow the locomotive, that they realized they had also left the greater part of the train behind at the tunnel. Evidently a shell had broken the coupling between the first carriage and the tender.

Pyat, the driver, the fireman and the two guards laughed in relief. The train sped on towards Kiev. Now there was a good chance that they would not be off schedule at all.

Pyat congratulated himself on the democratic impulse which, originally, had led him to join the men on the footplate. There were some advantages, it seemed, to democracy.

The Steam Yacht

Una Persson shivered. She wrapped her heavy black mink more tightly around her slim body. The silk Erté tea gown beneath the coat was cold and unpleasant against her flesh. She was feeling old. It was as much as she could do to stay awake. She smiled to herself and made a few long strides through the clinging fog, over the deck to the rail of the yacht.

She could see nothing at all of Lake Erie and she could hear nothing but the dull flap of the waves against the *Teddy Bear*'s white sides.

They were fogbound. They had been lying at anchor for days. The wireless had broken and there had been no reply to signal rockets, sirens or shouts. Yet Una was sure that a dark launch had passed close to the yacht at least twice in the last twenty-four hours. She had heard the purr of its engine several times during the previous night.

The yellow-white fog shifted and swirled like something sentient and malevolent. It was as if she were trapped in some dreadful Munch lithograph. She hated it and wished bitterly that she had not accepted the owner's offer of this cruise. It had been so boring in New York, though. She really disliked Broadway much more than she disliked the West End.

She drew the red and black silk scarf off her tightly-waved, short-cropped hair and wiped the moisture from her hands and face. Why was everything so frightfully bloody?

She went back to the companionway behind the wheel-house, paused, shivered and then daintily began to descend on high-heeled slippers, trying to make as much noise as possible on the iron steps.

Arriving in the corridor leading to the guest cabins, she noticed that some wisps of fog had at last managed to creep in. Now it was scarcely warmer here than it had been on deck. A 'brooding' silence. Were they to die here, then? It began to seem likely.

She tried to pull herself together, straightening her shoulders, putting a bit of bounce into her long step, bearing up manfully.

She went into the owner's large cabin, remarking, not for the first time, the incredible American vulgarity of it. It had been designed to look like a Tudor hall, with oak beams on the roof and pewter plates on the walls, claymores and tapestries. An electric Belling heater, built to resemble a log fire, only barely managed to take the chill off the cabin. The cabin had looked like this when the yacht had been purchased from its previous owner, but no attempt had been made to change it. It made her feel ill. It made her nervy.

The owner stood with his back to the cabin, staring out of the square, diamond-leaded porthole, into the fog. Once he leaned forward and, with his handkerchief, wiped condensation from the glass.

'Do you see any faces you recognize?' asked Una, attempting to sound friendly.

'Faces in the fog?' He glanced back at her and smiled. 'All faces are foggy to me, my dear. It's my loss, I suppose.'

Una gave vent to a dramatic sigh. 'You and your old angst, darling! What would you do without it, I wonder?' She bent forward and pecked him on the cheek with her carmine lips. 'Oh, it's so *cold*.' She crossed to the genuine Tudor sideboard and picked at a dish of mixed nuts. 'when *will* this boring fog lift?'

'Why don't you make the most of it? Relax. Pour yourself a drink.'

'A tot of rum? I can't relax. The fog's so *sinister*.' She ended this sentence on her famous falling note but then she let it rise again, almost without pause. 'I like to *do* things, Lob.' The pathos and the warmth in her voice was so strong that Prinz Lobkowitz was quite startled, as if he had found himself once again at the theatre where he had first seen her act. 'I don't mean silly things,' she continued. 'Worthwhile things.'

'Good causes?' He was ironic.

'If there's nothing else.'

There was a sound on the water. The faint putter of a motor.

She crossed eagerly to the window and, standing beside him, peered out. She moved her head this way and that as if there was a particular angle at which she would be able to see through the fog. She saw a gleam of water, a shadow.

He put his arm around her shoulders. She was so womanly at that moment. But she shrugged him away. 'Can you hear it? A motor-boat?'

'I've heard it frequently. It never comes very close.'

'Have you tried shouting to it? Using your loud-hailer, or whatever it's called?'

'Yes. It never answers.'

'Who can it be?'

'I don't know.' He spoke almost in a whisper.

She went back to the sideboard and helped herself to a Balkan Sobranie cigarette from the silver box, lighting it with a flourish at the flamingo-shaped table lighter. Puffing pettishly, she began to pace.

He watched her. He loved to see her act. She was so talented. He was glad they were marooned, for it meant he could watch her almost all the time.

'You're wonderfully selfish,' he said. 'I love you. I admire you.'

'I love you, too, Lob, darling, but couldn't we go and love each other somewhere warmer? Couldn't we go back to one of those cities? Chicago or somewhere? Couldn't we risk the fog?'

'There's a lot of hungry people waiting on the docks for unwary yachts. I'm afraid it wouldn't be wise.'

The motor-boat started up again and went away.

'If he can move, why can't we?'

'He's smaller. He's got less to lose. I mean, there's less risk for him.' From the pocket of his white silk dressing-gown he took a white box. He opened the box and took a pinch of white powder from it, sniffing it vigorously first

203

into one nostril and then into the other. He put the box back and continued to stare out of the porthole.

She went to the big radiogram and picked up a record. It was her own, from last year's hit *Only You*. She put it on and listened to herself singing the blues number which came in the middle of the show, *Gonna Kill That Man*.

She smiled wistfully.

> 'Gonna kill that man, if I can.
> You have to be cruel to be kind.
> I can't get him out of my mind.
> He's the worst sort of guy you could possibly find
> To his vices, I guess, I am utterly blind.
> But if he should try to two-time me
> He'll discover that I won't sublime be.
> I'll take out my gun
> And I'll stop all his fun,
> I'm gonna kill that man –
> If he loves a she who ain't me.'

It was not her usual sort of material, yet it had been the number they'd liked best, especially in London. She'd used a sort of Hoagy Carmichael technique for it. But she still didn't think much of it herself. She stopped the record and turned it over to *Dancing on the Clouds* which was much more *her*: bitter-sweet but essentially gay. Yet even this reminded her of the fog outside and she turned the Bakelite volume knob off with a snap, though she could still hear her voice, very, very faintly from the turntable. It was like a ghost. It made her shiver.

Her lover came towards her.

Was it all over? she wondered. The whole thing? Was she finished?

He was handsome in his white sweater, his white gown and white flannels, but he was pale. Another ghost in this foggy purgatory.

He embraced her.

'Una.'

The Flying Boat

They were going back.

Captain Nye steered the DoX over the choppy waters of the harbour. Behind them, Rowe Island lay in ruins, her airship masts buckled, her hotels blasted, her streets wasted, her mines and mine-workers buried under the tumbled granite of the great volcanic hill. The placid Indian Ocean, a sheet of burnished blue steel reflecting a brazen sun, remained.

'Well, that's bloody that, then,' said Frank Cornelius, stripping off his coolie blouse to reveal a loud, orange pullover. He wiped the best part of the make-up from his corrupt features. 'And that's Jerry down the drain, if he isn't very careful indeed.'

'I hope not.' Catherine stood behind the two men who had already taken their seats. She dried her face with a Rodier towel. 'It's such a beautiful day, isn't it?' She wore an opened-necked white shirt and white jodhpurs. Her calf-length riding boots were light tan. Her longish hair fell in two tight waves to her shoulders. She wore little make-up. She looked wonderful.

'Best weather in the world on Rowe Island,' said Captain Nye. 'A great pity.'

Miss Brunner was absent, as was the skeleton of the child. Nothing had gone right, really.

Captain Nye switched on all the engines and opened up the throttle, roaring out to sea. The floats began to rear beneath them, the wing-flaps whistled, and up they went into the clear, blue yonder.

Catherine wandered into the ballroom which had been refitted as a spacious lounge. Nobody felt like dancing at the moment. There were violently coloured Bakst murals on the walls. She looked enviously at the rich, fantastic scenes of fairyland forests and exotic Oriental princesses and Nubian slaves. It was a world she would feel happy in at the present moment. She was exhausted. She needed a rest, but she wanted a voluptuous rest. Hashish, honey and a handsome Hindu lover.

Professor Hira appeared, climbing the steps into the lounge and yawning. 'I was asleep. I hadn't realized we were taking off so soon.' His round, genial face held a faintly puzzled look. 'How long have we been up?'

She nodded out of the nearest window. 'Not long. You can still see the island. Look.'

'I won't thanks. I've seen quite enough of Rowe Island now. A terrible fiasco. I feel so guilty.'

'Guilty? You shouldn't feel guilty.' She closed her eyes, leaning back on the Beaumont tapestry cushions. She wished he hadn't come to interrupt what had promised to be quite a thrilling reverie. He was always too talkative when he got up. She pretended to doze.

'Yes,' he said soberly. 'It was all my fault. The ritual was infallible, in itself, and with the right *sort* of cosmic energy, we should have succeeded. But how was I to know that the majority of the coolies had been replaced by Malays? Those Muslims, they're the next best thing to an atheist. And then there was all the trouble with the time-concept, nobody quite agreeing on that. Again, the Malays . . .'

'Well, then – ' She took a deep, lazy breath and drew her legs up on the couch. 'It was their fault. It doesn't matter now. Though it's a pity about the Governor's residence. Wasn't that a charming building?'

'Did you like it? I've had to look at a spot too much of that type of thing in Calcutta, I'm afraid.'

Catherine caught only the last words. 'Afraid? It's a relief to know someone else is.'

'Afraid? What of? I've never seen you looking better.'

'The future, I suppose. And yet I hate the past. Don't you?'

'I've never quite understood the difference. I don't see it like that.'

'A woman – well – I'm forced to. In some ways, at least. I know it would be better for me if I didn't.'

'If time could stand still,' said Hira reflectively, 'I suppose we should all be as good as dead. The whole business of entropy so accurately reflects the human condition. To remain alive one must burn fuel, use up heat, squander resources, and yet that very action contributes to the end of the universe – the heat death of everything! But to become still, to use the minimum of energy – that's pointless. It is to die, effectively. What a dreadful dilemma.'

Captain Nye stepped from the pilot's cabin into the lounge. 'Your brother's steering. He picks things up fast, doesn't he?'

'Anything he can get.' Catherine regretted her waspish tone and added: 'He's very intelligent, Frank.' She looked into Nye's blue-grey eyes and smiled.

'Well,' he said. 'I'm going to get some sleep.'

'Yes,' she said. 'I think it's time I hit the hay. It's been a long – long . . .' She yawned.

She nodded to Hira and followed Captain Nye to the stairs, down past the cocktail bar, the cabin area and into the cabin. As he kissed her she held him tightly, saying: 'I'd better warn you. I'm very tired.'

'Don't worry.' He unbuttoned his jacket. 'So am I.'

She saw him shiver slightly. 'Are you cold?'

'A tiny touch of malaria, I shouldn't wonder,' he said. 'Nothing to worry about.'

'I'll cuddle up to you and keep you warm,' she said.

Professor Hira, feeling both lonely and jealous, joined Frank in the control cabin. Frank was wearing his fur-trimmed tinted flying goggles and looked a bit like a depraved lemur. He patted Hira's knee as the Indian physicist sat down. ''Ello, 'ello, old son! How goes it?'

'Not so dusty,' said Hira. 'Are you sure that chap Nye's all right?'

'What? Nye? One of the best. Why?'

'Well – going with your sister . . .'

'He's been sweet on her for years. Cathy knows what she's doing.'

'She's such a lovely girl. A generous girl.'

'Yes,' said Frank vaguely. 'She is.' He laughed. 'I quite fancy her myself. Still, I'm not the only one, eh?' He nudged Hira in the ribs. Hira blushed. The plane veered and started to dive, banking to starboard with the engines screaming. Frank inexpertly righted her, but didn't seem worried by the near-miss; he continued to chat cheerfully, telling Hira a succession of bad dirty jokes (mostly about incest, bestiality and Jews) until Hira thought he would cry.

He changed the subject as soon as he could. 'I wonder what the political climate's like, back there.' He motioned towards the west.

'Bloody hell! Not worth thinking about. That's as good as finished, anyway, nowadays, isn't it?'

'Does it "finish"?'

'Well, you know what I mean. We've got our plane, we've got our health, we've got the Cornelius millions – or will have soon. We've got each other. Why should we worry?' Frank moved the joy stick from his left to his right hand and stretched out towards Hira.

'I was thinking of the moral question,' said Professor Hira.

'Oh, fuck that!'

Frank's hand dived into Hira's lap and squeezed.

The Indian physicist shrieked and was his.

The plane flew perilously close to the water and then began to climb as Frank took it up towards a cloud.

The Raft

Sun-baked, salt-caked, it lay in the middle of the Arabian Sea on a waterlogged raft made of oil-drums, ropes and rush matting. The raft had no mast, held nothing but the shapeless heap of flesh and rags which might have been dead save for the spasm which occasionally ran through it when a small wave lifted the raft or swept over it, so that it sank a little further into the warm sea. One of the drums had been holed by what looked like a series of machine-gun bullets; it was this which had helped to deprive the raft of its buoyancy.

The flesh was blistered as if it had been exposed to fire; it was blackened in places. In other places bones stuck through at odd angles. There was a flake or two of dried blood. From time to time there were sounds: a grunt, a moan, a few babbled words.

The raft was drifting out to sea. The nearest land was now Bombay, 400 miles away, where a great sitar master, dying of cholera, was the only man with any notion of the raft's whereabouts. There was not much chance of rescue, even if rescue had been desired.

Jerry felt nothing. He was one with the flotsam of the great sea; almost one with the sea itself. He was content, listening absently to the odd voice; remembering the odd image. If this was dying, it was a relaxing experience, to say the least.

'Remember the old days?' said Miss Brunner's voice. 'Or were they the new days? I forget. The usual tense toruble.' She laughed gently. 'Echoes.'

'Nothing but,' murmured Jerry.

'But echoes from where?'

'Everywhere?'

'They would be, I suppose. Lapland won't be the same. Caves. Large bodies of water. The sky. The pleasures are constant, even if the problems change.'

'Yes.'

'Are the simple pleasures the *only* realities?'

Jerry couldn't reply.

'Oh, what a lovely, drifting sea this is.' The voice faded away. 'Who are we, I wonder?'

'Resistance,' said a child, 'is useless.'

'Absolutely,' Jerry agreed.

'The schizophrenic condition finds its most glorious expression in Hinduism,' remarked Professor Hira. 'Whereas Christianity is an expression of the much less interesting paranoid frame of reference. Paranoia is rarely heroic, in the mythical sense, at least.'

But Jerry found this argument barren. He didn't encourage a discussion. Instead, he remembered a kiss.

'Feeling seedy? I know I am.' Karl Glogauer came and went. Jerry had confused him with Flash Gordon.

'Time,' said the sad voice of Captain Cornelius Brunner, 'ruins everything.' They would not be meeting again for another thirty-five years. 'So long, Jerry.'

'I love you,' said Jerry.

With an effort he raised himself on his wounded hands.

'I love all of you.'

He looked at the sea. The sun was setting and the water was the burning colour of blood.

'Oh!'

A few tears dripped from his awful eyes. Then the head sank back. The night came and the raft dropped lower in the water until an observer might have thought that the body floated unsupported on the surface. The sun rose, pink and mighty on the western horizon, and Jerry raised his head for one swift glimpse. The sea ran through his burnt hair and made it float like weed; it washed his torn flesh and moved the rags of his black car coat; it ran into his reddened mouth and the sockets of his eyes, and Jerry, at peace, hardly noticed.

A little later, lizard-like, he crawled to the edge of the raft and slid quietly into the water, disappearing at once.

It was going to be a long century.

... and in spite of their maudlin sympathy, self-interest finally dominated everything else and so I was betrayed again, left alone. I think it must have been the final straw. Certainly, I ceased to trust anyone else for several years, then when Monica came along I forgot all that. I trusted her absolutely. And, of course, she let me down. Perhaps she didn't mean to. Perhaps it was too much of a strain. She should have kept the baby. I don't know how long I stayed in the kitchen with her after I'd done it. You could say that the balance of my mind was disturbed. I mean, what's a country for? What do you pay taxes for? What do you give your patriotism to? You expect something from your own country, your parents, your relatives. And then they don't deliver. Nobody cares. Every promise society makes to you, it doesn't keep. They kill babies before they're born, after they're born, or they do it the slow way, prolonging the moment of death for scores of years. I am not pleading guilty. By pleading insane, I am pleading innocent. Surely, I'm the victim. What does it mean? But I want to die. It's the only solution. And yet I love life. I know that seems strange. I love the lakes and the forests and all that. But it seems unnatural now. We've got to go, haven't we? I never asked to be born. I tried to enjoy it, I tried to be positive and optimistic. I'm well-educated, you know. It was mercy-killing. And killing is, if you look at it one way. I am trying to control myself. I'm sorry I'm sorry.

MAURICE LESCOQ, *Leavetaking*

SHOT FOUR

Police Dig Up More Human Remains

Police digging at Leatherhead (Surrey) where a woman's hand was found on Thursday found more remains yesterday in a navy blue zip bag at a shallow depth.

Wrapped separately in polythene were two portions of thigh, a left leg and a foot with a blue slipper on it. Police said they thought other parts of the body were 'somewhere else'.

Morning Star, September 4 1971

Observations

'There's a future in chemicals, if you ask me,' said Lieutenant Cornelius. He lifted binoculars to his bleak eyes and stared without interest at the Indian aircraft carrier his CA class destroyer *Cassandra* had been tracking for two days.

Overhead flew five or six small helicopters of different nationalities, including a British *Wasp*; below floated three or four of the latest nuclear submarines, among them the *Remorseless*, the *Concorde* and the *Vorster*. The Mediterranean fairly swarmed with busy bits of metal. Not too far off, a frigate of the imperial South Russian Navy was keeping its eye on Lt Cornelius's ship and a Chinese 'flying ironclad' – an armoured airship of obscure origin – observed the Russian.

'Chemicals and plastics,' Cornelius's No. 2, Collier, agreed, leaning over the rail of the bridge and looking down at the rather dirty decks where bored seamen lounged in each other's arms. Under the barrel of the forward 4.5 gun, the deck cargo creaked in its ropes. It was a single box, marked AMMUNITION/DANGER. 'That's what I'd put my money in. If I had any.'

'Buy the plants,' said Frank Cornelius. 'Take over. Go for the durables. Oil. Water. Steel. Air. Chemicals. Plastics. Electronics. That's survival. My brother's got the right idea – or had – or will have . . .' He frowned and changed the subject, handing the glasses to Collier. 'See if you can spot any change.'

Collier was happy to get a turn with the binoculars. He straightened his shoulders and peered self-importantly through the eyepieces. 'Are they having a party or something on deck?'

'They've been up to that since this morning. It's disgusting. I think it's meant to distract us from whatever they don't want us to know about.'

214

'Big girls, ain't they?' said Shaky Mo.

'Hermaphrodites.'

'I thought they were on our side.'

Frank went down into the Operations Room and consulted his grubby charts. He could have done with something a bit more up to date. He'd inherited the charts from his father and the political boundaries shown were nothing less than ludicrous. He moved a couple of counters to cope with the recently arrived South Russians. There was hardly space on the chart for another marker. Fragment split into fragment. Was it society or himself that was breaking up?

He was getting tired of the whole thing. A bloody great Prussian dreadnought had been after them for a week, taking a particular interest in their deck cargo. That meant a leak. Frank wondered if it wouldn't be wiser to turn round and go back to their Marseilles base or, failing that, make straight for Aden. With radio silence, there was no chance of getting his orders changed until he reached a port. He wished he hadn't taken on the responsibility of the cargo, now. If he could have been somewhere suitable when word came, he might have been able to turn a profit, given a slight shift in the balance of power at home. That was why he'd volunteered. Now he realized what a stupid idea it had been. He was never any good at the big deals. At little deals, he was great. He should have stuck at what he knew he could do well. Here he was, in the middle of the bleeding Med, while his nearest customers were at the other end of the North Sea. Fuck a duck, it was just his luck. He rubbed his greasy chin, flipping through his *Boatswain's Manual* for the right order to give the coxswain and the engineers. He'd make for Hamburg and hope for the best.

Idly turning the binoculars on to his own ship and its crew, Mo Collier focused on the big box and noticed for the first time that it seemed to be moving to a different rhythm from that of the waves. It was pulsing, like a rapid heartbeat, as if, Mo Collier grinned at the thought, two people were fucking in there. Well, that was impossible. On the other hand if the contents of the box were about to go critical, he'd better warn his captain. He let the glasses fall on their string and knock against his pelvis. He took the lift down to the Operations Room. 'Sir? sir?'

Frank looked up from his manual. 'What?'

'The deck cargo. It's sort of bouncing. It might be going to blow up.'

'Oh, shit.' Frank put the book down and followed Mo up to the deck. He took the glasses and looked. 'Oh, shit. I should have shifted it right at the beginning. He who hesitates is lost, Collier.'

'Fire drill, sir?'

'Bloody hell. What's the point?' They went slowly back to the Operations Room. 'Let's have a look at a map,' said Frank when they got there. 'No. We'll make for Sardinia and dump it. Break radio silence. Tell them our deck cargo hasn't been picked up on schedule and we're abandoning it on the nearest dry land.'

'Can't we just dump it in the sea, sir?'

'Are you out of your mind? We don't want more trouble than we've got already. Oh, shit.' Frank slumped down in a chair. 'Oh, fuck it to buggery.' He was the picture of whining impotence. Feeling this made his whine louder. At a certain pitch, his whine was echoed by a sound from the deck; the sound was almost in perfect tune, but constant where Frank's was punctuated by his need to draw breath.

Soon the two brothers were howling in unison as night fell and the destroyer steamed for Sardinia.

Guarantees

Major Nye had his trousers off. He sat on a canvas stool with an old towel round him. Mrs Nye spoke through clenched teeth as she stitched at the patched trouser leg. 'It's not as if we could afford it,' she said. 'All I seem to do is *mend*. And you're so clumsy. You must have known about the barbed wire on the beach.'

'Supervised its installation, I'm afraid,' admitted Major Nye. 'All my fault. Sorry, lovey.'

It was late in the afternoon and they were outside the beach-hut where they had been billeted. After being turned down by his old regiment (now an armoured vehicle corps), Major Nye had volunteered to help with the Brighton coastal defences. The Ironmaster House, some twelve miles inland, had been requisitioned as the headquarters of the local territorials, so he and Mrs Nye had had to move into the beach hut. Major Nye was not particularly upset by the takeover. The beach hut was not nearly so much of a burden and it was less effort tending the barbed wire than it had been looking after the market garden. Major Nye felt a bit ashamed. The war was proving something of a holiday for him. For all she would never admit it, even Mrs Nye seemed relieved. Her wind-reddened face had taken on something of a bloom, though this might have been the result of the cold. It was winter and the beach hut was heated only by a malfunctioning oil-stove. Their daughters had not joined them; both girls had voluteered for work in London. Isobel, the ex-dancer, was looking after her brother, who was still at school. Sometimes, at weekends, one or both of the girls would bring the little boy down to see his parents.

'Nearly Christmas.' Mrs Nye finished the darn with a sigh. 'Is it worth doing anything at all about it this year?'

'Maybe the girls will have an idea. ' Major Nye went into the beach hut and drew on his trousers. He folded the tattered towel and hung it neatly over the back of the deckchair. The trousers, like his jacket, were khaki, or had been before the elements and all the patching had turned them into a garment of many indistinguishable colours. He lit the remaining third of his thin cigarette. 'Tum-te-tum. God rest ye merry gentlmen, let nothing ye dismay, et cetera, et cetera, pom-pom.' He put the tin kettle on top of the oilstove, realized it was dry, and came outside to fill it at the tap which served his and two other huts. All these huts were now occupied by coastal defence volunteers. Many volunteers were older than Major Nye. With a loud, rasping sound, the kettle filled. The tap squeaked as he turned it off. Mrs Nye shivered in his greatcoat and, stamping with cold, got up, collapsing both their canvas stools and hurrying inside.

'A strong cuppa's what you need after that, m'dear,' he said.

'Don't throw away the old leaves this time,' she said. 'They'll last for another brew.'

He nodded.

They watched the kettle boil and when it was ready he flipped the lid off the mock-Georgian, mock-silver teapot and filled it half-full. 'Just give that a minute or two to stew,' he said. He made a corned beef sandwich for her, using thin sliced bread and even thinner slices of meat. He put the sandwich on one of their plates, taken from the tiny rack above the tiny card table on which their provisions were laid. He handed her the plate.

'Thank you very much,' said his wife. She nibbled at the sandwich. It was her tea. They were going to have a full tin of pilchards for supper.

'Well, I'd better go and check the searchlights before nightfall,' he said.

'Very well.' She looked up. 'See if you can get a paper.'

'Rightho!'

Whistling the half-remembered tune of the *The Bore o' Bethnal Green*, he ambled down the stony beach, following the course of his barbed wire, stopping at intervals to inspect the seachlights set on small pedestals every thirty feet. The lights had originally been used to illuminate the Pavilion during the summer months.

The sky was grey and promised rain. The sea was also grey and even the beach had a greyish tinge to it. That always seemed to happen in wartime, thought Major Nye. Above, on the promenade, he noticed that the odd fish-and-chip shop and coffee-stall hadn't yet closed. The shops were illuminated by oil-lamps and candles. All electricity was being saved for the defence effort. The places looked cosy. After making sure that all his lights were in good order, he left the beach and tramped up a ramp to the pavement, crossing the street to the shops. One of the ice-cream parlours was still open. These days, in spite of the plastic sundaes and knickerbocker glories in the window, it sold only tea and soup. The parlour also sold *The Weekly Defender*, the only newspaper generally available. A new issue was in. Large piles were stacked outside the shop. The paper's circulation was not very good. Those piles would remain virtually untouched and would be taken away when the new issue arrived. Major Nye was one of the few regular customers for *The Defender*. He picked up a copy from a pile and read the headline as he ambled into the shop, his sixty-pence piece in his hand. 'Evening, squire,' said the shopkeeper.

'Good evening.' Major Nye couldn't remember the man's name and he was embarrassed. 'The paper.'

'Sixty, please. Doesn't look too good, does it?'

The headlines read: *NEW GAINS FOR BRITAIN! SPIRITS RISE AS MINISTER ANNOUNCES PLANS. 'MORALE NEVER HIGHER' SAYS KING.*

Major Nye smiled shyly. 'I must admit . . .'

'Still, it can't last forever.'

To Major Nye it seemed it had already lasted forever, but he was, as usual, completely reconciled. You couldn't change human nature. You couldn't change the world. He smiled again. 'I suppose not.'

'Night, night, squire.'

'Goodnight to you.'

It was almost dark now. He decided to walk back along the promenade, rather than along the beach. The smell of fish-and-chips made his mouth water, but he resisted temptation, knowing what Mrs Nye would say if he brought back even a few chips. It was an unnecessary expense on food which was not nourishing; also it was 'not quite the thing' to buy hot food from a shop. They had to keep their standards up. Major Nye had always been fond of fish-and-chips. When he had worked in London, he had had them once a week. Of course, the fish was terrible now, and the chips weren't proper potato at all. And that was a consolation of sorts.

He began to go down the ramp which led to their stretch of gloomy beach. He paused and looked out at the black, gleaming water. The sea was so large. Sometimes it seemed foolish, trying to defend the coast against it. He wondered what would happen if the big anti-aircraft gun on the end of the pier ever had to fire. Probably shake the whole bally thing to bits. He smiled.

He thought he saw something bobbing on the water, quite close to the shore, about twenty yards from the pier's girders. He peered hard, wondering if it were a stray mine, but the object had passed out of sight. He shrugged and stepped on to the beach. The shingle rattled and grated as he crossed it. Further out to sea a steamer's siren moaned and the moan was echoed by the rooftops of the town so that it seemed for a little while that the whole of Brighton was expressing its misery.

Estimates

Una Persson made the plane just as it was about to leave Dubrovnik. She clambered up over the coffin-shaped floats and through the passenger doors. Inside, the plane was dark and crowded; people sat on the floor or, where there wasn't room to sit, clung to pieces of frayed rope fixed to the sides and roof. Refugees, like herself; though these were thin-faced civilians. She pushed through them, noticing the number of black-robed priests aboard, and found the companionways to the upper decks. There were people sitting on these, too, and she had to go up both flights of stairs on the tips of her battered boots. At last she reached the pilot's cabin. By that time they were already airborne, though two of the big wing-mounted engines were coughing on the starboard side. She wondered from what museum the plane had been resurrected. It was German, judging by its insturment panels. There was a lot of German junk around, these days. It wasn't surprising. Over the radio and heavily distorted came sounds she recognized as the Rolling Stones singing *Mother's Little Helper*.

The flying boat circled Dubrovnik once, dipping in and out of the thick, oily smoke from the burning city. 'We shan't be seeing that again,' said the Polish pilot. Colonel Pyat, who was seated in the co-pilot's chair, sighed. 'It'll be good to get home again. We are all ideas in the mind of Mars.'

Una gave him a puzzled look. 'So you say, general.'

'C – ' Colonel Pyat mopped his heated forehead. 'My dear Una, I thought you had taken the train.'

'Changed my mind. Back to Blighty, after all.'

'Just as well. Maybe our luck will change with you aboard.' He raised an imaginary glass. 'I salute Our Lady of Liberty.' He was eager to please, not sardonic.

'You're tired,' she said.

'Sing a song, Una dear. An old sweet song.' He was drunk,

but his white uniform was neat as ever. 'If those lips could only speak, if those eyes could only see, if those . . .'

'The European campaigns were wholly disastrous,' said the Pole, who was also a bit drunk. She could hardly hear him over the erratic roaring of the aircraft's engines.

'Why all the refugees?' she said. 'Where are the troops?'

'That's what the refugees wanted to know.' The Pole laughed. They weren't making much altitude as they flew out to sea. 'We *are* the troops.'

'*C'est la vie,*' said Colonel Pyat. 'My dear ones will have missed me.' He drew a flask from his hip pocket and tipped it up. It was empty. 'Thank God,' he said. 'You're right, Una. I am tired. I thought England would be the answer. A triumph of imagination over inspiration. Ha, ha!'

'He lost the box,' explained the Pole.

'In Ladbroke Grove,' said Pyat. 'It's been around a bit since then.'

Una sighed. 'So I gather. Well, it was just another straw, I suppose. Something to keep the fire going.'

'Feeling the draught?' said the Pole.

'I've been feeling it all century,' said Una.

From beyond the door came the sound of people at prayer, led by the droning voices of the priests. Even the plane seemed to be praying. Una went to find a parachute before they reached Windermere.

Applications

There seemed to be gratitude in Sebastian Auchinek's large brown eyes. He looked up as the security policeman entered his cell.

'Of course I understand that you have to do this job,' said Auchinek. 'And rest assured, Constable Wallace, I shan't make it difficult for you. Please sit down or – ' he paused ' – whatever you wish.'

Constable Wallace was a brute.

'I don't like spies, Mr Auchinek.' His skin was coarse, his eyes were stupid and there was a sense of pent-up violence about him. 'And should we prove that you're one . . .'

'I'm a loyal citizen, I assure you. I love England as much as anyone, for all that I was not born here. Your countryside, your democracy, your justice . . .'

'You're a Jew.'

'Yes.'

'There's been a lot of Jewish spies.'

'I know.'

'So . . .'

'I'm not one. I'm a businessman.'

'A poof?'

'No . . .'

'You go abroad a great deal. Macedonia?'

'Macedonia, yes. And to – well, to Belgium, Holland, Assyria . . .'

'Where?'

'Abyssinia, isn't it?'

'You've got *something* to hide,' said the red face, sweating.

'A poor memory.' Auchinek whimpered in anticipation.

'And I'm going to get it out of you.'

'Of course. Of course.'

'By force, if necessary.'

'I'm not a traitor.'

'I hope not.'

Constable Wallace had completed the necessary rough and ready warming up ritual and he grabbed Auchinek by his grey prison jacket and pulled him to his feet. He balled his red fist and punched Auchinek in the stomach. Auchinek vomited at once, all over Constable Wallace's uniform.

'Oh, you filthy little animal.' Wallace left the cell.

Auchinek had had enough. He sat back on his bed, careless of the vomit on his lips, chin and clothing. He gasped and cried and wished he hadn't had his breakfast. He should have known better. Or had he planned it? He had never been clear about his identity, his own motives, at the best of times, and now he was completely at sea. For all he knew, he might be a traitor. He should have retained his military role. It was easier.

The sound of rifle fire in the passage outside. Shouts. Running, booted feet. A clang. More shots. The bolt was withdrawn outside. Auchinek cringed as the door opened.

Catherine Cornelius, looking like a young Una Persson, stood in the doorway, an MI6 over the shoulder of her brown trenchcoat, a green tam-o'-shanter on her golden curls.

'Are you the chap we're to rescue?' said Catherine. 'Mr A?'

'Auchinek.'

'Shall we release the lot?' She indicated the other cells in the corridor.

'I don't know,' he said, watching out for Wallace, who was sure to appear in a minute.

'This isn't my normal job, you see,' explained Catherine pleasantly as she coaxed him from the cell and into the corridor of twisted iron and broken corpses. He saw Wallace. His red throat was cut by rifle bullets. He was dead. Auchinek gazed at him in wonder.

She led him past the corpse towards the outer door, which was off its hinges. 'I normally get the nursing jobs, but we're short-staffed, at present.'

'Who are you?'

'Catherine Cornelius.'

'No – your – outfit?'

'Biba's.'

'Who do you work for?'

'I work for England, Mr Auchinek, and freedom.' Self-consciously, she put the MI6 on automatic and rested it on her hip as they crossed the quadrangle of Brixton Prison and reached the main gate. 'There's a car waiting. Perhaps you could direct me? It's been a long time since I've been in South London.'

They stepped through the blasted gate and stood in a narrow street. A Delage Diane was waiting for them, its engine running.

'It's a bit of a waste of power,' she said apologetically, opening a passenger door for him, 'but I find the bugger rather hard to start.'

'Miss Cornelius . . .'

'Mr Auchinek?'

'I don't understand.'

'I'm afraid I can't help you there. The ins and outs of the revolution – if it *is* a revolution – are a bit beyond me. I just work for the cause.'

'But I'm not a revolutionary. I'm a businessman. I think you know more . . .'

'Honestly, no . . .'

'Perhaps I should go back? A mistake.' He hesitated beside the car.

'Don't you remember Macedonia?'

'Were you there?'

'You were an idealist. A guerilla.'

'I've always been in show business. All my life. Promotions. Management.'

'Well, there you are, then.' She opened the door of the car for him. 'Nobody's going to beat you up any more.'

'I'm tired.'

'I know how you feel.' She got into the driving seat and fiddled with the gears. The car seemed unfamiliar to her. 'We've still got a long journey ahead of us.' They began to

225

move slowly forward. 'Modification of species and so on. Perhaps it isn't really a revolution at all.'

Auchinek saw misery in Catherine's mouth. He began to cry. She reached the main road, crashing the gears as she turned the Delage towards the Thames.

Securities

'Good ole England!' said Mrs Cornelius, raising her pint of ale and saluting a picture of a bulldog painted on the glass behind the bar.

'Oh, yore 'opeless, Mrs C.!' Old Sammy in the corner guffawed, opening wide the black, wet circle of his toothless mouth and shaking all over. He lifted his own pint and poured its contents into his wasted, cancerous body.

''Ere come on, I mean it,' she said. 'There'll orlways be an England. We've 'ad our ups an' darns, but we'll pull through.'

'Well, *you* might,' said Old Sammy bitterly, losing his good humour as the beer in his glass disappeared.

''Ave anovver,' she said, by way of rewarding him for the compliment.

He brought his glass over to the bar where she sat on a high, saddle-shaped stool, her massive behind spilling over, so that the dark wood was all but hidden. ''Aven't seen too much of you, lately,' he said.

'Nar,' she said. 'Bin away. Visitin' an 'at, in' I?'

'Go somewhere nice?'

'Abroad. Went ter see me son.'

'Wot, Frank?'

'Nar! Jerry. 'E's ill.'

'Anything bad?'

She snorted. 'Iber-bleedin'-natin' 'e corls it! Mastur-fuckin'-batin', *I* corl it!' She turned as a third customer entered *The Portobello Star*. 'Oh, it's you. Yore late incha?'

'Sorry, my dear. Delays at immigration.' Colonel Pyat wore a cream-coloured suit, lavender gloves and white spats over tan shoes. He had a pale blue shirt and a regimental tie. His light grey homburg was in the same hand that carried his stick. His manner was hesitant.

'Sammy, this is ther Kernewl – my hubby.'

'How do you do?' said Pyat.

'How do? Jerry's dad, eh?'

Mrs Cornelius shook with laughter again. 'Well, 'e might 'ave bin once! Gar-har-har!'

Colonel Pyat smiled weakly and cleared his throat. 'What will you have, sir?'

'Same again.'

Pyat signed to the wizened old bat behind the bar. 'Same again in these glasses, please. And I'll have a double vodka. Nice morning.'

'Nice for some,' said the old bat.

Mrs Cornelius stopped laughing and patted the colonel affectionately on the shoulder. 'Cheer up, lovie. Yer *do* look as if yer've bin in the wars!' She opened her shapeless handbag. 'I'll git these. Pore ole sod.' She cast her eye about the gloomy bar. 'Where's yer bags?'

'I left them at the hotel.'

'Hotel!'

'The Venus Hotel, in Westbourne Grove. A nice little place. Very comfortable.'

'Oh, well, orl right!'

'I didn't want to put you out.'

'Well, you *ain't*!' She paid for the drinks and handed him his vodka. 'But I would a thort . . . First day 'ome . . . Well . . .'

'I didn't mean to upset you, my dear.' He rallied himself. 'I thought I'd take you out somewhere tonight. Where do you suggest? And then, later, perhaps, we could go on a family holiday. The coast or somewhere.'

She was mollified. 'Crystal Palace,' she said. 'I ain't bin there fer a donkey's.'

'Excellent.' He swallowed his drink and ordered another. 'Welcome austerity. Farewell authority!' He saluted himself in the mirror.

She looked critically at his clothes. ''Ad a run o' luck, 'ave yer?'

'Well, yes and no.'

''E orlways wos a very smart dresser,' said Mrs C. to

228

Sammy. 'No matter 'ow much 'e 'ad in 'is pocket, 'e'd orlways be dressed just so.'

Sammy sniffed.

Colonel Pyat blushed.

Mrs Cornelius yawned. 'It's better ter go away in the autumn. If the wevver 'olds.'

'Yes,' said Colonel Pyat.

'I've never 'ad an 'oliday in me life,' said Sammy proudly. 'Never even let 'em evacuate me!'

'That's 'cause yer never worked in yer life!' Mrs Cornelius nudged him. 'Eh?'

Sammy bridled. But she put her fat hand round the back of his neck and kissed him on his wrinkled forehead. 'Come on, don't take offence. Yer know I never mean it.'

Sammy pulled away and took his glass back to his table in the corner.

Colonel Pyat climbed on to the next stool but one. His eyes kept closing and he jerked his head up from time to time as if afraid to got to sleep. He didn't seem to have the energy, these days.

'I 'ope yer brought somefink ter eat over wiv yer?' said Mrs C. 'Everyfink's runnin' art 'ere. Food. Fuel. Fun.' She bellowed. 'Everyfink that begins wiv 'F', eh?'

'Ha, ha, ha,' he said distantly.

'One more for the road an' then we'll be off,' said his wife. 'Yer never reely liked pubs, did yer?'

'Excellent.'

'Cheer up. It can't be as bad as orl that!'

'Europe's in a mess,' he said. 'Everywhere is.'

'Well, we're not exactly at the 'eight of our prosperity,' she told him. 'Still, fings blow over.'

'But the squalor!'

'Ferget it!' She guzzled her light.

'I wish I could, my dear.'

'I'll 'elp yer.' She leant across the empty stool between them and tickled his genitals. 'Tonight.'

Colonel Pyat made a peculiar giggling noise. She took him by the arm and led him through the door and into the stinking streets. 'Yer'll like the Crystal Palace. It's *orl* crystal. Well, glass, reely. All different sides. Made o' glass. An' there's monsters. It's a wonder o' the world, the Crystal Palace. Like me, eh?'

Mrs Cornelius roared.

Children are stoning a tortoise. Its shell is already cracking open. It moves feebly, leaving a trail of blood and entrails across a white rock.

A 17-month-old baby girl was shot dead in Belfast tonight, Army sources said, by an IRA gunman's bullet meant for an Army patrol. A seven-year-old girl who was with her escaped injury although another bullet tore through her skirt.

Morning Star, September 24 1971

A drug given to women during preganancy may cause a rare type of cancer in their daughters many years later, the British Medical Journal warned yesterday. The cancer has been found among girls aged 15 to 22 in New England and has been linked to the drug stilboestrol, which was given to their mothers for threatened miscarriages ... Treatment has proved successful so far in the majority of cases, but one girl has died.

Guardian, September 10 1971

A boy aged three was knocked down and killed by an army vehicle near the Bogside district last night. As the news spread, crowds began to stone army units in the area. Several shots were fired at the troops and petrol bombs were reported to be thrown. The army did not return the fire.

Guardian, September 10 1971

Nothing survives, said Una Persson, who was older, more battered and wiser than Jerry had ever seen her, nothing endures.

While there's lives there's hopes. Jerry finished stripping the Banning cannon and immediately began reassembling it. The ruby had not, after all, been faulty. It was just wearing out. The gun wouldn't last much longer. Still, it wasn't needed for much longer. He was more worried about his power armour. Some of the circuits, particularly those on his chest, were looking a bit frayed. They were holed up in the basement of a deserted old people's home in Ladbroke Grove. They listened to the scuffling of the rats with intense interest, expecting an attack.

It's almost over now, isn't it? she said without regret. Civilization's had it. The human race has had it. And we've bloody had it. Are these all you've got? She held up a cerise Sobranie cocktail cigarette with a gold tip.

He opened a drawer in the plain deal table on which his cannon was spread. Looks like it. He rummaged through a jumble of string, coins and postcards. Yes.

Oh well.

You might as well enjoy what's left, he said. Take it easy.

It isn't easy to take. What with everything speeding up so fast. It's all burning too quickly. Like a rocket that's out of control, with the fuel regulator jammed.

Could be. He slotted one piece of scratched black metal into another. He fitted the cumbersome ammunition feed and worked a couple of slides. He didn't bother to put the safety catch on as he turned the cannon on its swivel mount so that it pointed towards the barred window. I don't know. He sighted along the gun; he stroked back his long, straight hair. Times come and go. Things re-cycle. The Jesuits . . .

Did you hear something?

Yes.

She went to the corner where her Bren lay on their mattress. She picked the Bren up and drew the strap over her leather-clad shoulder. She flipped a switch at her belt. It even took her power armour a few seconds to warm up now. After the village . . . she began.

You survive, Una. It wasn't something he wanted to hear about again. It disturbed him.

She looked at him suspiciously, searching his face for a sardonic meaning. There was none.

Alive or dead, he said and fired an explosive shell through the window and into the shadowy area. Magnesium blazed for a moment. Cold air came in. A shape darted away. Jerry flipped his own switch.

Beesley, Brunner, Frank and the rest, Una said, peering cautiously upwards. All the other survivors. I think some are trying to get into the house.

It had to come. In the long term there's never much safety in numbers.

I'd always believed you worked alone. A bit of a bourgeois individualist on the quiet.

Assassination's one thing, Jerry said primly. Murder's quite another. Murder involves more people and a different moral approach and that, of course, ultimately involves more murders. A reflex. People get carried away. But assassination is just the initial preparation. The ground work. Like it or not, of course, everything boils down to murder in the end. A grenade burst in the basement and the rest of the glass flew into the room, rattling against their power armour.

There's self-defence.

I've never been able to work that one out.

Jerry pulled the table nearer to the window, then angled the Banning upwards through the bars, firing a steady, tight sweep of shells. Two of the attackers flared up and fell. Karen and Mo, said Jerry. Not for the first time. They heard footsteps over their heads and then a few creaks on the cellar stairs outside their inside door. Una opened the door and, with her Bren, took two more lives. Mitzi Beesley and Frank Cornelius. Frank, as usual, made a lot of noise, but Mitzi died quietly, sitting upright with her back against the wall, her hands in her blood-stained lap, while Frank rolled and writhed and gasped and cursed.

Two more grenades came into the room and exploded, temporarily blinding them, but hardly denting their power armour.

This is almost the end, said Jerry. I think it's down to Miss Brunner and Bishop Beesley. It had better be. Energy's getting low.

Miss Brunner rushed down the stairs, her face twisted with rage, her red eyes blazing, her sharp fangs bared. She was awkward in her tight St Laurent skirt. She tried to get her Sten to fire. Una killed her, shooting her in the forehead with a single bullet. Miss Brunner staggered back without grace.

Bishop Beesley appeared in the area outside the window. He was holding a white flag in one hand, a Twix bar in the other. Even from here Jerry could see that the chocolate was mouldy.

I give up, said the bishop. I now admit I was ill-advised to quarrel with you, Cornelius. He crammed the Twix bar into his mouth and then reached towards his breast pocket. May I? He took out a delicate box of Chinese jade and opened it. From the box he removed a couple of pinches of sugar which he snorted into his nostrils. That's better.

Okay. Jerry nodded tiredly and pulled the Banning's trigger, plugging Beesley in the mouth. The face flared in a halo of flame and then disappeared. Jerry abandoned the gun and went to Una, who was pale and exhausted. He kissed her gently on the cheek. It's all over, at last.

They switched off their armour and lay down on the damp mattress, fucking as if their lives depended on it.

The ruins were pretty now that the fronds and lichen covered them. Birds sang. Jerry and Catherine Cornelius walked hand in hand to their favourite spot and sat down on a slab, looking out over the fused obsidian that had been the Thames. It was spring. The world was at peace.

Moments like these, said Catherine tenderly, make you feel glad to be alive.

Well, he smiled, you are, aren't you?

She stroked his knee as she lay stretched beside him, supported by one of his strong arms. It's so relaxing to be with you.

Well, familiarity, I suppose, is a lot to do with it. He, in turn, stroked her golden hair. I love you, Cathy.

You're good, Jerry, I love you, too.

They watched a spider cross the broken concrete and disappear into a black crack. They stared out over miles and miles of sun-drenched ruins.

London looks at her best on a day like this, Cathy said. I'm glad the winter's over. Now the whole world is ours. The whole new century, for that matter! She laughed. Isn't it paradise?

If it isn't, it'll do.

A light wind ruffled their hair. They got up and began to wander towards Ladbroke Grove, guided by the outline of the one complete building still standing, the Hilton tower. Black and white monkeys floated from broken wall to broken wall, calling to each other as the two people approached.

Jerry reached into his pocket. He turned on his miniature stereo taper. Hawkwind was half-way through *Captain Justice*; a VC3's synthetic sounds shuddered, roared and decayed. He put his arm round her slender shoulders. Let's take a holiday, he said, and go somewhere nice. Liverpool, maybe?

Or Florence. Those twisted girders!

Why not?

Humming, they made their way home.

Late News

Five teenage pupils from Ainslie Park School, Edinburgh, and a trainee instructor of outdoor pusuits, died near Lochan Buidhe in the Cairngorms yesterday in the worst Scottish mountain accident in memory. The tragedy was heightened by the fact that the party was found within 200 yards of a climbers' hut which could have ensured their survival.

Guardian, November 23 1971

A schoolboy in a party of 21 teenagers is believed to have died on a mountain in central Tasmania. A police and helicopter search is to resume at first light for the boys who are thought to be huddled together as blizzards break over the mountain.

Guardian, November 24 1971

Two babies died today in a fire at a tented tinker's camp – hours after their grandfather died in a road accident. Peter Smith (2) and his ten-month-old baby sister Irene, died as fire ripped through their makeshift canvas home at Ferebridge Camp, near Barnbroe, Lanarkshire. Earlier, their grandfather, farm labourer Mr Ian Brown (54) was killed when he was involved in an accident with a car as he was walking near the camp.

Shropshire Star, December 18 1971

Farm worker Alan Stewart, who had a lung transplant at Edinburgh Royal Infirmary on Thursday – his 19th birthday – died last night. Alan, of Kirkcaldy, drank weedkiller from a lemonade bottle a week ago.

Shropshire Star, December 18 1971

Reminiscence (H)

A man wearing a papier-mâché mask in the form of a skull
enters the doors of a pub.
   A drunk screams and attacks the wearer.
   Mother's eyes.

The Forest

'It's like a magic wood.' Cathy's voice was hushed and delighted. 'So many soft greens. And, look, a squirrel! A red one!'

Frank Cornelius sniffed the air. 'Lush,' he said. He tested the ground with his patent-leather foot. 'Springy, Give me the good old English broad-leafed tree any day of the week.'

'Oo, wot luverly flars!' said Mrs Cornelius, ripping some wild orchids from the moss and holding them to her face. 'Thus is wot I *corl* a wood, Kernewl!'

Colonel Pyat gave a modest, proprietorial, smile, and wiped his forehead with a large handkerchief of coarse linen. 'This is the English forest at her best. The oak. The ash. The elm. And so forth.' He was pleased to see her happy.

'I 'ope yer remember where we left ther motor,' said Mrs C. fiddling with the controls of her little tranny and failing to find a station. She gave up. She put the radio back in her bag. She cackled. 'We don't wanna be like ther fuckin' babes in ther wood!'

Mellow sunshine filtered through the leaves of the tall elms, the strong oaks, the aristocratic poplars and the languid willows, filling the flowery glades with golden beams in which butterflies, mayflies and dragonflies sauntered.

They wandered on over sweet-smelling moss and grass and feathery ferns, sometimes in silence, sometimes in a babble of joy when they saw a pretty animal or a bank of beautiful flowers or a little, shining brook rushing between mossy rocks.

'Something like this restores your faith,' said Frank as they paused to watch a large-eyed doe and her faun nibbling delicately at some low-hanging leaves. He took out his rolled gold cigarette case and offered it round, quoting: ' "It is from the voice of created things that we discover the

Voice of God never ceasing to woo our love. Gaudefroy."' It was a quotation to which he would become particularly attached in the coming years, especially over the Christmas period of 1999, shortly before he and Bishop Beesley would pay the final reckoning in the Ladbroke Grove Raid, at a time when their theological disputes would have brought them close to blows. 'Time stands still. Man is at peace. God speaks.'

'I orlways said you wos the one should've gorn inter ther Church,' said his mother sentimentally. She took a cigarette, a Sullivans, and waved it in a vague, all-encompassing gesture. 'And wot would our friend Jerry make of all this, I wonder. Turn up 'is nose? Nar! Even 'e couldn't knock this.'

'Jerry . . .' said Catherine defensively, and then could think of nothing more.

'Jerry's far too involved in the affairs of the world to spare time for the simple things of life,' said Frank piously.

'You'd fink 'e'd write a p.c.' Mrs C. puffed at her fag. 'Oh, look over there!'

It was a pool overhung by willows and sapling silver birches with big white boulders all around it. A tiny waterfall cascaded into the pool from high above. They all walked towards it, listening to the water. Colonel Pyat followed behind. He didn't have the energy any more. He, too, was wondering what had become of the missing member of the Cornelius family. There had been conflicting rumours. One rumour had it that he had been resurrected. Another said he had been returned to the sea. They had all relied too heavily on him, as it turned out. So much for the optimistic slogans. Messiah to the Age of Science, indeed! Now it was plainly too late for action. The opportunities had passed. It was all fragmenting. Even this silly attempt of his to keep the family together was a reaction to the real situation which he could no longer hope to control. Messiah to the Age of Science! A bloody Teddy boy, more like. But Colonel Pyat was reconciled, really. This holiday might be the last of his life and he wished to make the most of it. He only regretted that he could not go back to die in the Ukraine. The Ukraine no longer existed. With his homeland destroyed, there was little to live for, his love for England being entirely intellectual.

Frank turned back to see what had happened to Pyat. 'Come on, old boy.' Frank's holiday seemed to be doing him good. His face glowed with a vitality that was almost healthy. 'Don't want to miss the beauty spots now we're here, do you? Where on earth did you find this little corner of England? I didn't think places like it still existed. If they ever did.'

'Oh,' Pyat shrugged. 'You know how it is. Strangers sometimes discover things in a place where the people who've lived there all their lives have never looked.'

'Well, you've turned up trumps with this one, I must say. It's like bloody fairyland. Titania's wood.' Frank was in a literary as well as a religious mood today. 'I'm expecting a visit from Puck at any moment. Can you lay that on, too?'

Pyat smiled. 'It isn't the wood that's enchanted.' But Frank hadn't heard him; he joined his mother and sister. The two women were unrolling plastic raincoats and spreading them on the rocks. Mrs Cornelius began to unload her string bag, taking out a vacuum flask and two packets of sandwiches.

''Ere we are. Git stuck inter these, you lot,' said Mrs C.

No wasps or ants came to disturb them as they ate their picnic beside the shady pool. Catherine was fascinated by the water. It was so dark and deep, but there was nothing sinister about it. It was tranquil and seemed to offer peace to anyone who considered entering its still waters. Because she didn't much care for these cheese and pickle sandwiches anyway, she left the other picnickers and climbed down to stand on a rock beside the pool. The conversation above sounded a long way away. She stared at her reflection for some moments until she realized with a shock that it was not quite her face which looked at her. There were strong resemblances, certainly, but this was a man's face and its hair was black. It smiled. She smiled back. She turned to remark on the phenomenon to her relatives but they had

242

disappeared out of sight on the other side of the rocks. She felt, then, that she had been standing here much longer than she had realized. She started to climb back. There was a slight afternoon chill in the air.

'Catherine!'

The voice came from above. She looked up and was surprised when she recognized the man who had called her name. He was clad in rather tattered evening dress. He stood offering his free hand to her. His other hand held a Smith and Wesson .45, rather loosely, as if he really didn't mind if he dropped it.

'What a strange coincidence.' Cathy smiled as she put her palm into Prinz Lobkowitz's. 'How are you? It's been an age.'

'How are you, dear?' His voice was low and intense, his expression melancholy and affectionate. 'I hope you are well.'

'Very well. But you, my dear, you look so tired. Are you running away from someone?' She reached up and brushed his hair back from his wrinkled forehead.

He held her to him. 'Oh, Catherine.' He was crying. 'Oh, my dearest. It is all over. This is defeat on every level.'

'We must get you something to eat,' she said.

'No. I haven't much time. I came here for a reason. Colonel Pyat is here?'

'Yes – and mother, and Frank.'

'I'm sorry,' he said, 'but . . .'

'Well, look who it isn't!' Frank Cornelius emerged from around a rock, his mother and step-father in tow. 'So you know about this place, too. What a sell! It's getting like Piccadilly. Perhaps this is the real heart of the Empire, eh? We went for a little walk. Hello, Prinz L.'

'Good evening.' Lobkowitz was embarrassed. 'I'm sorry to interrupt.' Birds began to sing everywhere and red-gold sunlight flooded the scene. Prinz Lobkowitz cast a startled glance over his shoulder. 'I wanted a word with Colonel Pyat.'

Pyat stepped forward. Then he changed his mind and

began to retreat, climbing up the white boulders until he stood looking straight down at the pool.

'Wotcher doin' up there?' said Mrs Cornelius loudly. And then she fell silent.

There was a smear of dark green on the elbow of Colonel Pyat's suit. Catherine was glad that Pyat himself didn't know about it. Or did he?

Colonel Pyat sighed and turned to look down at them all.

'Prinz?' he said.

Lobkowitz reluctantly raised the heavy gun with both hands, drawing in a deep breath before pulling the trigger. Pyat seemed to bow in acknowledgement, receiving the shot courteously in the heart. Then he fell backwards and dropped into the pool. The waters closed over him.

'Oh, blimey!' said Mrs Cornelius, looking with nervous disapproval at the gun. 'Oh, Gawd!'

Frank stepped prudently back into the shade of an oak.

Prinz Lobkowitz looked miserably at his old sweetheart. Then he began to climb up the rock on which Pyat had stood. Catherine watched, feeling only sympathy for both the murderer and his victim. Lobkowitz reached the top, turned, raised the revolver to his lips, kissed it and tossed it to Catherine. She caught it with instinctive deftness. At long last Lobkowitz had learned a style.

He jumped into the pool. There was a splash and a silence.

Catherine tucked the Smith and Wesson into the waist band of her skirt and walked past her mother and brother. She entered the cold wood.

'Where's she off ter?' said Mrs C. 'In one of her bloody moods agin, is she?'

'Let's see if we can find the motor,' said Frank, frowning. 'She'll turn up again when she's ready.'

'And wot are we gonna do abart cash, I'd like ter know,' said his mother, practically. 'Talk abart ther end o' a perfict day!' She snorted. 'An' I'm a bleedin' widder agin,' she said, as if suddenly realizing the essence of what had happened beside the pool.

She cheered up, nudging Frank in the side.

'Still, yer've got ter larf, incha?'

He looked at her in horror.

The Farm

Sebastian Auchinek, bringing home the cows for their evening milking, heard the shot quite clearly and looked out across the fields to see where it came from. Hereabouts, people rarely hunted at this time of the year, though possibly someone was potting a rabbit or two for his dinner. Beyond the fields, where the wheat sheaves stood waiting for the next day's attention, he could see the great, green wood, almost a silhouette now in the late afternoon sun. The shot had probably come from there. Auchinek shrugged and trudged on. He flicked at the rumps of his cows with a light willow stick. 'C'mon Bessy. Git a move on there, Peg.' The phrases were mumbled automatically, for the cows had trodden this path more often than he had and they needed little encouragement. They plodded up the rutted track of red earth between the sweet-smelling hedgerows full of briar roses and honeysuckle, towards the stone milking sheds which lay beside the farmhouse with its warm cobble-stone walls and its thick, thatched roof.

When Auchinek had first gone to earth, he would not have believed that he could have taken so easily to farming. In his old corduroy trousers, his rubber boots, his pullover, leather jerkin and flat, dirty cap, a quarter of an inch of stubble on his tanned ruddy face, he looked as if he had farmed these parts all his life; and he felt it, too. The shot didn't bother him. Poacher or gamekeeper, human or animal, what happened beyond the confines of his farm was none of his concern. He had a lot to do before dark.

It was almost dusk by the time he had milked the cows and poured the milk into his electric separator. He drove the cows back into the nearest field and returned to man-handle the milk churns on to his cart. He harnessed up Mary, his old shire horse, and started off along the track towards the railway.

When he got to the railway, he lit the oil lamp which hung on its usual post. He had to see to get his milk onto the little wooden platform. In about an hour's time the train would stop here and pick the milk up, delivering it at the local village station for the dairyman.

Night sounds had replaced the sounds of day. A few grasshoppers chirped in the long grass of the railway embankment. An owl hooted. Some bats flapped past. Now that his work was over Auchinek felt pleasantly tired. He sat on his cart and lit a pipe, enjoying a smoke before returning to the farm. It was a warm, clean night, with a good moon rising. Auchinek leaned back in the seat and breathed in deeply. The old shire twitched her huge flanks and flicked her tail but was content to wait until he was ready to go. She leaned down in her yoke and began to tug at the grass with her large yellow teeth.

Auchinek heard a noise in the neighbouring field and identified it as a fox. He'd have to be careful tonight if a fox was on the prowl, though he hadn't really had much trouble from predators since he'd taken over the farm. Then the rustling grew louder and more energetic. Had the fox already found its night's meat? There came a peculiar strangled whimper – perhaps a rabbit. Auchinek peered over the hedge, but the light from the lamp cast only shadows into the field. For a moment, though, he thought he saw an animal of some kind – a savage face that might have belonged to an ape rather than to a fox. But then it was gone. He picked up the reins. He had grown eager to get home to his supper.

'All right, Mary. Come on now, girl.' The country accent came naturally to him. 'Come on, old girl. Gee up, there . . .'

When he had turned a corner of the track and could see the yellow warmth glowing from his own windows he felt completely at ease again. It was funny what you sometimes thought you glimpsed at night. All that was over now. He'd never be involved again. And the war couldn't touch him. The countryside was eternal. It was a good job, however, that he wasn't superstitious. He might start to have silly fantasies about his past catching up with him. He smiled. He'd boil some eggs for his supper and have them with some of that new bread, then he'd go to bed and finish Surtees' *Hillingdon Hall*. Of late, his whole reading had been devoted to eighteenth- and nineteenth-century novels of rustic life, as if he were subconsciously determined to steep himself in even the metaphysical aspects of country lore. He had already read *The Vicar of Wakefield*, *Romany Rye*, *The Mill on the Floss*, *Clara Vaughn* and *Tess of the D'Urbervilles*, as well as other, more obscure titles. He didn't seem to enjoy anything else. Sometimes he would sample a more modern work by Mary Webb or R. F. Delderfield and he found them enjoyable, too. He was going off George Eliot and Thomas Hardy, though. He didn't think he would read anything more by them.

He drove into the farmyard and got off the cart, unharnessing the mare. As he led her past the milking shed towards her stable, he heard the milk separator going, the big blades swishing and clacking. He smiled to himself; he was more tired than he had realized. As it sometimes happened when you were feeling a bit worn out, the sound seemed to form a word.

He remembered Una Persson. What ever happened to her? It had been a dream, that period in Macedonia and Greece. A nightmare. He'd done some funny jobs in his life before finding the one which suited him.

Ch-ch-char, went the blades. *Traitor – traitor – traitor*.

He closed the stable door, stretching and yawning. The air had turned very cold. They could be deceptive, these autumn nights.

Traitor – traitor.

He went inside. It wasn't very warm in the house, even though the range had been lit in the kitchen. He flicked open the doors of the stove to let more heat out. He could still hear that damned separator going. He shivered. He'd be glad to get under the blankets tonight.

The Village

The train picked up the churns and took them to the village station where they were unloaded by the dairyman who put them in his van.

The van rattled happily as it drove down the peaceful street from the station, past the cheerful windows of the two pubs, *The Jolly Englishman* and *The Green Man*, past the village hall, where music was playing, past the church, down the alley and round the back of the little bottling plant where the milk would be readied for the morning's deliveries. Thank God the monopolies didn't control the farm produce in this part of the world, thought the dairyman. There were still a few corners of old England which hadn't yet been overrun by so-called progress. The dairyman left his van in the yard and strolled back towards the village hall. There was something special on tonight – a break in an otherwise acceptable routine.

He pushed open the doors and saw with some pleasure that they had already got the parachutist to start to strip. She was quite a good-looking woman, if a bit on the slim side for his taste. A cut over her left eye didn't improve her appearance, either. Had that been necessary? He nodded to the other village men and smiled at Bert and John, his brothers, as he took his place near the front of the stage. He licked his lips as he settled back in his chair.

Una Persson had been captured two days earlier but had had to wait, a prisoner in George Greasby's barn, while the village decided how best to use her. She was the first parachutist they had ever caught and they understood the conventions involved: a captured parachutist became a sort of slave, the property of whoever could find and hold one. Nearby villages had several male parachutists working their fields, but this was the first woman.

Conscious of George Greasby in the wings with his

249

brazier and red-hot poker, Una had already unbuttoned her long flying coat and dropped it to the floor. She didn't much care if he burned her; all she really wanted to do was take the easiest way out and get the whole business over with as soon as possible. It was their idea of dignity and individualism that was central here, not hers. Stripping to *King Creole*, the tinny single on the cheap record player, seemed the easiest thing to do. Not that she'd ever cared much for Elvis Presley. She took off her shirt, staring into the middle-distance to avoid looking at all the fat, red heads with their bristly haircuts who made up her audience. She'd had worse. She didn't waste time: off came her boots, her trousers and her pants until she stood passive and naked, showing the few yellow bruises on her left breast, her right thigh and her stomach. It was a bit chilly in the hall. There was a slight smell of damp.

'All right, now give us a song,' said George Greasby in his high-pitched voice. He waved the poker, holding it in a big, asbestos mitten.

Fred Rydd settled himself at the piano, running his stubby fingers over the keys and then thumping out a series of discords with his left hand while he struck up a rousing chorus of *A Little of What You Fancy Does You Good*.

Una had played the provinces often enough before. This wasn't very much different. She tried to remember the words. Charley Greasby, the old man's son, jumped up on the stage and slapped her bottom. 'Come on, lovey, let's 'ear yer!' With lewd winks at the others, he cupped her breasts in his hard hands and pinched her nipples and yelled in her ear while performing a sort of obscene Morris dance: 'I never was a one to go and stint meself. If I like a thing, I like it, that's enough. But there's lots of people say, if you like a thing a lot, it'll grow on you – and all that stuff.' His breath smelled of onions.

'I like my drop of stout as well as anyone,' sang Una, now that he had started her off. She felt faint. All the villagers were on their feet now, laughing and stamping and clapping. 'But a drop of stout's supposed to make you fat.' The whole hall seemed to be shaking. More of the thickset countrymen were clambering onto the stage. Her vision was full of corduroy, leather and woollen pullovers. The piano played maniacally on. 'And there's many a lah-di-dah-di madam doesn't care to touch it, 'cause she mustn't spoil her figure, silly cat!'

They all joined in the chorus. 'I always hold in having it, if you fancy it. If you fancy it, that's understood. And suppose it makes you fat – well, don't worry over that. 'Cause a little of what you fancy does you good!'

'Come on,' said Tom Greasby, who was still wearing his police constable's trousers, 'let's have all the verses, my pretty. I haven't heard that one in years. The old ones are the best. Haw, haw!' He put a horny finger into her vagina. She knew it was there but she didn't feel it much as she went into the next verse.

She finished the song and was half-way through *Someday I'll Find You* when they lost control of themselves and got their corduroys and flannels down, pushing her on her back as they began, in hasty turns, to rape her.

The greatest discomfort she felt was in trying to breathe beneath the weight of their heavy, sticky bodies. She had never cared for the country and now she knew why. From the distance came the sound of the record player starting up again with Cliff Richard's *Living Doll*. She realized that her eyes were still open. She closed them. She saw a pale face smiling at her. Relieved, she smiled back.

It was time to split.

As the fifteenth rural penis rammed its way home, she left them at it.

The Hill

'There's lights on still in the village hall,' said Mrs Nye, closing the bay window. 'Maybe they're having a dance down there. There's music.'

'I'm glad they're enjoying themselves,' said Major Nye from where he lay in crisp sheets in the topless Heal's four-poster. He had gone yellow and his lips were flaking. His pale blue eyes shone from deep cavities and his cheeks were hollow. 'Say that for the English. They know how to make the best of things.' He had just recovered from an attack of malaria. He was dying.

They had had to leave Brighton when the malaria got really bad. It had been disappointing, after building everything up there. They had moved further west, to his father's old place, a large Frank Lloyd Wright style house built on the hill. On one side the house overlooked the village, on the other, the sea. From its windows it was possible to view the valley, with its farm, forest, village and streams, and the little harbour town and the beach. There were very few fishing boats in the harbour, these days. But holidaymakers still came from time to time. It was all very picturesque. 'The very best of England,' as Major Nye's father had often said. But for some reason Major Nye was ill at ease here.

'I wonder where the doctor could have got to,' said Mrs Nye. 'I sent Elizabeth in the Morgan. It was the last of the petrol, too.' Her own complexion was beginning to match her husband's. Many of the village women were convinced that it would not be long before she 'followed him'. Once he had gone, she would be glad to follow. She had had quite enough. He, on the other hand, was uneasy about dying in his bed. He had never imagined that he would. It seemed wrong. He felt vaguely ashamed of himself, as if, in an obscure way, he had failed to do his duty. That was why, from time to time, he would try to get up. Then Mrs Nye would have to call her daughter to help put him back in the four-poster.

A fat, jolly girl bustled into the room. 'How's the patient?' demanded Elizabeth Nye. She had become very attached to her parents just lately. A month ago she had been kicked out of the girls' school where she had been teaching and it had given her the opportunity to come home and look after them. 'Shall I take over now, mums?'

Her mother sighed. 'What do you think?' she asked her husband. Major Nye nodded. 'That would be nice. D'you feel up to reading a bit of the book, Bess?'

'Happy to oblige. Where is the damned *tome*?'

Her mother brought it from the dressing table and handed it to her. It was a large red book called *With the Flag to Pretoria*, a contemporary account of the Boer Wars. Elizabeth settled herself in the bedside chair, found her place, cleared her throat, and began to read:

'Chapter Twenty Three. The March on Bloemfontein and opening of the railway to the south. With the capture of Cronje in the west, and the relief of Ladysmith in the east, the first stage of Lord Roberts' campaign may be said to have ended. The powerful reinforcements sent out from home, and the skiful strategy of the commander-in-chief had turned the scale.'

She read for an hour before she was sure he was asleep. In a way she felt it was a pity to encourage him to sleep when he had so little time left. She wished he was just a bit stronger so that she could take him out for the day in his wheelchair, perhaps to the village, or to the seaside. There was no chance of using her car again. The trip to the doctor's had used up the last of the fuel. She no longer despised her father and had come to feel very close to him, for his weaknesses were her own in a different guise. Simple-minded loyalty was one of them. And he, too, she had discovered only yesterday, had been crossed in love as a young man.

As she was putting the book back on the dressing table he opened his eyes, smiling at her. 'I wasn't asleep, you know.

I was thinking about the little chap and what's going to become of him. You'll make sure he stays at school?'

'If there's a school to stay at.' She felt sorry for her cynicism. 'Yes, of course.'

'And Oxford?

'Oxford. Yes.'

'He's a bright little chap. He was a cheerful lad. I wonder why he's so melancholy, these days.'

'A stage,' she said.

'No. I know it's the school. But what else could I do, Bess?'

'He'll be all right.'

'But not the Army, eh? It's up to him to break the chain. Get a good civilian job.'

'Yes.'

'Could you get me a glass of water, do you think?'

Elizabeth poured him some water from the decanter on the bedside table. The room was so unfriendly. She tried to think of ways of making the atmosphere warmer.

'I heard on the wireless the other day that they can't find the ravens,' he said.

'Ravens? Where?'

'Tower of London. All flown off. When the ravens go the White Tower will fall and when the White Tower falls, my dear, England will fall.'

'There'll always be an England,' she said.

'The chances are good, I admit that. Even Rome lasted in a way, and Greece and Persia before her. Even Egypt, really. But Babylon and Assyria. Well, well ... I'm rambling.' He sipped the water. 'And America. So short-lived. But very powerful, Bess.'

'It's all been fined down, I'll grant you,' she said. 'The barbarians don't come from outside the walls any more, do they?'

'We breed our own cancers,' he said. 'And never a cure. But perhaps that's always been the case.' He let her take the glass. 'Merry. Hectora. Garvey. Kalu. Grog. Brorai, I think. And Jet.'

254

'What's that?'

'The names of the ravens.'

She laughed. 'Aha!'

His voice was tiring. It was little more than a croak as he continued. 'I've led an ill-disciplined sort of life. No moral fibre. It's something about the Army. There were thousands of people in my position. Perhaps it was just the standard of living, or something. My old colonel was a drunkard, you know, before he died. And penniless. I used to stand him the odd drink. Decent old boy.' His head trembled and he shut his eyes tight. 'All failures. To a man. He – ' His pale lips tried to speak but could not. She bent over him.

'What was that?'

He whispered. 'He committed suicide. Chucked himself out of a bally window at the Army and Navy Club.'

'Maybe it was for the best.'

'It's all gone, Bess.' His face was horribly white, like a skull. His moustache looked incongruous, like a piece of weed which had caught on the skull. 'I'm sorry.'

She said awkwardly: 'Nothing to be sorry about, I'd have thought. You've done your best for the family. For the country, too, if it comes to that. You've put more in than most. You deserve – '

She knew that the next sound was a death-rattle, but it didn't last long.

Her mother came in.

'He's dead,' said Elizabeth. 'I'll go into town tomorrow and make the arrangements.'

Mrs Nye looked down at the corpse as if she couldn't recognize it.

'It's all over,' said Elizabeth. She patted her mother's shoulder. The action was mechanical and for a moment it seemed to both of them that Elizabeth was actually striking her mother. Elizabeth stopped and went to the window. The lights were off in the village hall. The village was silent.

Mrs Nye cleared her throat.

'Well,' she said. 'Well.'

The Seaside

Next morning, Elizabeth cycled down to the harbour town to make the necessary arrangements. While she waited in the funeral parlour, she thought she saw Catherine Cornelius go past with two other people, a thin man and a fat woman. Elizabeth knew this was less than likely. It was just her mind playing her another morbid trick. Earlier she had had the impression that her father was still alive in the house. She would never see Catherine again. Everything was over now. Her sex-life was over. Having a sex-life involved too much responsibility and now she had her mother and her little brother to think about. She looked through the dark glass of the window at the gleaming sea; she listened to the children playing on the beach. And quite suddenly she felt full of strength; suddenly she was confident that she would have sufficient moral resolve to win through against all the difficulties which faced her. She prayed that the feeling would last.

'Clotted cream and strawberrry jam and loverly choccie biscuits,' said Mrs C. 'That's wot I feel like, kids. That bleedin' hotel thinks we're bloody budgies, if yer ask me. The size o' them meals! Fuck that!' She led them towards the beach, much relieved by her recent discovery that Colonel Pyat had left his wallet in the car and that the wallet had been stuffed with tenners. There would be no trouble about paying the bill or having a bloody good time while they were down here. They deserved it.

They stopped at the cafeteria near the beach while Mrs Cornelius had her elevenses. The cafeteria smelled strongly of candy floss. Frank and Cathy shared a knickerbocker glory, looking rather wanly at the bright, yellow sand.

'It's a tidy sort of beach,' said Frank. 'Not like Margate, for instance. Very middle class, wouldn't you say?'

Catherine felt too warm, even in her light summer frock.

She removed her blue cardigan and put it in her gay beach bag. She noticed that both Frank and Mum were sweating, too.

''Urry up an' scoff that darn, you two,' said their mother, who had finished three times as much in half the time. 'Eat it all up. Don' wanna waste it. It's all paid for.'

They crammed the rest of the tinned strawberries, the chocolate syrup, the nuts and the ice cream into their-mouths and munched while their mother busied herself with her toilet, touching up her carmine lipstick, laying on a little more scarlet rouge, another coating of pink powder, and patting at her perm with a comb. Then she took each of her children by one of its hands and led the way from the cafeteria, down the asphalt slope to the beach.

'Deckchairs, Frank.' She surveyed the beach, hands on hips, like Rommel planning a campaign. 'The sea's lovely, innit?' Frank went to the neat stack in the little green shelter by the wall of the promenade and got three brand new candy-striped canvas chairs. 'Right,' she said. 'This way.' She led them towards a breakwater. Not far from the breakwater were four little children, two boys and two girls, at work on an elaborate sand palace, with turrets and towers and minarets and everything. They were digging a moat round it. Elsewhere, in a rock pool, twin girls, aged about eight, with blonde page-boy haircuts, studied crabs and starfish and seaweed.

'It's like the bloody *Rainbow Annual*,' said Frank with some approval. 'Tiger Tim at the Seaside. It's almost too perfect.' He set up the chairs and got them just so. Then he stripped off his jacket, his shirt, his vest and his flannels to reveal a pair of yellow and black silk boxer-style bathing trunks. He stretched his thin body in the chair and drew on a large pair of wrap-around mirror sunglasses. But he was still not ready. He got up again and found the Man-tan lotion in his jacket pocket. He began smearing the stuff on his pale, spotted flesh. Meanwhile Mrs C. had applied all her various creams and had lifted her loud print dress to reveal her pink satin directoire drawers and her huge, white thighs. She sat with the her legs spread, as if to catch the sunbeams in her lap. Cathy was reading a copy of *The Rescue* by Joseph Conrad. 'This'll do,' said Frank, regarding the distant sea. 'We can come here next year. Now we've discovered it.' Merry laughter rippled from the throats of the children around the sand palace. They were digging a deeper and deeper trench. A few happy seabirds wheeled and screamed. A red-sailed boat drifted by on the horizon. A small black and white cat began to walk demurely along the breakwater. Frank picked up a pebble and chucked it at the cat. He missed.

'Are you going in, love?' said Mrs C. 'It must be loverly for swimmin'.'

Frank shuddered. 'I don't think so. Currents and that. Riptides. Undertows.'

'But there's others bathing over there,' Catherine pointed. 'They seem to be okay. There'd be signs if it was dangerous.'

'Maybe later, then,' said Frank. 'I might have a bit of a summer cold.'

'Oh, all right.'

Everything was so ideal that Frank almost expected to see a jolly face painted on the golden disc of the sun, or even on the buckets and spades. The sand might have been dyed that bright, clean yellow; the sea might have been stained that bright, clear blue. Well, there was no point in looking a gift-horse in the mouth, was there? He leaned back and began to study the pictures in his body-building magazine.

'We'll go ter that pub fer lunch,' said Mrs C. 'The on'y complaint I got is there's no bleedin' Bingo. That's a issential part of an 'oliday, I reckon. An' bumper cars. I like 'em. An a bit o' fish-and-chips. Yum yum.'

Cathy suddenly felt funny. 'I just had one of those lurches,' she said. 'You know. *Déjà vu.*'

Frank's mirror shades regarded her. 'Reels within reels.' he said with a thin smile. 'Don't worry, love. It happens to me all the time,' he sniggered.

'Frank.'

'Yes, mum.'

'Go an' git us an ice, there's a love.'

Frank got up slowly. 'I'll want some cash.'

She handed him a tenner. 'All the jack you need,' she said. 'I never bin a *rich* widder before. Git one fer yourself an' Caff.'

But he returned quite quickly, empty-handed. 'Sold out,' he said. 'They say they weren't expecting a heat-wave. Personally, I don't find it that hot.'

'I'm boiling,' said Cathy.

'Fuck,' said their mother removing the tenner from Frank's fingers. 'I don't call this much of an 'oliday resort. I mean, they don't seem ter want ter cater fer visiters. An' we 'ave got money ter spend. We're not paupers. I could git through this lot in a day at Brighton.' She put the money back in her large red and yellow plastic bag. 'I could do wiv a cuppa,' she hinted. 'Anyway, I don't like 'ome made ice cream.

Frank and Cathy were pretending to be asleep. They lay stretched in their deckchairs, facing out to sea.

Mrs Cornelius shifted in her chair, wondering whether to get up or not. She looked with some admiration at the huge sandcastle the kids were building. It was going on five feet tall and was elaborately detailed. She could almost have believed it was a real castle if she'd seen it in the distance. And the moat would soon be the size of an army trench. The energy of these kids! Where did they get it all from? They were working like beavers. They were moving about so fast! The sand was fairly flying from the ditch. The castle grew and grew. Turrets and galleries and towers appeared. The children laughed and shouted, carrying their buckets of sand to key points, patting down a tessellation with their little wooden spades. It must be very good sand, thought Mrs C. vaguely. It must be very easy to work with. Now two of the boys were actually burrowing into the castle, hollowing it out. A Union Jack flew proudly from the highest tower. She took a deep breath of ozone. She hadn't smelled sea like that since she was a kid herself. She reached for the radio in her bag, but changed her mind. It wasn't too bad, this beach. Her hunger and thirst diminished; she stopped fidgeting. It was peaceful. She closed her eyes, listening to the sound of the surf, the cries of the gulls, the distant chatter of the happy children. Poor old Pyat. She still wondered why he'd married her. He must have been after something. It wasn't the sex, more's the pity. She hadn't done badly out of him. She'd got something out of all her husbands, really. Not to mention the others.

Frank got up and pulled on his shirt. 'Don't you feel cold, Cath?'

'What? Sorry. I was miles away.'

'Aren't you chilly?'

'I was thinking it was too warm.'

'You must be running a temperature.' He sniffed. 'Or I am. Maybe we're sickening for something.'

She yawned. 'It would be a shame to have our holiday cut short. Still, in a way I wouldn't be sorry. I feel a bit guilty, really. Poor Colonel Pyat.'

'It was a private issue. Nothing we could do. An accident as far as we were concerned. Unavoidable. I expect he died for a cause or something. Is that a boat on the horizon? A warship?'

'I'm not sure I believe in accidents, as such.' She looked to where he was pointing. 'Could be. Oh, dear, I feel so lazy. And yet, at the same time, I feel I should be doing something. Aah!' She stretched. 'Fancy a game of cricket, eh, Frank?'

He sneered.

She glanced at the towering sandcastle. The children had found the little cat and were pushing it into the hollowed out main entrance. They didn't mean any harm and, in fact, the cat seemed to be enjoying himself as much as the children. Soon Cathy saw the amused black and white face staring at her from one of the upper windows. She smiled back at it, remembering the pool in the forest. She dug her bare feet into the sand and wiggled her toes.

A huge, reverberating snort came from the other deckchair. With a great dopey grin on her face, Mrs C. was snoozing. She looked as if she were having a happy dream.

'Well, she's all right, anyway,' said Frank. He held his arms round his body, leaning forward in the deckchair and shivering. 'I'll have to split back to the hotel if this goes on. What's got into those kids?'

There was a slight note of alarm in the children's voices. Cathy rose from her chair and walked towards them. 'Anything the matter, boys and girls?' But now she could see what was wrong; the roof of the castle had caved in completely. They had got too ambitious and ruined their creation. Also the moat was beginning to fill with foaming water. The tide was coming in.

'That cat's in there,' said one of the little girls in panic. She twisted at her hair with her fingers. The roof's fallen on him, miss.' The other children were all in tears, shocked by what they had done. It was plain that they thought they had killed the cat. Only one boy was trying to do something about it, digging frantically into the side of the castle with his small wooden spade. Cathy picked up the largest spade she could find and started to dig from the other side, listening for any sounds which the trapped animal might be making. She was afraid it was dead already. 'Block that stream,' she said, indicating the channel which fed the moat. 'We don't want to be flooded any sooner than we have to.' She dug and dug, getting her frock all smeared with wet sand, while the other children stood in a silent semi-circle watching her. 'Come on,' she cried. 'Get your spades and help.' Nervously, they came forward. Evidently they would much rather have gone away and forgotten the whole incident. They picked up spades or buckets and began to dig. Sand flew in all directions. Frank came up. He stood there with his hands on his hips, his mirror shades glinting. 'What the hell are you doing, Cath?'

'Trying to get the cat. Can you give us a hand, Frank?'

'I would,' he said. 'But this cold's got worse.'

She panted. Her dress, her arms, her legs, her face and hair were now all covered in sand. 'Then go back to the hotel

261

and keep warm.' Not for the first time she felt annoyed and let down by him.

But he just stood there, shivering and watching as they dug on. Soon the whole castle was down and there was no sign of the cat.

'Could it have escaped?' Cathy spoke to the boy who had first started digging. 'Before the roof collapsed?'

'I don't think so, miss. He might be in the cellar.

'What?'

'We dug a cellar – underneath.'

Catherine wiped her hot forehead. Her arms and back were aching terribly. She summoned more strength and began to dig below the surface of the beach. She was quite surprised how strong she was, considering how much energy she had already expended.

By the time they had dug a hole some six feet deep, it had become difficult to work, for water kept dripping and sand would fall back into the pit. Cathy looked for Frank but he had retreated. Her dress and hair were soaked and gritty. She must look a mess. Then she felt her spade strike something solid, something hollow. She sank down and gasped. 'Phew!' She looked up. The children were all peering over the edge at her. 'Phew!' she said. 'I think I've reached some sort of old breakwater. That was a waste of energy, eh? That cat *must* have run out of one of the doors or windows. What a lot of excitement for nothing.' And then she heard a sound which was almost defintely a cat's mew. It came from under her feet. She scraped sand away from what she had thought was a breakwater, revealing pale polished timber. 'We've found a treasure,' she said with a grin. The children's eyes widened. 'Really and truly, miss?' said one.

'I'm not sure.' She dug away more wet sand and then felt a spasm of anxiety as she exposed the whole of the box's surface, including the blank, brass plate. 'You kids had better find your mums and dads,' she said. She ran her hand over the surface of the coffin, wondering how it could be so warm.

'Oh miss! Please!'

She did her best to smile. 'Go on,' she said, 'I'll let you know if it's a treasure chest. Don't worry.'

Miserably, reluctantly, they fell back from the edge of the pit.

Catherine wondered if the coffin were really an unexploded bomb. A booby trap? She'd heard of such things. And it *was* warm and there was a regular, slow ticking sound coming from inside it.

'Frank,' she called. 'Mum?' But neither answered. A gull squawked. Or had the sound come from inside the box? She had the impression that the beach above was now deserted. She looked at the sides of the pit. 'Oh, God!'

Water was seeping down. The sand under her feet had the consistency of a quagmire. She was sinking into it. 'Frank? Mum?' Gulls replied. They were miles away. How had she got into this situation? It was ridiculous.

There was nothing for it, she decided, but to free the box completely. If it floated, she might be able to climb on it and drift to the surface as the pit filled. If not, she could put it on its side and perhaps climb up over it. She dug as fast as she could, but wet sand kept falling back into the holes. At last she was able to grab one of the brass handles and heave it, with a disgusting, sucking sound, upwards. Something heavy bumped about inside. The ticking stopped. A muffled screech replaced it. A bird? Could the cat have got inside somehow? She looked at the four bolts securing the lid and she had an idea. The Smith and Wesson .45 was still in her waistband. She took it out and screwed up her eyes, aiming for the first bolt. She pulled the trigger. The bullet hit the bolt and knocked it out. She aimed and fired three more times and by what seemed sheer luck managed to shoot all the bolts free.

She put the gun down and then, on second thoughts, picked it up again.

She pulled away the lid of the coffin.

A dreadful stink of brine and human excrement flooded from the box. She covered her mouth, staring at the creature she had revealed. Its eyes glowed, its lips curled back from

263

its stained teeth, its fingers curved like claws as it wrenched at the bonds securing its wrists to the sides of the coffin. First one hand came free. Then the other. And Cathy, recognizing her poor, mad brother, fainted.

'Cathy?'

She opened her eyes. She was lying on the edge of the pit. She could only have been insensible for a few seconds. She looked down and saw that the pit was full of bits of weed and pebbles and shells, as well as splintered pieces of wood which had comprised the coffin.

'Cathy?'

He was standing over her, on the other side. But he had changed completely. He was dressed in a white pierrot suit with big red bobbles on the front. He had a blue comical clown's hat on his head, a triumphant grin on his face. He looked down at his costume and brushed a speck or two of sand off the front. He was once again her favourite brother. 'Gosh,' he said, glancing up at the sun, 'is that the time? I must have been dreaming. Hello, Cathy.'

She was still a bit nervous.

'Sorry about the first sight,' he said. 'I didn't want to alarm you. But I had to have your help, you see.'

Her alarm faded. She was suddenly delighted. She might have guessed he'd do something like this. 'What a wonderful surprise!' She stood on tiptoe and kissed him warmly on his lips. 'You are a one, Jerry.'

'Mum and Frank about?'

She looked for them. 'Somewhere. Frank got cold.'

Her brother grinned. 'I thought it was Frank. I had to get the fuel from somewhere. And Mum?'

Cathy laughed and clung to his arm. He was the best big brother in the world. 'Look,' she said, pointing. 'There they are. Poor old Frank!'

Frank was virtually under their feet, but in a little dip in the sand and so out of sight. He was curled into a tight ball and his flesh was all blue. His mirror sunglasses stared sightlessly from the top of his head. Cathy couldn't help smiling. 'It's time Frank had a turn,' she said. 'I shouldn't laugh, really.'

Mrs Cornelius was still sprawled in her deckchair, her legs wide, her arms folded under her breasts, her chins shaking with each mighty snore. 'She's having one of her happy dreams,' said Jerry. 'Do you think the tide will come in this far?'

'Just,' said Cathy, pointing at a mark on the breakwater.

'It'll wet her feet. Nothing more. Let's leave her there to enjoy herself.'

'It does seem a shame to disturb her,' said Jerry. He looked up at the sky. The gulls were still circling cheerfully overhead and the sea still sparkled, but the air was darkening a bit, though there wasn't a cloud to be seen. 'We could be in for some rain.'

'Leave her anyway,' said Cathy.

'All right.' He peered towards the horizon. 'If you think it's a good idea.' He frowned.

'There's that boat Frank saw,' said Cathy. 'It's geting closer.'

'Ah, well, she'll have to take her chances,' said Jerry. 'Yes, I noticed that. It's a destroyer.' He spoke absently looking tenderly down at her. 'Do you want to go for a sail, Cathy?'

'Lovely,' she said. 'Or a swim?'

'I think I'll hold off swimming for a while. I'm still a bit stiff.' He brushed the sand from his costume and, with long, easy strides, led her up the asphalt ramp to the promenade. 'This way,' he said. 'It's in the harbour.'

It wasn't far to walk to the old stone harbour. There was only one ship moored there and Cathy recognized the white schooner at once.

'It's the good ole *Teddy Bear*!' she cried. She was delighted. All its brasswork shone and bright bunting danced in the rigging. 'Oh, how wonderful!' They raced along the jetty and up the gangplank. The engines were already running. A small crowd of children stood on the quay, staring at the ship with mute curiosity. They cheered as Jerry picked Cathy up and carried her the last few paces onto the deck.

Almost as soon as they were aboard, the ship upped anchor, moved away from the jetty and out of the harbour, heading for the open sea. The children waved their pocket handkerchiefs and cheered again.

In her deckchair Mrs Cornelius stirred. The tide had begun to lap at her toes. It had already covered Frank. Behind her, the shops were beginning to close up for the day and the main street was deserted, save for Elizabeth Nye, pedalling slowly up the hill towards her home. A woman, wrapped in an old sack, turned the corner and signalled to her, but Elizabeth Nye was intent on her cycling. She didn't notice Una Persson. Una looked out to sea and recognized the destroyer. She sat down on the pavement and waited.

On the sun-deck of the yacht, Jerry found a ukelele. He collapsed into a steel and canvas Bauhaus chair and began to strum the uke while Cathy swayed peacefully in a hammock under an awning and sippd her lemonade. The coast sank slowly behind them as the *Teddy Bear* steered a course for Normandy.

'I'm not stuck up or proud. I'm just one of the crowd. A good turn I'll do when I can!' Jerry sang his favourite George Formby medley. It had been a long time. 'The local doctor one night needed something put right and he wanted a handy man . . .' Cathy winked at him and tapped her feet to the rhythm. Jerry rolled his eyes at her and wagged his clown's hat as he went into a fast ukelele break. She laughed and clapped.

A few moments later they were interrupted by a dull roar from behind them. 'Sounds like thunder,' said Cathy. 'I hope we're not in for a storm.'

Jerry put down the uke and pushed back the wide cuffs from both wrists, checking his watches. 'No,' he said. 'We're all right.' He yawned. 'It's been a bloody long haul, all in all. You don't mind if I get half an hour's kip in, do you? Clausius summed it up in 1865. 'The entropy of the universe tends to a maximum.' I suppose that's when it all started. Did anyone celebrate his centenary? One idea leads to another. Ho hum.' His feet up on a canvas footstool, his hands folded in his lap, his healthy face at peace, the light wind tugging at the ruffles, folds, pleats and pom poms of his red, white and blue pierrrot suit, Jerry Cornelius fell asleep.

Catherine Cornelius got out of her hammock. She kissed her fingertips and put them on his smooth forehead. 'Dear Jerry.' She went to the rail and looked back towards the vanished coast. 'Goodbye, England.' The sound of thunder was fainter now. Perhaps the storm was moving away.

Dropping anchor a short distance offshore from the razed and smoking resort, the destroyer fired a few last rounds over the hill and got a direct hit on the village on the other side. A 4.5″ shell took out the house. Four Sunstrike missiles turned the forest into an inferno. The farm, however, had been burning since the previous night.

THE CONDITION
OF MUZAK

This book is dedicated with gratitude to the following people who, at different times, encouraged me through the eleven years this tetralogy took to complete:
Clive Allison, Hilary Bailey, Jimmy Ballard, Edward Blishen, Alan Brien, John Clute, Barry Cole, Mal Dean, Michael Dempsey, Tom Disch, George Ernsberger, Giles Gordon, Mike Harrison, Doug Hill, Langdon Jones, Richard Glyn Jones, Philip Oakes, Keith Roberts, Jim Sallis, Norman Spinrad, Jack Trevor Story, Jon Trux, Angus Wilson.

CONTENTS

All art constantly aspires towards the condition of music. For while in all other works of art it is possible to distinguish the matter from the form, and the understanding can always make this distinction, yet it is the constant effort of art to obliterate it.

– *Pater*

What's more in HERCULES than HARLEQUIN
One slew the Hydra, this can kill the Spleen;
In him Behold the Age's Genius bright;
A Patch-Coat Hero, this great Town's delight.
With Craft and Policy, his humour tends
To publick Mirth, and profitable ends.
Let Envy gnash her teeth, let Poets rail
Whilst PIERO is his Guide he cannot fail.

– Satirical print: *The Stage's Glory*, 1731

Each flower and fern in this enchanted wood
Leans to her fellow, and is understood;
The eglantine, in loftier station set,
Stoops down to woo the maidly violet.
In gracile pains the very lilies grow:
None is companionless except Pierrot.
Music, more music! how its echoes steal
Upon my senses with unlooked for weal.
Tired am I, tired, and far from this lone glade
Seems mine old joy in route and masquerade,
Sleep cometh over me, how will I prove,
By Cupid's grace, what is this thing called love?

[*Sleeps*]
– Dowson, *Pierrot of the Minute*

Hop! enlevons sur les horizons fades
Les menuets de nos pantalonnades!
    Tiens! L'Univers
    Est à l'envers . . .

    – Tout cela vous honore,
    Lord Pierrot, mais encore?
                Laforgue, *Complainte de Lord Pierrot*

Tuning Up (1)

As Major Nye tried to brush some green and brown stains from the collar of his tropical combat jacket a little damp earth fell from his neck and struck the fused stone of the timeless causeway. Around him what remained of the ruins of Angkor merged with the blackened boles of a defoliated jungle; the area was at peace; it had ceased to be of strategic importance. About fifty feet away a huge stone head of Ganesh, elephant god of trade and good luck, lay on its side where a 105mm shell had shot it between the eyes, blasting a deep gash in the stone above the base of its trunk: the wound glinted white and crystalline against the surrounding mossy grey of the forehead; the god seemed to have acquired a disenchanted third orb. Though a few monkeys and parrots (no longer the rowdy insouciants of more glorious pre-war years) crept about in the higher terraces, pausing cautiously if they disturbed a fragment of plaster or dislodged a twig, there were few sounds of life in the city.

Major Nye had at first found the city peaceful but he was becoming increasingly uneasy with the tensions which had gone to produce that peace. He lifted his head towards his right as, from the twisted and fire-blasted turret of a wrecked tank, a poor copy of a Vickers Mark I Main Battle (the 'Shiva'), emerged the chubby khaki bottom of a small Brahmin. Behind the tank the jungle brooded. 'It's no go, I'm afraid, Major.' The Brahmin wiped fat hands on his oily fatigues and wriggled round so that he could face Nye. 'Not a scrap.' He flourished an empty picnic hamper.

This was the Shiva which had scored the hit of Ganesh: its occupant was the only survivor of retaliatory rocket fire which had, in turn, taken out the tank. He called himself 'Hythloday' but Nye knew his real name. 'Hythloday' had been a technical advisor with the Indian mercenary mechanized cavalry in its now famous sweep from Darjeeling to Saigon. Some months earlier, having no room for passengers, the cavalry had left him behind with his broken tank, and two days ago Major Nye, making a routine search and destroy operation in the area on behalf of his Khmer employers, had found him, recognizing him as a former acquaintance. Major Nye had not reported his capture – there would have been little point, for yesterday he had intercepted a radio report: Phnôm Penh had sustained a tactical nuclear strike, possibly Tasmanian in origin. Without question it was curtains for the Khmers.

Unemployed again, bereft of the loyalties he needed so badly, Major Nye stroked his ancient tash and drew grey brows together. His pale hair, thin and sandy, his pale blue eyes, stood out in contrast to the heavy tan on his near fleshless face and neck. 'Ah, well,' he said in answer to Hythloday's statement, 'there are always the emergency rations. I must say the world is not the one I knew as a boy.' He lowered his Armbrust 300 anti-tank weapon to the ground and unpacked the box at his belt. 'Still, peace has been restored and that's important. Though at a price, of course.'

From behind a crackling mass of fried foliage a third figure climbed up the masonry and sat beside him on the slab: a young man in tatty out-of-date clothing, haunted and demoralized by something more than war. The major offered him a strip of pemmican. 'You seem cold, old chap. Are you sure you haven't picked up a spot of fever?'

'It depends what you mean, Major.' Jerry Cornelius turned the ragged collar of his black car coat so that it framed his face. He accepted the dehydrated meat and raised it reluctantly to his lips. His eyes were hot, his skin flushed. He was shivering.

Professor Hira joined them. 'You've had the last of the medical kit, I regret to say, Mr Cornelius.'

Cornelius had revealed himself to them on the previous day. From what he had told them he seemed to have been hiding in the ruins for a long time, since well before the final battle. Today he was, physically, slightly better than when they had found him, though he continued to deny that there was anything wrong with him. He had accepted the morphine, he said, because he hated to look a gift horse in the mouth. Similarly the quinine, the penicillin and the Valium. There was at least a score of recent holes in his forearms.

'It's industrialization I need.' Jerry shifted himself so that he squatted at Major Nye's feet. 'I've developed this horrible antipathy towards peasant communities. Particularly Slavs and South East Asians. What makes them so cruel?'

'It's hard to sympathize, isn't it?' Professor Hira nodded his head. 'Original sin, I suspect. The devil come to Eden. It can't be the climate or the terrain.' He had decided to skip the jerky and was gnawing, instead, on a root. 'It can't be poverty.'

'The very opposite, in my view,' said Major Nye. 'The richest New Guinea tribes were always the nastiest. Don't Kiev and Bangkok have a great deal in common with Crawley or Brighton?'

'Or Skokie,' said Professor Hira with a certain amount of feeling.

They looked at him in surprise. He shrugged. 'It was a long time ago.'

Major Nye carefully packed up the rest of the rations. 'I wouldn't mind getting back to Blighty myself. Better the devil you know, eh? A return to reality.'

'Oh, Christ.' Jerry began to shiver again. He rose. 'That's the last thing I need.'

As Errant Knight of Table Round,
In high resolve shall Harlequin fulfil his quest;
And thus his judges all confound.
    Harlequin Disguised as a Warrior (French print c. 1580)

Mother and Three Children Die from Asphyxia

No definite explanation for the cause of a fire which swept through two attic rooms in North Kensington on 14 January, killing a mother and her three young children, was forthcoming at the resumed inquest on Wednesday. Verdicts of 'Accidental Death' were recorded. 'I left the three children sleeping there when I went to work that morning,' said Mr Colum Cornelius who had been staying in the house at the time. Fire Officer Cyril Powell said after the fire had been put out the bodies of the mother and her three children were found in the front attic room. Pathologist Dr R. D. Teare said that the cause of death was asphyxia due to the inhalation of fire fumes.

KENSINGTON POST, 12 February 1965

J.C.

*Affluence and poverty are here in their extremes. Bohemi-
ans and traders, prostitutes, millionaires and famous
actresses, writers, painters, street singers, drug-pushers,
pop-stars, rag-and-bone dealers and antique dealers, immigrants from every part of the world – West Indians, Greeks,
Pakistanis, Irish, Italians, Americans – and rich women
from South Kensington come to London's finest vegetable
market to shop cheaper. Just a few of the types in one of the
world's most exotic streets . . .*

The Portobello Road, *Golden Nugget*,
September 1966

Some two miles north of the abandoned shell of Derry and
Toms Department Store (now, like the ruins of Tintagel and
Angkor, a mere relic) there once stood a grey-brown collection of nineteenth-century brick buildings surrounded by a
high wall, also of brick: the Monastery of the Poor Clares
Colettines, Westbourne Park Road, established in 1857 at
the request of Dr Henry Manning, Superior of the Oblates
of St Charles. The buildings themselves were erected in
1860, modelled on those of the Convent of the Poor Clares
at Bruges which supplied the first nuns. Notting Hill,
according to *The Building News* of the period (quoted in the
Greater London Council's Survey of North Kensington,
1973), was nothing more than a dreary waste of mud and
stunted trees, where the convent shared 'the sole interest'
of this desolate district with 'Dr Walker's melancholy
church' of All Saints', then still unfinished, and a lonely
public house, now called the Elgin, in Ladbroke Grove. A
number of 'low Irish' had settled in the vicinity, and already
there had been 'a plenty crop of Romish conversations
there'. The convent looked East on to Ladbroke Grove,
North on to Westbourne Park Road and South on to Blen-

heim Crescent, while to its West were rows of run-down Victorian terraces separated, back-to-back, by tiny yards.

During the decade 1965–75 (the period during which the major part of our story probably took place) the convent was sold to the Greater London Council who subsequently built on the site a number of blocks of flats and a multi-storey car-park to serve the needs of their richer tenants. The nuns were moved to Barnes, across the river.

Before the convent was demolished it had been possible for people living on the upper floors of the surrounding houses to glimpse occasionally the activities of the nuns, members of an enclosed order, in the convent gardens, where vegetables and flowers were grown. In the summer the nuns would enjoy a game of rounders on the lawn or take picnics under the shade of the many elm trees whose old branches could be seen by those who passed by on the other side of the time-worn brick. The walls provided the nuns with a tangle of rambling roses and ivy and on their reverse offered the public slogans, some cryptic (VIET-GROVE) and some relatively clear (QPR RULE OK), as well as the usual spray-painted selection of quotations from the works of Blake and Jarry. For those residents of Blenheim Crescent, Ladbroke Grove and Westbourne Park Road who found themselves with time on their hands the convent represented a regular diversion. At any one time during the height of the summer at least fifty pairs of eyes would be trained on the convent from a variety of angles, from windows, balconies and roofs, waiting for a glimpse of a figure at a window, the sight of a black habit crossing from a residential wing to the chapel or, more rarely, the spectacle of a cricket match. The convent proper, being, according to local legend, forbidden to any man (apart from the confessor, the electrician and the plumber who attended to the failing central heating) and most women, represented an ideal, a mystery, a goal, a challenge. Some doubtless hoped for a glance of flesh, a suggestion of illicit love between the nuns, while others were merely curious as to how the inhabitants spent their time. To certain ladies the convent represented a haven, a sanctuary from the complication of children, husbands, lovers, relatives and jobs.

On one particular summer afternoon, at the beginning of the decade already mentioned, a young man sat on the ledge of a window of a wretched tenement in Blenheim Crescent staring intently at the door of the chapel from which, in five minutes, almost all the Poor Clares would emerge together. The young man had lived most of his life in the three-room apartment and had an intimate knowledge of the nuns' movements as well as an affectionate proprietorial attitude towards them: several had nicknames – Old Ratty, Sexy Sis, Bigbum, Pruneface – for he had grown up with them; they were his pets. Given the opportunity, he would probably have died to protect them. He did not, of course, regard them as human beings.

From behind the young man and in the next room came the sound of crockery being washed; a noise accompanied by a rhythmic almost sub-vocal litany which was familiar and restful to him, like the drone of insects in a country garden, the tinkle of water over rocks.

Jerry Cornelius yer kin jest git yer shitty littel finger art an' do an 'ands turn like ther rest'v us, yer bugger. Fuckin' 'ell, yer dad woz fuckin' lazy but yore ther fuckin' world champion you are. If it wosn't fer me eyes I'd be doin' a bleedin' job, I worked fer years fer you lot and where'd it fuckin' get me, look at this bloody place it's a pigsty, an' Frank keeps promisin' me 'e'll git us a noo flat an' thass bin four years NAR!

A totter's cart, piled with the discarded debris of a score of slum houses, turned into Blenheim Crescent. It was drawn by a brown and white pony. Jerry automatically found himself inspecting the junk from where he sat, high overhead: it was an inbred instinct of all children born in the district. There were two old gas-stoves, a wooden bedstead, a water-heater, a tin bath, some boxes of rusty cutlery. The pony's hooves clattered on the tarmac of the street. The driver, in a stained brown overcoat, his eyes owl's eyes behind thick lenses, had propped his main prize of the day, an old set of stag's antlers, behind him so that for an instant it seemed that he himself was horned. He gave a throaty instruction to the horse and it turned right, vanishing into the nearby mews.

Jerry yawned, stretched, and settled a thin shoulder against the window frame, swinging his legs above the tiny balcony formed by the house's front porch. The balcony had once been painted green but most of the paint had peeled. It contained dilapidated window boxes, some of which managed to sustain a few weeds in their sour earth; a collection of grimy plastic woodland animals and gnomes; part of a black Raleigh roadster bicycle which Jerry had begun reconstructing two years before; a deck-chair whose canvas had rotted and which had ripped when, with a yell, his mother had fallen through three days earlier. Sooner or later, Jerry had reassured her, she would not recognize the balcony. He planned, eventually, to turn it into an ornamental conservatory with semi-tropical plants.

The afternoon was very warm for early summer and was relatively still, for it was a Thursday, when almost all the local shops and stalls closed down. Jerry could turn his head to the right and see, at right angles to Blenheim Crescent, a tranquil, deserted Portobello Road, or to the left a Ladbroke Grove with about half its normal volume of traffic. It was almost as if, for a few hours, an aura spread from the convent and made the world outside as tranquil as the world within.

Before the nuns emerged, Jerry's attention was distracted to the street by the chuckling drums of some Pakistani love song which almost immediately stopped and became the last few bars of a Rolling Stones number. Three black youths, in jeans and jazzy jumpers, were springing down the steps of the house immediately opposite Jerry's, a house even more dilapidated than his own, of tired red brick. The tallest youth swaggered, holding in his hand a transistor radio which now played the Beatles' latest hit; the other

284

two were jostling him, trying for possession of the radio. The tall boy pulled away from his companions. 'Lay off me, man.' He made loose, dancing movements. The volume rose and fell as he moved the radio. 'Come on, man — let's have it.' One of his companions grabbed and the station was lost. Jerry could hear the static. 'You broken it, man!' They paused, seeking the correct wave-length. 'No, I ain't!' They found the programme just as the song faded. They began to scuffle again. 'Give us a go, man.' The tall boy broke and ran with the radio, up towards Portobello Road. 'Get your own. It's mine, ain't it?' The other two caught him almost immediately, tackling him around the legs, bringing him down.

As the fight became more serious a policeman turned the corner from Ladbroke Grove. He was young, pink and all the character seemed to have been scrubbed from his sober features. Without altering his pace he raised his voice:

'Oi!'

Unheeding the boys began, almost amiably, to kick and punch their companion, who lay on the ground, his knees drawn up, the tranny hugged to his chest. It was playing Jimi Hendrix now.

'Oi!'

The policeman loped towards them. They turned. The two shouted a warning and ran towards Kensington Park Road. The third picked himself up and followed them. The policeman stopped, drew a couple of breaths and wiped his forehead with a navy-blue handkerchief. Then he continued to pace in their wake, obviously not in pursuit.

'There's never a copper around when you need one!' Jerry found himself shouting into the silence of the street. Startled by the loudness of his own voice he turned his head in the opposite direction. When, after some seconds, he turned his head back he saw the policeman glaring up at him. Jerry winked.

'Wot's 'appenin'?' His mother entered the bedroom and saw her son on her ledge. 'Git off a there! Yer'll fall!' She neared the window and saw the policeman. 'Blimey! Wot's 'e want?'

'Dunno, Mum.'

'Nosey bloody parkers the lot of 'em.'

Mother and son contemplated the policeman. Eventually he became self-conscious and resumed his beat.

Mrs Cornelius cocked her head. 'Someone comin' up. Are yer *sure* . . . Oh, it's Frank.' The door opened.

Frank came into her room. Frank wore a blazer with polished steel buttons, grey flannels, an open-neck white shirt, a yellow cravat with a horse-shoe motif. He stared in affected contempt at his brother whose own costume was a red satin shirt with the words *Gerry and the Pacemakers* imprinted in yellow on the back, skin-tight drainpipe jeans and suede desert boots. His black greasy hair had almost grown out, but was still streaked with blone dye at the ends. 'Bloody hell.' Frank placed a large bar of Cadbury's Fruit and Nut on the confused dressing-table. 'They should never have abolished National Service. Look at you!'

'Piss off.' Amiably Jerry took in his brother's gear. 'What was the regatta like? Just come up from Henley, have you?'

'I've been *working*.' Frank ran a hand down his waist.

'Conning some poor ignorant foreigner, eh?' Jerry looked speculatively at the chocolate on the table.

'I've made an important sale this afternoon.' Frank produced a huge roll of dollar bills from his trouser pocket. 'Don't knock it, Jerry.'

Noting the expressions of the faces of both his brother and his mother he quickly slipped the roll back where it had come from.

'Not a bad little bundle,' said Jerry. 'Did you sell some of them authentic Chippendale vases you antiqued up last week?'

Frank tapped his forehead. 'Intelligence got me that.' He preened himself. 'Information. Property. That's my commission.'

'You can be had up for playing Monopoly with real

money.' Jerry swung his legs into the room. 'Say, lend us a couple of bucks, will ya, bud?'

'Oh, Christ!' Frank returned to the living room/kitchen. He glared around him at the crowded, ruined furniture, the half-done washing up, the piles of magazines and broken china ornaments. 'Don't let him talk in that fake Yank accent, Mum. He's so *common*.'

'Make it ten bob, then,' said Jerry reasonably, in his own voice.

'Piss off.' Frank sniffed. 'Get a bloody job.'

'I'm organizing this beat group,' said Jerry. 'It takes time.'

'What is the time?' Frank glanced at his wrist. 'My watch has stopped.'

'Is that the bargain that fellah sold you in the pub?' Jerry was triumphant. 'Solid gold, wasn't it? Fifty jewels? Con men always make the best marks, don't they?'

'I didn't come to see you.' Frank slid his white cuff over his malfunctioning watch. 'I came to see Cathy – and mum, of course. Is she here?'

'That's Mum, by the sink.'

'How childish,' said Frank.

'What you doing then?' Jerry asked with genuine curiosity, ignoring his brother's last remark. 'Following in Rachman's footsteps?'

'Tenements?' Frank was shocked. 'This is *property development*. Offices and that.'

'Round here?'

'It's going up all the time. A rising residential area, this is. All the people from Chelsea and South Ken are moving in.'

'Buying themselves nice little ragshops in Golborne Road, are they?'

'Multiple tenancies are giving way to one-family houses. It's council policy.' Frank savoured the sound of the words.

Jerry looked out of the window over the sink. He had missed the nuns. 'You know what I'd do, if I had the chance? I'd buy that bloody nunnery.'

'I've got news for you,' began Frank. 'The GLC . . .'

'Just to own it,' said Jerry dreamily. 'Not to do anything with it.'

'Well, you'd better start saving up, hadn't you?'

Jerry shrugged. 'Wait till our group gets to number one.'

Frank laughed. 'You'll be lucky if you're all awake at the same time.'

Absently, Jerry popped a mandy into his mouth. 'It's idealists like me the world needs. Not grafters like you.'

This seemed to improve Frank's spirits. He put a condescending hand on Jerry's forearm. 'But it's a grafter's world, my son.'

'Yeah?'

'Most definitely, young Jerry.'

Jerry sniffed. 'I'll let you get on with it, then.'

He turned to his window.

Frank wandered to his mother's side. 'Hello, Mum. Any chance of a cup of tea?'

Major Nye

'I'm afraid it's not quite the thing for our little theatre.' Major Nye tried to sit on one of the bar-stools and then decided to remain at attention. Gingerly he sipped his pint of shandy, revealing shiny cuffs. The suit was twenty years old at least. 'I really am sorry, old chap. What is it? A pint?' His pale eyes were sympathetic.

'Thanks, major,' said Jerry. 'I'm sorry I can't get you one.' He was scarcely any more fashionably dressed than Major Nye. He wore his black suit with the high, narrow Edwardian lapels and the slight flare to the trousers, which he had got Burton's to make up for him, albeit reluctantly, when he had been flush. The only black shoes he had were the elastic-sided cuban-heeled winkle-pickers pre-dating the suit and he felt awkward in his rounded, button-down-collar white shirt, with the black knitted tie. 'But you've only heard the cassette on a cheap player. If you heard it over proper speakers you'd get our full sound, you know.'

'Surely you can get bookings in these pop clubs they have everywhere these days?' He caught the attention of the purple-cheeked barman. 'Pint of best, please.' He leaned cautiously against the mahogany counter, looking beyond Jerry at Hennekey's other customers crowding around the pub's stained wooden benches and big tables. It was evident that while he did not judge the shaggy young bohemians he was mildly curious about them. He fingered the ends of his cuff. 'I thought they were mushrooming.'

'They're not interested in us,' Jerry told him. 'You see, we're a bit more than an ordinary rock group – we're trying for something that combines a story, a light-show, spoken words and so on. That's why I guessed you might be interested, since you're local. The only local theatre. And it's more of a theatrical show, you see.'

'I'm just the secretary, old chap. I'm probably the least

powerful person in the whole outfit. And acting, unpaid, at that. It was my daughter got me involved, really. I'm retired, you see. I was adjutant of the – well, we got kicked out – the regiment was incorporated – no room for old fogies like me. Anyway, she's an actress. Well, of course, you must know that already, since it was through your sister . . .'

'Yes,' said Jerry. 'I do know. But you're the only person connected with the Hermes Theatre who'd even bother to listen to me.'

'They're a bit old-fashioned there, by and large, though I think they're going to do Pinter next year. Or is it Kafka? *A Night at the Music Hall*'s about as far as they're prepared to go, eh? The boy I love is up in the gallery . . .'

'I see,' said Jerry. 'I suppose you don't know anybody else I could approach?'

Major Nye was disappointed at not being allowed to finish the line. 'Not really.'

'Everybody's hopes are pinned on this, you see,'

Major Nye said seriously, as a group of newcomers jostled him against Jerry's chest: 'You shouldn't stop trying, old chap. If you've got something worthwhile it will be recognized eventually.'

Jerry sighed and sipped his bitter.

Una Persson

'Bloody hell,' said Jerry miserably as he backed into the corner of the white room, his elbow almost dislodging a particularly ugly china dog on a shelf, 'there must be every trendy in the King's Road here, Cath.' The party bubbled about his ears. There was a great deal of blue and orange, of op and pop and pastel plastic, of the Tilsonesqueries loading the walls, of coloured Strobescopes and Warholian screen-prints, light screens displaying shapes of an oddly Scandinavian neatness, hunt-ball whoops and giggles, stiff upper-class bodies in a terrifying parody of vitality. His sister shook her head. 'You're such a snob, Jerry. They're nice people. A lot of them are friends of mine.'

Jerry tasted his punch. He had got his new brown and white William Morris shirt wet ladling the stuff into his cup. He had only come because Catherine had told him he would be able to make the right sort of contacts. The trouble was that every time someone spoke to him in one of those high-pitched voices his throat tightened and he could only grunt at them. The strobes turned the whole scene into a silent movie – something about decadent modern times called *Despair* – as the hearty girls in their shorts and mini-skirts danced with pale young men in neat neckerchiefs and very clean jeans who puffed at machine-rolled joints and staggered against the chrome and leather furniture in an unaesthetic danse macabre.

The Rolling Stones record finished and was replaced on the deck by a fumbling drunkard who lurched against the amplifier and knocked it half off its shelf. The amplifier was saved by a tall girl with short hair and sardonic grey eyes. The girl wore a long calf-length skirt and a rust-coloured jumper to match; she had an assured elegance possessed by no one else in the room. She squeezed past the drunkard as he let the pick-up fall with a crunch on the record he had selected: *Elvis Presley's Golden Hits*, already much scored. 'Oh, fab!' cried more than one melancholy soul.

Jerry watched the girl until she looked back at him and smiled. He turned his head to find himself face to face with the dark young man whom Catherine had introduced as Dimitri, doubtless one of her many Greeks. At least Dimitri wore a suit, albeit a 'Regency' cut. Dimitri's eyes widened in panic at the prospect of a further exchange of grunts. The elegant girl entered Jerry's field of vision again. She was carrying a glass. 'You seem as much out of place as I am.'

Jerry's being flooded with gratitude but he hoped it didn't show. 'Chelsea wankers,' he said, playing it cool. He tossed back his drink. 'What's a nice girl like you doing here?'

'I came with a friend.'

Jerry was disappointed. 'One of those blokes?'

'One of these – chicks.'

He wondered if she was foreign.

'Liz Nye,' explained the girl.

'She's a friend of my sister's.'

'Catherine's a great pal of mine.'

'Who are you, then?'

'My name's Una.'

Jerry smirked, in spite of himself. He knew all about Una Persson. 'You're a legend in your own lifetime,' he said. 'You're not like I imagined.'

Her smile was for herself but she replied quickly to save him embarrassment. 'Catherine sees just one side of me.'

'Have you got a lot?' Jerry asked. 'Of sides.'

'It depends what you mean.'

Jerry's smile broadened and became a grin which she shared. She winked at him and stood beside him, shoulder to shoulder, so that they both faced the party. 'They should be putting the Vivaldi on soon,' she said. 'And begin to "smooch".'

Somehow she had given him courage. 'Do you want to split?' he asked.

She frowned. 'You mean "leave"?'

'Yes. Sorry.'

'There are so many levels, aren't there? I'll have to find out what Liz wants to do. She's in the next room.' Una Persson touched his arm. 'But I'll be back.'

Jerry began to come to life. Gracefully he reached towards his guffawing hostess and accepted another punch.

Sebastian Auchinek

Fingering the hand-stitching on his blue velvet Beau Brummel jacket Sebastian Auchinek bent an ear towards the Dynatron cabinet stereo to which was attached, five pin DIN to five pin DIN, Jerry's little cassette tape recorder. 'Well, it's certainly different, isn't it?' He added: 'Man.'

'It's underground music,' Jerry explained.

'Yeah, ther bleedin' eight-forty-five ter Aldgate, by ther sarnd o' it!' Mrs Cornelius laughed as she put two cups of cocoa on the surface of Jerry's battered amplifier. They were in Jerry's room at Blenheim Crescent. The untidy bed was littered with magazines, of a different kind from his mother's, and most of the rest of the space was given over to valves, wires and speakers, the majority of which didn't work. 'Sorry, I'm shore!' said Mrs Cornelius. She departed, closing his door in a pantomime of courtesy.

Luckily Sebastian Auchinek's sense of humour functioned only in direct relation to his own sense of despair. He puzzled over the music. He removed his little hat. He sucked at his huge lower lip. He rubbed his monstrous nose. 'But will it catch on with the general public? That's what we have to think about – Jerry? You don't mind?'

'No, no. 'Course not.' Jerry looked anxiously into the liquid eyes of the handsome promoter. 'You've heard of The Pink Floyd, haven't you? They're getting quite popular.'

'Oh, yes. I don't doubt it. But you know what public taste's like. Twinkle one week, Mojos the next. Whether this sort of music's got any future – I honestly don't know. I can see you're serious. But are you commercial? I'm sorry.' Sebastian Auchinek held up a shapely hand as if to ward off a light blow. He put his cap down. 'It's what we have to think about, *if* we're going to back you. It still boils down to investments. You're a talented boy, I don't doubt it. I mean, what we have to say to ourselves is – How do we promote this kind of music? All right; we can get a minor record company to do one LP – but it's the singles market that's important. I can't see any of this as single material, quite frankly. Miss Persson led me to understand that you were more of an R&B group. Like Graham Bond and Brian Auger. We're considering them at the moment.'

'We don't do that sort of thing any more,' said Jerry with a certain disdain. 'Una said you were into progressive stuff.'

'We are. We are. But we have to *see* it. In context. We have to be able to feel we can do something positive for a group. It wouldn't be fair to you, would it, if we just took you on and then did nothing?'

'Yes, I can see that . . .'

'Maybe if I came along and heard you at your next gig?'

'That's why I'm talking to you. We can't get any gigs.'

'Not even locally?'

'There aren't any local venues, are there?'

'It's difficult, isn't it?'

Jerry turned the recorder off. The hissing had begun to irritate him. 'Some people think we're ahead of our time.'

'Could be. When's you next rehearsal?' Auchinek was eager to prove to Jerry that his mind was still open.

'I'm not sure. We have trouble finding places.'

'Well, look, get in touch with me when you know what your plans are. Maybe I can fix up a rehearsal room for you.'

'It'd be something, anyway. Thanks.'

Sebastian Auchinek removed a leather-bound note-book from his inside pocket. He clicked a ball-point with his thumb. 'What's the name of the group?'

'The Deep Fix.'

'You might have to change that a bit. It's not really – you know . . . The BBC's still a power in the land, eh? They don't like drugs. Have you thought of any other names?'

'Yes,' said Jerry. 'The Cocksuckers.'

Sebastian Auchinek managed a small smile. 'Well, we'll talk about that when the time comes.' He tore a page from the book. 'Here's my office number. Keep in touch. Leave a message with my secretary if I'm not there. Don't think I'm being negative. And remember – I'm not the only promoter on the beach.'

He looked around for his corduroy cap. He had put it on top of his cocoa.

Mrs C. and Colonel P.

'Of course,' said Colonel Payat as he poured Mrs Cornelius another gin, 'we lost everything in the war, including our titles. My uncle had a very big estate not far from Lublin. And his father, you know, had an even bigger one in the Ukraine. He was shot by Makhno who in turn was shot by Trotsky who was killed by Stalin.' He shrugged and his smile was crooked. 'So it goes.' He fell back into Mrs C.'s best armchair, the white plastic one, his eyes fixing on the silent television screen. The warped monochrome picture displayed a nurse, a nun and a black man in a hospital bed.

'We're surpposed ter be related ter *'im*,' said Mrs Cornelius, brushing crisp crumbs from her pink cotton lap. 'Shouldn't eat crisps. They make yer sweat.'

'My uncle?'

'Nar! The ovver one. Trotsky, innit? Though I 'eard 'e corled 'isself somefink else. Brahn or somefink.'

'Bronstein. His real name was Bronstein. Jewish, you see.'

'Nar! It woz nuffink forin'.' She raised her glass. 'Darn the 'atch then.'

Bemused, the drunken colonel imitated her action.

'It's more comfy 'ere, innit, than ther pub?' said Mrs Cornelius. She could see that Colonel P. was a gent (even though currently in need of a spot of luck) by the cut of his greasy tweed jacket, his shiny flannels: but his breeding was revealed by his bearing rather than his clothes, she supposed. And he hadn't hesitated to fork out for a half bottle of gin when she'd taken a fancy to him and suggested coming back here. Tonight wasn't the first time she had seen him in the Blenheim, of course, but it was the first time she'd had a chance to have a decent chat.

'Definitely Brahn,' she said. Her expression softened. She moved closer to Colonel Pyat. He looked at her through

wary, red-rimmed eyes. He stroked the stubble of his chin.
'Is Pyat yore real name, then?'

'Well, it's my official name, you know. In the last war . . .'

From the next room, Jerry's, there suddenly came the ear-
splitting squawk of a feeding-back amplifier. She was
shocked. It hadn't occurred to her to check if her son was
in. Automatically she lifted her great red head and raised
her voice:

'I thort yer said you woz garn art ternight! Turn that
fuckin' thing darn!'

'Pardon?' thickly said Colonel Pyat.

'Not you, Kernewl. Sorry. Turn it darn, carn't ya!'

'I meant to go back after the war.' Colonel Pyat raised a
sorrowful glass to his lips. 'I was in intelligence, you know.
Liaison officer for your chaps. Stuck here when the war
ended. But, naturally . . .' He shrugged.

She was vaguely sympathetic. 'The Russians, eh?'

'Worse than the Germans.'

'But I thort you said you *woz* Russian.'

'No, no – I was *with* the Russians.'

'Oh really? Where woz that?'

A high-pitched shriek filled the flat.

'My God!' Colonel P. covered his ears. His eyes hunted
about the room. He stared through the window as if he
expected the sky to fill with planes.

''Ang on a sec.' Carefully Mrs Cornelius got to her broad
feet. 'Ooo.' She coughed. 'It's me kid,' she said.

Before she could reach Jerry's door the sound from behind
it had changed again, rising and falling, so that now it
resembled the distant wailing of some demented creature of
the sea.

Early Reports

Scotland Yard will keep up its drive to recruit black police-men despite the failure of the campaign so far. Revealing this yesterday Metropolitan Police Commissioner Sir Robert Mark said: 'We won't take No for an answer. We shall keep at it.'

Daily Mirror, 31 March 1976

The chances of our moderate climate changing soon to a prolonged cold spell, but not glacial, are high, Dr E. J. Mason, FRS, director of the Meteorological Office, suggested last night. With the caution of a man carrying ultimate responsibility for the precision of the official day-to-day weather forecasting methods, he added: 'There is no real basis for the alarmist predictions of an imminent ice age, which have largely been based on extrapolation of the 30-year trend of falling temperatures in the northern hemisphere between 1940 and 1965. Apart from the strong dubiety of making a forecast from such a short-period trend, there is now evidence that the trend has been arrested.'

Guardian, 18 March 1976

The annual meeting of the National Front voted in London at the weekend to expel all members who are mixed race, non-European ancestry or coloured. About 20-25 members are affected. But yesterday, Mr Eugene Pierce, an Anglo-Indian accountant who has been a member of the National Front and walked out of the meeting in protest at the vote said: 'I was immediately assured by members of the direc-torate that the vote was only a recommendation . . .' Mr Pierce, 65, whose British grandfather married an Indian, earlier told the meeting: 'I was a member of the British army, along with thousands of other Anglo-Indians.' But the meeting became increasingly noisy and his words were drowned in the uproar. 'We have to be 100 per cent racialist in the National Front,' said the mover of the resolution, Mr Bert Wilton, of Southwark, London, to loud applause: 'If people who are half or quarter coloured are allowed in, it will kill everything.'

Guardian, 6 January 1975

Police frogmen were hunting for more bodies yesterday after the cut-up remains of two teenage sisters were found in a lake in the Catskill Mountains, 110 miles north of New York. The self-styled 'Bishop of Brooklyn', 51-year-old Vernon Legrand, leader of a bizarre cult, has been charged with the murders.

Daily Mirror, 15 March 1976

Two members of a British-based religious sect are believed to have been the victims of ritual killings. Police think that they were hypnotized – and then vital organs in their bodies were crushed. The probe began after the body of artist Michel Piersotte was found at the foot of the 250ft Citadel in Namur, Belgium. Michel was a member of the Children of God sect, whose international headquarters is at Bromley in Kent. A post-mortem revealed that his liver and kidneys were crushed, as though in a vice. Police decided to re-open an inquiry into the death of another member of the sect. This was 20-year-old Jean Maurice, who was found dead at the foot of the Citadel in Dinant, Belgium, in December. Again police established that vital organs had been crushed. The men were close friends. They were believed to be trying to break away from the sect. A Belgian police spokesman said last night: 'We're studying a Scotland Yard report about the sect.' The report says that hypnotism is used at indoctrination ceremonies. Youngsters are encouraged to break off all ties with their parents.

Daily Mirror, 15 March 1976

Tuning Up (2)

Jerry hauled on the reins to bring the lead dog to a sudden stop. At once the other dogs lay down in their traces, the breath from their pink panting mouths melting the surrounding snow. The small red sun overhead was the only bright colour in the dark grey sky, the only light, yet it was possible to see for miles over the twilight landscape to a range of mountains in the north-west, to the black line of the horizon elsewhere. It had taken him months to reach Lapland, travelling mostly by sled. He hauled a sack from the wicker rack behind him and began to walk along the line, throwing the dogs chunks of skinned half-frozen wolf. As he reached the lead dog and produced a larger than average lump of meat from the sack he heard in the distance a bass drone, coming from the direction of the mountains. He recognized the motor of an old Westland Whirlwind and automatically looked for cover. There was none, save the sled. He pulled his bow and his quiver of arrows from beneath the furs and bric-à-brac on the main section and prepared for the worst. Things were waking up a little sooner than he had anticipated. He supposed that, in spite of the immediate problems, he was relieved. At least the birth (or re-birth, depending how you look at it) had been relatively easy this time.

The big chopper appeared in the sky, black and glimmering, and the dogs looked up from their flesh, eyes bright, ears pointing. One of then snarled; Jerry was sure that they had not responded to any specific stimulus. They were a strange breed of huskies, with red eyes, white coats and red-tipped ears.

Snow began to fly. Clouds seemed to form just above the surface. The helicopter came down heavily, still only partially powered, bumping and groaning. The motor switched off. In the stillness the rotors clacked slowly to a halt. Jerry saw muffled figures moving inside the breath-clouded canopy. He fitted an arrow to his bow as a door in the Whirlwind's body opened and a woman descended. She had a large 7.63mm Borchardt automatic pistol in her gloved right hand. Her face was hidden in the hood of an ankle-length panda-skin parka. Her breath coiled from shrouded lips as she peered towards the sled. She walked with a kind of Sarah Bernhardt limp.

'Mr Cornelius?' The voice was sharp, demanding.

'Which Mr Cornelius would that be?' Jerry recognized her at once.

Miss Brunner was her usual petulant self. 'Oh, don't be silly. What have you got in your hands?'

'A bow and arrow.'

She buried her pistol in her clothing. 'I understand. Put it away.' She held up her heavy arms.

'Oh sure.' Jerry indicated the swivelling gun-turret in the chopper.

She shrugged. 'Merely a gesture. You know there's little chance of a gun working in the current moral climate. What are you doing in Lapland? Looking for someone?'

'Just trying to recapture the past.'

'That's not like the old Jerry.'

'I can't say the same to you. But then I always admired your consistency.'

'There's a bit more mass than there used to be.' It was obvious that she had taken his remark for a compliment. 'You look like a mountie. Well, what do you want from us?'

'Nothing,' he said. 'I didn't even know you were out, did I?'

She became suspicious. 'Aha.' The snow crunched. She moved tentatively forward. The dog snarled again, pricking its peculiar ears. She stopped, glaring at it in considerable dislike. 'You won't be able to get to the laboratory. Not for a while. It'll be frozen up. Is that where you were thinking of going?'

'I haven't been thinking much at all. You don't in these conditions. I suppose I was making for the lab. Instinct.'

'Instinct!' She cackled. 'You!'

She had hurt his feelings. 'It's the only explanation I can think of. You were heading south. Does that mean you've been to the lab already?'

'That's how I know about it. We came via Russia. And before that Canada. We've been flying for ages.'

Luxuriously Jerry inspected the vast sky, half expecting to see a formation of geese, but it was still empty. 'It's probably the spring,' he said.

INTRODUCTION

On New Year's Night, 1091 a certain priest called Gauchelin was terrified by a procession of women, warriors, monks, etc. who swept past him, dressed in black, half-hidden by flames, and wailing aloud. Astonished and dismayed, the priest said to himself: 'Doubtless this is the Cornelius family. I have heard that it has formerly been seen by many people, but I have mocked at such tales. Now, indeed, I myself have truly seen the ghosts of the dead.' Gauchelin was, indeed, neither the first nor the last to see the notorious 'maisnie Cornelius' (Harlequin-troupe), which appeared so frequently both in mediaeval France and England. For Harlequin (Harlechin, Hellequin, etc., are all variations of the same word) appears first in history or legend as an aerial spectre or demon, leading that ghostly nocturnal cortège as the Wild Hunt.

Enid Welsford, *The Fool: His Social and Literary History*,
London, 1934

Prince Philip Opens Dream Flats in W.10

Trains roared behind a VIP canopy, the sun popped out suddenly and children whistled from the roof-tops when the Duke of Edinburgh arrived in dreary North Kensington on Tuesday afternoon (to open) Pepler House, the biggest project to date by the Kensington Housing Trust.

KENSINGTON POST, 12 November 1965

1. The dog-fight missile designed to dominate its decade

Jerry struggled into his pink tweed Cardin suit. The waist-coat was a little tight and he had to undo the shoulder holster by a notch but otherwise he looked as sharp as he had always done. He pulled his needler free and checked that the magazine was full, each hollow dart containing a neat 50ccs of Librium: a perfect hunting charge. He smoothed his long, fine hair about his face as he stood in front of the looking-glass, well-satisfied, in the circumstances, with his appearance. He checked his watches. Both waited at zero. He crossed his wrists and started the watches. The hands moved at a steady rate.

'Pretty,' he said. He smirked. He faced the room, squinting in the glare from the white, plastic furniture, the neon, the ivory walls. He took mirror shades from his top pocket and slid them over his eyes. He sighed. 'Nifty.'

He sailed out into the currents of the days, high on pain-killers and a sense of his own immortality, swinging his hips to the sound of Eleanor Rigby from the receiver built into his unfashionably rigid collar, down Holland Park Avenue beneath the tall spring trees, stepping wide on two-inch Cuban heels. The bravest dandy of them all: he had a smile for everybody. Under his breath he sang along with John, George, Paul and Ringo and turned right into Camp-den Hill Square where his great big Duesenburg, chocolate and cream, waited for him alone. He unlocked the door, slid behind the wheel, started the perfect supercharged straight-8, let go the brakes and was on the move. A masterpiece to equal any one of its European contemporaries, the 1930 SJ Torpedo Phaeton was the most elegant car America had ever produced. Euphorically, both mind and body in ecstatic unity, he cruised between the labouring corpse-waggons which parted so that he could pass through them, as if by divine command. He offered a friendly wave to all he overtook, then he reached the top of Ladbroke Grove's hill and began the descent into the mythical netherworld of Notting Dale. The road was suddenly almost deserted; sounds were muffled; the sun was hotter.

Turning right into Westbourne Park Raod he stopped outside the main gate of the Convent of the Poor Clares. He did not bother to lock the car. He knew he could rely on its aura to protect it.

Sister Eugenia, the Mother Superior, herself greeted Jerry as she opened the grilled steel door which led directly into the shadowy Visitors' Chapel with its hideous green, yellow and pink Crucifixion above the green marble tiles, the brass, the tasselled purple of the altar. She spoke in carefully modulated tones like a consultant psychiatrist and when she smiled it was sweet and good. Jerry admired her smile in particular, as he admired professionalism wherever he found it.

'Father Jeremiah.' She gestured for him to precede her while she supervised the tender young novice locking the gate. They followed single file behind him as he headed through the side exit and on to a gravel path, making for the main building, smelling the air, admiring the blooms and the well-kept lawns, the peculiar, ingrown dwarf elms. He was not sure but he thought he heard, somewhere in the chapel on his left, the second part of Messiaen's *Turangalila Symphony*. He pressed his head against his collar and cut off the Beatles, looking enquiringly back at the Mother Superior. 'A record?'

'Oh, no!' The Mother Superior was amused. Behind her the soft little novice giggled.

They reached the main building and climbed steps into quiet passages, arriving at last at the second floor and the Mother Superior's office which looked out on to the garden. It seemed to Jerry, surreptitiously sniffing the air, that the infirmary was nearby. At her desk the Mother Superior lowered herself into her high-backed Windsor chair, signing for Jerry to sit in the chair's twin facing her. 'It is a very

308

great pleasure to see you again, Father Jeremiah. You are looking well.'

'And you, too, Sister Eugenia. Congratulations on your appointment . . .'

'I pray that I will fulfil . . .'

'. . . there can be no question . . .'

'You are kind. It seems such a short time since you took confession at Harrogate. How greatly our lives have changed. Your own responsibilities . . .'

He dismissed them. 'I'm very grateful for what you've been able to do.'

'The poor child. I was glad to help. She's perfectly safe here and will be until – ?'

'Eventually, of course, it will be possible for her to leave.'

'How is Father – ?'

'We no longer communicate, I fear. But I hear he is in good health. In France.'

'He has similar duties to your own, then? There were rumours of dissolution . . .'

'Nobody's perfect.'

She was full of sympathy. It was almost as if she restrained herself from reaching across the desk and touching his hand. 'The burden . . .' she murmured.

'It's born of joy.'

Her eyes shone. 'You have a vocation.'

'I'm due for one. I hope so.'

'Oh, you have!' Her smooth features were radiant. 'You're an inspiration to us all.'

He accepted this with modest dignity.

She reached into a desk drawer and produced a ledger. 'I regret the formality.' She found the appropriate page and offered him the book. He removed a large Mont Blanc fountain pen from the inside breast pocket and signed his name and title in full, giving his usual tasteless flourish to the initials S and J. She looked with pleasure upon the signature for a moment before putting the book away. She took some keys from the desk. 'These are such dangerous times. You risk so much in coming.'

'I gain much.' Once again he heard the sound of music. This time they were playing Schoenberg's *Pierrot Lunaire*.

'You're too kind.'

They left the office, passed the infirmary, descended three flights of steps. Jerry realized, by the articial lighting, that they were underground. This passage, with its stout doors at regular intervals on both sides, all painted the same olive green, was much colder. The Mother Superior stopped at the end of the passage, the last door. She unlocked it. 'I'll leave you with her. She needs your help. I am so glad . . .'

'Thank you.'

'When shall I . . .?'

'In two hours.'

'Very well.' Another admiring, insinuating smile and she had departed. Jerry pushed the door open.

His sister Catherine looked up from her iron-framed bed. A little daylight entered the cell from a small window near the roof, a single exquisite ray, but she had been reading with the help of an electric lamp, its 40 watt bulb shielded by a shade of green glass. She looked much better than when he had last seen her. Her hair was pure blonde again and her skin was rosy. She was wearing her shift and she automatically reached for her white habit, hanging over the chair beside the bed, before she grinned and dropped her hand. She spread her arms wide. He closed the door and bolted it. He stood over her, grinning down, all his lost innocence momentarily restored.

'You don't half look sinister,' she said. 'What are you playing at today?'

'I'm the tortured priest, aren't I?' With a flourish he removed his shades.

'Did you come to add another sin or two to your conscience?'

He sat down beside her. He hugged her warm, yielding body. 'You've really improved.'

'I couldn't have had a nicer rest. You told them I had amnesia?'

'To save explanations. Anyway, I was right, in some

310

ways.' He bent away from her, studying her face. 'Not a bad resurrection job, though I say it myself.'

She frowned. 'I'm steering clear of hard drugs in the future. It's taught me a lesson. Nothing stronger than coke from now on.'

'I think you're wise.'

She stroked his hair. 'No. You're the wise one. What a lovely pink suit. Omniscient old Jerry.'

'Don't say that. You'll bring all my anxieties back.' He removed his jacket and threw it on top of her habit, leaning across the bed so that he was resting against the wall. 'I must say I envy you the peace and quiet.'

'You've never liked peace and quiet.'

'I envy it, all the same.' He stroked her right breast through the coarse linen of her shift. She seemed unusually disturbed. 'Is anything wrong?'

She held his hand against her breast. 'I was wondering why you sent that other bloke along to see me. He didn't look like one of your usual friends.'

'I didn't send another bloke.'

Her lovely shoulders slumped. 'The gaff's blown, then. Frank will know where I am now.'

'Blokes aren't normally allowed in at all. What did he look like? How did he get in?'

'Fat and oily. Purple shirt. Gaiters. Dog-collar. Definitely clerical gear. Plummy voice. Apparently he was surveying the place for some reason. He knew me. So I realized . . .'

'Beesley?'

'That's the name.'

'Sod.' Jerry sighed as he drew off his pink tweed trousers and folded them over the back of the chair. 'You're right, Cath. He's Frank's mate. The Bishop of North Kensington. Though how he managed to get to see you is still a mystery.'

'Pulled strings.' She removed her shift and handed it to him as he unbuttoned his waistocat. Absent-mindedly he held the shift in one hand and unstrapped his shoulder holster. He put everything in a bundle on the chair and began to remove his shirt and tie, then his socks and

311

underpants. He drew trim brows together. 'He's good at pulling strings.'

Jerry paused, hands on hips, trying to order his thoughts. Then he glanced up, noticing that her expression had changed to one of open astonishment. Her wide blue eyes stared at his lower torso.

'What's the matter?' he asked her.

'When on earth did you get yourself circumcised?'

In puzzlement he fingered his penis. Vaguely he shook his head, grinning. He shrugged, dismissing the problem as he squeezed in beside her. She switched off the light. The ray of sunshine, like the light from some new-found grail, fell upon their hands. He took her bottom in both his large hands. 'You're not the only one prone to amnesia, you know.'

2. Matra ubiquity with 2nd and 3rd generation missiles

The gate of the convent closed behind him and Jerry adjusted his eyes to the light, resuming his shades, making for his Duesenberg. As he had half-expected Frank was sitting in the back seat. 'Watcher, Jerry. Long time no see.' He grinned through the wound-down window, his drug-ravaged lips twisting in peculiar directions. 'Your education's certainly coming in useful, these days.'

Jerry sighed. He looked down at Frank. 'What are you doing here?'

'I was just passing, recognized the motor, thought I'd give you a surprise.'

'It's no surprise. I already know your mucker's been in the convent.'

'Oh, really? I haven't seen Dennis for ages.'

'Get out of my car,' said Jerry. 'You're coming to bits all over the upholstery. You used to be such a nice young man, too.'

'I'm a martyr to science, that's my trouble. I abandoned a lucrative profession in the property business in order to further my researches and thus become a slave to tempodex.' Frank's skin twitched all over. Then, as Jerry watched, he changed to the colour of grey flannel. Frank had always had a penchant towards respectability. 'I feel sick.'

Jerry opened the door and bundled his brother to the pavement.

Frank went to lean with one hand against the convent wall. 'Come on, Jerry. Blood's thicker than water.'

'Not in your case. There's no need for you to be out on the street. You've got a home to go to. Several.'

'I'm having an identity crisis. How's Catherine?'

'Much better.'

'Better? That's funny.' Frank pulled his cracked plastic

flying jacket around his shivering chest. His horrid head lifted like a pointer on the scent. His eyes glazed but seemed to fix on an invisible target. He began, stiff-legged, to walk in the general direction of Lancaster Road. 'Well, see you around, Jerry. Got to – um . . .'

Jerry sank into his car and watched Frank march like a zombie across Ladbroke Grove and into the Kensington Park Hotel. The KPH had not been used as a hotel for some years and was now merely a large pub. Surely Frank hadn't come down to scoring from dealers in public houses? Jerry felt that his family pride was under attack but he resisted the urge to follow. Probably the KPH was no more than one of Frank's bolt-holes. Doubtless it led somewhere else.

At this, Jerry became suspicious. He recalled a rumour he head heard from a fourteen-year-old biker speed freak who had given him a lift when his Phantom had been shot up by local vigilantes just outside Birmingham. According to the biker there was at least one ancient tunnel running under Ladbroke Grove from the Convent of the Poor Clares. The tunnel, the speed freak had told him, led into all sorts of other dimensions. It was a familiar rumour. A family legend hinted at something similar. Jerry had paid the story very little attention; he had been only too glad that a little romance was coming back into the lives of the younger generation. But now he recalled Bishop Beesley's excuse for visiting the convent. Something about a survey. Perhaps Beesley had had a double purpose for going there.

Jerry stepped out of the Duesenberg with the intention of ringing the bell of the convent but then changed his mind. He had already tipped off Catherine and there was not much else he could do until he found a new hideout for her, at least until her amnesia was completely cleared up.

He returned to the driving seat, started the car, reversed into Ladbroke Grove, drove as far as the KPH, stopped and got out. He entered the ill-lit pub. Frank was there, talking to a couple of undersized girls who, by the look of their skins and eyes, had been helping him in his experiments. Even as Jerry came in he saw Frank stoop and kiss one of the girls full on the mouth, seeming to suck the last of her substance from her. Now she was in pretty much the condition in which Frank had been a moment or two ago. She stumbled towards the door marked Toilets and disappeared. Frank wiped his mouth and grinned. 'Hello, Jerry. What are you having?' He put a seedy elbow on the damp bar and attracted the landlord. 'Sid!' Through the gloom came service.

'I thought you might want a lift,' said Jerry.

'I've just had one. Two pints, please, Sid,' said Frank. 'Could you manage to get these, Jerry?'

Jerry put a ten-pound note into the pool of alcohol on the greasy counter. 'You know I don't drink beer.'

'It's for Maureen.' Frank winked at the remaining grey girl. The beer arrived and Frank handed over his brother's money. 'You can have Barbara, if you like. When she comes back from the lavatory.'

'Well,' said Jerry. 'Don't you want a lift, then?'

'How far would you be going?'

'How far do you want to go?'

'Get you!' said Frank. 'France?'

'Don't be silly.'

'I was thinking of taking up residence in the old place. The Le Corbusier château. There's a lot of ideas I've got. Following in father's footsteps, following the dear old dad. There again I could open it to the public.

Jerry shuddered. 'It's not a real Le Corbusier château.'

Frank shrugged. 'There's no need to be so fucking literal-minded, Jerry.'

'I'll take you as far as Dover, if you like.'

Frank's eyes narrowed. Mucus semed to squeeze from the corners. Red irises shifted in decaying sockets. 'I wasn't thinking of leaving for a day or so.'

Jerry folded his arms. 'It's now or never.'

'You're right.' Frank looked vaguely around for a clock. 'It always bloody is.'

3. Acquire targets simply, reliably and accurately with inland direct-drive tracking and guidance servo elements

They had reached a compromise. Dropping his brother off at the Army and Navy Club near Waterloo Station, wondering when Frank would try to get hold of Catherine, Jerry drove back to his house in Holland Park Avenue. Frank would almost certainly act in the next couple of days: he ran in old grooves; he would want to take Catherine with him to France. Jerry couldn't blame him. The weather was perfect. There was, in fact, something remarkable about the whole season. He had never known the world so fresh. Jerry smacked his lips.

London was alive with flowers; gigantic hydrangeas and chrysanthemums, monstrous carnations, vast tulips and looming daffodils; sweet williams, peonies, cornflowers, snapdragons, hollyhocks, foxgloves; their scent hung like vapour in the beautiful air. And people were wearing such pretty clothes, listening to such jolly music; the first ecstatic flush of a culture about to swoon, at last, into magnificent decadence, an orgy of mutual understanding, kindness, tolerance and refusal to maim or kill. Jerry turned on the Duesenberg's stereo and got Jimi Hendrix singing *Waterfall*. He leaned back, a casual hand on the wheel. The Dubrovnik disease certainly had its compensations. It was all a matter of how you looked at things. As he entered Hyde Park he found other signs of the improving times as gangs of men and women in bright blue municipal uniforms dismantled the gallows on either side of the road. He reached towards the spring-clip on the dashboard and removed the half-full paper-cup, swallowing a snazzy fifth of Glen Nevis to unclog the jam of uppers and downers in his throat. For a moment he had an urge to turn back the way he had come and shoot a few pins in Emmett's but decided, after all, to go home. He had to do something about his head lice.

He had stashed the car at the side entrance of his fortress and had walked round the tall white walls and up the steps to the black front door before he saw a movement behind one of the pillars on his right. His head swam for his needler but dropped. He smiled instead. 'Afternoon, Mo.'

''Ullo, Mr C.' By way of apology Shakey Mo Collier shrugged in his filthy denim suit. His bright, kitten's eyes, greedy for violence, shifted, and his scrubby moustache and beard twitched like the whiskers of a rogue beast. 'Can I come in?'

Jerry put his hand against the print-plate and the door opened. He led the way to a wide, mosaic hall, turning off strobes and substituting limelight. Mo panted behind him muttering to himself. 'Oh, fuck. Oh, fuck.' He scuttled for a side door and entered Jerry's back parlour, a tangle of electronics and dirty, expensive upholstery. The room was dark, only a little light coming through the thickly curtained french windows. Mo crawled into the comfort of a huge mohair sofa, feeling down its sides for something to sustain him, slipping pills and capsules at random into his mouth. 'What's it all about, I ask myself.' Quickly he achieved a philosophical equilibrium. 'Eh, Mr C?'

Jerry pulled the curtains back a fraction. 'You don't mind?' Light sidled into the room

Mo nodded. 'I came with a message, actually. Shades is on the dole and wondered if you had any ideas.'

'I though he was in the States.'

'Things have dried up there, as well. You know how fashions change. Last year it was all assassinations, this year it's all sex scandals and religion. Could we have a little music?'

Jerry fiddled with an already glowing console. Faintly Zoot Money's band gave them *Big Time Operator*.

'That'll do,' said Mo. 'It doesn't need to be loud. Just there. Anyway, Shades thought you might be looking around.'

Jerry smiled. 'You have to, don't you, with Shades. Tell him I'll probably be in touch.'

Mo nodded. 'He says all he needs is a pair of kings.'

'It's good news for everyone else.' Absently Jerry toyed with a decaying packet of Chocolate Olivers. 'Though his interpretations are all his own.'

'And I saw Mr Smiles. He says to get in touch sometime. It's about what Simons and Harvey are after, he says.'

Jerry shrugged. 'All that's in the past.' He glanced through an electron microscope. 'Or maybe the future.'

Mo had lost interest in the conversation. He began to move slowly about the room, experimentally fingering any loose wires he discovered. 'Oh, and I saw your mum in the pub. When was it? Tuesday?'

'Did you tell her I was back?'

'What do you think? But she's heard you was living around here. She was more interested in knowing where Cathy was.'

Jerry smiled at this. 'They always were close.'

'She said Frank was doing very well for himself but was looking a bit tired. What is he doing with himself, these days, anyway?'

'Services,' said Jerry. 'Power and communications.'

'Only I heard he was dealing.'

'It's the same thing, isn't it?'

'Everything is . . .' Mo returned to the sofa and curled up. He went to sleep. Jerry pulled a huge silver metallic sheet over him to retain what heat was left in his body and headed for the kitchen. He searched amongst the collection of Coronation biscuit barrels and jugs and cottage-shaped tea-pots until he found the half-full bottle of Prioderm. He climbed the stained white carpet of the curving staircase and went into the bathroom, glad to find that the hot water was working in the shower. He stripped naked and, bottle in hand, stepped into the stall.

Soon his head was engulfed in hellfire.

4. Introducing a new dimension of realism in visual simulators, Vital III

Jerry rarely visited his father's fake Le Corbusier château and this was probably the first time he had used the front entrance, but he was in unusually high spirits as he eased his Phantom V up the weed-grown drive and depressed the horn button to let his father's faithful retainer know he had arrived. Beyond the broken outline of the house was the grey Normandy sea. Rain was coming in from England and with it waves of inspirational music interspersed with the babbling voices of that crazed brotherhood of the coast, the pirate deejays. Jerry stepped out of the car and took a deep breath of the cold, moody air. His father – or the man who claimed to be his father – had died without leaving a will, so Frank (who was convinced that he was both the only legitimate and the true spiritual successor to the old man) had claimed the house and its contents as his inheritance; but John Gnatbeelson swore the dying scientist had bequeathed his roof and its secrets to his namesake Jeremiah (there was even a rumour that old Cornelius had changed his name to Jeremiah soon after his son's birth). The matter had been settled, in Jerry's view, by his letting Frank use the place whenever he wanted to. In spite of the complications, Jerry had been glad that his father had died. It removed an uncomfortable ambiguity. Jerry hated keeping things from his mother.

Before he could put his palm against the print-plate the grey steel door moved upwards and John Gnatbeelson, in tattered Norfolk jacket, grey moleskin britches and scarlet carpet slippers, greeted him awkwardly. He was thin, his cancerous skin given a semblance of life by the many broken blood-vessels spreading purple and red beneath it. His chin sprouted a few long, grey wisps of hair, perhaps the remains of a beard, and his cheek-bones were set so low as to give his head an oddly unbalanced look. A stooping six-foot-four, he looked fondly down on his young master who strode into the dark interior. Originally the house had possessed enormous windows, but these were now shielded with steel-plate. As old Cornelius's suspicion of the outside world had increased he had introduced more and more modifications of this sort.

'Have you come to stay, sir?' Gnatbeelson whispered habitually. His former employer had hated the sound of the human voice and had communicated almost entirely by a variety of mechanical means, never leaving his heavily guarded laboratories. Neither Jerry, Catherine or Frank had ever met their father personally, though they had all lived here from time to time. The house trembled with profound and unusual memories; it stank of the experiences of a hundred lifetimes, centuries of technomania tinged with the desperate eroticism of those who cast desperately about for their lost humanity and found only flesh.

'Just a flying visit,' Jerry said. 'I'd have phoned, but you've been cut off.'

'The bill seemed unreasonable, sir. It was all Mr Frank's reverse charge calls. I did write to you . . .'

'As long as the generators are working.'

'I tested them last week. They're just fine.'

'I want you to activate the defences as soon as possible,' Jerry told him. He walked rapidly through haunted galleries, Gnatbeelson, his limbs moving irregularly, lolloping in his wake. 'Particularly those towers.'

'The hypnomats, sir?'

'Set every one at go.'

'Are you expecting trouble, Mr Cornelius?'

'From Mr Frank. He's on his way. I don't know what he's up to, but I know it involves this place. He mustn't get in.'

'I thought you didn't mind, sir.'

'I don't normally.'

'Is anything up, sir? Some sort of situation?'

'It's all instinctive. I couldn't really pin it down.'

'I've been reading about it in the book, sir. The millennium and so on.'

Jerry stopped as the corridor opened on to another gallery. He looked down through filthy light at the scattered shells of computers, the innards spread at random over the large black and white tiles of the floor. 'That wasn't here last time.' He put his hand on the balustrade, close to a fragment of canvas on which had been painted a patchwork of red, yellow and blue diamond shapes, faintly bloodstained. His foot struck a gilt frame on the floor. 'The sod's eaten it!' He was shocked. 'Watteau!'

'What ho, sir . . .' Gnatbeelson's face sagged a litle lower. 'Mr Frank was looking for something, I think. He kept sucking at those vacuum tubes in the corner. He said the marrow was good for his piles. He's not himself, sir.'

'Then who is?' Jerry put the scrap of canvas into his pocket and continued his inspection of the house.

'I'm glad you've decided on a firm line at last, sir.' Gnatbeelson's legs bent and straightened, bent and straightened. 'I took the liberty of saving one of those books you gave me to put in the furnace. *The Million Spears and the Coming Corruption.* Do you think – ?'

'It's lies. It's your moral duty to burn it.'

'Then of course I shall, sir. But are you sure this isn't to do with that?' It's all a question of how you look at it. What about the reactor?' Jerry peered over the rail of another gallery. Below was a swimming pool, the water stagnant, filled with every kind of rubbish. Something living seemed to move just below the surface. 'I've changed my mind. Things are settling down. They've never been better.'

'Then why are you so anxious?' The whisper came from miles away but when Jerry turned Gnatbeelson was at his shoulder.

'Because I want to maintain the balance. I've a right to take a few precautions.' Jerry was defensive. 'What's wrong with that?' He peered down at the far wall. Written in a substance resembling, in colour, the ichor of spent batteries, were the words:

Encore un de mes pierrots mort;
Morte d'un chronique orphelinisme;
C'était un coeur plein de dandyisme
Lunaire, en un drôle de corps.

Jerry became sentimental. 'How we loved to luxuriate in terror.' There had been good times here, when the three of them had spent their holidays, at play amongst their father's discarded inventions, stretched upon heaps of confused circuits, with a bag of apples and a Wodehouse or a Sade. Simpler, if not sunnier, days.

'I'm in full agreement with you, sir.' The old retainer's voice seemed closer now, almost normal. 'But why have you rejected all those books out of hand?'

Desperately Jerry rounded on Gnatbeelson, displaying glowing eyes. 'Can't you see? It's my last bloody chance to achieve a linear mode!'

5. Need actuators that won't freeze, burn, dry out, or boil?

It might be 196 – , thought Jerry, but the countryside beyond Dover had returned with incredible speed to its mediaeval state. Kent was wild and beautiful again; so lush that few would have guessed it had sustained and recovered from a major nuclear bombardment during the 'Proof of Good Faith' contests between the major powers. There were disadvantages: poor roads and slow progress; but his car wasn't badly affected, even when it was forced to inch through bramble thickets or cross small patches of ploughed land where angry peasants occasionally appeared, to pelt him with pieces of rock or crude spears. The people of Kent, happy at last in their proper primitive state, were much more at one with themselves.

A fairly unspoiled stretch of road took him close to the remains of Canterbury where skin-clad monks had erected a timber reproduction of the Cathedral, almost the same size as the original. The unseasoned scaffolding still surrounded it and more monks were at work with what was probably liquified chalk, painting the exterior in an effort to make it resemble stone. Elsewhere a project to restore the shopping precinct was in hand; soon Canterbury in facsimile would flourish again: triumph of Man's optimism, of his faith in the future. Jerry hooted his horn and waved, turning up the stereo, to give them a friendly blast of *Got To Get Into My Life*, pursing his lips regretfully as one of the monks lost his footing on the scaffold and fell fifty feet to the ground.

Soon he was nearing London. In the evening light the city was phosphorescent, like a neon wound; it glowed beneath a great scarlet sun turning the clouds orange and purple. And Jerry was filled with a sudden deep love for his noble birth-place, the City of the Apocalypse, this Earthly Paradise, the oldest and greatest city of its Age, virgin and whore, mother, sister, mistress, sustainer of life, creator of nightmare, destroyer of dreams, harbourer of twenty milion chosen souls. Abruptly he left the middle ages and entered the future, the great grey road, a mile wide at this point, gradually narrowing to its apex at Piccadilly Circus. Now, as night drenched the tall buildings and their lights burst into shivering life, he could again relax in his natural environment.

Against all the available evidence he was betting everything on simple cyclic time, on cause and effect, on karma. He passed through the first toll-check; now the road was covered; its perspex roof reflected the myriad colours of the headlamps below. He took the first exit up to the fast tier and joined the hundred and seventy mph stream; within a minute or two he was leaving it again, spiralling down the Notting Hill exit and making for home through the crowded park. The booths and tents of the nightly fair were only, he noticed, doing moderate business. At his favourite roadside fish and chip bar he stopped and paid four pounds for a piece of warm carp and some fried reconstituted mash potato. It had been days since he'd had any real food. He wasn't looking after himself properly. There were too many fresh shadows. He enjoyed the meal, eating it off the passenger seat as he drove, but felt sick afterwards and had to munch a couple of Milky Way bars to make himself better. He was already improving by the time he drove through the back gates of his house and garaged the Phantom beside the Duesenberg.

He went into the house and found his old black car coat, his black flared trousers, his high-heeled boots, his white linen and, as he dressed, he became depressed. It was probably association, he thought. Dark clothes often brought him down. He turned away from the wardrobe, seeking a stereo, and at last found a deck and amplifier where he must have shoved them under an old-fashioned bentwood and china washstand. He switched the kit on. From the ceiling came the miserable, neurotic drone of the Everly Brothers. He let it play, deepening his mood. If a mood was worth having, he thought, it was worth having profoundly.

He went downstairs and turned up some mail which must have come with one of the last runners to get through. There was a letter from Mr Harvey, one of Frank's wholesalers, saying that he had some information which might be useful to Jerry and Mr Smiles, Jerry's sometime business partner. Although he had made at least a million in the last job he was disinclined to work with Mr Smiles again. Smiles usually claimed to have a 'purpose' to his ventures and thus tended to confuse Jerry. He crumpled the letter, wondering why Harvey should wish to double-cross Frank, an excellent customer for any new chemical to come in.

Jerry began to worry about Catherine again. She was his ideal, his goddess, his queen; he loved her and she represented everything else he loved, no matter how she changed, whereas Frank represented everything Jerry hated: greedy hypocrisy. If Frank got hold of Catherine again Jerry knew that he would have to risk repercussions and kill his brother. It would be a shame, since events were just beginning to stablise into a fixed pattern, like a clockwork train on its little oval track. After a while one got to know the dodgy bits of line. Any deaths at this stage would produce a whole new train set, with all kinds of bends and twists, moebius strips and dead ends: exactly what he was hoping to escape. He gave in to his instincts' demands. He must check to see if Catherine were all right, no matter how irrational the impulse was.

He left the house, taking the Duesenberg to Westbourne Park Road and stopping outside the convent. There was no other traffic. The walls of the convent seemed higher than usual in the darkness.

Against every desire his mind had filled up with prescience, with a knowledge of the futures he refused to accept.

With a groan he went straight over the wall, using the hooked nylon ladder from the back of the car. He dropped amongst runner-bean poles, scraping his shin, trod as lightly as possible through the flower-beds and vegetable patches, crossed the garden, hit his shoulder on the corner of the potting shed, and arrived at the main door. There was some sluggish movement from within, but not much. He got the door open and went inside; raced on tip-toe through the corridors until he came to the top of the flight of stairs leading underground. So far he had not been spotted by a single nun. He went down the stairs and reached the cold corridor. There were stirrings, now, behind many of the doors; they were conclusive. As he approached, lights went off one by one in the cells until only the light in Catherine's cell remained. Her door was open. He looked in on a discarded habit, an unmade bed, an empty lipstick case, an unread paperback with the cover reproducing an Adolphe Willette poster, the smell of Guerlain Mitsouko. He was too late. Frank had struck already. He would have reached the fake Le Corbusier château just after Jerry left. There would have been no time for John Gnatbeelson to activate the defences. Sister and house were now Frank's.

Jerry howled. His eyes blazed red in the gloom of the convent cell. His lips snarled back from wolfish teeth. An era had ended for him and he was never to know such innocence again.

Rebellion or insurrection, on the other hand, being guided by instinct rather than reason, being passionate and spontaneous rather than cool and calculated, do act like shock therapy on the body of society, and there is a chance that they may change the chemical composition of the societal crystal. In other words they may change human nature, in the sense of creating a new morality, or new metaphysical values.

Herbert Read, *Revolution and Reason*

It is essential to take the greatest pains to rouse the might of the German people by increasing its confidence in its own strength and thus also bringing a stability into the minds of our people to assist their appreciation of political problems. I have often, and I have to add this in speaking to you, felt doubts on one single matter, and that is the following: if I look at the intellectual elements of our society, I think what a pity, unfortunately they are needed; otherwise, one day one might, well, I don't know, exterminate them or something like that. But unfortunately one needs them. If now I take a good look at these intellectual elements and imagine, and check, their behaviour towards me, and towards our work, I feel almost afraid.

Adolf Hitler, private speech to German Press, Munich, 10 November 1938 (day after Kristellnacht).

S.A.B. Zeman, *Nazi Propaganda*

6. In the beginning was the flight – today it's security and security means chiefly electronics

Jerry clambered out of his stockings and suspenders and threw them on top of his Courreges suit. All he had left now was his perm; he wondered why he had ever thought red hair would suit him. He needed a complete change of identity. He searched through the heaps of clothes he had brought with him to the deserted convent but could find nothing he wanted to wear. He walked the length of the cool guest room, with its hard beds and green radiators, to the pine writing table where he had placed his little Sony cassette player. He pressed the play button. Slow, heavy sounds crept from the speaker; the batteries were exhausted.

He switched off. For a second he thought he had heard footsteps in the passage outside, but it was unlikely that anyone could have traced him here now that London was almost entirely depopulated. The exodus had been a huge success. He touched his forehead, glad to find that his temperature was dropping at last. Whistling, he stirred a skirt with his toe just as the door opened and Miss Brunner came in.

She glanced disapprovingly around at the mess. She wore some kind of standard Slavic peasant costume and had an MG42 tucked under her muscular right arm. Crossing to one of the beds she lowered the heavy machine gun onto the grey blanket which was as neat and clean as the last occupant had left it.

'There's evidently been some confusion,' she said. She sat down beside her gun and began to stroke its stock. 'What on earth are you doing?'

'I'd heard you were dead – or, at least, transferred.' He picked up the nearest pair of underpants – Daglo yellow – and put them on.

'You more than anyone should know about temporal

shifts, Mr Cornelius. Everything's well and truly up the spout.' She drew in a sour breath. 'I thought I had you under control this time. There's a rumour about your black box, that you've got it back. If that's true you haven't really used it to your advantage, have you, eh?'

'I've been resting.' He began to sulk. He found two orange socks that almost matched. He sat opposite her and pulled them on to his grubby feet. 'Anyway, if we're accusatory, what happened to you? I thought we were going to be together always.'

'It's your sentimentality I can't stand.' She rose like a disturbed wasp, leaving her gun where it was. 'It's your main drawback. You could have been a brilliant physicist. If you'd only had a better grip on the scientific method.'

'My black box . . .'

'Your father's invention, and you know it. You developed it, certainly, but to ends that were completely irresponsible. Think how much better things could be if you hadn't started experimenting for your own amusement rather than for the good of the world.'

'People get what they want out of my box.'

'What they think they want. And its power source is ludicrous. Utterly wasteful.'

'It's not much different to yours.'

She clicked her tongue.

'What they think they want is usually what they do want,' he added. 'Is there anything wrong – ?'

'God almightly, you don't know what morality is, do you?'

'I tried to find out. I became a Jesuit . . .'

She turned over his clothing with her pointed foot. 'Is this junk all yours?'

'You can have it, if you like.'

'What would I do with it? You've no ambitions, have you, Mr Cornelius? No sense of purpose? No ideals?'

'Since Catherine was killed . . .'

'I don't think necrophilia counts as an ideal.'

'Standards change.' Jerry was miserable. 'And we're proof

enough of that, aren't we? After all, we didn't need to become divided . . .'

'We've discussed that already. The scheme didn't work out. Too many regressive genes – put us straight back to square one.'

He shrugged and stooped to pick up a black T-shirt.

'Everything's fluxed up, thanks to you,' she said. 'I had this perfect programme all plotted and ready to go, then suddenly the co-ordinates are haywire. I didn't need to make too many enquires to find out where the interference was coming from. I had to abandon the whole programme because you were playing games with your silly little box.'

'Well, you needn't worry. I haven't got it any more.'

'It's too bloody late now, isn't it! Where is it?'

'I lost it. Or lent it.'

'You're lying.'

'I had a touch of my old trouble. Didn't you have it, recently? Paramnesia? Paramnesia?'

'That wouldn't – '

'Then it developed into ordinary amnesia. I'm not even sure how I got here. There was a party at Holland Park . . .'

'I don't know what you're talking about,' she said.

'Then maybe it hasn't happened to you yet,' he told her reasonably. He paused to think. 'Or maybe it hasn't happened to any of us yet. Maybe it won't happen, after all.'

'Oh, you shifty little sod.'

'That's another thing I was wondering about . . .'

'I came here to try to clear up the confusion.' She found a wallet and began to search through it, emptying company credits and luncheon vouchers on to the floor. She turned a fifty million mark silk banknote in her fingers and absently touched it to her lips, licking it. 'Why did you choose this mausoleum, anyway?'

'I forget.'

'You usually stay with your mother in a crisis.' She picked up another wallet. It contained nothing but a bundle of over-stamped Rhodesian guinea-notes.

'Is she around?'

'Apparently.'

'I'm tired.' He reached for her gun.

'Steady on, Mr Cornelius.' She became alarmed.

'I only wanted to look at it. I've hardly ever seen one. Are they still making them?'

'How should I know?' She shook out the pockets of a black velvet jacket and began carefully to inspect each worn piece of paper. 'Where are your weapons, by the way?'

'In store somewhere.' He was vague. 'Do you want to look at them?'

'Certainly not.' She had discovered a huge perfectly cut diamond and was holding it up to the green-shaded light bulb. 'This is real.' She inspected the facets, one by one. 'Where did you get it?'

'It's only a model.' He put his legs into a pair of purple bells.

7. Optics for defence

Grass and moss were growing over the paving stones of Westbourne Park Road. Jerry saw Miss Brunner to the gate and took in the scenes of soft decline, much more congruent, at last, with the rural atmosphere of the convent's garden. Even the air was relatively fresh. 'It's lovely now, isn't it?' He watched her walk to her Austin Princess. 'It smells so rich.'

'Stagnation's no substitute for stability.' She wrenched open the car's door. 'I hope you're pleased with yourself.' From behind the façade of deserted houses on the opposite side of the street a few small dogs barked. 'It's going to take England a long time to get back on her feet. And as for the rest of the world ...' She entered the car. He saw her through the clouded glass as, aggressively, she put the engine into gear. For someone who had so much to do with machines she displayed a stern hatred for most of them. He waved as she swerved into Ladbroke Grove, still puzzled as to why she had taken the laundry box with her; it had been full of his old junk – a broken watch, tickets, empty matchbooks, old calendars, torn note-books, catalogues, useless maps, out-of-date maintenance manuals; all had gone into her box. Perhaps she thought she could feed the information into a new computer and thus reproduce his lost memory. He was quite grateful to her; there was nothing, he felt, of his past he wished to retain. He had been glad to offer her his clothes and tapes, but she had declined most of them with the air of someone who had already researched them thoroughly. Deciding against returning to his room, he locked the gate behind him and walked round to Blenheim Crescent, peering up at his mother's flat as he passed but making no effort to see if she was still there. He was sure that Mrs Cornelius, of all people, wouldn't have moved. He turned left at the antique shop with its smashed windows, its contents on the pavement, where Sammy, his mother's lover, had once sold pies, into Kensington Park Road. Assegais, brass microscopes, elephants' feet, bits of sixteenth-century armour, the innards of clocks, broken writing chests, Afridi rifles inset with copper and mother-of-pearl, their stocks crumpled by woodworn, rotting books and fading photographs lay in heaps all across the street, exuding a sweet, musty smell that was not unpleasant. He entered Elgin Crescent, going towards Portobello Road, and found a shop that had once specialized in theatrical costumes and musical instruments. The door was ajar and the bell rang as he entered. Most of the costumes were still intact, in boxes or on hangers depending on racks from both sides of the showroom. He tried on the full dress uniform of a captain in the 30th Deccan Horse, discarded it. He dressed himself as Zorro, as Robin Hood, as Sam Spade. He tried the Buffalo Bill outfit and felt a little more at ease in it; he forced himself into a lurex Flash Gordon, a Sherlock Holmes deerstalker and ulster, a Zenith the Albino dress suit, a Doctor Nikola set, a Captain Marvel costume, even a Tarzan loincloth; a suit of motley, a Jester, seemed better, but he was seeking security at present, so he also discarded the Harlequin trickster set, but eventually decided upon an elaborate black and white satin pierrot suit, the main colour being black, the pom-poms, ruff and cuffs being white, the skull-cap being white also, a reverse of the usual arrangement. He was pleased with his appearance. He found a pure white wig, perhaps originally for an old lady character, and put this on under his skull-cap. As an afterthought he picked up some greasepaint and blacked his face and hands then, for an hour, he sat in front of the long mirror playing a Walker five-string banjo to himself, raising his spirits still further: *On the road to Mandalay-ee, Where the flying fishes play-ee* . . . It was all so much more comfortable than the stockings, suspenders and girdle of his earlier disguise, so much more tasteful than the bright colours of vanished youth. Indeed, it was the nicest of any of the disguises he

334

had assumed since his boyhood. Nobody made any demands on a pierrot. All in all things weren't looking too bad, really.

'Hide your tears behind a smile.' He said blithely as he searched through the wicker baskets. 'Hide your fears inside a file.' He found two or three more pierrot costumes, two harlequins, a columbine and some masks, and bundled them all into a hessian sack.

He had decided, once his new equipment was installed, to open up the convent as a kind of health-farm. Sooner or later London would come back to a version, at least, of its old self, and this time he would be ready for it.

He paused once more beside the mirror. 'I could be happy with you,' he said, 'if you could be happy with me.' He gave himself a big kiss and left a smear of make-up on the glass.

8. The BL 755 cluster bomb is highly effective against tanks and other armoured vehicles, aircraft, transport, patrol boats, and personnel

The convent was coming along a treat. Jerry had signed a formal lease for the place and had been lucky enough to secure the services of some ex-nuns. He had left the outside pretty much as it had always looked, but the buildings inside had been thoroughly restructured. Now wide picture windows looked out into old English gardens where pious and apple-cheeked Poor Clares worked with hoe and rake as they had worked since time immemorial. Jerry expected his first customers soon. So far his only client had been his financial backer, his sister's friend Constantin Koutrouboussis, the Greek millionaire who had inherited the family business on the death of his older brother Dimitri. Koutrouboussis was rarely satisfied with anything but miracles and Jerry hadn't been in business long enough to gain experience enough to provide them. But when the Americans started arriving things should look up.

Koutrouboussis stopped off one day, on his way through to his Soho headquarters. He was carrying a new line in riding crops and was keen to show one to Jerry. 'Look at that!' He swished it through the beam of dusty sunlight which entered Jerry's spacious office by way of the half-closed blind. 'The secret's in the weight of the handle.'

Jerry was searching white plastic drawers in his desk. Of late he had affected a great deal of white. He wore a surgeon's smock at this moment, and a chef's hat. It contrasted nicely with his freshly stained skin. 'What?'

'The handle.' Koutrouboussis put the crop back in his case. 'How's your sister keeping, by the way?'

'Oh, all right. I checked this morning.'

'Are you sure – ?'

'There are no certainties in this business, Mr K.'

'I suppose there aren't. A science in its infancy.'

'It'll stay that way, if I have anything to do with it,' Jerry promised. 'Adult science doesn't seem to produce a satisfactory variety of results.'

Mr Koutrouboussis fingered his new beard. His hands wandered down to his expensive collar, his neat lapels, his dapper buttons. 'You won't tell the clients that?' He moved towards the wall and stared at the tastefully framed French prints showing characters from the Commedia dell'arte.

'There aren't any clients for our kind of science. You're too much of a cynic for this sort of clinic . . .' Jerry stopped himself quickly and inspected his watches. 'A drink? I've a wide selection of Scotches . . .' He gave up.

'No time.'

Jery wondered why Koutrouboussis always made him feel aggressive. Maybe it was the tension the man carried with him; it could even be that Jerry resented his financial involvement, his power.

Mr Koutrouboussis reached the door and lifted his gloved hand in a moody wave. 'No time.'

'I'll be seeing you,' said Jerry.

Koutrouboussis chuckled to himself. 'At this rate you'll be raising me, too. Cheerio for now, Mr Cornelius.' As an afterthought he said from the passage: 'And if you should discover the identity . . .'

'I'll let you know.'

'I would be grateful.'

Jerry put his elbows on his desk and rubbed at his face. One thing was certain: he was under an obligation and it was making him uncomfortable. Then he consoled himself with the knowledge that Koutrouboussis was no idealist. His interest in the whole affair was connected with Catherine alone and justified by a profit motive. If Jerry was going to make his clinic in any way successful he would have to forget both his sister and her admirer for a while. He was sure he was on the right track this time around. He had found hope again. If these new machines couldn't beat the human condition then nothing could.

A tasty young nun knocked and entered. 'You're looking tired, sir. You've so much on your shoulders.'

He straightened his back. Automatically he checked his lapels for nits. 'Lice,' he murmured, to explain.

'The world is full of them, sir. But the truth shines through.'

He glanced at her faithful face. 'The trouble is,' he said, 'that we're at least a hundred and fifty years old. How many generations need to comply in a fallacy before it becomes accepted as truth?'

She was untroubled. 'Can I bring you a nice cup of tea, doctor?'

'It would certainly help.'

'Your machines . . .'

'They're not oracles, you know. They just get rid of the demand for oracles. Abolish the future and you lose the need for faith. Familiarity, by and large, banishes fear . . .' He clutched, again, at his head. 'I wish I knew how the damned things worked.'

'I was going to say. They're moaning again.'

'They haven't got enough to do.'

'Soon,' she reassured him.

'The whole idea is that we should do away with "Tomorrow" . . .'

'I'll make the tea immediately.' The door closed on her whispering gown.

He got up and drew the blind so that he could see into the quiet garden. 'Heritage. Inheritance. The secret's in the genes. Chromosomes. Chronos zones. It always comes down to those fucking flat worms.' He really needed a chemist at that moment, but he was buggered if he was going to bring his brother back. Frank would have a vested interest in the status quo; his whole identity depended on its preservation. The same could be said for Miss Brunner and the rest. He couldn't blame them. They thought they were fighting for their lives.

The phone began to ring.

He uttered a disbelieving laugh.

9. The Strim antitank rocket launcher is light (4.5Kg), accurate (very high single shot hit and kill probability), easy to use, low-cost instruction — no maintenance, no overhaul . . . complementary rockets, smoke/incendiary, 1,000 meters, illumination, 100 to 2,000 meters, antipersonnel, up to 2,000 meters

With only a few reservations Jerry watched the new arrivals as they were herded from the big white bus through the narrow gates of the convent. There were only three men; all the others were women under thirty — or, at least, they resembled women. Some of the patients, he gathered, had already made a few faltering steps towards a crude form of self-inflicted transmogrification, some of it involving quite terrifying surgery.

He had decided not to present himself to his patients until the evening, during the Welcome Ceremony (which would be held in the ballroom, once the twin chapels) since, at this stage, he would be bound to make them feel self-conscious. Even as the white bus disappeared into the new underground garage a black Mercedes two-tonner took its place, unloading amplifiers and instruments, music for the ball. He stepped back from his window. As the population increased, so, in direct proportion, would his clients. He went over to his new console, turning the master switch to make every television monitor screen work at once, showing a clinic now satisfyingly busy. He was particularly pleased with the way in which the nuns had adapted to their new nursing work. He looked for a moment at the reception desk where guests were cautiously signing their names (most fictitious) in the gold-embossed green leather register. Their faces, haunted by hope and anxiety, were familiar to him. For many of them the treatment, even if partially successful, could not come too soon.

The thing he was looking forward to, however, was the ball. It had been a long while since The Deep Fix had played together. As soon as he could he would go down for the sound check. It would be good if he could get some rehearsing in before the event.

His eye was drawn back to the screen. He was sure he had seen the old military-looking character quite recently. He recognized the frayed cuffs. 'We are all offered a selection of traditional roles,' he murmured. 'The real problem lies in finding a different play. In the meantime we attempt to console as many of the actors as possible by finding them the parts in which they can be as happy as possible.' His voice was carried over the PA to all parts of the building, interrupting the Muzak.

'You're becoming a regular telly freak, ain't ya, Mr C.'

Shakey Mo Collier now stood there, arms folded, most of his weight on one leg. He was wearing a yellow and red paisley shirt, a light suede waistcoat, filthy with the remains of a thousand fruitful meals, a tattered green and blue Indian silk scarf, patched and faded jeans and scuffed cowboy boots with white decoration. His hair was longer than when Jerry had last seen it and he had grown a Mandarin moustache. Jerry was pleased to see him. 'Where have you been, Mo? The first I heard you were around was when someone brought me your postcard.'

'I've been asleep, haven't I?' said Mo. 'Up in the Lake District mostly. It's nice up there. Good roads. Plenty of shale. All dead. Lovely. You want to go.'

'I know it. Grasmere. Daffodils and dope. Or that's the way it used to be.'

Mo was unusually astute. 'That scene's shifted, hadn't you heard? To Rydal. But the best days are over.'

'Well, a word's not worth much these days. I heard the town had gone all chintzy.'

'Quincy?'

'Chintzy.'

340

They giggled together. Mo sat down on the posh carpet, cross-legged, and began to roll himself a joint. 'Anyway you seem to be doing all right with this lot.'

'I can't complain. There's no profit in it, though.'

'Aren't they paying?'

'All the takings go to my sleeping partner, Mr Koutrouboussis.'

'Well, well.' Mo licked his papers. 'So, really, you could leave here any time you liked?'

'I've got responsibilites, Mo.'

Mo looked at him in some disappointment. 'Blimey!'

'How long has the group been back together?'

'Not long. We all met up in Ambleside. Tried out a few things – acoustically, of course. You can get some of those old reed organs to sound just like electronics if you work at it. But we need power, so we trucked back to London, hoping we'd find some. Of course we hadn't realized everything was coming alive again. We picked just the right time, for once. We must be the only beat group around. We're getting a lot of work. Too much, really. The tensions . . .'

'It's done your ego a lot of good,' said Jerry. 'You're your old cocky self again.'

'Thanks. I feel cocky. Yes.' His grease-stained fingers explored a waistcoat pocket for a match. He lit his joint. 'I just wish they'd bring back the money system. All this fucking bartering's getting beyond a joke. Half our wages rot before we can eat them and we can't trade them because nobody's got the kind of stuff we need.'

'I don't know what you want.'

'Cheap tat, of course. And weapons. Just like the old days. Colour tellies. But don't worry. This gig's free.'

'We've got a few new drugs.'

'Nar,' said Mo. 'We're not into drugs any more. Well, not at the moment, anyway. We're into beer.'

'You don't mind me . . .?'

'Smashing. It'll be like the Friendly Bum days. You remember?'

'My memory isn't what it was.'

'It's a fucking opium den now. For the tourists.'

'I've been staying away from the centre. My work . . .'

'Oh, sure.' Mo was suddenly embarrassed. Hesitantly he offered Jerry the joint.

Jerry enjoyed a drag. He went to sit on the ledge of the open window, looking towards Blenheim Crescent then up into the sharp blue sky. 'I think we should see an improvement, soon. It's a bit early, though.' He cocked an ear to the East, detecting a whine. He smiled. 'They're here, at last.'

Mo joined him at the window as the first black wave of Starlifters shrieked in at minimum altitude, banking slowly until they had located Heathrow.

'Far out!' said Mo in delight, as soon as his voice could be heard. 'Those jobs carry over a hundred and fifty troops apiece. There are thousands coming in. Oh, it's all going to liven up! The Yanks are back!'

Jerry moved to the intercom. He must warn his staff to be ready for the extra volume.

10. Rapier, ultra low-level air defence system in service with the British Army and RAF Regiment, ordered by the Imperial Iranian Government, lightweight, direct-hitting missile, high kill-to-engagement ratio, optional 'add-on' blindfire unit, outstanding cost-effectiveness

Jerry rubbed more of the dye into his skin, regretting once again that his machines simply weren't up to handling his own problem. It was high time that they were overhauled, anyway, since the convent had been placed off-limits to all advisory forces: though it had only been civilian auxiliaries who had been coming in the first place; patronizing the clinic now counted, on General Cumberland's orders, as fraternization with hostile personnel.

Jerry couldn't complain. It meant he could expand his own activities if he wished. In the meantime the money-system had been re-introduced, Koutrouboussis had been paid back and was receiving an excellent dividend; Jerry was no longer beholden to the Greek who had, on his own initiative, formed a consortium together with his younger brother Spiro, to exploit the Cornelius patents world-wide, offering Jerry a flat commission on every client, including those who wished to change nationalities as part of their transmogrification. Jerry intended to take more of an interest in this international aspect of the enterprise now that the original clinic was running so well. Spiro, by mutual consent, would act as chief liaison man.

When he had finished with his face he picked up a tangled sheaf of traumograph printouts, leaving black smudges on the semi-opaque paper, and crammed them into one of his desk drawers. He was wearing a white German suit, black shirt and no tie, as part of his current disguise. His hair was bleached bone white. For the moment, too, he had discarded his needle-gun and wore the more comfortable vibragun which, he felt, was a trifle better in tune with the zeitgeist. Currently, he felt, the world could accept any ambiguities so long as he retained a certain dramatic resolution to events.

He left the office and strolled through his pale blue corridors, amiably greeting his nuns, nurses and doctors as he passed them. Most of them had already made preparations to leave for the country; only a skeleton staff was to be retained in London.

His Phantom VI was already at the gate, its motor running. He stepped into the driving seat and drove up Westbourne Park Road, turned right into Kensington Park Road, heading for Notting Hill and beyond.

He arrived in Church Street just in time to see a silver Cadillac disappearing into Holland Street. The area was otherwise deserted of cars, although a few M-75 armoured personnel carriers were parked here and there, their crews lazily giving his Phantom the once-over as it went by. He turned into Kensington High Street and parked outside Derry and Toms which he had acquired only recently in the deal granting Koutrouboussis full control of European exploitation rights of his father's original patents. Jerry disembarked and entered.

Within, the department store was hushed as usual: middle-aged women moved slowly from counter to counter; murmuring assistants in dove-grey uniforms addressed them respectfully. When re-opening the store Jerry had made it clear to his staff that only a certain sort of customer was to be encouraged. He had always been very strong on tradition.

He took the lift to the sunny tranquillity of the roof-garden and crossed a few feet of crazy-paving to enter the restaurant whose wall, facing the gardens, was completely of glass. He was keeping an illicit rendezvous with Captain Hargreaves. He sat at his usual table, completely alone, for the restaurant had not begun to serve lunch, watching the pink flamingos wading about in the tiny rivers and fountains, listening to the whistlings and chirrupings of the less flamboyant birds in the foliage.

Any intimations of trouble which he might have had during his drive here were now dispersed. He relaxed and looked over his shoulder to see Captain Hargreaves, very smart in tailored olive fatigues, come through the plate glass doors. He stood up, smiling. He pulled back a chair and Captain Hargreaves sat down.

'Thanks. I got that stuff for you. Gnatbeelson's alive and in London.'

Jerry resumed his chair. He frowned. 'What about his memory?'

'It's a typical case of amnesia – of the sort you described to me. He believes his name to be Beale. And, as you guessed, he's taken a job in a library.'

'The books are there?'

'At least one copy of *Times Search*.'

'Then it's conclusive.' Jerry leaned forward and slid a friendly fingernail along the inside of Captain Hargreaves's thigh. 'Do you want lunch now?'

Captain Hargreaves's hand fell on Jerry's. 'Afterwards, I think.'

'There might not be time. They know where I am – or should do.'

'I'm not too hungry.' The captain reached into a large satchel and drew out a piece of paper. 'The address.'

Jerry tucked the paper down inside his holster, rising slowly. 'Give me a moment. I've got to change my clothes. I'll join you in the Dutch garden, if you like.'

'Okay.' Captain Hargreaves stood up, kissing him on the cheek. 'You'll be quick?'

'Don't worry.'

But he was frowning as he went through the back of the restaurant into the cloakroom and began slipping into the costume he kept there.

There was no doubt about it, he thought. Things were looking black for the English assassin.

Early Reports

Editors: Hitler stopped too soon! He should have gotten rid of the Ginzburgs and the Borosons and a lot more like you. Indeed we should have a Hilter in America to rid the country of the merchants of filth, pervertors and corruptors of morals, and muckrakers!

Mrs John W. Red, Memphis, Tennessee;
letter to Fact, Jan-Feb 1965

Contrary to the national trend, crime decreased in the Notting Hill area last year.

Kensington Post, 8 January 1965

The one thing you can say about Hitler is that he was a damned sight more pro-British then M. Pompidou.

Kingsley Amis, Speakeasy (BBC Radio), 18 July 1971

Even in these enlightened days cancer continues to be a disease evoking dread and horror in the general public. Perhaps because of this peculiar emotional response to cancer, quite unlike that seen with other diseases, there has always been a fringe of unorthodox practitioners specializing in unusual treatments to lead to dramatic 'cures'.

M. A. Epstein, *Times Literary Supplement*, 16 January 1976

Tuning Up (3)

'I feel like a right ponce.' Jerry climbed gingerly into the large rowing boat, seating himself in the stern, glaring miserably at the misty lake. The boat's name was on the back-rest behind him: *Morgana le Fey*. He arranged the skirt of his lilac jacket around him; he plucked at the knees of his lilac flares to reveal daffodil socks, daffodil cuffs; he was cold.

'Well, I think you look lovely.' Karen von Krupp unshipped the oars, handing one pair to Miss Brunner, one to Una Persson. 'Doesn't he?' she asked the others.

'Lovely.' Una Persson's back was to him but Jerry could imagine her expression. Miss Brunner, in russet Ossie Clarke battle-dress with matching boots and bush-hat, was silent. She seemed to think that Doktor von Krupp should be doing some of the rowing.

'I wish you'd all stop taking the piss out of me. I've had a hard time of it.' Moodily, Jerry tugged at a tiller line. 'Who's going to shove off?'

Karen von Krupp sighed to Mitzi Beesley; Mitzi was to remain on the bank as look-out until they returned. She pouted and swung her customised Winchester .270 over her shoulder, lifting her white Dorothee Bis skirt to her thighs so that she could wade into the shallows, feet protected by Paulin espadrilles. The mother-of-pearl in the rifle's stock clashed a trifle with her skirt as the butt bounced against an angry bottom and Jerry felt her heavy breath on his head as she shoved. The boat shifted a little in the shingle. Mitzi pushed blonde marcel-waved hair back from her face and tried again. Gradually her face grew almost scarlet to match her horrible Maple Red Max Factor mouth. Karen von Krupp rocked the boat at the other end. Suddenly they all slid out into the lake and Mitzi waved her arms, barely recovering her footing. Petulantly she waded back to the shore and swung the Winchester into both hands. She kept her spine displayed to them. She wasn't much for vocalizing her displeasure. In reply to Mitzi's gesture Doktor von Krupp wrapped her dove-grey C&A trench-coat more firmly around her large body. 'That way,' she said, gesturing beyond the reeds in the direction of the island, a dim outline, already being obscured by the thickening mist, in the middle of the lake. 'Are you sure you know how to steer, Jerry dear?'

Jerry dragged the line hard over so that the boat moved suddenly to starboard.

'We don't need demonstrations from anyone else today, Mr Cornelius.' Miss Brunner was panting. 'I think we're sitting the wrong way round, by the way.'

Una Persson had first pointed this out when they had entered. But she remained as patient as ever. Una wore her usual light-weight khaki under an open black maxi-coat; though the coat tended to hamper her movements, she was evidently reluctant to remove it. Crouching, she turned herself carefully so that she was looking up at Jerry. She winked grey eyes, first one, then the other, and sat down again, taking hold of the sweeps. Behind her, Miss Brunner swivelled, much more awkwardly, her legs held by her red-brown midi. Her long bottom struck the seat somewhat heavily and the boat responded dramatically, rocking from side to side, shipping a little water to port. 'I don't think much of this thing's construction,' she said. Then they were rowing again.

'Let's try to keep the same rhythm this time, shall we?' Miss Brunner hissed as one of her oars reared from the water, weed driping from its blade.

The morning was very misty. They moved through a strip of clear water between thick reeds, not yet on the lake proper, but already the heavily wooded bank was invisible. Some ducks flapped low over the grey surface, as if trying to keep below the mist-line. A light drizzle formed rather than fell around them. They rowed into shrouded silence, their own sounds muffled.

'You're the only one of us familiar with the island, Mr Cornelius,' said Doktor von Krupp. 'You'll have to keep us on course.' She picked up the Remington 700 Mitzi Beesley had loaned her and placed it carefully across her knees. Both Miss Persson and Miss Brunner were armed with identical Smith and Wesson .45 revolvers. Jerry had a heater on one hip, his vibragun on the other hip and his needler under his arm-pit, but none of these gave him much sense of security.

'I hope we bloody find something after all this.' Miss Brunner had caught another crab. Una Persson leaned on her oars as she waited for the woman to start rowing again. Jerry was glad of her friendly, resigned face, even though it had been Una who had tipped the others off about the island (but it had been Mitzi Beesley who had tracked him down to where he had hidden his naked body in Gaping Gill pot on Ingleborough in the West Yorkshire Pennines, and Miss Beesley and Karen von Krupp who had dressed him in this outfit before he had had a chance to revive; he was still not quite sure what was going on). Una seemed somewhat regretful. She wiped the clinging moisture from her cheeks with the back of her hand – a mixture of mist and sweat. It was playing hell with the others' make-up.

The boat began to move again. Jerry couldn't remember what they were looking for on the island. He knew that something important had happened there once, perhaps to him, perhaps in his childhood, and he could certainly remember the stone barn very well (he had always been curious about the function of the place), but the rest was mysterious. 'There was a sun once,' Miss Brunner had said, just as he had woken up. Or had she said 'son'? He glanced into the water, seeking the source of the bad smell, like dead fish. Terror blossomed in the back of his brain. He tried to speak but could not. He searched the cold mist. There was no escape.

The three women were all staring directly at him, each lost in her own thoughts, as the boat moved on through the Grasmere clouds.

He looked down at his hands; he realized for the first time

that they had turned a funny colour. The pain in his spine made him want to bend double, to go on all fours. He grunted. His nostrils shivered. A small primitive noise formed in the back of his throat.

'Oh, god,' said Miss Brunner. 'It's starting again.'

Poor Gauchelin was much alarmed by his experience, but as time went on – at any rate in France – the Hunt lost some of its terrors, and the wailing procession of lost souls turned into a troupe of comic demons who flew merrily through the air to the sound of song and of tinkling bells. Nor did it always remain a mere nebulous, ghostly phenomenon. I have suggested, elsewhere, that the mummery probably originated as a miming of a Wild Hunt led by a certain Mormo, a child-devouring ogress of Greek origin, not unlike Perchta, the mythical patroness of the Perchton. That the Harlequin-Cornelius troupe was also sometimes mimed is suggested by the fact that it makes a partial appearance in Adam de la Halle's *Jeu de la Feuillée*, which, as we have seen, had for its central theme the entertainment of fairies by the citizens of Arras. 'Already I hear the Harlequin-troupe approaching,' cries Croquesot (Biter-of-fools), 'a little bearded man,' who having cheerfully enquired of the audience whether his 'hairy phiz' doesn't become him well, proceeds to woo the fairy Morque on behalf of his mighty master Cornelius, the Harlequin, who, though still supernatural, has obviously developed into a more substantial and more comic figure than his ancestor, the demonaic leader of lost and wandering souls.

Enid Welsford, The Fool, ibid

The jingle-cap is such a great grinner,
He will dance for you, not well, but with vigour,
His jingle-head full of coloured beads.

Maurice Lescoq, Postumous Poems

Triomphe et que l'envie en crive de depir,
Brave Arlequin queton nom plein de gloire
Soit, pour test faits, ton bel esprit,

A l'avenir en lettres d'or ecrit
Dans la temple de la memoire.

The Stage's Glory, ibid

Fairy Benigna: *Poor Afric's children sigh for liberty.*
Alas! That task was not reversed for me.
Furibond; or, Harlequin Negro, Drury Lane, 1807

Notting Hill Doomed to be Racial Battlefield

The 1962 Commonwealth Immigrants Act came immediately after the racial trouble from campaigns against immigrants from the West Indies, Africa and Asia. One of the centres of racial violence then, and earlier, was Notting Hill; indeed this area's name is now almost synonymous with racial prejudice . . . Notting Hill seems doomed to be the battlefield of racial discrimination: the Government's White Paper will not stop the battle. But sense and responsible reaction from the people against whom legislation is directed should at least let us know what the causes of the war really are.

KENSINGTON POST, 3 September 1965

1. Seven years for bank-raid vicar

From Sumatra it wasn't too hard to get back to Sandakan and something like sanity, though the sari could not safely be abandoned until he could look down on his yellow palace, last remnant of a great personal empire, his inheritance, in the dark green hills above the desert harbour. Quite a lot of jungle had grown around the building since he had last visited it; trees and architecture were rounded, their contours softened by the hazy light, seeming to merge, and in the distance were the great blue and purple mountains of the island's interior, the 'real Borneo' as Major Nye had once termed it. To see if there were any signs of danger Jerry flew twice over the red and grey town. There were a few steamers at anchor against the broken concrete of the quays; some were already sinking into the emerald water, others were entirely discoloured by rust. On the quay he saw three isolated figures looking up at his giant Dornier DoX flying boat. Perhaps they recognized the sound of the twelve Curtiss Conqueror engines spluttering and misfiring around him as usual. He flew out to sea towards the Philippines, to make a wide turn so that he could begin his landing approach. He now wore a white one-piece flying suit, trimmed with ermine, gold-trimmed goggles and a white kid helmet. He had always been expected to show a little face in Sandakan.

The plane began to drop too steeply. Jerry pulled her up a bit; she responded as poorly as usual, but he managed to keep to his original path until he was almost on top of the broken mouth of the harbour. The Dornier's huge floats touched tranquil water, bounced, swerved; he was taxi-ing between sagging, extinguished light-towers, forcing his heavy craft away from the protecting walls which formed an almost perfect circle and towards the mass of rotting steamers and water-logged fishing sampans, the deserted

354

house-boats and the junks. It began to occur to him that he had not been paying attention to his real responsibilities. He let the flying boat drift in crab-wise until it was bobbing against the side of a junk which seemed relatively intact. He shut off the engines and clambered from the door of the cockpit on to the forward floats, clutching a strut to keep his balance as the machine rocked badly, and from the floats boarded the junk, testing its timbers carefully as he crossed the deck to walk slowly down a bouncing, flaking gang-plank still resting on the quay. Empty moulding buildings presented themselves to him, a mixture of Victorian Gothic and Malaysian-Dutch stucco. Rats watched from ledges and windows. Sadly he walked up the hill, through ruined streets where timber-merchants' and rubber-planters' offices, shipping companies, importers, exporters, chandlers, money-lenders, insurance brokers, restaurants, bazaars, stall-holders, silk-sellers, paper mask sellers, puppet sellers, sellers of acrid pastries, savoury dumplings, sweetmeants, carved wooden boxes and bird-cages, had flourished in lazy competition.

Now a few starved Chinese and Dyak faces disappeared from doorways as he passed by. It was evident that nobody recognized him in his new costume and this saddened him.

The gates of the palace, which stood on its own hill outside the town, were slabs of grey marble on slender white tapering posts. They were exactly as he had left them, their pristine carvings and decoration reflecting a strong Islamic influence. He took a large key from his pocket and with considerable difficulty turned it in the great iron lock, pushing the gates open to find richer colours within. The gravel drive had been freshly raked and the lush shrubs had been trimmed and tended. Even the fountains of the ornamental lake were playing, perfectly orchestrated. Clear water ripled against a background of jade and lapis lazuli. Exotic birds looked carelessly at him as they dragged their glinting plumage about the perfect lawns where bowls, croquet and even cricket had been played in the old days. He reached the house, with its three terraced verandahs, climbing quartz steps between monstrous tigers and dragons of coloured ceramic and polished limestone, noting that the bronze doors, only recently dosed with considerable quantities of Brasso so that it hurt his eyes to look at them, were open, as if in welcome. The doors were twice his height; he pushed them back a fraction and squeezed through, entering the cool shadows of his palace, pausing in the very centre of tha hall's bright mosaic floor, facing towards the main staircase, of graduated shades of marble. There was no dust. He cleared his throat. There was a discreet echo.

'Dassim Shan?'

His major domo did not appear. The deities of a dozen different faiths, bronze, ebony, porcelain, regarded him, some glowering, some tranquil, from alcoves. Diffracted light, entering through coloured patterned glass set close to the ceiling, filled the hall with delicate shadows.

Jerry took a step or two towards the stairs, then paused, hearing a movement overhead in the gallery behind him. A light but perfectly pitched voice, a bitter-sweet voice sang:

'Oh, Limehouse kid, oh, Limehouse kid, going the way that the rest of them did. Poor broken blossom who's nobody's child. Haunted and taunted, you're just kind of wild. Oh, Limehouse blues, I've the real Limehouse blues, learnt from the Chinese those sad China blues. Rings on my fingers and tears for a crown, that is the story of Old China Town . . .'

Languid as one of the peacocks outside, Una Persson leaned against the carved marble balustrade. She wore a long Molyneaux evening gown of the thinnest yellow silk and her hair was cut short in a coolie crop with a fringe at an angle on her forehead, framing her oval face, emphasizing her ironic grey eyes. She began to move as he looked up. She was smoking a cigarette without a holder.

Jerry had never seen her like this. 'What?'

The gown caused her to stride in a peculiar swaying gait. She walked round the gallery, her heels ticking, until she came to the stairs. 'Shall I come down?' she spoke softly, laying a significant hand on the balustrade.

Jerry scratched his head under his helmet. He undid the strap and removed it, shaking out his long hair. 'Maybe I'd better come up. I'm a bit more mobile.'

'What's been going on in the big world?' she asked as she accompanied him to his study which lay almost at the end of the gallery. Some Guerlain perfume or other hung about her, making him uncertain of her identity as well as his own. He unlocked the door, intricately carved from local hardwood, and held it open for her. 'It's delightful.' She went directly to the french windows and opened them, admitting a certain amount of light and one or two insects began enthusiastically to explore the large room. She swayed out into the sunshine, on to a balcony providing a view of the sea in one direction and the distant Iran Mountains in the other, all dark greens, blues and purples. The sky was perfect; blue with a touch or two of pink in it. 'Oh, Jerry! This is the loveliest view!'

In the study there was a great deal of dust, as if it had all gathered in one place. Jerry wiped it from his desk with his white gauntlet, making long smears across the mother-of-pearl inlay. 'Have you seen anything of Dassim Shan?'

'He's probably near the swimming pool. He spends most of his time there, I gather.'

Jerry frowned. 'Is he all right?'

'Well, he seems to have a rare form of hydrophilia which tends to make him a bit introspective. I shouldn't go to see him, if I were you, until I've had a chance to warn him. The shock could kill him.'

'How long ago did this happen?'

'Soon after the resumption of hostilities.'

'Sod,' said Jerry. With a decisive gesture he threw off his flying helmet and reached to take a pre-wound ornamental turban, of red, green and yellow stripes, from the bottom drawer of his desk. He pinned up his hair. 'It's my fault, as usual.'

'You take too much on yourself,' she said. She returned to the interior but then, when she saw that he intended to

357

go onto the balcony, made a few backward steps so that she was outside again, her hands behind her, supporting her slim body as she rested against the rococo rail.

Adjusting the turban on his head he moved to join her. From where he stood he could see the lawns at the side of the palace, the cypresses which hid the servants' cottages, empty now. To his left he could make out the roofs of the deserted town. On his right loomed foothills, then mountains. 'There are demands on one here,' he told her. He tapped the turban. 'There is more to this than a few privileges, Miss Persson. There is, perhaps, even a destiny.'

He drew a deep breath of the sweet, heavy air.

'Duty?' She became immediately attentive.

2. Society hostess death riddle

'It's silly, I know,' said Jerry as he and Una lay close together, knee to knee in the massive and uncomfortable bed, listening to the waves and the wild-life of the Sandakan dawn, 'but I do miss America. I have ancestors there, you know.'

'You're obsessed with your relatives.' She reached for the silver filigree thermos jug and poured herself an inch or so of iced lime juice. She lifted the jade beaker to her lips. Already their affair had taken one or two turns for the worse.

He shrugged his blue silk shoulders. He flashed her a grin, his teeth unnaturally white against his unnaturally dark skin. 'I have so many, Una.'

The electrics were working unexpectedly well. As the dawn continued to bloom the four-bladed fan overhead hummed in sympathy with the voices of a thousand waking insects.

Jerry pulled back the netting and walked in bare feet to his dressing room next door and from there to the toilet. The suite was almost all polished mahogany, Victorian, designed, it appeared, to resist the Orient. He sat down on the elegant seat, at last able to relax. But within a moment or two she had joined him, quite naked apart from two ivory bangles on her left wrist, an Egyptian cigarette in one hand, the jade beaker in the other. She leaned against the door jamb, sipping from the glass. She studied his naked lower quarters. He regretted now that he had not locked himself in.

'I wish to god we could get some news, Jerry.' She took a brief, nervous puff on her cigarette. 'How's Dassim coming along with the radio?'

'He's had to cannibalize. From the plane. No luck so far.'

'I'm frightfully bored, you see.'

'I understand.'

'I thought you'd be rounding up your faithful retainers, getting everybody back to work, clearing the harbour, sorting out the rubber and so on. There isn't one horse left in the stables. No ostlers or anything. You've done nothing except write in your notebooks.'

'There's nobody to round up, you see,' he explained. 'They've either gone inland or else they're mentally deficient. The only people left in town are idiots.'

'I quite agree. You couldn't give me a lift to the mainland, could you?'

'This is the mainland.' He pointed through the door to the dark map on the wall behind her. He took a sheet of music manuscript from the floor and began to crumple it, soften it. He stood up and wiped his black bottom.

'Of Borneo, though, darling.'

He was still disorientated by the role she had adopted. He dropped the paper into the bowl and operated the lever to flush it away. 'Where would you want to go?'

'What about – where is it? – Australia?'

'We'd have to stop for fuel before we reached Darwin. That DoX is a very greedy aeroplane, for all I've converted a lot of her passenger accommodation to fuel reserves. The only station I know of that's safe, because everyone's forgotten it, is Rowe Island. Moni?'

She sighed. 'Too many skeletons.'

'I must admit that's my feeling. One too many, at least.'

'What about the other way?'

'We've only got a flying boat, don't forget.'

'Singapore?'

'Singapore's out.'

'Bangkok?'

'Bangkok's completely out.'

'Anywhere else? Hong Kong? Formosa? Shanghai?'

'They're all out, too.'

'Well, the Philippines, then.'

'I told you what happened to the Philippines. Besides, I'd

still have to come back and fuel would be a very serious problem.'

'We'd be all right in the Philippines, wouldn't we? We could explain.'

'I couldn't. I've had enough of that.' He rolled his eyes and began to Charleston from the toilet. Gradually the Charleston turned into a cake-walk and from a cake-walk became a coon-dance. 'I know where I'm well off.' His arms flapped and jogged. 'What do you think I was after in Sarawak? And I only left there in time!' He retreated into his netting again, peering at her through it. He stretched out on the bed. 'I've no objection if you take the plane yourself.'

'Oh, I'd never learn to fly.'

'The last time I saw you – I think – you had a licence. Didn't you?'

'I may have told you something like that.' She was vague, upset by the reference.

'It'll have to be Rowe Island, then. I've got to get back. I wouldn't be allowed into Australia under any circumstances.'

'But your son . . .?'

'I shouldn't have mentioned it.'

'Ghosts,' she said.

'You wouldn't recognize them now,' he told her, parting the curtain and taking her hand. Tenderly he drew her back into the net.

3. An important message to every man and woman in America losing his or her hair

The lean steam yacht sailed fastidiously into Sandakan harbour, furled her white sails and dropped anchor. A little cream-coloured smoke drifted from her gleaming aristocratic funnels; her white sides were turned greenish blue, reflecting the water.

Watching from his balcony Jerry recognized the *Teddy Bear* and pursed his lips, in no doubt that his radio signals had been intercepted. She had hoisted a complicated collection of signals from her masthead, triatic stay, starboard yardarm and port yardarm, the simplest of which read *Coming to your assistance*. As Jerry looked, she ran the Red Ensign up her ensign staff. He made out the letters HBC in the fly and his suspicions were confirmed. There were few who would sail under the flag of the Hudson's Bay Company unless they had to.

He returned to his study to take from the table, on which there also rested a Harrison naval chronometer and a large globe of the world, his telescope. Once more on the balcony he focused the lens on the *Teddy Bear*. A number of sailors were at work on her decks; most of them wore uniforms closely resembling the tropical kit of the United States Navy. They were armed with Springfield rifles of an old-fashioned pattern; Jerry couldn't identify them. A moment later the flash of a maple-finished Remington stock confirmed everything he had suspected. He collapsed the telescope and went to find Una Persson.

She was in the swimming pool, bathing under the unseeing eyes of Dassim Shan. Her brown body flickered against shady jade, lapis lazuli and Tuscan marble. Dassim Shan, in his elaborately embroidered coat of office, his small turban and his silk britches, sat where he always sat when not specifically employed, occasionally glancing up at the crystal dome of the roof, cocking an ear if he detected some slight difference in the sound of a fountain.

'It looks as if you'll soon be able to say goodbye to Borneo.' Jerry squatted on the mosaic tiles at the edge of the pool. 'Una. There's a ship turned up.'

'British?'

'It might as well be. Beesley's tracked me down. I knew I hadn't really shaken him off in the States. He's been to Sumatra and picked up the steam yacht.'

Her head came sliding over the surface to stare into his eyes. 'Are you sure?'

'Quite sure. I recognized his daughter's butt.'

'That he's come for you?'

'I suppose there's a slight chance he's run out of provisions and is hoping I've got the odd Tootsie Roll stashed away, but however you look at it the holiday's definitely coming to an end.'

'I didn't want to go back to *work*.' She pouted. 'I'm far too tired. Besides, I'd do no good.' She squeezed water from her eyes.

'You could always sing for the troops.'

'Don't be vulgar, darling.' Her head sought the depths.

'By and large,' Jerry reflected, dabbling his fingers in the water, 'I prefer a post-war situation to a pre-war one. But I was hoping to miss the current conflict altogether.' He stared wistfully at Dassim Shan. The major domo seemed to have found a solution.

She was on the other side of the pool now, shaking liquid from her short hair. 'What will you do?' she called.

'I'm a fatalist, these days. I'll play it by ear.' He realized that his silk trousers were becoming damp. He rose. 'What will you do?'

She wiped her mouth. 'Look up Lobkowitz, I suppose. He usually has a fair idea of what's going on. This must mean the peace talks have broken down, eh?' Already she was beginning to sound like her old self.

'I don't think they've got to that stage yet.' Jerry took a silver cigarette case from his jacket pocket, removed one of the last of his Shermans and lit it with a brass Dunhill lighter.

She clung to the side. 'Beesley has some kind of official backing, you think?'

He drew on the brown cigarettello. 'He's definitely not alone.'

From far away there came the sound of a ship's siren.

Una pulled herself from the pool and wrapped a thick brocade robe about her. It was Chinese, in blue and gold. Dragons embraced her.

They waited for some time at the bronze doors of the palace before they saw Bishop Beesley marching through the gates towards them. He was at the head of a small party of marines in blancoed webbing, belts and puttees. Recognizing Jerry and Una, Beesley stopped, signalling to his men who came immediately to attention, presenting arms. From behind them all Mitzi Beesley peeped out, waving the fingers of a malevolent imp.

Bishop Beesley was in full kit. His white and gold mitre, his bone and silver robes, were evidently fresh on, perhaps to impress any natives he might encounter. He held a rococo crook in one plump hand, a half-eaten bar of Zaanland Coffee Brandy Chocolate in the other.

'Still crawling away from the gibbering darkness are we, Mr C? You should relax. Nothing's as bad as it seems.' Bishop Beesley began a portly apporach.

'Afternoon, Bishop,' Jerry fell back on old dodges. 'What brings you to the Islands?'

'Missionary work, my boy. We got your message and came as soon as we could. You wouldn't, by any chance, be able to offer us some refreshment?' He swallowed the remains of the Zaanland.

'We're a bit short-staffed, just now. More primitive than I care for myself.' Jerry offered his arm to Una who took it. Together they led the way back into the palace.

'I thought you enjoyed living amongst the head-hunters, Mr Cornelius. After all, you and they have so much in common.'

Jerry was genuinely puzzled. 'There aren't any head-hunters in Sandakan. All that sort of thing's much further south. You're thinking of the Dyaks and their bloody oil-fields.'

Bishop Beesley waddled in. 'What a lovely home. I'll just leave the boys outside, shall I? Mitzi! You don't mind if my daughter joins us?'

Mitzi Beesley was wearing a rather cheap rayon ensemble, loose sailor blouse and wide, baggy trousers, almost certainly a bad Schiaparelli copy of the sort obtainable from any second-rate tailor's shop in Bombay or Calcutta. Even the shade of pink was slightly off. Her golden hair was waved tightly against her mean little skull. She placed her small tongue on her thin lower lip and smiled at Una. 'We've met before, haven't we?'

Una released Jerry's arm. 'I don't think I'd be likely to remember,' she said innocently. 'How do you do, Miss Beesley?'

Mitzi sniffed. 'Not bad. Not now. But times have been a bit chaotic until recently, when daddy got this new job.' She removed her Remington from her shoulder and looked around for somewhere to put it.

'I'll take it,' said Una hospitably.

Mitzi handed her the gun and Una crossed the mosaic to the large Ming ceramic umbrella stand, dropping the rifle, barrel first, among the walking sticks, sunshades and riding crops. 'It'll be all right there, will it?'

'Fine,' said Mitzi absently.

Bishop Beesley raised beringed fingers to his rosebud lips and uttered a little wind. 'I hear they do a very pleasant dish in these parts. A local version of the baclava, eh?'

'I think there are a few cold ones in the storeroom,' Jerry looked towards the door under the staircase. 'Shall I show you where it is?'

'That's very kind of you, Mr Cornelius. You seem, rather cleverly, to have adopted the manners as well as the style of a gentleman. Congratulations!'

'You're too kind.'

'Standards are slipping everywhere. Credit where credit's due, sir. And, of course, I bear no grudges.' His breathing became deeper. He was almost snoring by the time he had waddled to the door to the lower regions. 'This is deliciously opulent, isn't it? The barbaric splendour of the East. You must feel much more at home.'

'I can't complain, Bishop.'

'Is Miss Brunner with you?' asked Una suddenly of Mitzi Beesley. It was as if she remembered a name and nothing else.

'Not this trip.' Mitzi moved closer to her. 'That's a nice dressing-gown. Is it a man's?'

'I'm not sure.' The two women followed Jerry and Bishop Beesley through the door and down stone steps cut from the living rock. It was suddenly much cooler.

'And as for Frank,' continued Mitzi intimately, 'Jerry's brother, you know – we couldn't get him to do a thing. It's as if there's a spell on everybody. Almost. You've met Doktor von Krupp, too, have you?'

'I think I might have . . .'

'She's almost completely retired, now. Gave herself to the cause body and soul. Bishop Beesley has had to continue the work virtually single-handed. I help as best I can, of course, but he complains that I don't really understand the importance of it all. He thinks my loyalties are sometimes divided.' They were quite a long way behind the men. Mitzi smirked. 'Of course, that's impossible. I haven't any loyalties at all.'

'What a relief.' Spasmodically, Una smiled down on the minx. She found that she was lying and enjoying the sensation. 'How refreshing.'

The minx began to stroke her exposed ribs.

The party descended still deeper into the darkness. From the gloom ahead Una could hear the sound of Bishop Beesley's awful breath.

'It's high time you were back in harness, Mr C.'

4. Cross country rape and slay spree of the frustrated bondage freak

'There's still a touch of vulgarity about you which I like,' said Bishop Beesley. His marines had taken up permanent positions within the palace grounds and the bishop had almost completed his inventory of the building's contents. The two of them strolled between peacocks and birds of paradise and pedigree Sinhalese bantams, over the lawn towards the larger fountains which cast faint, flickering arabesques everywhere on grass and shrubs. The bishop was eating something sticky from one of Jerry's silver plates, holding the plate in his left hand while with his right he lifted the honey-flavoured food to his glistening lips. 'What a riot of colour, those flowers and shrubs!' Flies were settling hopefully on his mitre. 'America and Europe are getting along fine. Say what you will about President Boyle, he's a dedicated internationalist. He's given the British authorities his whole support.'

'It's the Islamic influence, I suppose,' murmured Jerry. 'I've always been a bit prone . . .'

'Security is at a premium, Mr Cornelius. Of course, it's given a tremendous boost to the navy. Britannia Resurgent!'

'We're a bit behind the times here.' Jerry prised a determined mosquito from his cheek. 'I'm afraid.'

'How we'd all love to live in the past, particularly a past so splendid.' Bishop Beesley expressed sympathy. He waved a cake. 'No one understands all this better than I.'

Jerry was doing his best to remember what had been going on. 'I don't think I could go back to Britain,' he said. 'Not now.'

'I would be the first to admit that there are, for certain people, difficulties. But with the proper papers you'd be quite safe. Restrictions aren't merely negative, you know. They work for you, too.'

'They don't like me over there any more.' He made a vague gesture towards the West. 'Do they?'

'Nonsense. You can prove a change of heart!'

Jerry laughed. He put both his hands into a lattice of water, causing the fountain to alter its note. 'That's the only thing that hasn't changed, Vicar.'

'Come, come, come.' Bishop Beesley clapped him on the back. For a few moments his fingers adhered to the silk of Jerry's pale blue kurta then came away with a small sucking sound. 'You must be positive!'

Jerry said doubtfully: 'I'll try. I have tried.'

'I'll get my daughter to have a chat with you. She's helped you in the past, hasn't she?'

'I can't recall . . .'

'It will come back.' Bishop Beesley looked around for somewhere to put his empty plate. In the end he found a green soapstone sundial. 'There isn't a great deal of time to spare. The box is still in England, I take it.'

'Oh, yes,' said Jerry dreamily, to be agreeable. He was incapable, just now, of thinking that far ahead.

'And with the box in the right hands, mankind will prosper again. A major war will be averted. The world will greet you as a saviour!'

'I thought I'd already turned the job down.' Jerry found some seed in his pockets and began to throw it to the birds. From one of the upper floors of the palace came the strains of King Pleasure singing *Golden Days*. 'That's a bit anachronistic, isn't it? Or is it me?'

For a moment Bishop Beesley's huge face became sober. 'There is no need . . .'

'Well, that's a relief, at any rate.' Jerry rambled on. Ahead of him, on the other side of an ornamental hedge, two sailor hats drew down for cover. 'What does Una say?' He sniffed a sweet magnolia blossom. 'She's the brains of the outfit.'

'I don't know how she feels but, as you say, she's an intelligent woman. My daughter's dealing with her. They are more sympatico.'

'She'd feel all right about going back to Blighty. She wants to. Maybe you should just take her.'

'Does she know where the box is?'

'I'm sure she does.'

Bishop Beesley wiped his face with a red spotted handkerchief. He flicked at the flies and returned it to his back pocket. He inspected his left gaiter. 'Is that a scorpion?' He pointed to the small insect crawling up his leg.

Gently, Jerry cupped his hand around the creature and held it on his palm, looking down at it. 'It seems to be a wingless butterfly. Isn't that odd?'

Bishop Beesley glared around him. 'Where's Mitzi?'

'Upstairs somewhere, with Una. Can't you hear the music?' King Pleasure was now singing his own *Little Boy, Don't Get Scared. Little fellow, don't get yellow and blue*, he sang.

Bishop Beesley smiled to himself. Jerry was still looking at the butterfly. 'Hadn't you better kill it?' said the bishop. 'I mean, it can't be happy.'

'It doesn't look too unhappy, though.' Jerry's hand shook a little. 'I shouldn't worry.' He placed the insect inside the scarlet rhododendron flower. 'It might as well enjoy the time it's got.'

Bishop Beesley evidently disapproved of these sentiments. He was about to speak when his small ears caught a sound from on high. Jerry heard it too and they both looked up.

Through the shimmering, heated sky there came a large, dark shape and, for some reason, Jerry became immediately more cheerful, even as he felt his last grip on consecutive thought slipping. 'Well, well, well. An airship. From Rowe Island, I shouldn't wonder.'

'Airships are – ' Bishop Beesley clutched at his jowls. 'Airships are – ' His hand went to his back. His brow contorted. 'Ah!'

Jerry began to jump about on the lawn, waving mindlessly to the massive black ship with its crimson markings. Disturbed, the peacocks and the bantams scattered screaming and clucking. Macaws filled the air, red, yellow, blue and green, shrieking.

'My back! Back!' moaned Bishop Beesley.

'It's tensions, I expect,' suggested Jerry, turning for a moment, but the bishop was already hobbling for the house. Jerry sat down on the lawn. There was a silly grin on his face. 'Gosh! I never thought I'd be glad to see one of those buggers again!'

5. Spirit voices help me – Peter Sellers talks about the strange power that has entered his life

King Pleasure was doing *Tomorrow is another day* as, half his togs abandoned, his mitre over one sticky eye, Bishop Beesley rolled out of the palace, dragging Mitzi. His daughter was soft and naked, reluctant to leave, trying to work the bolt on her Remington, to remove a malacca cane from the barrel, slapping at his hands which seemed to be covered with feathers from a pillow. 'Okay!' Her father shouted to the marines. 'Okay!'

Bishop Beesley dragged Mitzi past Jerry. Her heels were making unsightly scars in the gravel. 'I hope to god, Mr Cornelius, none of this ever gets into the primary zone! I would like to remind you that this is the seventies.'

'Almost a hundred, I'd have said. Phew, what a scorcher!' Jerry had begun to pick himself a bunch of flowers. 'Blip,' he added.

'It's all your fault,' wailed Mitzi at him. 'You and your rotten engines!'

'Blip!'

The dark shadow of the circling airship passed over them for the fifth time. The birds of paradise were particularly disturbed by the commotion, running this way and that. The macaws and bantams had completely disappeared. Only the peacocks had settled down and were screeching aggressively at the big vessel. For a moment or two Jerry imitated them, evidently for the fun of it, then he began to mumble, dropping his flowers. 'Five. Birds. Water. Messiah. Ice.'

Una emerged, in trench-coat and khaki, buckling on the heavy military holster containing her S&W .45. 'That airship's come for us. Somebody's running a horrible risk. We'd better bloody take advantage while we can. I'm pissed off. What's Beesley got to do with me?'

'I'd thought airships were extinct,' said Jerry. 'Or not invented yet. I'm slipping. Blip.'

'We're all slipping. Everybody's slipping,' screamed Bishop Beesley, untangling his daughter from a jacaranda. 'Monstrous anachronisms! Come along, Mitzi, please. The co-ordinates haven't jelled yet, so there's a chance we can escape before complete chaos results. Men! Men! Men!' The marines began to emerge from peculiar hiding places, like children interrupted in a game. 'Deviants!'

'It's not my fault,' said Jerry, 'about Rowe Island. At least, I don't think it is.' His vacant eyes glanced questioningly at Una Persson. 'Is it? It was dormant.'

Her smile was brave and reassuring. 'You'll be all right, I expect.'

Tomorrow is the magic word. It's full of hopes and dreams . . .

'Lovely.' Jerry turned a seraphic face upwards. 'I've always thought they were, thought they were, thought they were, thought they were, thought they were, thought they were . . .'

A long rope ladder fell from the centre section of the gondola and almost hit him on his poor head. He continued to stand there, mumbling, even as, from the other side of the wall, rifles began to bark. 'Get up it, you silly bugger!' shouted Una Persson. The Smith and Wesson was now in her hand. For the moment the marines were contenting themselves with pot-shots at the hull as they retreated down the road and back through the town. 'Get up! Get up!'

'Yes, mum.' He grinned a daft grin. He wondered why he felt so happy. 'What about you? Ladies first?'

'You've got a job to do, sunny jim,' said Una grimly and slapped him on the bottom. 'Go on!'

He took hold of the rungs and began to climb the swaying ladder, chuckling childishly. The airship's engines shouted and screamed as her crew manoeuvred her to maintain their position in the air over the garden. Like the Dornier, she had forward and backward facing engines, the nacelles capable of turning through ninety degrees. A late mark

O'Bean, thought Jerry, as he lived and breathed, but he did not know what he meant by the thought. He was almost half-way up the ladder, giggling to himself, when he looked down. The golden dome, main roof of the palace, half-blinded him. 'Get up!' cried a determined voice. With one arm hooked in the rungs, Una Persson was sighting along her revolver, picking off marines in the white, tree-lined road below. So he called to the riggers peering at her from the open hatch through which the ladder had been lowered: 'Take her up. Lift. Lift. I'll be fine.' A winch creaked. The ladder rose a foot or two.

Jerry felt the wind in his hair. He had never had a better view of the island. 'This is heavenly,' he said. 'What a smashing way to finish. Or begin.' The rope swayed wildly. He almost fell off as he neared the top and the waiting gondola.

Hands found him: it was a disapproving Sebastian Auchinek, all scowls and moody, who hauled him in the last few feet. 'You've got a long way to go yet, Mr Cornelius.' There were a number of dark figures in the bare aluminium interior, evidently a storage hatch. It reeked of high octane fuel. Through the gloom Jerry crawled towards the nearest bench, also of aluminium, bolted to the bulkhead. Out of the fresh air his high spirits had dropped away again and he was mumbling. 'Airships. Human remains. Empires. War. Ideals. Science . . .'

As Una Persson was dragged in, firing a last round or two at the marines, Prinz Lobkowitz sprung into the light from the entrance, reaching for the lever, closing the hatch-doors. 'Thank god.' He and Auchinek embraced the woman they loved. Lobkowitz wore riding britches, brown boots, spurs, a white rollneck sweater, as if he had been taken away suddenly from a polo match. Auchinek wore a rather loud check suit that seemed to belong to the turn of the century.

Una frowned at them. 'Should you be here, at all?'

There was a movement above and a pair of thin legs in dark green trousers with a red stripe climbed down the metal ladder into the hold. 'We shouldn't.' Major Nye was in the uniform of the 3rd Infantry, Punjab Irregular Force, rifle-green with black lace and red facings. 'It's more comfortable above, by the way. This is just for stores, and we haven't any, of course.' He looked over to Jerry, who drooled and simpered. 'Poor old lad. We're dodging and weaving a bit, hoping for the best. He was due in England weeks before the *Teddy Bear*, you know. Everyone was contacted at very short notice, had to down tools and jump to it. Shoulders to the wheel, lads, shoulders to the wheel . . .'

'What else could we do?' Gently Lobkowitz stroked Jerry's bewildered head. 'Besides, he won't remember a lot. Neither shall we, for that matter. We'll drop him off in London and hope for the best.'

Auchinek was sullen. Evidently he had taken part in the raid against his will.

'But California first stop. It's important that we all check our bearings again before we progress any further.'

'Are you sure it's in California?' said Major Nye. 'I thought it was in London, now.'

'Not at the present,' said Auchinek.

'Blip.'

Tom McCarthy's patrol was supposed to round up a group of Rhodesian African guerrillas. Instead, he claims, it wiped out a village. There were about sixty victims – the entire population of a tiny village near the Mozambique border. McCarthy, a 22-year-old Londoner, who served in the Rhodesian Light Infantry, told the full story of the atrocity for the first time yesterday. McCarthy himself confessed that he shot a young terrorist as he lay wounded. He was ordered by an officer to shoot the boy. The death-mission began when the Rhodesian Special Branch was given a tip-off that the guerrillas would be slipping into the village to collect £1000 towards their 'funds'. McCarthy and his patrol, including black scouts and members of the Rhodesian Special Air Service, were ordered from their base at Mount Darwin in the troubled border area north of Salisbury. They arrived at the village below the Mavuradonha mountain range, about 30 miles away, in darkness. Through their 'night-sights' they saw 17 guerrillas arrive. But the Rhodesian soldiers did not move into the village to arrest them. Instead they illuminated the village with flares. Then they bombarded the huts with automatic fire and rockets. McCarthy maintained he could hear the screams of the villagers 300 yards away. Then he was called in to help with the 'mopping-up operations'. Thirteen of the terrorists died with the villagers. Four escaped but three were picked up later. McCarthy went into graphic detail of the alleged murder rampage by the Rhodesian troops. He said: 'We were also told that the only prisoners we wanted were the terrorists. We were also told we were after the money. There was this boy of about seventeen. There was no doubt he was one of the guerrillas because I recognized him from the night-sight. He had been shot but he wasn't too bad and the medic was working on him. Someone must have decided

375

that he knew nothing because the medic was told to move away.' McCarthy was sending a radio message when an officer called him over and ordered him to shoot the youth. 'I was frightened and asked if he wouldn't be any good. I was told: "Certainly not." I was shaking quite a bit and the officer said: "Are you worried?" I knew that if I disobeyed a lawful command in an operational area I faced four years in the stockade. I remember putting the safetly catch to 'rapid fire' and put my rifle to my shoulder. But I turned my face away before I fired. I missed by a foot – that will tell you how bad I was. He just lay there and put his arms up against his chest. I don't know why but he didn't say a word. He just looked at me and I'll always remember that as if it were just this morning.' The officer than came behind McCarthy, grasped his head in both his hands and said: 'You useless — bastard.' McCarthy continued: 'He forced my head down to look at the man on the ground and said: "Now shoot the bastard." This time I hit him between the nose and the mouth and his face just seemed to cave in.'

Ellis Plaice, *Daily Mirror*, 27 February 1976

THE REUNION PARTY

377

William Randolph Hearst's monumental pile had first been displayed to the public on 2 June 1958 and since then had become one of California's greatest attractions, on a par with Hollywood and Disneyland, under the supervision of the California Department of Parks and Recreation, in accordance with Hearst's legacy after he had died, aged 88, on 13 August 1951; a mock Hispano-Moorish haven, crammed with the greastest collection of second rate art ever assembled in one private building, it lay on top of a hill once known as Camp Hill, now rechristened The Enchanted Hill and a visit to it was, according to the official guide book, 'an experience unsurpassed by the other great dwellings built in a fabulous era when American tycoons were erecting imposing structures and importing art treasures found throughout the world. A walk through its grounds with terraced gardens, paths lined with camellia hedges, great banks of azaleas and rhododendron, more than 50 varieties of roses and the soft tinkling of water dripping from marble fountains, is a stroll through the epitome of beauty and grandeur. A great dream, never quite completed.' The building began in 1919, nearly twenty years before the Derry and Toms Roof Garden, an echo, an exquisite miniature, had been opened in London. 'There are,' the guide book tells us, '100 rooms in the main building, including 38 bedrooms, 31 bathrooms, 14 sitting rooms, 2 libraries, a theatre and an area that was meant to contain a complete bowling alley.' Work on this building continued to 1947, when it was abandoned. There is no real evidence for the legend that in a year sometimes given as 1955, sometimes as 1985 and sometimes, obviously erroneously, as 1918, an important and secret meeting was held there of a number of men and women, representatives of most schools of thought and of many nations in the world. This has been variously described as the 'Veteran's Meeting' or the 'Reunion Party' and, of course, a number of books have been written in an effort to 'explain' the legend. So far a satisfactory book has yet to appear, though all accounts are agreed on the authenticity of one piece of evidence, a guest list, giving the names of the guests in order of arrival, 'with one notable absence, impossible to remedy at this stage' (as a pencilled note on the card points out). Accounts by local people concerning a huge concourse of ghosts on a day and a night in midsummer 1951, when shadowy figures were seen laughing and talking in the grounds, swimming in the Neptune pool, playing music of bizarre and unrecognizable origin, chiming the thirty-six carillon bells, housed in the twin Hispano-moresque towers of the Casa Grande; feasting in the huge refectory, with its silk banners representing the seventeen wards of Sienna, its Gothic tapestries and its fifteenth-century Spanish choir stalls, whilst seated at long tables of rich, old wood, burning oddly coloured lights, to ride off in a great flurry of hooves shortly before dawn, heading for the sea, have been independently confirmed and described, according to the taste of the teller, as a meeting of vampires, witches, devils or the Wild Hunt itself. Reports also agree that there was nothing sinister about the haunting, that, indeed, a great sense of peace and tranquillity pervaded the surrounding countryside on that Midsummer Night, a peace which those ancient Californian hills had not experienced for many a century, and the ghosts were generally thought to be 'lucky' rather than 'evil' (Butler, *Haunted California*, 1975). 'Men and women from all sides of the conflict would meet on common ground and exchange information in the timeless halls and passages of the four castles, in the peaceful groves of this noble Tanelorn' (Butler, ibid).'Their voices were hushed and relaxed and there wasn't one who showed any animosity he or she might feel . . .' (Hall, *The San Simeon Mystery Explained*, 1971). 'The time of the final conflict was not yet. Their garments, their manners, their languages, their gestures represented the best that the twentieth century had been able to offer, the inheritance of

Golden Age on Golden Age. Every enthusiasm was repre-sented; every beast was in its prime. And, for a day and a night, there could be no question of invasion, even from within.' (Morgan, *Law v. Chaos; The Last Great Meeting*, 1975). 'Time travellers? Visitors from space? Ghosts? Or just a bunch of hoaxers – a gang of kids having fun? Then how to explain music that was years ahead of its time, fashions that were not seen until twenty years later, snatches of conversation referring to events occurring towards the end of this century?' (Fromental, *San Simeon, the Flying Saucers and Patty: Who is getting at who?* 1976).

The note of guests attending the 'coven' or 'sabbat,' as others have called it, was found under the billiard table in the Game Room, written in longhand, not evidently American and probably English, headed 'Manifestations' and, under that, 'Arrivals in order of appearance.' The names included the following:

Mr J. Daker, Mr J. Tallow, Mr E. De Marylebone, Mr Renark, Mr E. Bloom, Mr C. Marca, Mr J. Cornelius. Prof. I. Hira, Mr Smiles. Mr Lucus. Mr Powys. Miss C. Brunner, Mr D. Koutrouboussis. Mr Shades. Mrs F. Cornelius. Mr J Tanglebones. Rev. Marek. Duge D. von Köln, Mr K Glogauer, Cpt. Arflane, Mrs U. Rorsefne. Prof. Faustaff, Mr U. Skarsol, Bishop D. And Miss M. Beesley, Dr K. von Krupp, Captain C. Brunner, Mr F. G. Gavin, Prince C. J. Irsei. Mr E. P. Bradbury. Mr J. Cornell. Mr O. Bastable. Miss U. Persson. Cpt. J. Korzeniowsky. Mr V. I. Ulyanov, Gen O. T. Shaw, Major and Mrs G. Nye. Captain and Mrs G. Nye. Miss E. Nye. Miss H. Nye. Master P. Nye. Col. F. Pyat. Mr S. M. Collier. Mr M. Lescoq. Mr M. Hope-Dempsey. Mr C. Ryan. Prinz Lobkowitz. Mr S. Koutrou-boussis. Mr C. Koutrouboussis. Mr A. Koutrouboussis. Mr R. Boyle, Mnr P. Olmeijer. Mrs H. Cornelius. Mrs B. Beesley. Mr S. Cohen. Miss H. Segal. Prof. M. O'Bean. Mr R. De Fete. Mr C. Tome. Captain B. Maxwell. The Hon. Miss H. Sweet. Mr S. Vaizey. Miss E. Knecht. Lady Sunday. Mrs A. Underwood. Mr J. Carnelian. Lady Charlotina Lake. Lord and Lady Canaria. Miss Q. Gloriana. Miss M. Ming. Mrs D. Armatuce. Gen. C. Hood. Lady Lyst. Mr E. Wheldrake, Lord Rhoone. Lord Wynchett. Baroness Walewska. Sir T. Fynes. Dr J. Dee. Captain Quire, and a great number of other experienced people.

Notting Hill's annual Summer Carnival is unlikely to take place this year in its traditional form. The Royal Borough Council has told its organizers to find a fixed assembly point for this year's Carnival – preferably the White City Stadium in Shepherd's Bush. Alternative venues like Wembley Stadium and Wormwood Scrubs were also mentioned. But all the proposed sites are outside the Royal Borough, and the organizers have rejected these suggestions as boding 'total destruction of the fundamental concept of what the Carnival should be.' Their objections to deputy council leader Ald. Peter Methuen's 'compromise' solution to the carnival problem were raised at a closed meeting between Royal Borough officials and various concerned parties at Kensington Town Hall last week. Cllr Michael Cocks, who called the meeting, said it was vital to decide in good time how to avoid the controversy which followed last year's massive three-day celebrations. Nearly a quarter of a million people (mainly West Indian) flooded into the borough for last August's carnival – the tenth. But the aftermath of complaints from residents, the police and from certain councillors themselves, prompted the council to insist on a change of attitude to recognize that this once local event has now reached 'national proportions'. The objections of local residents, itemized in a 196-signature petition to the council, include noise (particularly from steel bands playing late into the night) and dirt and litter left after the week-end's festivities. Their petition called for 'the immediate and effective prohibition of amplified music and vocal performances in the Westway and W.10 and W.11 areas and for the re-siting of the Notting Hill Carnival in 1976 and subsequent years.'

The police added that the crime rate had increased seriously during Carnival time and that traffic congestion had blocked access for ambulances and fire engines. The council said that the event was now too large for them to provide adequate hygiene and litter amenities ... 'To move to the White City would totally destroy the event as we know it,' Mr Palmer said ... 'The festival is a street carnival and the whole atmosphere would be lost if it were moved out of the streets of North Kensington,' said Labour leader Val Wallis ... But Mr Anthony Perry, Director of the North Kensington Amenity Trust, warned that if the Carnival were to go ahead without approval, then the Trust, on whose land much of the festivity takes place, would not make the land available. 'We are eager that it should be used by the community,' Mr Perry said, 'but not against the wishes of the community.'

Kensington News and Post, 6 February 1976

6. BAC cools hopes of airship boom

Jerry was still shivering as he waded out of the dirty Cornish shallows on to Tintagel's ungenerous beach. A careful search of all the caves in that half-eaten bay, of the ruins of the castle, of the deserted town beyond, had turned up nothing but debris, seaweed and dead fish. Now his cold feet struck something white and mushy lying on the shingle and, glancing hopefully down, he discovered only a bundle of quarto paper, secured by green admiralty tags, typewritten. He went to turn the pages but they disintegrated at once, like the flesh of a rotten sole. He folded his arms for warmth, his ancient oilskins creaking and cracking at armpits and shoulders. He rid himself of his stiff sou'wester, throwing it behind him, into the Atlantic.

As he looked above the looming cliffs at the petulant sky grey rain fell on his face. He tramped for the dangerous steps leading up the south face of the cove, beginning to regret overreacting and giving in to the impulse to smash all his equipment, to rely entirely on metaphysical methods for a final solution to his sister's malaise. Now his foot slipped on a piece of rotten granite. He paused. A darkness had entered the bay. His upward climb became hastier. There was no use crying over diffused plasma (or ectoplasm, for that matter): the world was splitting up, like so many dividing cells, and the energy was unlikely to be concentrated in any one place for much longer. He had been foolish to believe that his remedy had been any better than the others.

He reached the top of the cliff and made his way to the old wooden café shack where he had left his camouflaged jeep. It was still there, parked at an angle of forty degrees on the rutted path. He climbed in, thinking of Captain Brunner and wondering if the noble old anachronism's sacrifice had been worth anything in the long run. He took a yellowing packet of Black Cat cigarettes from the map compartment and lit one with the brass Dunhill he had found there; the lighter's flame was very low. He put the Black Cats in his pocket and abandoned the Dunhill. He turned the ignition key. The starting motor rolled sluggishly a few times but the engine failed to fire. Jerry had expected this. Even the American equipment wasn't what it had been; the mainland had sent no new supplies for months. In the back seats of the jeep he found his fur hat and mittens, his heavy P&O Norfolk jacket. He stripped off the oilskins and dressed himself more warmly, buckling the jacket's belt tightly around the waist.

He left the jeep behind, walking up the steep path towards the town. His search was proving entirely fruitless and he was tempted to give it up altogether, retiring from any kind of involvement, and yet his instincts had to be satisfied; he was resigned to continuing his quest. After all, most of his old enemies had themselves retired to safer zones. On the surface it seemed that the field was completely open.

The town had never been anything more than ramshackle, built primarily in response to the late 19th century tourist boom which had owed far less to Coleridge than to Tennyson and the Pre-Raphaelites. Even ruin could not make it picturesque. The streets were awash with weather-stained postcards, bedraggled and muddy King Arthur tea-towels, broken plastic Holy Grails, Excaliburs carved from chalk, tiny Round Tables to hang on the wall, with polystyrene crowns. In the reign of one Elizabeth the ideal had reached perfection and, in the reign of another, it had achieved its ultimate degradation. Jerry sniffed to himself. It had to happen sometime. Perhaps that was what he had failed to understand before.

He began to check the few parked cars, but all were in poor condition. The exodus had been made in less than a day, when the area had been, like so many, declared a non-civilian zone. Something to do with the Cornish Nationalist Movement. But the military had lost interest in the site almost immediately and had never established anything more than a few yards of barbed wire here and there.

Personally, Jerry thought the Americans had been a trifle naïve in thinking they had scored significant points in recruiting the CNM, a notoriously unreliable outfit whose members remained loyal only until they were trained and re-equipped when they deserted, returning to their rented farms and tied-cottages to await the calling of the traditional landlord leaders. A few of them still worked freelance for the Americans but, Jerry had heard, the military advisers were reconsidering the system of paying scalp-bounty, since the scalps in question were always difficult to identify and, on more than one occasion, had proved to originate with their own personnel stationed in the remoter parts of West Penrith. Scalp-hunters had been reported in the area only a few days ago, so Jerry kept a wary hand on his vibragun and gave close attention to the shadows, though it was unlikely that any hunter would bother with Tintagel which was known to be abandoned.

Eventually Jerry gave up inspecting the cars and stepped through the smashed plate-glass window of a tea shop. From the counter a curious rat looked up and, for an instant, Jerry mistook him for the proprietor. Casting a prudent glance over its shoulder the rat beat a leisurely retreat. Jerry found himself a Coke in the powerless ice-box and took it to a grimy table to consider his transport problems. The Coke tasted peculiar, having undergone some sort of transmutation, but he swallowed it anyway. It could always be that his own metabolism had changed, there had been so many fluctuations recently. At least the temporal shifts had become less crude, flowing smoothly one into the other, layer passing almost imperceptibly through layer so that it was not always possible to tell exactly what one's bearings were. Although it made his job harder, he couldn't complain. After all, much of it was his own fault. It was only demonstrating his theories.

He was awakened from this somewhat tranquil mood by the distant sound of an ageing engine.

7. UFOs – occupants and artifacts in Eastern Indiana

It was a broken-down Bedford two-tonner with a tattered canvas canopy; definitely a pre-war job. It moved slowly up the street as if searching for something. Jerry couldn't recognize the driver but, since this was his only chance of a lift, he decided to expose himself.

He ran to the fractured window and climbed carefully out to the pavement. The lorry stopped. Through the wound-down window a tired military face was presented to him. 'Colonel Cornelius?'

'Well – ' said Jerry doubtfully. 'I think he's . . . Can you give me a ride?'

The man had kindly but confused pale blue eyes. He was in his fifties or sixties, wearing a shiny blazer, a frayed shirt with washed out pink stripes, a regimental tie. He had a small grey moustache and thinning grey hair. 'I'm Major Nye.' He took a small photograph from above the driving mirror and looked from it to Jerry. 'I'm to take you to Grasmere, I believe?'

Jerry, trusting the major's identification better than his own memory, walked round the lorry and opened the door on the passenger's side. He put a foot on the step as Major Nye cleared various maps and documents from the worn leatherette upholstery. He climbed in and sat down, shutting the door with a slam. The Bedford's engine was still running. Major Nye put it into gear and began to back slowly up the street. 'You came ashore here, did you?'

'In a manner of speaking,' said Jerry.

'You knew about Grasmere?'

'I know *about* Grasmere, certainly.'

'You'll be briefed there. Sorry we couldn't give you something more sophisticated, but the Americans took their best stuff with them or else they destroyed it.'

'The Americans have gone?'

'Didn't you know, old chap? Certainly. Pulled out altogether. Given Europe up as a bad job. Can't say I blame 'em. It means chaos now, of course. But, still . . .' He stopped reversing and moved forward up the B road for Camelford. 'It's going to be a struggle to get through. As you can imagine, communications are breaking down left, right and centre.' He turned on the windscreen wipers as the rain grew heavier. 'But so far no one group has displayed any sort of significant gain.'

'Do you mean it's Civil War?' said Jerry in astonishment.

'It hasn't come to that yet.'

Jerry smiled to himself. 'It was always a game of Roundheads and Cavaliers for years, wasn't it? If you look at it one way.'

'Oh, I quite agree with you.' Major Nye was concentrating on his driving. 'Come on, old girl. Come along then, beauty.'

The Bedford responded with a little extra speed. Major Nye smiled. 'The last lot of bombing didn't improve matters for us. There's scarcely a stretch of road left that hasn't been – ' The lorry began to bump over potholes. 'That's nothing compared to the destruction closer to London. Still, we'll be able to skirt London, that's one consolation.' The rain crackled on the roof. In spite of the major's words, Jerry felt considerably safer in his company that he had felt for a very long time, particularly when he began to hum *The Ballad of Sexual Dependency* from *The Threepenny Opera*. The smell of petrol in the cab gradually became less noticeable and Jerry reached into his Norfolk for the ancient packet of Black Cats. He offered one to Major Nye. 'No thanks, old chap. Roll my own. I say, you wouldn't mind rolling one for me, would you?' He reached for a Rizla tin on the ledge above the dashboard and handed it to Jerry who tried to remember how to use the rolling machine, balancing it on his knees, putting the paper, tobacco and filter into the rubber pad, licking the sticky edge of the paper, closing the lid and producing a fairly reasonable-looking cigarette.

With some pride he gave the result to the major who looked at it a little critically. 'Thanks, old chap. Thicker than my usuals, but still . . . Want one?'

'I'll stick to these,' said Jerry. With his steel Dunhill, almost a match to the one he had left in the jeep, he lit the major's and then his own.

'Bloody rain,' said the major. 'You mustn't mind me. I've got awful habits. My wife says so. Swear all the time. India, I suppose.'

There was silence for a while until they had gone through Camelford, witnessed by the supicious eyes of the residents, and were on a road heading for Tauton and the M. Whereupon, Major Nye, to Jerry's amazement, suddenly began to sing in a slight mellow voice: 'Moonlight becomes you. It goes with your hair. Did anyone ever tell you how pom-pom ta-tee.' He seemd unaware of his audience, peering placidly through the shets of rain as the lorry bravely bucked along. 'I'll see you again, whenever spring comes through again – through again? Something like that. Da da da dee-dee da-dum. In those old familiar places, with those old familiar traaaaa-taaaa . . .' He went through a dozen song fragments in less than four minutes, like a malfunctioning juke box. 'You're the cream in my coffee, I'm the milk in your tea.' He finished his cigarette and wound down the window sufficiently to throw the butt away. 'If you knew Peggy Sue . . .' Then he seemed to remember Jerry. He opened the glove compartment to take out a large newspaper-wrapped packet. 'Sandwich, old boy? Cheese and tomato probably, worst luck. Help yourself. There's far too many for me. The old ulcer. I can't eat much at a sitting. Little and often, that's the motto. Tuck in.'

Jerry pulled away the paper and removed a sandwich. He relaxed in his seat, scarcely paying any attention even when three or four bright explosions lit the evening skyline to the east.

Major Nye did not seem particularly troubled, either, but regarded the explosions rather as confirmation of his earlier forebodings. 'There you are,' he said. 'That's what the Americans have left us to handle.'

'A bastard,' said Jerry.

'The least of it,' said Major Nye.

8. The girl next door could be a witch

There was no doubt about it, thought Jerry, there had once been a time when he had been able to call at least a little of the play. Nowadays even the smallest decisions had been taken out of his hands. He yawned, searching the grey road ahead for black patches that would indicate shell holes. He didn't really care, because his interests were becoming increasingly private as time went, if not on, then at least backwards and forwards. Major Nye was still singing. 'Them good ol' boys drinkin' whiskey an' rye . . .' Perhaps it did have something to do with his losing faith in rock music. The best performers had either died, decayed or fractured, leaving behind them a vocabulary of muscial ideas, lyrical techniques and subject matter, styles and body languages which had never been given the opportunity to mature but had, instead, been aped by the very world of Showbiz against which they had originally revolted. And everything else was just the same – a load of oily entrepreneurs with their hair a little longer, their clothes occasionally a little easier on the eyes, their language an eager combination of professional slang and adman quasi-technical. It forced you, whether you liked it or not, into a classical stance, to long for a world when fiction really was stranger than truth because there were no films, television, magazines, newspapers to prove differently, to find consolation in the great Romantics of those far-off hazy days – Schoenberg, Ives and Messiaen – to hang in a sticky web of conflicting freedoms, finding an acceptable discipline only in Art, and if you were not an artist then the only alternative, as in Mo's case, was a nihilistic war against the sole injustice you could identify, the tyranny of Time and the human condition . . .

Once again Major Nye rescued him from this sentimental reverie. 'Here we are, old chap.'

Jerry looked up, recognizing tranquil Grasmere lake on

his left, the gigantic mock-gothic hotel which had sheltered so many ecstatic old ladies from Minnesota before rocket fire had blown its roof away. Major Nye steered the Bedford carefully off the road to the right and into a small macadamized car-park surrounded by a stone wall. A twisted sign read *Car Park For Wordsworth's Cottage Only*. Dove Cottage was to Jerry's right. As Major Nye switched off the engine and sighed with relief someone appeared at the gate and walked round into the car-park: a tall man of about the same age as Major Nye but with a self-conscious dignity that was just a little Teutonic. He wore an old-fashioned grey three-piece suit and had a daffodil in his lapel. He was settling a grey homburg on his distinguished patrician head, knocking the ash from a cigarette which he smoked in a six-inch holder, cupped in the Russian manner between thumb and fingers.

Lost in a cavern of self-pity, Jerry remained in the cab when Major Nye had walked through the drizzle to shake hands with the newcomer. 'Am I glad to see you, old boy. We've been travelling the best part of two days – rained the whole time. Nearly missed the petrol dump outside Coventry. I'm afraid my passenger's become a little depressed. Is your phone working? I'd like to tell my wife we've arrived safe and sound.'

'There are no lines, I fear.' The man in grey spoke softly. He had a pleasant foreign accent. 'But your daughter is here.'

'Splendid.' Major Nye gestured to Jerry. 'Time to disembark, Colonel Cornelius.'

Jerry roused himself. It was quite possible that the petrol fumes were affecting him. He felt the need of a pick-me-up. A Jimi Hendrix track or a few minutes of *Moses und Aron* would be enough to do the trick; but he had lost hope. He did his best to put on a more cheerful face, opening his door, sliding to the ground, stretching his legs and arms as he approached the pair. The rain fell on his unprotected head. He had left his hat in the cab.

'I am Printz Lobkowitz.' The handsome man stared hard into Jerry's face. 'You know me?'

'No,' said Jerry. 'Do you know me?' He could have ridden for ever in Major Nye's company. He was resentful that the journey was over.

'Oh, it's probably just a touch of *déjà vu*,' said Prinz Lobkowitz. 'Come.' He led the way up the crazy-paving path and into the cottage. 'I think Elizabeth has the kettle on.'

The cottage had not been used as anything but a museum for some time. The uncarpeted rooms were full of glass cases and miscellaneous objects marked 'Probably Wordsworth's stick' and 'The kind of pen Wordsworth would have used'. Most of the genuine things had been sold off to the occupying troops years before. In a room at the back of the cottage was an ordinary table with a blue and white chintz cloth, a gas-stove on which boiled a large iron kettle, a gas-fire in the grate. Two women sat at the table, looking up as the three men entered.

Major Nye smiled. 'Hello, young Bess.' He embraced his rather plump and pretty daughter who wore a multi-coloured Afghan dress and who accepted the embrace with a degree of condescension.

'This is my friend Una,' said Elizabeth Nye. 'Una Persson.'

'I think I've heard of you, my dear. How do you do?'

'How do you do?' said Una Persson.

Jerry was not sure he had ever seen a more beautiful woman. She wore a black trench-coat and beneath it a long suede riding skirt, black knee-length boots, a white polo-neck sweater. There was a cartridge belt around her waist and attached to it a holster for a large revolver. She shook hands with Major Nye and then with Jerry, giving them both a small but friendly smile. Her short chestnut hair fell into her eyes as she sat down again. She brushed it back with a long hand.

'I expect you've a good idea why we contacted you, Colonel,' said Prinz Lobkowitz, sitting close to Miss Persson, 'but we ought to fill you in about the Scottish position as soon as possible. They'll be coming through for you shortly.'

'Aha,' said Jerry, looking for the radio.

Elizabeth Nye got up to pour hot water into a teapot.

'Just what I could do with,' said Major Nye, rubbing his knotted hands together near the gas-fire. 'This is Calor gas, I suppose, isn't it?'

'That's right.' His daughter laughed. She took the pot to the table and put it down amongst the mugs and the milk and sugar already there. 'Who likes it weak?'

'I'd better have it weak,' said Major Nye. 'Thanks, girly.' He accepted the mug.

'As strong as it comes,' said Jerry. 'I'm afraid I've lost my memory.'

'That's what I like to hear.' Printz Lobkowitz had responded to his first statement. 'Eh?'

'My memory,' Jerry said.

'Oh, sod it.' Impatient air hissed from Miss Persson's clenched teeth. 'He must be the most unreliable medium we've used. Every bloody time we need him he cops out – goes and loses his memory again.'

'Sorry.' Jerry was anxious to placate this lovely woman. 'My mind's been taken up with my sister, you see. She's all I have.'

Una Persson's expression softened. With her own hands she gave him a mug of tea. 'Sugar?'

'Not for me. Just milk.'

She poured a little milk into the mug.

'I don't know what I can do for you, really. I'm a fast learner though. In some things, anyway.' Jerry smiled at her, accepting the tea.

'It's not for us,' said Prinz Lobkowitz. 'It's the Scots. We promised them you could advise them. None of us has any experience in physics. Not yet. Not in a practical sense, at any rate.'

'I've put all that sort of thing behind me,' said Jerry.

Una Persson stood up and went to the window.

'I thought religion might help, you see,' he continued. 'If

394

I redefined things in supernatural terms. It can sometimes work. In the short run.'

He looked to them for confirmation and saw only bafflement.

'You'd better dredge up whatever you can,' said Una Persson. 'They've arrived.'

The five people crowded to the window, staring through the trees and the ruins out towards the lake. In the centre of the lake was a small island, hilly and wooded. Hovering over the island was a bulky hull. On its tail-fins was painted the blue cross of St Andrew. The ship's entire outer skin was covered in the brilliant scarlet sett of the McMahon clan.

'Why me?' said Jerry miserably.

'Just your bad luck, I'm afraid,' said Prinz Lobkowitz. 'We're hoping that Scotland will hold, you see. Everything else is disintegrating rapidly.'

'Politics?' Jerry became wary. 'Is this some sort of manipulation?'

Major Nye patted Jerry on the back.

'Cheer up, old chap. It won't be for long, after all.'

'I thought I was regressing, but this – Christ!' He let them push him towards the door.

'In the meantime,' said Una Persson suddenly, a little brisk sympathy in her tone, 'we'll be helping you look for Catherine. How's that?'

Jerry spread his hands. 'Out?'

9. A Bicentennial celebration. The 1976 Guns and Ammo Annual. It's all new . . . it's informative . . . it's authoritative . . . Start your 'Bicentennial' celebration today!

Dodging and weaving as usual Jerry slithered down the mound of refuse, his kilt left behind him like a forgotten fleece where it had snagged on the barbed wire and pulled free. Below him was what remained of the road and, on the other side, the ruins of the Convent of the Poor Clares. He was relieved to see that the row of houses on the South side of Blenheim Crescent, although boarded up, had escaped any major damage. He had jumped ship as the *James Durie* lost height over what had been the Mitcham Golf Course, had made it as far as the Bangladeshi ghetto in Tooting, where, under the hastily invented pseudonym 'Secundra Dass,' he had been accepted and passed on through Brixton and as far as Pimlico before the chain had broken and he had found himself alone. From Pimlico he had to cross the desolation of Knightsbridge before he was in sight of home. Knightsbridge was the notorious of all quarters, its inhabitants so vicious that they were feared even by the infamous denizens of Mayfair. Moreover Jerry in his kilt and turban had had the odds stacked as high against him as was possible, short of having a wooden leg as well. He had been fortunate in retaining his claymore and kris and with these weapons had been able to score himself a serviceable Lee-Enfield from a tall and muscular young lady in a silk headscarf and a necklace of black human ears.

Now, in grubby underpants, his legs running with cuts and half-healed gashes, the .303 cocked, he reached the Convent, drawn towards the blasted chapel by the faint strains of Buddy Holly singing . . . *my heart grows cold and old* . . . on a tiny cassette machine. It was a signal. The song faded and became *You've Got To Hide Your Love Away*. It could not be a trap. He relaxed by a fraction and put the rifle under his arm so that he could stoop and pull up his socks which had slipped down inside his stolen wellington boots (another prize from the lady in the headscarf). A shadow moved behind a mock Gothic window. The music stopped. Jerry raised his rifle and advanced. Pieces of broken plaster stirred as Sebastian Auchinek, in a neat set of fatigues, a Browning automatic in his inexperienced fist, broke cover, his free hand held palm outwards without much hope. His large brown eyes were wary, antagonistic, ready, as ever, for compromise. Instantly the Dixie Cups began to sing *Chapel of Love*.

'You're looking pale, Mr Cornelius. You've lost your usual camouflage, eh? What's the matter – is the famous survival instinct shot at last?'

'I can't help the opinions people hold of me,' said Jerry. 'Your message came through days ago. I'm sorry I couldn't get here sooner.'

'Don't give it a thought. There's not an awful lot of danger around at the moment. It's as quiet as the grave. Almost rural in some respects.' He sounded wistful.

'It always was,' said Jerry. 'Enervating, isn't it, conventional warfare?'

'You're not fooling me, my son. I'm hip to any Pied Piper tricks.' Auchinek holstered his Browning. 'I'm acting on behalf of Miss Persson. As her agent. She asked me to do this.'

'Still in the promotion business, then?' Jerry followed the Jew into the shadows of the chapel and found a seat on the cold ugly marble of the altar. 'What sort of acts are going down with the London public at the moment?' He began to shiver. 'You couldn't lend me a costume, could you?'

Auchinek was pleased with the situation. 'Sorry,' he said casually, 'all the props are gone.'

'You could lend me your guerrilla suit. You won't win the girl by making a monkey of yourself, king. Aping her's not going to help the state of the Empire. Aaah!' Jerry opened his mouth and screeched with laughter, displaying his broken, pie-bald teeth.

'And you'll never get away with that material.' Auchinek shook his head. 'Not these days. Tastes are changing. The public wants sophisticated romantic comedy. You're offering them amateurish street theatre. Things have come a long way since the mummer's plays. It won't do, Mr Cornelius.'

Jerry scratched his neck. 'So it is an audition, after all?'

'Of sorts. I can help you. There might be room for a brother and sister act in our final programme.' He studied Jerry's eyes and seemed satisfied by the reaction he received. Jerry got down from the altar. Sebastian Auchinek turned over the tape to its reverse side. *I believe in yesterday* sang Paul McCartney, his voice finding an echo in what remained of the roof. With a sudden burst of malicious energy Auchinek flung the player against the wall. It smashed at once and there was silence. 'I'm Miss Persson's manager, as you know, but I do sometimes handle other people . . .'

'You don't have to tell me. Are you talking about Catherine?'

'I am. My spell in the USAF . . .'

'I don't want to know about your introduction to black magic . . .'

'. . . proved useful in that I was able to acquire certain rights . . .'

'I told you . . .'

'. . . and in turn come to possession . . .'

'You're not listening. Your religious convictions are your own. All I want to know – '

'. . . of a number of flies – files – pertaining to the activities of informants operating in this area.'

'Narks? Stoolies? Squealers?'

'One of whom was a friend of yours, I believe. Gordon Gavin.'

'Flash Gordon.'

'I was able to interview him, just before the big pullout. He knew the whereabouts of your sister. She's still here.'

'She can't be. I moved her, didn't I? I had her – I had her –
that's what I can't remember. But I was sure . . .'

'Only the surface suffered much. The underground sec-
tions are still almost entirely intact and functioning. Why,
there's a rumour that some of these tunnels go all the way
to Lapland.'

'So she was under my nose before, before, before . . .'
Jerry's head was aching badly. 'Have you got her safe?'

'She doesn't look too good to me. But Miss Persson
assured me . . .'

'She's an expert at that.' Images filled his poor battered
head. He left the chapel and ran across to the main building,
up the fractured stairs, over the demolished threshold,
waist-deep in lath and plaster, brickwork and shattered
timber, wading towards his only hope, his goal, his faith,
flailing around him as, with his last reserves of energy, he
shifted muck and rubble.

'Catherine!

'Catherine!

'Catherine!'

In critical awe Sebastian Auchinek watched the wasted
body of the wailing barbarian disappear in a chaos of dust.

10. High intensity colour (that's actually good for your eyes!)

'Airship? You never bin on a bleedin' airship – not since you woz a boy at ther bloody Scrubs Lane fair!' Mrs Cornelius had a good laugh before looking down on her son and shaking her huge head, freshly permed, freshly gold. Her mouth was a handsome crimson, an exotic blossom, its tints echoed in her cheeks, contrasted by her eyelids of midnite blue, the pink powder. She belched and her breasts wobbled as she patted at her belly. 'Pardon.' She tugged at the waist of her cotton frock with its pattern of maroon and yellow nasturtiums. 'Ah. Thass better. Wot's 'appened ter Frank?'

'He went off with the colonel, Mum,' said Jerry meekly. 'You didn't tell him about Cathy, did you?'

'Fink I'm daft. Silly bugger! 'Course I didn't. We don't wan' the 'ole fuckin' world ter know, do we?' Although not altogether sure what was wrong with her daughter, Mrs Cornelius had a strong suspicion that it was connected with something scandalous. When Jerry had brought her home his mother had immediately suspected him of having attempted an abortion on her. It had been Colonel Pyat, with his connections, who had known of the fortified hospital at Roedean and arranged for the girl to be taken there. Catherine had been in the worst condition Jerry had ever seen her – more than a little frost-blackened. The hospital, however, was the best there was. The doctors had every confidence, they said, in an early revival. Jerry had had to borrow four cases of 12.77mm machine-gun ammunition from Colonel Pyat to add to his own store, and that had been for the hospital's down payment only. He wasn't sure where he was going to find the BTR-50PK armoured personnel carrier he would need to secure the release of his sister once she was up and about. Again Colonel Pyat had been reassuring, promising that he would underwrite Jerry until the situation improved for him.

Jerry had wanted to go straight back to London from Roedean but his mother insisted on making a day of it. Frank was living in Brighton now, running a small general shop, and Mrs Cornelius wanted to see how he was getting on.

'It 'asn't arf changed,' declared Mrs Cornelius as she stood regarding the twisted pier, most of which had tipped itself into the sea. She pointed at a distant girder. 'There where the ol' dodgems useter be, innit?'

Jerry turned up the collar of his black car coat. He put his hands deep into his pockets. It was very cold for May, although the sky was blue and clear and the water as calm as the Mediterranean. He was worried in case Colonel Pyat told Frank something which would start the whole trouble all over again. He looked back towards the darkened dolphinarium in time to see the colonel and his brother ascending the steps to the street. Colonel Pyat shook his head calling: 'Nothing I'm afraid!'

'Orl I bleedin' want is a bag o' fish an' chips!' said Mrs Cornelius with a gigantic sigh of dismay. She patted her son a the shoulder. 'Up yer get, Jer'.'

Jerry rose from the bench, moving his weight from foot to foot, running his tongue round the inside of his mouth. 'I'm a bit worried about the lorry,' he said. 'What with the scavengers and that.'

'It'll be safe enough where it is,' she reassured him. 'I wish ther bloody trains woz still goin'. Cor! Wot a cumdarn, eh?' She cast a disgusted eye over the wrecked façades, the faded signs. 'Yer carn't even go on there fuckin' beach for bleedin' bar' wire!'

Frank and Colonel Pyat arrived to stand beside them. Jerry was disturbed by the fact that Frank wore a black coat almost identical to his own. His brother's eyes were warm and cunning as if he had recently sniffed prey. 'Not a chip to be had,' said Frank. 'Sorry, Mum. It's what I thought. Nobody's catching any fish, for one thing.' He anticipated

401

his mother's next question before she asked it. 'And, of course, there hasn't been a pub open since the ordinance. You'd better take me up on that sandwich.' He nodded towards the twitterns of the town's cold interior. 'Back at the shop.'

Mrs Cornelius sighed. 'I used ter love this place. It woz reelly fun. Remember ther races, Ferdy?'

Colonel Pyat, who wore a cavalry twill military-style over-coat, nodded his heavy Slavic head. 'Everything is gone now.'

'It's not as bad as all that,' said Frank. 'A lot of the old residents are still here. We've quite a flourishing community, really. We've kept our identity, which is more than you can say of some. We can't offer the facilities to visitors nowadays, of course, but perhaps that's for the best – so far as the indigenous population's concerned. But you'll see. Brighton'll be back to normal before you know it.'

Jerry removed a dirty handkerchief from his pocket and loudly blew his nose. Frank darted him a weary look. 'Cool it, Jerry.'

Jerry put his handkerchief away. 'I shouldn't've thought it could have got any cooler.'

For the first time Mrs Cornelius noticed the cold. 'You're right. It's bloody freezin'. You got anyfink I c'n put on, Frank?'

'I've got some lovely coats back at the shop. Real mink. I'll lend you one of those.' Frank began to walk along the front and they followed.

'Mink?' said his mother. 'Bloody 'ell! You must be doin' orl right, as usual!'

'There's not a lot of call for luxury goods just now. But that'll change in time. I accepted them as barter.' Frank laughed. 'I must have every decent mink coat on the South Coast. I've literally got a back room full of them. The trouble is, though, that they attract rats.'

'Aaawk!' said Mrs Cornelius ritualistically.

Frank stopped and then fell in beside Jerry. 'And how's life treating you?' His bleak eyes stared out to sea, giving the horizon a shifty once-over. 'Getting by, are we?'

'Under the circumstances,' said Jerry.

'A bit more realistic, these days, I should think.' Frank was almost euphorically triumphant. He tapped his head. 'Got the old imagination in check at last. You're staying with mum?'

'I've been a bit queer,' said Jerry.

'So she's looking after you, is she?'

'Well, my own place . . .'

'A direct hit, I heard. Shame.'

They were some distance ahead of Mrs C. and Colonel P. Now. Frank led the way up King Street. 'You had your head in the clouds, you see. Now I saw the way the wind was blowing. I've got my shop. In real terms I'm probably the richest man in Sussex. Surrey, too, I shouldn't wonder. Got four Pakis working for me. Kept my head down, see, and my nose clean and here I am. I don't deny I'm well off. I don't fell guilty.'

'Guilty?' Jerry had never heard his brother use the word. He cheered up a fraction. 'Blimey! You must have done some terrible things. Brighton's getting to you, then?'

'What?' Frank was puzzled. 'I'm happy, Jerry. Not many can say that, these days. Got my pick of anything I want. Any *body* I want.' He nudged his brother in the ribs. 'Some of those people'll give anything for a bit of fresh liver. Their little daughters. Eh? What! They never learned to fight, you see – only complain. I must have had every "Disgusted" in the Home Counties in my shop! Well, I ask you!' He paused. Mrs Cornelius and her escort were a fair way behind, labouring up the hill. 'You want to work for me? Is that why you came?'

'Mum wanted to see how you were doing. I just drove the lorry.'

'Your lorry, is it?'

'The colonel's. He was in the last government for a few days.'

'Did all right for himself, then?'

'He reckons he was sold short.' Jerry spoke listlessly as he looked at a sea bereft of boats, a sky without ships, a street without music. Catherine remained and he was helpless to give her comfort or take any direct part in her destiny. He swayed as his mother came closer. She was bent almost double, rubbing her thumb against her index finger, making peculiar smacking noises with her lips. He felt very dizzy indeed. Frank glanced at him. 'You've gone all yellow.'

'I'm tired,' said Jerry.

'Totch-totch,' said Mrs Cornelius. 'Come 'ere, yer littel bleeder. Totch-totch-totch.'

Through rapidly blurring vision Jerry saw that she was addressing a small, mangy black and white cat in the gutter. The animal walked slowly and amiably towards her, rubbing its flank against the kerb, its tail erect.

Jerry sat down on the pavement.

His mother didn't notice what was happening to him; but the cat turned to look at him, its intelligent green eyes piercing his own.

For a moment it seemed to Jerry that his entire being was about to be drawn into the body of the cat. Then Mrs Cornelius had pounced and seized the animal. 'Gotcha, yer little bugger!'

'This is a fine time to start playing the Fool,' said Frank.

Jerry passed out.

Early Reports

Many bathing deaths were reported from seaside resorts yesterday. Two men and a boy were drowned while bathing near Llanelly, and Bertie Crooke, sixteen, son of a soldier, was drowned at Exmouth. Mr Duncan McGregor (twenty-four), a chemist, of Coatbridge, while bathing at Spittal was carried away by a strong current and drowned, despite the brave attempts to rescue him made by Mr James Webster, of Airdrie. Two young munition workers named Griffith Robert Jones and Richard Morris were drowned while bathing at Buryport.

Sunday Pictorial, 22 July 1917

The following notice announcing the adoption of a system of air-raid warnings for London by 'sound bomb' was issued last night: – The experiments made on Thursday with sky signals showed the value of sound bombs for the purpose of warning the population of London ... The signal will consist of three sound bombs fired at intervals of a quarter of a minute ... having regard to the speed at which aeroplanes now travel, the warning at the point attacked can only be of a few minutes' duration.

Sunday Pictorial, 22 July 1917

The *Bourse Gazette* states that the Premier, Prince Lvoff, has resigned. M. Kerensky has been appointed Premier, temporarily retaining the portfolios of War and Marine. M. Kerensky has sent a message to Reval, Helsingfors, and other points, saying: The disturbances have now been completely suppressed. The arrest of the leaders and of those guilty of the blood of their brothers and of crimes against the country and the revolution is proceeding ... I appeal to all true sons of democracy to save the country and the revolution from the enemy without and his Allies within.

Sunday Pictorial, 22 July 1917

Aliens living at Folkestone and Margate have been given notice to leave the towns ... under a new Home Office Order which prohibits their presence within 20 miles of the coast. At Folkestone 130 foreigners are affected. They must be out of the town by midnight tonight. At Margate 238 have been given three days' notice.

The Times, 5 June 1940

The trial began before Mr Justice Atkinson at the Central Criminal Court yesterday of Udham Singh, 37, an Indian engineer, who is charged with the murder of Sir Michael Frances O'Dwyer, a former Governor of the Punjab, at the close of a lecture at Caxton Hall, Westminster, on March 13. He pleaded 'Not Guilty'.

The Times, 5 June 1940

Prefabs, with people clinging to the roofs, floated past bedroom windows at Felixstowe, where disaster arrived when the River Orwell burst its banks two miles away. Survivors told of nightmare screams and shouts for help as they watched people slide to their deaths from floating prefabs. Mrs Beryl Hillary ... said they were awakened by screams. 'As I looked out of the window I saw a little girl washed off the roof of a prefab and drown.' In Orford Road, where the Hillarys lived, a mother, father and two young children were drowned in a downstairs flat. People in the top flat were rescued. Mrs Katherine Minter, of Lauger Road, said: 'In the darkness all that could be heard was the roaring of the water and the screaming of terrified women. The housing estate was like an ocean.' ... Two-year-old Valerie – she could not tell nurses her surname – cried in hospital for her parents. They are listed among the missing.

Daily Sketch, 2 February 1953

A baby died in a basement blaze in Sorcham Street, North Kensington on Saturday after two passers by had hurled themselves into the burning front room when they heard her screams.

Kensington Post, 19 February 1965

Fire danger in North Kensington has become a controversial issue between the LCC and KBC. They sharply disagree on the code of fire prevention for lodging and rooming houses. Kensington Council say that the LCC Code of Escape from Fire is impracticable and expensive. They claim it would mean an average cost of £300 per house ... Kensington Council have not yet revealed their own plans for fire prevention, but there is no doubt they envisage a much cheaper and simpler code.

Kensington Post, 19 February 1965

Jimi Hendrix, the pop musician, died in London yesterday, as reported elsewhere in this issue. If Bob Dylan was the man who liberated pop music verbally, to the extent that after him it could deal with subjects other than teenage affection, then Jimi Hendrix was largely responsible for whatever musical metamorphosis it has undergone in the past three years. Born in Seattle, Washington, he was part Negro, part Cherokee Indian, part Mexican, and gave his date of birth as 27 November, 1945.

The Times, 19 September 1970

Part-time soldiers have been on manoeuvres with a Nazi 'secret army' it was claimed yesterday. The troops were members of a Territorial Army unit. Special Branch investigators have been told that TA men linked up with a Nazi paramilitary group known as Column 88 for exercises in the Savernake Forest in Wiltshire. At least one TA officer – said to be a secret Nazi group member – is alleged to have helped to set up the operation. Members of the 20-strong TA unit thought the Nazis were another TA group. During the exercise the soldiers acted as mock terrorists, while the Nazis played the role of defenders of an important military target.

Daily Mirror, 19 April 1976

Tuning Up (4)

'What infernal bad luck!' As he walked along the deck in his glittering white uniform Colonel Pyat tossed his racquet in the air and caught it again. 'We lost all our balls.'

'Overboard,' said Catherine, indicating the Mediterranean. She, too, wore white, a boater with a blue and white band, a simple silk shirt-waister with a pale blue broderie anglaise bodice. The shirt of the dress was cut just on the ankle of her kid boots. She and he had been playing tennis in the yacht's court, astern. 'Entirely my fault. I'm terrible.'

Jerry shifted his weight in the blue and white deck-chair, putting his newspaper on the matching canvas stool at his elbow. 'I'm sure we'll be able to get you some more. In Alexandria, perhaps.' He ran a finger round the inside of his hard collar.

'Is it far, Alexandria?' she asked him. She sat in the chair next to his. Colonel Pyat hovered, then went to stand by the *Teddy Bear's* rail.

'Not too far.' A tiny breeze found his face. He sighed with pleasure.

Colonel Pyat laid a finger on one side of his small moustache and peered out from beneath his cap. The peak shaded his eyes completely. Indeed, the only strong feature visible was his neat Imperial. 'Shouldn't you be getting ready? It's almost tea time.'

'So I should.' Jerry rose from the canvas chair. He gathered up his books and papers. 'And you, too, Catherine, eh?' He raised his Panama. 'I'll see you later, then.'

'Fine,' said the colonel.

Jerry crossed to his cabin. It faced forward – a bedroom, a sitting room and a dressing room. It was full of light from the large port-holes on three sides, simply furnished with Charles Rennie Mackintosh designs. Even as he changed into his costume he heard eight bells ring for the dog-watch;

time for tea. Slipping on his domino Jerry hurried out, making for the stern and the quarterdeck where a piano had already been set up by lithe Lascar matelots. On the rest of the deck were little gilded bamboo tables with lace cloths; they had matching gilded bamboo chairs, upholstered in blue plush.

As Jerry approached the quarterdeck, racing down the companionway, he almost bumped into Miss Brunner, the governess, who made a clicking noise with her tongue before she guessed who he was. Dyak stewards, in white turbans, red Zouave jackets and blue sarongs, were setting silver-ware and teapots on the tables. Jerry ascended the last companionway just ahead of Bishop Beesley and Karen von Krupp (wearing her usual Brunswick coffee-coloured gown), two of his guests on the cruise, and just behind Una Persson who was smoothing the folds of her elaborate Columbine costume, gold, white and scarlet, and adjusting her own domino mask. She stood beside the piano, protecting her head with a Japanese sunshade. Jerry winked at her and sat down at the piano.

'Shall we try it, then?'

Una Persson looked at Bishop Beesley, Karen von Krupp and Miss Brunner who were arranging themselves at the farthest table, near the rail. 'Why not?' she said. She cleared her throat. Jerry lifted the lid of the piano and played a few notes, exercising his fingers, folding back the flounced cuffs of his red, white and blue pierrot suit. 'Where's Catherine?'

'On her way.' Jerry spread his new music.

'And Prinz Lobkowitz?'

'On his way.'

'Auchinek?'

'You'd know better than I, my dear.' Jerry put his thumb on middle C.

'Your Mr Collier?'

'Doubtless on his way.'

'They're all arriving, the audience. Oh, I hate bad time-keeping.' She folded her sunshade and put it behind the piano.

Jerry played a ¾ tango rhythm with his left hand. 'We might as well start, I think. It's only an amateur show, Una.'

She put one hand on the quarterdeck's port rail, glanced at the smooth sea, raised herself on the points of her ballet slippers, twirling in her three-quarter-length skirt. She began to smile. It was the professional in her. To encourage his companion, Jerry played a white note glissando and began to hum the tune of their song as Major Nye, Mrs Nye, the Nye daughters and the Nyes' little boy, Pip, took their places at two tables near the front. Major Nye was smiling in delight. 'How jolly!' Mrs Nye did her best to smile, but she was not Una's class. The girls looked a trifle embarrassed and the little boy seemed astonished. He wore a sailor suit, as did his sisters. The Dyaks bent over them to take their orders. Mrs Cornelius, in a huge cream and strawberry day dress and a lopsided Gainsborough hat, arrived on the arm of her son Frank who wore an orange, blue and green blazer, white cotton trousers and a yellow boater. Una began to sing in her high, sweet voice:

> *My pulse rate stood at zero*
> *When I first saw my Pierrot.*

Jerry sang to her over his right shoulder as he continued to play:

> *My temperature rose to ninety-nine*
> *When I beheld my Columbine.*

Catherine ran onto the deck, arriving just in time to join Una. Catherine, too, was masked, dressed as Harlequin in colours to match Una's. She had her magic wand in her hand, Harlequin's slap-stick with which, traditionally, everything could be transformed into something else. They all sang the chorus:

411

Sigh, sigh, sigh . . .
For love that's oft denied.
Cry, cry, cry . . .
My lips remain unsatisfied
I'm yearning so, for my own Pierrot.

Catherine took Una about the waist and they danced together for the last line of the chorus.

As we dance the En-tropy Tan-go!

Jerry played the chorus through again, making it more lively and giving it strict tango rhythm now, for Auchinek had reached them. He was in white from head to foot, half his thin face covered in an expressionless white mask, the rest caked in dead white make-up, a false grey beard, huge glasses, crowned by an elongated silk hat. He was old Pantaloon, as orthodox as ever in the traditional dell'arte costume.

Una and Catherine were cheek to cheek. ' Sigh, sigh, sigh . . .' Their eyes were fixed on the audience. Auchinek went to stand awkwardly on the other side of Jerry, evidently trying to remember the lyrics. When Jerry had told him of the plan he had gone from Naples to Rome by train to buy his costume. 'For love that's oft denied.' Jerry stared mournfully at Columbine. 'Cry, cry, cry . . . My lips remain unsatisfied . . .' Facing Jerry now, Una sang perhaps a mite too sardonically: 'I'm yearning so for my own Pierrot.' And altogether: 'As we dance the En-tropy Tan-tan-go!'

Colonel Pyat sat down, raising his cap in jovial, if uncomprehending appreciation. Nearby, Frank Cornelius frowned as he tried to make out the words, comprehending all too well. He began to look a bit alarmed.

Prinz Lobkowitz came up at last, all in black velvet save for a white frill around his neck, a beribboned mandolin in his hand, his eyes merry behind his mask, as Scaramouche, and behind him was Shakey Mo Collier, panting, scrambling, swaggering as soon as he was in sight of the audience, in a gorgeously elaborate military uniform, festooned with braid, blazing with brass, a great Wellington hat on his head, sporting strich and peacock feathers, wearing false moustachios which he twirled rather too often, monstrous eyebrows which threatened to blind him, jackboots and sabre, a perfect burlesque bantam dandy, Captain Fracasse.

Assembled they sang the next chorus with wavering gusto:

> *I'll weep, weep, weep*
> *Till he sweeps me off my feet.*
> *My heart will beat, beat, beat,*
> *And my body lose its heat.*
> *Oh, life no longer seems so sweet*
> *Since that sad Pierrot became my beau*
> *And taught me the En-tro-py Tan-go!*

Harlequin tango'd with Pantaloon, Columbine with Scaramouche, Pierrot with Captain Fracasse, until Jerry had to return to his place at the piano for his own verse:

> *So flow, flow, flow . . .*
> *As the rains turn into snow.*
> *And it's slow, slow, slow . . .*
> *As the colours lose their glow . . .*
> *The Winds of Limbo no longer blow*
> *For cold Columbine and her pale Pierrot,*
> *As we dance the En-tro-py Tan-go!*

Frank was groaning and looking about him as if expecting attack from all sides, as if he contemplated ducking under the table. His face had turned a colour that was ugly in contrast to his blazer, but his mother merely shook her head. 'Ai deown't know ai'm shewer.' She was using her posh voice. 'Yew cern't unnerstand a word of the songs these days, cean yew?' She waved a tea-cake. Crumbs cascaded over her strawberry flounces. 'An' wot they doin', ai wondah, puttin' on a bleedin' pentomime et Easter?' She pushed back the brim of her hat as her eye caught something in the distance. She tugged at a Dyak's jacket. 'Blimey! Wot's that?'

Absentmindedly Frank swallowed his whole cake. His eyes popped. He choked. 'What?'

Although they had planned another chorus, Mrs Cornelius's cry was so loud that even the performers turned to stare in the same direction.

Sebastian Auchinek's eyes were weeping, doubtless from the toxic effects of the make-up. He removed his topper. 'Where?'

'What?' said Shakey Mo, twirling a disappointed moustachio. He had only just begun to enjoy himself for the first time since Nice.

'That!' said Mrs Cornelius dramatically.

Miss Brunner, Karen von Krupp, Bishop Beesley and the whole Nye family rose to their feet.

'That smudge over there!' Mrs Cornelius crammed another tea-cake into her mouth. She made a further remark, also, but it was entirely muffled.

Prinz Lobkowitz put his mandolin on top of the piano. He seemed relieved. 'That's Africa.'

Mais Arlequin le Roi commande à l'Acheron,
Il est duc des esprits de la bande infernale.

Historie plaisante des faits et gestes de Harlequin etc.,
Paris, 1585

Once, the giant huntsman was Odin, the Norse god of the dead, who rode through the night skies seeking the souls of the dying. Though his name was changed with the coming of Christianity, his role did not. Often he was thought of as the Devil himself, but in different parts of France he was identified as the ghost of King Herod, or of Charlemagne. In northern England he was sometimes called Woden, while other counties saw him as Wild Elric, who defied the Conqueror, or even as Arthur. The phantom hounds were the spirits of unbaptized children, or of unrepentant sinners . . . Some critics have pointed out, however, that their cries, as they seek the souls of the damned, closely resemble those of migrating geese.

Folklore, Myths and Legends of Britain, London, 1973

Filth and Noise: Portobello Residents Complain

Portobello Road Market is a disgrace say some local residents – and they are backed up by Sisters of St Joseph's Convent. The cause is the junk and litter left by second-hand dealers – the Steptoes and 'trotters' of North Kensington. It's not just the noise and the Borough Council workmen clearing up the rubbish that is annoying the Catholic Sisters. By day, says the Mother Superior, people throw old shoes, suitcases and other unwanted articles over the convent wall. 'The main door is thick with filth sometimes,' she said. 'It is quite degrading' ... Mrs Anna Marks, a Portobello Road shopkeeper, described the northern part of the market as 'shameful'. It was a disgrace to London. ... Her husband, Mr W. Marks, added: 'I have lived here all my life – I remember when they used to drive sheep down the Portobello Road. The market has gone downhill lately.'

KENSINGTON POST, 23 April 1965

1. The God from the machine

'The new century,' said Major Nye, 'doesn't seem awfully different from the old.' He stretched his arms in his stiff drab jacket, settled his topee on his grey locks, and clumped in booted feet out onto the verandah to salute the flag as it was raised for the morning. In the fort's quadrangle a squadron of troopers in the uniform of the 3rd Punjab Irregular Rifles, a squadron of Bengali riflemen in red and dark blue, with red and yellow turbans, and Ghoorka infantrymen in gun-green and red, saluted the Union Jack. Young Cornelius was in charge of the guard. 'Sir!' He, too, wore drab, with black lace and red facings, a solar topee wound about with the regiment's green, black and red colours.

'Morning, Cornelius. Happy New Year to you. Looked for you last night.'

'I was still on my way back from Simla, sir. I've just had time to change.'

'Of course. Any news?'

'Not much sir.'

'Ha!'

Major Nye yawned. Then he craned forward to inspect first the British and then the native troops who stood to attention on three sides of the parade ground as the bugle began its traditional call. Currently he and Cornelius were the only white officers here. He raised his eyes to the great hills beyond the walls. He had faith in his Sikhs and Ghoorkas. Secundra Dass and his Chinese allies might be threatening from the East, while Zakar Khan, the old hill fox, could be on his way from the North, with Russian machine guns and officers, but they'd be no match for a couple of battalions of these chaps, plus a squadron or two of the 3rd Punjab Cavalry. Major Nye frowned.

'Cavalry didn't travel with you, after all?'

Cornelius dismissed the guard. 'Yes, sir. But I was on

418

duty, so I had to ride ahead. They shouldn't be more than an hour or two at most, sir.'

'Jolly good.' Major Nye moved his head. 'Mind coming inside for a moment, Cornelius?'

Major Nye retired into his gloomy office. It was almost cold. On the wall hung the photograph Major Nye usually referred to as his 'personal touch': a picture of Sarah Bernhardt as she appeared in her white costume in Richepin's *Pierrot Assassin* at the Trocadero in Paris on 28 April 1883, just before her marriage to M. Damala broke up. She had married Damala in London the previous year and Major Nye had been on leave at the time and witnessed it, almost by accident. Overhead the punka swept back and forth, disturbing some of the dust on the piles of papers stacked everywhere. Major Nye rarely replied to communications but he did not have the heart to file anything before it had been officially answered. 'Sit down, old chap.'

Cornelius sat in the rattan armchair on the other side of the desk. Major Nye removed something from his own chair before seating himself. 'Had that fellow of yours in yesterday, Cornelius. What's his name? Hashim?'

'Really, sir? Did he tell you anything worthwhile?'

'Wouldn't talk to me. Wouldn't talk to Subadar Bisht. Wouldn't talk to Risaldar S'arnt Major. Would only talk to you. Trusts you, I suppose. Couldn't blame him. But he seemed to have an urgent message for you. Worried me a bit. Could mean trouble coming, eh?'

'Quite likely, sir. He was riding with the Chinese until they stopped to recoup at Srinagar. He reported their position and then returned to their camp. I'd guess that the horde's on the move again.'

Major Nye frowned. 'It means that Secundra Dass and his men have joined them now.'

'That's the report we had while I was in Simla, sir.'

'We're going to need some Lancers, Cornelius.'

'Yes, sir. And a bit of artillery too, sir, I'd have thought.'

'Artillery would help. Still, I feel sorry for the Chinese if our Ghoorkas get at them. They're not a fighting people, the Chinese.'

419

'No, sir.'

'Like the Americans. No good at it. They should leave fighting to the British, eh? And the Ghoorkas and the Sikhs, hm? And the Dogras and Mahrattas, what?'

'Who would we fight, sir?' Cornelius was amused, but Major Nye didn't find the question sensible.

'Why, the bloody Afridis, of course. Who else? He'll always give you a good scrap, your Afridi.'

'True, sir.'

'Damned true, Cornelius.' Major Nye became nostalgic and querulous. 'Why'd the blasted Chinese want to interfere? Waste of time. Waste of everybody's time.'

'They've conquered Tibet and Nepal and Kashmir and Iskandastan so far, sir.'

'Certainly they have. But they haven't crossed the border yet, have they?'

'They must be about to, sir.'

'Then they're blasted fools. And Secundra Dass is a blasted fool to tie himself down with a lot of Chinese.'

'They outnumber us by about a thousand to one, I should think, sir.' Cornelius spoke mildly. He was trying to read a partially exposed report on the major's desk. The report was yellow, several months old at least. 'If they attack while we're at our present strength, we should have quite a hard time of it.'

'Certainly. It won't be easy, Cornelius. But with the Cavalry here we should do it, what?'

'It could be the largest army on the march since the time of Genghis Khan.' Cornelius got up and looked through the blinds at the glinting hills.

Major Nye lit his pipe. 'But Genghis Khan was a Mongol, not a Chinaman. Besides, he didn't have the British to deal with – or the Ghoorkas, or the Jats or Baluchis, or Madrassis, or the Ranghars or Gorwalis or Pathans or Punjabis or Rajputs – or, for that matter, the 3rd Punjab Irregular Rifles. Not just the best trained soldiers in the world, not just the bravest and most spirited, but they're the fiercest, too. Volunteers, you see. There's nothing more terrifying, more

420

"unstoppable", than a force of British lancers. That's why we get on with them so well – they're as civilized and no-nonsense savage as we are. It's why we got on well with Arabs, too, you know. It's why we *don't* get on with Bombay brahmins . . .'

'The Chinese and Secundra Dass are sworn to sweep every European from Asia, sir.'

'Excellent idea.'

'Sir?'

'What? Ah!' Major Nye smiled in understanding. Dropping his voice he spoke slowly, as if he didn't wish to startle Cornelius. 'We're not Europeans, after all. Never have been. We're British. That's why we've so much in common with India.'

'They seem to hate us just as much as any other – non-Indians – sir.'

'Of course they do. Why shouldn't they? Good for them. But they won't beat us.'

'It seems, sir, that the Chinese . . .'

'The Chinese are a peasant race, Cornelius. The British and their fighting Indian allies, do you see, are not peasant races. The Slavs, the Germans, most Latins, are natural tillers of the soil, makers of profits. They like to preserve the status quo above everything else. But we, like the Sikhs and Ghoorkas, are naturally aggressive and pretty rapacious. Not brutal, you understand – it's peasants make brutal soldiers. Russians, Chinese, Japanese, Americans, Boers – all peasants and burghers. The infantry, at any rate, while the cavalry are full of ideas of swagger and glory – parvenu Uhlans the lot of them, Hussars-manqués, that's what I think. Peasants – panicky butchers at best, and sometimes crueller than any Pathan – war's an insanity for them, you see, no part of their way of life – they'd rather be at home doing whatever it is they do with the cows and pigs and shops. We're cruel, arrogant, often ruthless, but we've lived by war for too long not to have become somewhat more humane in the way we wage it. We make quick decisions. We make our points hard and fast. We don't have to hate

421

our enemies to kill 'em, we do it decently, on the whole, with respect and economy.' Major Nye rang a bell on his desk. 'Feel like some tea?'

'Thanks, sir.' Young Cornelius seemed somewhat depressed, probably because he had been up all night on the train from Simla.

'Same goes for your Arab, your Pathan, your Sikh. It's self-interest, it's efficiency, and sometimes it's a sort of practical idealism, but we rarely have to work ourselves up to hatred, to find a Cause, a reason for loathing those we wish to kill. Practicality – it's why we're good at running an Empire. And as long as people don't give us trouble, we look after 'em. The Dutch and the Belgians, for instance, take too much out of their colonies, and so do the French – the peasant instinct, again, a tendency to overwork the land, you might say. Also, of course, they were unfortunate enough to belong to the Continent of Europe. Then there's the Cossacks. I've a lot of resepct for your Cossack, by and large, though he's inclined to get a bit carried away from time to time. Now if it was Cossacks we were dealing with I'd be looking forward to a good, professional scrap, but most Russians are tame. Most Europeans are tame. Most Americans, God bless 'em, are very tame indeed. I hope the British never become tame. It would be the end of us.'

'Well, I suppose if we ever lost a major war . . .'

'It's not the winning and losing of wars that tames a nation – it's the love of property, the acquisition of too many comforts for their own sake, the cossetting of oneself, that tames you. Thank God the bourgeoisie don't run England yet, the way they run the Continent. Internationalism could ruin us. Stick to imperialism and you can't go far wrong. A country should be in charge of its workers and its aristocrats. Farmers, shopkeepers and bankers have far too much regard for their cosy firesides to be trustworthy guardians of a nation's pride or its well-being. Your aristrocrat has no respect for wealth because he's inherited it. Your common man has no respect for wealth because he's never experienced it. See what I mean?'

'I think so, sir. But shouldn't the army have a voice . . .?'

'Doesn't need a voice if the country's being properly run. No part of the army's job, politics.'

An Indian orderly entered with a tray of tea. 'No fresh milk today, sir. All cows gone.'

'Damn,' said Major Nye absently as he reached for the pot, 'that'll be their advance raiding parties, I shouldn't wonder. Better lock up as soon as the Lancers arrive, Cornelius. Post extra guards and so on. And send some sort of message to Delhi, would you?'

Cornelius accepted a cup. 'Should we do anything else, sir?' looking through the window again it seemed to him that the hills were obscured by a huge cloud of white and yellow dust.

Major Nye knocked out his pipe and picked up his cup. He chuckled as he raised the tea to his cracked lips. 'Write letters to our nearest and dearest, I suppose.' He lifted a white handkerchief to his sleeve and brushed away a fly. 'I shouldn't think this will last too long, do you?'

2. With the flag to Pretoria

'Bleck is bleck ent wide es wide, my dee-arr,' said Meneer
Olmeijer comfortably, puffing at his large pipe. The tubby
Boer, in khaki shirt and jodphurs and wide-brimmed bush-
hat, surveyed the tranquil plaas through twinkling eyes.
'Airr you stell intirrested on de oostrrich, Miss Cornelius?'

'Perhaps . . .' she said. She had difficulty crossing the yard
in her long tropical skirt. She had chosen a drab brown so as
not to show the dust. Her hat, too, was brown and its brim
teneded to obscure her vision. 'Perhaps later?'

'Cerrtinly, cerrtinly – lader or niverr – y'ave all de tame
in de woahld 'ere. Yooah ön 'oliday! Ya doo whadiver ya fill
lake – Liberty Kraal, eh? Heh, heh, heh!' He displayed his
stained teeth. 'En corrl me Cousin Piet. Efterr all, we'rre
rrelitivs, ain't we?' He placed a tanned, red hand on her soft,
wincing shoulder. 'Ther woah's övah – we'll all be Afrikan-
ders soon – Brridischerr oah Hollanderr – farrms oah mines.'
They had halted by a white wooden fence, marking the
northern limits of the plaas. On their left were the huts of
the native workers' kraal. Piet Olmeijer lifted a booted foot
to the lowest rail; a mystical light had entered his eyes as
he inspected the infinite veldt, most of which was his, won
from the Matabele with blood and bibles and an inspired
hypocrisy which filled Catherine with admiring awe but
caused her companion, currently back in the house, considerable confusion. Una had been unable to face this morning's tour; neither, to their host's dismay, had she
breakfasted. She continued to suffer, Catherine had said
when presenting Una's excuses, from the heat – but the fact
was that Una, furious and frightened not so much by the
condition of the native Africans as by the peculiar attitude
of the whites towards them, was almost incapable now of
speech in the presence of Olmeijer or his overseers. Moreover the farmer had taken a fancy to Una and had dropped

several hints concerning his need for a wife and sons who could inherit all he had created. Olmeijer had told Jerry, whom he knew from Johannesburg days, that Una Persson looked strong and healthy, the sort of help-meet an Afrikander farmer needed. Olmeijer's first wife and most of the rest of his family had contracted typhus during interment some years previously, when the Witwatersrand dispute was at its height. However, Una's bouts of ill-health, as she explained them, were causing him to relax his attention as time went on. The only unfortunate consequence of this was that gradually the farmer was beginning to speculate about Catherine's capacity for filling the role. The introduction of Christian names was, Catherine guessed, a significant step forward and, perhaps, a bold one for a widower Boer of forty sweating, self-restraining summers. It could also explain his sudden expressions of tolerance towards someone who, while they had a name that sounded comfortingly Dutch, was still an Uitlander. He had been reassured by Una herself when they had first arrived: at that point she had been anxious to recall her pro-Boer convictions in England, to disassociate herself with the gold-diggers, critical of the foreign invasion of the Transvaal, full of the romance of the Great Trek, of the courage of the Voortrekkers and their struggles against the savage Matabele. Una had always found such mythologies attractive and, Catherine thought, always sulked in bitter disappointment when the reality contradicted her imaginings. But Catherine was determined not to be critical of her friends. Una's idealism had dragged her up from despair more than once.

'Just think,' said Catherine positively to Meneer Olmeijer, 'only seventy years ago there was nothing here but lion and wildebeeste! And now . . .' The veldt rolled to the horizon. 'And now there's hardly any lions or guns at all!'

'Doan't ya bileef et,' chuckled Piet Olmeijer. 'Ger rridin' by yerself an' find ert!'

'Well, at least there's no wild natives to worry about any

more,' said Catherine, still doing her best, but feeling increasingly that she was somehow betraying Una.

'Det's a fekt,' agreed Olmeijer with some satisfaction. 'Neow, Ah prromist Ah'd lit her see some o' da tebacca bein' pecked in da feealds, ya?'

'Oh, yes,' said Catherine reluctantly. 'Or the oranges, you said.'

'Certainly — oah de örrinjis.' He chose to detect in her manner an enthusiasm for his life and its loves. As they left the fence he reached a hand towards her but dropped it as, from the other side of the bungalow, there came a pounding sound which shook the ground and round the corner raced a tall black and white ostrich, its eyes starting, its beak enclosed in a peculiar harness, its broad feet stirring the dust, while on its back, whooping and giggling in a dirty, crumpled European suit, his white hat over his face, was Catherine's brother, followed by upwards of twenty grinning blacks in loincloths or tattered shorts and shirts.

'Heh, heh, heh,' laughed Piet Olmeijer. 'Oh, look at det berd rrun! Heh, heh, heh!' He removed his pipe from his mouth and waved it. ''Ang ern, Meneer Cornelius! Excellent!' The ostrich reached the kraal fence, stopped and then swerved, running the length of the enclosure. Jerry slipped further from the saddle, yelling with joy like a five-year-old, the loose-limbed blacks clapping and shouting. 'Ride 'im, baas!'

The bird's panic increased. It began to run in circles, its long neck undulating, attempting to free itself from the halter.

'Ride 'im!'

'Hokai!' cried Olmeijer jovially. 'Hokaai!'

Jerry fell heavily on his back and was dragged a short way by one stirrup before he could free himself. His face was bruised purple and yellow, covered in dust; his suit was torn and he was limping, supported by the blacks as he came back towards Olmeijer and his sister. 'That was great fun.'

'I don't think I'll try it now.' Catherine was concerned for him. 'What's wrong with your leg?'

426

'Turned my ankle in the stirrup, that's all.'

'Foei tog!' said Olmeijer sympathetically. He spoke in Afrikaans to the blacks holding Jerry, ordering them to take him to the stoep, ordering others to capture the ostrich and return it to its pen. At the door to the house Olmeijer dismissed the boys and he took one side of the hobbling Englishman while Catherine took the other. Olmeijer was in fine humour.

'I hope the ostrich is all right,' said Jerry.

'Dit is vir my om't ewe!' Olmeijer was admiring. 'Ye'ave te've gets to rroide them oostriches . . .' He remembered himself. 'Excuse me, Miss Cornelius. Eouwt 'ere, wivart vimenfolk arahnd, ya git a liddel sleck wid de lengvij.' They entered a large white kitchen, seating Jerry in a high-backed wooden chair. 'Olly! Olly! Waar die drummel – weah de deuce es det houseboy?'

The houseboy emerged grinning. He had evidently heard what had happened. Olmeijer told him to bring cold water and towels for Jerry's ankle.

Catherine helped Jerry to remove his jacket, looking about for a cloth. 'I'll clean your face.'

'Nar, nar,' said Olmeijer pleasantly, 'lit one av der serrvants do et! Det's wod dey're paid fer, efter all!'

Catherine left the kitchen, entering a shady hall, on her way to Jerry's room to get him a fresh shirt and jacket. As she passed the door of the room she and Una were sharing, she heard her friend's voice raised in song. Glad that Una seemed more cheerful, she went in. Una was bathing. As an uncomprehending black girl poured warm water over her perfect back she rendered an old Gus Elen music hall song of several seasons before:

I wonders at th' ig'rance wot prevails abaht th' woar,
Some folks dunno th' diff'rance wot's between a sow an'
Boar!
Roun' Bef'nal Green they're spahtin' of ole Kruger night
an' day,

An' I tries to put the wrong-uns right wot' as too much
to say . . .
W'en I goes in 'The Boar's Head' pub the blokes they
claps th'r 'ands,
They know I reads a bit, an' wot I reads I understan's;
They twigs I know abaht them Boars an' spots the'r
little game
'Cos they bin an' giv' yer 'ighness 'ere a werry rorty
name!
I finks a cove sh'd fink afore 'e talks abaht th' woar,
There's blokes wot talks as dunno wot they mean,
But yer tumble as yer 'umble knows a bit abaht th' Boar

–

W'en they calls me nibs 'The Bore of Bef'nal Green' . . .

'Ssshh,' said Catherine smiling, 'he'll hear you. He's only
in the kitchen. I thought you hated that song. You were
saying . . .'

'I do hate it,' Una agreed, sponging her breasts, 'but it's
the only thing that'll cheer me up at the moment.'

'You're such a pro-Boer! You could hardly get work . . .'

'Yesterday's underdog is tomorrow's tyrant.' Una stood
up, taking the towel which the pretty servant girl handed to
her. 'That must be even more obvious on the Dark Continent, I suppose.' She raised her voice and sang louder:

In this 'ere woar – well strike me pink – ole England's
put 'er 'eart,
Them kerlownial contingints too 'as played a nobby part,
Some people sez we ain't got men – I ain't got no sich
fears,
An' it's me wot fust suggested callin' out th' volunteers!
Anuffer tip o' mine's ter raise a Bef'nal Green Brigade,
Th' way they scouts for 'coppers' shows them blokes for
scouts is made –
But I 'ears as 'Bobs' 'll eat them Boars – an' now I twigs
th' use
Of sendin' out a Kitchener to cook ole Kruger's Goose!

428

Naked, Una swaggered around the room, watched by a spluttering Catherine and a wide-eyed black girl.

But for shootin' at th' women – well I 'opes they'll get it
stiff.
'Cos ain't they bin a-firin' shells at that poor Lady Smiff!

Spontaneously, Una linked arms with Catherine and then with the servant, to march them back and forth across the carpet. 'Altogether for the chorus!'
'We don't know it, Una.'

But yer tumble as yer 'umble knows a bit abaht th' Boar
W'en they calls me nibs 'The Bore of Bef'nal Green' . . .

Una stopped, put her hands on the back of the young servant's neck and kissed her full on the lips. The girl uttered a strangled yell and fled from the bedroom.
Catherine stared at her friend in despair. 'What did you want to do that for, Una? You'll give the whole game away at this rate.'

3. The Pathfinder

Only hours ahead of the Cossacks and the so-called 'Mohawks,' Una Persson reached the garrison at Fort Henry to find the place crowded with the Northwest Mounted police and a couple of regiments who, on first sight of their dark blue and scarlet uniforms, seemed to be the 5th and 7th Royal Irish Lancers. The four high concrete towers of the fort were thick with Maxim guns. There was also a generous display of medium-weight artillery all along the crenellated walls, while circling over the pines and crags of the heavily wooded pass which the fort defended, a Vickers Vimy biplane kept reconnaisance. As she dismounted and went to look for C.O. Una realized that her ride had been unnecessarily hasty – the plane would be able to warn the Canadians of an attack in plenty of time. The Cossacks, as usual, were not showing much caution. Her long Henry rifle in the crook of her arm, she forced her way through the lancers and mounties and ran up the concrete steps to the H.Q. building, saluting the healthy corporal on duty at the door. 'Captain Persson the scout. Who's your commandant, trooper?'

He returned her salute. 'District Superintendent Cornelius, at present, ma'am. Um. Is it urgent, Captain?'

She straightened his broad-brimmed hat on his head. She took a pace backward, cocking her eye at him. 'You'd probably have time for a couple of choruses of *Rose-Marie* before a Cossack sabre turned you into a soprano.'

He was shocked. He opened the door for her; he was still saluting. 'Scout to see you, sir.'

Una strode in. In the loose silk divided skirt of the Don Cossack, a wolf-skin trimmed riding kaftan, with cartridge pockets just above the breasts, an astrakhan shapka, she could be immediately identified as an irregular.

The District Superintendent greeted her: a wary wave of

his gloved hand. The scarlet of his tunic clashed horribly with his young face which bore an expression of callow sternness and which suggested that he was new to the job. His accent was a reasonable attempt to give Canadian inflexions to an otherwise nondescript English accent. 'You've news of the invasion?'

'They're done with Quebec and are on their way. I didn't expect to see you this far north, Jerry.'

'They posted me from Toronto two days ago. I was supposed to be in Niagara Falls by now. Do you think I've been set up? Is it going to be the Alamo, all over again? Or was it the Alma?'

'Don't forget Quebec intially welcomed the Cossacks. The French always think they can control their conquerors. There wasn't any resistance to speak of. And nobody was much interested in stopping them between the time they left Alaska until they landed at Ungava. Even then you all thought they'd be content to run around in the Northwest Territory a bit until they got tired and went home. But by that time the States had started to get worried. Those are American guns out there, aren't they?'

'Mostly. They've been very good about giving us support.'

'Then you've nothing to worry about. Why were you going to Niagara Falls? Honeymoon?'

'Oh, sure.' He scratched his red sleeve with leather fingers. 'No, I was meeting my father. I think. He's got business in Buffalo.'

'I thought your father was in Mexico.'

'Maybe he'll be going to Mexico later.'

'Are you sure he's — ?'

'No. But he says he is. It was worth checking.'

'I suppose so.'

'The bloody Cossacks have fucked everything up, as usual. Once they start — '

'You'll stop them. They'll never reach Kingston.'

He frowned anxiously at a map of the Great Lakes. 'We don't want the Americans moving in. And they will, unless . . .'

'They've left nobody behind – the Cossacks, I mean. The "Mohawks" aren't a problem. As long as they all attack Fort Henry, that's it. You'll blow them to bits.' She sounded sad. 'You needn't worry about the States.'

'It was bad enough when it was only sitting Bull. Or do I mean Notting Hill. What's that?'

'Since Roosevelt they've had it in their heads that the rest of America is really theirs, too, that they're leasing it to a lot of incompetent relatives and foreigners on condition that they look after it properly. But in this case there won't be much more interference.' She was decidedly regretful. 'A shame. I'd love to see the Cossacks in New York.'

'I heard that's where they meant to go. They thought the Ungava Peninsula was Nantucket.'

'You could be right. They're still not clear as to whether they're in the USA or Canada. There's only one or two of them can't speak any English at all – and the French "Mohawks" can't understand the Cossacks' French while the Cossacks can't understand the French's French. Apparently the accents create two virtually different languages.'

'You know a lot about them.'

'I should do. I've been acting as an interpreter since Fort Chimo.' She straightened her shapka. 'Well, I must be on my way.'

'You're not staying for the "fun"?'

'No point. You'll beat them. They're tired, over-confident, poorly armed. They'll have eaten badly and been sleeping in the saddle, if I know them. Most will probably be drunk. They'll keep coming at you until you've wiped them out. In the meantime the "Mohawks" will have run back to Quebec.'

'They can't have come all this way without a plan.'

'They got to Uppsala two years ago without a plan. They were wiped out. Four prisoners taken. It's their nature. And twenty years ago they reached Rawalpindi, couldn't find the British, hit the Chinese by accident and drove them back. Hardly anyone in England ever knew there had been a threat!'

'That was a bit of luck for someone,' said Jerry innocently.

'It usually is. Well, cheerio. You're bound to get a promotion if you hang around long enough after the battle.'

'I told you, I was on my way . . .'

'I can go via Niagara, if you like. Any message?'

'If you get a chance, find a man named "Brown". He's staying at the Lovers' Leap Hotel on the American side. Tell him I've been held up.'

'Okay.' She removed her kaftan. She had a buckskin jacket underneath. Hanging by a deerhide thong at her beaded belt was an old-fashioned powder horn. She reached for the horn, taking something from the bullet pouch on her other hip. 'Have you got a mirror?'

He removed the map of the Great Lakes. There was a large oval mirror behind it. She inspected her face. Then, tipping a little powder on to the puff, she began to cover her nose.

4. The outcast of the islands

'I remember the good old days,' said Sebastian Auchinek, his voice grumbling along with the twelve wing-mounted engines on either side of the cabin, 'when there was still a sense of wonder in the world.'

'That was before universal literacy and cheap newsprint,' Jerry spoke spitefully. Either Auchinek or the engines began to cough. They had not been getting on since Calcutta when the Russian policeman had demanded to see their documents and Jerry had shot him.

The Dornier DoX was cirling Darwin while they tried to make up their minds what to do. Nobody had expected the Japanese to strike so fast. As far as Whitehall had been concerned the problem had been whether or not to let them stay in Manchukao. When they had materialized simultaneously outside Sydney, Brisbane and other cities, pounding the settlements to bits with naval guns and bombs, resistance had been minimal. Help was on the way from Singapore and Shanghai, but it would be some time before the Emperor's armies were shifted.

'Besides,' said Moses Collier from the co-pilot's seat, 'it's the Aussies' own fault for being elitist. You know how eager the Japs are to be accepted everywhere at any cost. We'd better scarper, Jerry. Rowe Island's our only chance.'

'It's full of bones. It's haunted. I hate it.'

'No time for superstition now, Mr Cornelius,' said Auchinek with a fair bit of pleasure. 'It was you who believed the story about the waters of Eternal Life with their powers of resurrection. I never did.'

'You've never believed anything. A lot of people were as impressed as I was.' Jerry was defensive, but he responded without much spirit. 'I only said I hated the place . . .'

'That's hardly the point.' Mo took a tighter grip on his controls as the plane lost height for a moment. 'We've got to dump this bugger, get her repaired before she falls out of the sky. Listen to those engines!'

Jerry was looking moodily down at the Australian wasteland. 'I suppose so.'

'There's a couple of C-class Empire flying boats in reasonable nick there,' said Collier. 'I diverted them myself.' Mo had spent a lot more time than any of the others in this part of the world. Occasionally he would even claim to be an Australian. 'Lovely jobs. Better than this old madam any day of the week.'

Jerry was sensitive about his Dornier. He would never admit that he had been hasty in acquiring it while it was still in its experimental stages. 'They've got nothing like the range,' he said automatically. 'Nothing like.'

'Maybe not, but it'll take a plane in good nick to get us to Singapore, if that's where you want to go.' Collier buttoned up his helmet strap. 'What do we all think? Is it on?'

'For me it is.' Auchinek began to leave the cabin. 'I'll go aft and see what the others have to say.'

'See if you can get some more info out of the abo,' Collier suggested. They had found a black tracker in the ruins, before they had realized that the Japanese were still present in the city.

'Can't,' said Auchinek.

'He left,' Jerry explained. 'While we were going up. Opened the door and walked out. Said he had to find his mother and father. They'd been after an emu, apparently.'

'Funny little bloke, wasn't he?' Collier glanced at the Timor Sea. 'I hope he makes it.'

'They're marvellous, really,' said Jerry. 'They can find their way through anything.'

'Didn't seem to realize there was a war on.' Collier hummed to himself as he made adjustments to his panel. 'Number four's looking dodgy again.'

'It sounds fine to me.'

'Well, it's bloody dodgy. It's conked out twice.'

'It missed a couple of times, that's all.'

Collier sighed. 'All right. Christ I wish we had some

cannon with us. I don't half feel naked. We've seen a fair bit of the fleet, but what are they doing with all their bloody Fujis or Kawaskis or whatever it is they're flying these days?'

'Probably down near Sydney and Canberra or Melbourne,' suggested Jerry. 'This isn't a very strategic area, by and large.'

'Luckily for us. Why were they hiding in the ruins when we first arrived?'

'Probably thought we were military. Hoped to take us by surprise.'

'They did that all right.' Mo waved his grazed arm. 'Cor! It makes me want to vomit. All that fighting and no chance of hitting back. I'm joining up when we get to Singapore. Then I'll come straight to bleedin' Darwin with a great big Tommy gun. Except,' he said mournfully, 'that they always jam on you. Bastards, Tommies are.'

'What about a Schmeiser?' Jerry was glad that only blue water and sky surrounded them on all sides now.

'You're bloody talking, me old son!' Mo whistled through his teeth. 'There's even a couple of Yank machine-pistols I wouldn't mind trying. They don't have a lot of style, though, Yanks don't. Not in the military stuff. All their invention goes into the private sector. Funny that. Is it free enterprise, d'you think?'

'It's the cars I like best,' said Jerry. 'I'm going to miss the cars.'

'They won't stop making cars just because they've got a few problems on their borders.'

Jerry wasn't so sure. 'I can't bear to think what the Canadians will do with Detroit.'

'They might give it back. Swap it for that other place they want. Pig's eye, is it?'

'St Paul? Maybe. It doesn't seem a fair swap, though.'

'The wars can't last forever. Things are sorting themselves out already.' Mo was depressing himself as he tried to cheer up his friend. 'Eh?'

'It'll take ten years.' Una Persson shut the door of the

cabin behind her, sat down and put her elbows on the chart table.

'What's ten years?' said Mo.

'Bishop Beesley says he can see a pattern emerging already.' Una toyed with a map.

Jerry laughed. 'He's always seeing patterns. There aren't any. Not really. The disordered mind sees order everywhere – systems take shape from the movement of the wind in the leaves of the trees – patterns merge as the mad eye selects only what it wishes to see. Patterns are madness, for the most part. That's the bishop. He's barmy.'

'Oh, come on, Jerry.' Mo turned in his seat. 'There's some sort of shape to what's going on, isn't there?'

'If there is, I haven't detected any.'

'You've got to believe in some kind of order, man!'

'Order isn't patterns.'

'It's a perfectly easy shape, I think,' said Una Persson. 'But it – well, it shifts. It's a prism. A classically cut diamond, perhaps. It isn't strictly linear. By selecting a linear pattern from the larger design you certainly distort things. I think that's what you mean, don't you Jerry?'

Mo belched. Then he farted. 'Pardon,' he said.

Jerry gave up. 'All I know is that there's too much going on at once and I've had about enough. All the bleeding possibilities occurring at the same time. That's not what I joined for. I wanted a simple life. I remember. I wanted a set of nice straight tracks from A to B. And what did I bloody get? I wish I was out of it. I'm too old and this century's too familiar. Any bloody aspect of it. You can't win. Only the bloody Japanese can win.'

'It's worse than that,' said Una with a smirk. 'Nobody wins. Nobody loses.'

'That's life,' said Mo Collier. The engines began to falter, to rumble. He licked his teeth.

'You're wrong. The Japanese win. It's all in inverse proportion to the amount of ego you have. These days, at any rate. The bigger the ego, the more you lose. And it's big egos make the biggest, stupidest patterns. Look at Hitler.'

437

'I used to enjoy him,' said Mo cheerfully, 'in the *Dandy*. Or was it the *Beano?* Hitler?' Mo giggled. 'What, that little bloke in Berlin? The copper?'

Jerry raised his hands to his head. 'Sorry,' he said. 'I was forgetting.'

5. What is art?

There were fifty keels lying at anchor over Kiev when Prinz Lobkowitz woke up and looked out of the diamond-paned window of the house he had rented near the Cathedral of St Vladimir, with its view of the Botanical Gardens.

The artillery fire, which had been almost constant for the past week, was now only intermittent and, as a result, Lobkowitz felt a peculiar, unspecific anxiety, as one does when faced with the unfamiliar, however welcome. From several roof-tops, as he watched, rose puffs of grey smoke and he heard the crack of rifle shots. The defenders of Kiev were firing hopelessly at the airships which swayed overhead obscuring the thin morning sunlight. It seemed to Lobkowitz that the siege was as good as over, but he could not be quite sure which side had won. Then he caught a glimpse of a German uniform on the roof and guessed that the airships, silhouettes against the dawn sky and impossible to identify from any markings as yet, were here in support of the besieging Makhnoviks, returned at last to avenge the murder of their leader over twenty years previously. They were led now by a Don Cossack styling himself Emalyan Pugachev, claiming to be a descendant of the Peasant Tsar and (incidentally) renouncing all claim to the throne in the name of the Democratic Union of Free Cossack Anarchists. Although Pugachev refused a title he was universally accepted as Hetman by the Cossacks. Now, as one of the ships turned in the wind, Lobkowitz could make out a fluttering black flag inset with the blue cross of St Andrew. The Highlanders, having established their position north of the Clyde, had linked up with their Ukrainian brothers to push back the Russians and their German mercenaries and once more establish the Ukraine as an independent state. Lobkowitz, whose sympathies were with the Makhnoviks, reflected aloud to Auchinek who had wandered in, still in night-shirt and dressing gown, smoking a briar pipe, a copy of *The Master of Ballantrae* under his arm: 'Perhaps Kiev will come alive again. It used to be such a vital city.'

'It won't make much difference to the Jews,' said Auchinek with a shrug. 'Every new government winds up promoting a fresh pogrom. It's a wonder there's any Jews left.'

Lobkowitz frowned. He was forced to admit that his friend was right. 'I can't see Pugachev allowing such a thing.'

'Pugachev's a Cossack. Cossacks have a metaphysical and instinctive desire to butcher the members of any race originating East of the Urals or South of the Caucasus. They can't help themselves. I think they hate Jews most of all because they think of us as being a kind of decadent Tartar. Nothing to do with our habit of sacrificing Christian babies, raping Christian virgins, ruining Christian merchants or, of course, crucifying Christ. Their instinct goes back much further than that. They'll tolerate Teutons and maintain a wary trust for other Slavs who, in turn, are regarded as effete versions of themselves, but Latins belong to a caste hardly higher than the Jews . . .'

Lobkowitz was amused. He jerked his thumb behind him at the sky. 'What about Celts?'

'Honorary Cossacks. They can find many points of similarity, you see. The Highlanders were traditionally used to expand the frontiers of Empire, just as the Cossacks were sent into Siberia. From time to time they have done well in uprisings against the central government and have the same tendency to fling themselves willy-nilly into a conflict. Oh, you'd have to ask a Cossack for the rest.' Auchinek scratched under his eye with the stem of his pipe. Then he scratched his nose. 'I just hope the papers you got will see me through, Lobkowitz. Every time Kiev falls I get nervous. Still, I welcome it politically, this development. The Ukraine was the last major state to break free of the Russian Empire. And the Chinese have at last given up their attempts to expand their territories or to re-impose their

440

rule on Cochin China and Korea. And if the Japanese did nothing else, they broke the chain that held the British and American colonies to their masters, without actually managing to retain a foothold in those colonies themselves. All the Empires are going down at once. It's reassuring. Did I read that the Peuhl finally took Fort Lamy?'

'I seem to recall . . .'

'And Arabia is rising. Can it mean that the long era of empire building is over at last?'

'You think the world will learn to cultivate its own gardens? The wars continue. They are just as bloody.'

'It will take a while, I grant you, to achieve a reasonable status quo. But Makhno's dreams may yet become the final reality. The same equilibrium of anarchy.'

Lobkowitz was impressed by this new confidence in his old friend. He was heartened. 'I should work on your enthusiasm for Makhno,' he advised. There was a noise on the stair. 'Hello! Who's this?' The voice of his housekeeper rose up to them. Heavy feet ascended. 'It will stand you in good stead.'

Auchinek was grinning as the door of Lobkowitz's rooms burst open and Colonel Pyat, splendid in his white and green uniform, his boots shining with some dark liquid, came in, hastily removing his cap and gloves. 'We've lost everything,' he said. 'I know you're not sympathetic – but those fools of peasants wouldn't listen to reason.' Pyat had been acting as a go-between for the Russians and the Ukrainians. As a veteran of the Indian and Chinese campaigns he had some standing with the wilder Cossack elements and for a short time had served as one of their officers. 'The Germans are leaving, so we can't even negotiate from a position of relative strength. You've heard nothing from Prague?'

'We can't help, I'm afraid,' said Lobkowitz. 'I might as well tell you that it's my opinion Prague will recognize the Pugachev government as soon as they have official control of Kiev.'

Pyat nodded. He was fatalistic. 'Then can I ask you a favour?'

'Of course.' Lobkowitz felt an increased friendship for Pyat now that the man's efforts to maintain Russian rule had come to nothing.

'Make me a temporary member of your staff – until you get to Prague. I won't stay in Bohemia. I'll go to Bavaria, where I have friends. A great many of my old colleagues are already there and apparently have been decently received.'

Lobkowitz drew a dep breath. 'I think I can arrange it, so long as Prague is quick to recognize Pugachev. If that happens I'll probably have enough prestige to get away with one or two irregularities. You're not, after all, who they're really after. What about your cousin, the Governor?'

Colonel Pyat was bitter. 'He took the last train to Moscow yesterday evening, after he had announced that he was making me his deputy.'

'That creates complications, eh?' Auchinek looked sardonically to Lobkowitz.

Pyat smiled as he shook his head. 'I tore the order up. It would have been suicide to accept.'

Outside, the gunfire suddenly increased its intensity and then stopped altogether.

'Then who is governor now?' asked Auchinek. He had a passion for knowing the names of those in authority.

'Cornelius accepted the job.'

'But he's a known Makhnovik sympathizer!'

Lobkowitz went to the window again, staring across the frosty Botanical Gardens to the distant bulk of the new governor's palace. He laughed. 'Look,' he said, 'the Black Flag is already hoisted over Kiev.'

Pyat sat down in the large leather armchair. 'The man is a blatant opportunist. He bends with every wind. I wish I knew his secret.'

'Everyone envies him that.' Auchinek spat into the ashes of last night's fire.

Literature and art are not the field of the literary or art critic only; they are also the concern of the sociologist, of the social historian, or anthropologist, and of the social psychologist. For through literature and art men seem to reveal their personality and, when there is one, their national ethos.

Gilberto Freyre, *Brazil: An Interpretation*

Important writing, strange to say, rarely gives the exact flavour of its period; if it is successful it presents you with the soul of man, undated. Very minor literature, on the other hand, is the Baedeker of the soul, and will guide you through curious relics, and tumbledown buildings, the flimsy palaces, the false pagodas, the distorted and fantastical and faery vistas which have cluttered the imagination of mankind at this or that brief period of its history.

George Dangerfield, *The Strange Death of Liberal England*

... it is the image which in fact determines what might still be called the current behaviour of any organism or organization. The image acts as a field.

Kenneth Boulding, *The Image*

There have been studies of the higher intellectual sphere through which ideas flowed between the two countries, but the popular sources of these ideas have largely been overlooked. Probably the major source of ideas concerning India came from fiction set in that country. 'Literature is the one field of Indo-British culture which has provided a comparatively large harvest, though the average quality is not very good.'

Allen J. Greenberger, *The British Image of India*

You've gain'd the victory, Rome, it will not hold;
Britain when hist'ry shall her page unfold,
In future times, where're her flag's unfurl'd
Shall prove the queen and terror to the world.
Forward at least two thousand years we'll go.
And shew what London will be: and then shew
A pastime Britons then will pleasure in,
A chequer'd droll, its hero HARLEQUIN.

London; or, Harlequin and Time, 1813

The formal canonization of John Ogilvie, a Jesuit martyr, as Scotland's first saint in 700 years came a step nearer yesterday with the publication of details of a cure which is recognized as miraculous by the Catholic Church.

After years of investigation in Scotland and Rome, the Church now officially accepts that Mr John Fagan, aged 61, of Glasgow, who was dying in 1967 from a major stomach cancer, was saved through the intercession of John Ogilvie. The priest was hanged at Glasgow Cross on 10 March 1615, for refusing to recognize the supremacy of King James I in spiritual matters.

The detailed evidence showed that almost at the moment when Mr Fagan was expected to die, 'he developed a dramatic, abrupt, and uninterrupted improvement with return to full health.' A long sequence of examinations by doctors concluded that there was no possible medical explanation for the disappearance of the cancer.

Guardian, 12 March 1976

6. The Birth and Adventures of Harlequin

'Did you ever see greyer skies?' Miss Brunner had just arrived in a rattling old Ka-12 copter of the flying motorbike type, probably an experimental model. Doubtless she had been inexpertly looting museums again. Landing on the roof of a half-completed Royal Festival Hall, she had immediately turned her attention to the oily waters of the Thames where Jerry had managed to put down his own Princess Flying Boat, damaging the wings and tailplane as he had knocked over the Skylon and negotiated Waterloo Bridge. The drizzle seemed to have been falling on London for a decade; it brought a certain gleam to the overcast scene.

'Eh?'

Jerry had not been expecting her. He had come to the South Bank in the hope of finding the Dome of Discovery, but a Palestinian bomb (about the only one to hit London before the whole of their ramshackle air force had been blown apart) had left a huge crater in its place – indeed, there was no evidence that it had actually been constructed. When the Ka-12 had arrived Jerry had been bouncing up and down, clinging to a fallen girder, telling himself that this was the last time he would trust one of Flash Gordon's tips. Gordon had heard that Catherine had been transferred here from Roedean at the outbreak of the invasion, when half of Sussex had fallen to disaffected Kentish marines who had made a surprise mass attack along the whole coast between Hastings and Littlehampton. The Nursing Home, Sunny-dales, had actually driven back the marines, but not before it had sustained major damage and lost over seventy per cent of its charges.

The rolled up linen blueprints of the Festival site were already going limp. They stuck at an angle from the pocket of his military-style camel hair overcoat. Soon they would be useful as handkerchiefs. Rain dripped from the brim of his trilby on to his cheeks so that it looked as if he had been weeping. He began to tramp away from the Hall, over cracked concrete, towards the iron framework of Hungerford Bridge.

'Eh?' asked Miss Brunner again. She hurried behind. She wore an uncharacteristic Balenciaga New Look dress in avocado green velvet over which was pulled a black duffel coat. On her feet were ponyskin boots and on her head a peculiar astrakhan cap, as if she had tried to make a concession to several different ideas of taste at the same time. 'Eh?'

Jerry stopped. 'Yes, very grey. A chilly era altogether, wouldn't you say?'

Having obtained her response she was satisfied, turning on him immediately. 'You're being facetious.' Ostentatiously she studied the river again. 'Well, it's a shambles! I can't think what's got into the British Empire.'

'Corruption in high places?' Jerry felt his other pocket to make sure his cigarette cards were still dry.

'Rot!'

'I thought – '

'It's poor morale all round.'

'Not all round.' Jerry rubbed the water from his skin. 'Some people are fighting for their liberty for the first time ever.' He looked wistfully towards his ruined Princess.

Her foxy mouth snarled at him. 'Liberty! How I hate it! Given the chance I intend to establish a sane element of authority in this country again. I've put all my money into land. It's land that England's made of. Land is the only thing of importance. And the one who has most land has most power to revive England's greatness. Happy people, Mr Cornelius, are people who know where they stand. A responsible ruling class does not trade in ambiguities – it trades in facts and statements of fact. It tells people exactly what their position is and what they may do within certain well defined limits. People would rather not own land themselves, because of the responsibility. Therefore they are prepared to let those who own the land make their decisions for them. Owning land, you see, brings with it a great burden. By lifting that burden from the shoulders of the common man, by putting experienced managers in charge, we shall produce a stability this country has not experienced for fifty years. A hundred years. It is my dream, Mr Cornelius, to re-establish the Rule of Law in Great Britain before we see 1960 again. I shall need experienced people like yourself. That's why I looked you up. You have the makings of a fine manager.'

Jerry shook his head. 'All I want to do is keep my head down until this floppy decade's over. There's no other way to survive it that I know.'

'It's the key period, Mr Cornelius.' Her eyes were on fire. 'There is still a chance for us to stem the tide, re-divert the waters so that they irrigate the roots of a sane, tranquil, stable society – cottagers, villagers, townsmen and citizens all building for a common aim. Give each man, woman and child a place and a purpose and, as a consequence, a firm idea of identity – show them who the enemy is, what they must fight, and all this internal squabbling, this unhappy squeaking for revolution, will be finished with, once and for all. We reached the peak of our social evolution in 1900 and now we are devolving at a sickening rate. Can't you see it?'

'I appreciate your faith in the restoration of the status quo, Miss Brunner, but I'm not sure land values are the whole answer. I mean, by 2000 we'll probably all be living on Mars and Venus anyway, won't we? The future's in space, isn't it?'

'Space!' She was vicious. 'I don't believe in space! And neither should you. Our duty is to remember our heritage – and to make our fellows recall that heritage, too!'

She was giving him a headache.

'Rockets!' he said pathetically. 'Whoosh!'

She indicated the crater. 'That's what rockets do. Boom!' She drove her point home: 'They blow everything up.'

'Yes, well, they've got to, haven't they? First?' Against

her enthusiasm his logic, never very strong, disintegrated. 'Haven't they?'

She moved towards him, her boots squelching. 'You're very naïve, Mr Cornelius. I'm older than you . . .'

'I wouldn't say that.'

'. . . and I may seem a trifle old-fashioned. But mark my words our future lies in the yeomen of England, not in some half-baked fashionable creed of anarchistic scientific internationalism. There are too many "-isms" in the world already – and the result is Chaos. Come with me. Let me exorcise the demon of nihilism and breathe a new spirit into your troubled soul. There is only one "-ism" which will save us – the good old English penchant for pragmatism. We must reduce the number of choices facing the bewildered people of England. Choice produces confusion and confusion leads to social disintegration. And when we are strong again, strong enough to show the world that we know who we are and where we are going, we can extend the same salvation throughout the globe, bringing stability and order wherever we go. We stopped too soon, you see. We lost sight of our goals. We became afraid of responsibility – of the responsibility of Empire – we let other countries get away with far too much and, as a result, lost faith in our own authority.'

'I'm still not sure about my own identity, let alone what I should be doing.' As he walked on towards Hungerford Bridge Miss Brunner again began to follow.

'Strong authority produces a strong identity, personal and corporate.'

'It all sounds a bit too political for my taste,' Jery told her. 'I never did understand politics very well.'

'But that's exactly it.' They had reached the iron steps of the bridge and began to climb. The metal rang as Jerry's heels struck. She disapproved of his steel blakeys. 'I hate politics, too. I'm completely apolitical. I'm talking about faith – faith in one's country and its greatness – faith in common sense, in order, in justice – faith in traditional values which, say what you like, never let us down in the

449

past.' They were crossing the river now. Jerry regretted the damage he had done with his Princess. The noble flying boat was waterlogged in her starboard float and part of the wing was already under water, lifting the plane over.

'She's sinking,' said Miss Brunner. 'Isn't she?'

'It'll be a long time before that old girl goes down,' Jerry spoke sentimentally. It was this feeling for imperfect or misconceived machinery which had got him into trouble more than once before.

They reached the opposite side of the bridge and crossed the road to the fractured Charing Cross Underground Station, where a coffee-stall had re-established itself. The embankment at this point still had its big trees, its shrubs, it nameless statues. They joined the queue of wounded soldiers and derelicts moving slowly forward until Jerry heard a familiar voice from the counter. 'Garn, yer ol' bugger, toast's anuvver bloody tuppence!'

Jerry's throat contracted. His mother had returned to London. He broke from the queue.

'Eh?' said Miss Brunner, grabbing for him and missing.

He ran up Villiers Street towards the Strand as fast as he could go. At the top of Villiers Street he climbed the ruined wall of the mainline station and risked a look back. Miss Brunner was in friendly (and to him, sinister) conversation with his mother. It seemed that the most disparate people were forming alliances these days. He dropped from the wall and ran on, through Admiralty Arch, to the Mall. There were grey trees on either side of him; even the grass of he park looked grey and smelled sterile. He ran towards Buckingham Palace at the end of the Mall not because he thought he would find safety there but because its outline was the only one he currently recognized. He reached the roundabout outside the palace, the statue of the old Queen, and the fountains. To the left of the palace, the tall houses of Victoria and Pimlico looked attractive; they had hardly been touched by any of the wars. He decided to make for Buckingham Palace Road and Prince's Street, where he had once had friends, but, as he walked panting beside the railings of the palace, there came a shout from the other side and he turned his head to see a soldier in a scarlet and black uniform, a bearskin on his head, threatening him with what appeared to be a Lee-Enfield .303.

'Halt,' said the guardsman.

Jerry stopped. 'What?'

'Halt. 'Ow'd'yer get frew ther fuckin' barrier, chum?'

'Didn't know there was one,' said Jerry. 'I've been away ill.'

The guardsman's brutal, bloodshot eyes narrowed. 'Stay there,' he said. He called over his shoulder. 'Corp!'

A corporal ran out of a gatehouse at the side of the palace façade. It was Frank. His face was pale and covered in acne, emphasized by his scarlet tunic. He grinned broadly when he recognized his brother. 'Jerry! You come to see us, 'ave you?'

Jerry shook his head and was silent.

'Unlock the gate, soldier,' said Frank with some relish. The small wrought iron gate was opened and the guardsman stood back to allow Jerry to enter, but Jerry remained where he was. 'I didn't know you'd joined the army, Frank.'

'I was called up, wasn't I? It's me National Service. You oughta be in, too.'

'I've been ill.'

'Well, come on! We've a lot ter talk abaht!' Frank pretended enthusiasm. 'Seen Cathy, 'ave you? And Mum? She's runnin' – '

'I know.' Jerry shuffled through the gate. 'The coffee-stall.'

'That's right. Wiv ol' Sammy. Nil desperandum!'

'Who?'

The soldier locked the gate behind him. 'Are you allowed to have visitors, then?' Jerry asked.

'Me? I'm quite an important man round 'ere, these days. I'm expectin' to 'ave proper promotion any day now. I'm the senior officer, anyway. All the others are either on barrier duty or dead or wounded.'

'Who're they fighting?'

'You have been away a long time, me old son! The Miners

451

Volunteer Force, o' course. It's a terrorist organization, mainly from Durham and that way. They've been givin' us an awful lot o' trouble, but we'll lick 'em!' Frank opened the green-painted door in the white stone wall. They entered a small office full of dark polished wood. 'Cuppa?'

'Thanks.'

Frank filled the kettle from a big steel drum and placed it on a portable gas ring. He lit the gas. 'Yeah. I'm virtually second-in-command at the moment.'

'What? To the king?'

'The king! Do me a favour!' Frank laughed heartily and sat down in a comfortable leather armchair beside a small coal fire. It was warm and secure. Jerry took off his soaked coat and hung it on a big hook near the door. Frank's khaki greatcoat was there, too. He sat down on a straight-backed wooden chair on the other side of the fireplace.

'What's wrong with the king, then? Been deposed has he?' Jerry rubbed his hands and warmed them at the grate.

'Deposed? 'E's bloody dead, ain't 'e!' Frank was coarser than Jerry remembered him. It was probably the effects of army life.

'Then who's in charge?'

'The church took over, didn't they? Sort of care-taking capacity until order's restored.'

'The Archbishop of Canterbury or something?'

'Nar! They 'anged the poor old blighter months ago. The current boss is a bishop. Bishop Beesley. You must've 'eard've 'im!'

'Vaguely,' said Jerry. He loosened a soggy tie.

'You *must* 'ave. 'E's gonna bring back spiritual values into our way of life, in'e?'

'Oh, then Miss Brunner's working with him?'

'Do us a favour, Jerry! She's the one 'oo led the fuckin' miners on London, ain't she!'

'It beats me,' said Jerry. He watched as Frank rose to pour water into the teapot.

'You're dead lucky I spotted you.' Frank stirred the tea in the pot. 'I'll put in a word. On my recommendation you'll get a commission. Captain, at least. Bound to.' Frank reached out and turned the knob of a big table wireless. There was a lot of interference but through it all came the voice of Edmundo Ros. To a rhumba rhythm he was singing his latest hit. *Enjoy yourself, it's later than you think. Enjoy youself, enjoy yourself, it's later than you think.*

Jerry reached out for the mug Frank offered him. His hand was trembling.

'This is the chance for people like us to take advantage of the opportunities,' Frank was saying, 'and make something of ourselves. They need us, see.'

'What for?'

'Our will to survive,' said his brother. 'Our terror of poverty.' His grin was savage. 'Our rat-like rapacity, Jerry old lad. Our vitality. They'll pay anything for our protection.'

'Sort of Danegeld, you mean?'

'Call it what you like, mate. Not that they can't teach us a thing or two about 'anging on. As soon as we've got those bloody miners off our backs – and that's as good as done, at least for the time bein' – we'll be in charge. Then we'll show 'em!'

'It sounds a bit dodgy to me,' said Jerry. He was still unclear of the issues or of his brother's ambitions. 'They've had a lot more experience. They'll turn on you, Frank.'

'I know too many secrets.'

Jerry shrugged. 'Well, maybe you're right.'

'Are you on, then? Comin' in with me?' Frank grined an eager grin.

Jerry shook his head. 'I'll keep moving, I think. This isn't my decade at all.'

'You won't get a better opportunity.'

'I'll wait and see what the future brings.'

'The future?' Frank laughed. 'There isn't any future. Make the most of what you've got.'

Jerry scratched his damp head. 'But I don't like it here.'

'You never believed you'd be visiting your brother in Buckingham Palace, I bet.'

'I never believed in Buckingham Palace,' said Jerry helplessly. He began to smile. 'And I'm not sure I believe in you any more.'

'Oo, you snooty little sod.' Frank glowered. His pallid lips set in anger. 'You stupid, stuck-up shitty little bastard! And I was trying to 'elp you! Well, if that's the way you wanna play it. I've got powers to enlist you. And once you're fuckin' enlisted, me old son, you'll see the error of your fuckin' ways.'

Jerry drew his needle-gun from a pin-striped pocket. 'I think I'll have to borrow your uniform if I'm going to get through. I'll let you have it back later.'

Frank was hardly aware that his life was being threatened. He stared curiously at the needle-gun. 'What's that?'

Jerry said: 'The future.'

7. Harlequin Invisible; or the Emperor of China's Court

Jerry shrugged himself back into his frilly Mr Fish jacket and kissed Mitzi Beesley heartily on her exposed left buttock. Mitzi twitched. Her voice from beneath the pillow was lazy. 'You could stay another couple of hours. My dad won't be back yet. We haven't tried it with those bottles.'

'We'd only get stuck.' He made for the stairs. 'Besides, you're not nearly old enough.' It seemed to him, as he went down, that he was still surrounded by the aura of her juicy lust. 'See you.' He opened the street door.

He walked out into the Chelsea sunshine. The bishop, a popular local figure, had not done too badly for himself since the dissolution. King's Road was crowded with pretty people, with music, food-stalls, hawkers of disposable clothes, fortune-tellers, prostitutes of every possible persuasion, beautiful buttons and blossoming bows; soft bodies brushed against him on all sides, delicious perfumes swam into his nose; his flesh sang. He pressed through the throng, whistling an Animals tune to himself, on his way to The Pheasantry, which Mr Koutrouboussis had recently purchased. There was no doubt about it, thought Jerry, Utopia had been worth hanging on for. Everyone was happy. *Here, There and Everywhere*, sang the Beatles as he passed a daytime disco; they were the poets of paradise. *Turn off your mind, relax and float downstream* . . .

There was, Jerry found himself bound to admit, still a minority of people who would have preferred the euphoria of austerity to all this and, indeed, the King's Road was not what he would have considered his own natural environment, even on festival days such as this one. Nonetheless, if he missed an egg and chips there was always someone to provide a fantasy of more generous proportions, with a hurdy-gurdy and a rebuilt tram or two. If anything got to him here, then it was the self-consciousness, absent from his own territory further north, where hangovers of the poverty trance still operated to the advantage of the natives. And, too, it was in King's Road that he saw the seeds of disaster, of the destruction of everything he held dear. He put these thoughts from his mind and shouldered his way a little more aggressively up the road only to stop dead as he reached the stone gates of The Pheasantry and confronted none other than Miss Brunner. She wore a white angular Courreges suit with shorts, white PVC boots and a white PVC floppy hat and satchel. On her nose were huge, round sun-glasses and her red hair was cut quite short. A very noisy radio went by – *Jumpin' Jack Flash, it's a gas, gas, gas* – so he could not hear her greeting but, to his astonishment, he was sure she had mouthed the word 'Darling' at him. He stopped, leaned his thin body against the opposite gate-post and sniffed at her Young Lust. 'Swinging along okay, Miss B?'

'What? Oh, yes. Fabulously. You look pretty psychedelic yourself.'

'Thanks. I do my best.'

'No, I mean it. As tasty as anything. Are you going in?' She peered towards the gloom of the hallway. 'You live here?'

'I've a friend who does. Well, he's a friend of Catherine's really.'

'How is your sister? That job – or did she get – ?'

'She's resting at the moment.'

'Frank said something.'

'He's improving, then. Well, I'll be seeing you.'

'No!' She placed her white plastic fingers on his arm. 'I was actually looking for you. I know we've had our differences.'

'And our likenesses. There's no need to rake up the past.'

'Certainly not. I wouldn't dream . . . Could we have a chat?'

'You're not trying to recruit me for anything, are you?'

'Not really. I think we've more in common than we

456

knew.' She looked distastefully down at her body. 'As you can see, I'm quite "with-it" now.'

'What are you doing with yourself?'

'Ha, ha! I've been trained. I'm a fully qualified computer programmer. Shall we have some coffee?'

Jerry shook his head. 'It makes me too wary, eating in Chelsea. At best I can only do it if my back's well to the wall and my eye's on the door. You know how it is.'

'But there are some charming places.'

'That's what I mean.'

He moved into the courtyard, a zone of relative silence, and sat down on the lip of the pool. Blue, green, yellow and red water came at intervals from the fountain in the centre. After a pause, she sat beside him. 'I can't remember where it was we last met,' she began.

'Neither can I,' said Jerry. 'Perhaps it hasn't happened yet?'

'Well, yes, possible, certainly.' She had lost her old confidence while Jerry had gained quite a lot. She was evidently distressed.

'I know how interested you are in science,' she said.

'Not any more.' Jerry tried to catch a striped fish which floated to the surface. 'Sorry. Technological art now.'

'Oh, well. Even better. Technological art. Yes! Yes! Good. That. Well, science is the answer, I've decided, at any rate. I thought you'd be pleased. And computers are very definitely where we are going. My backers have invested in some of the absolutely lastest equipment. You'll be familiar with it, of course.'

'Don't judge me too hastily. I might leave it alone. I don't fancy . . .'

'Ha, ha. Now . . .' She removed a pearlite case from her white bag. She offered him a cigarette. 'Sobranie, I think. Are those all right?'

Jerry shook his head.

'Oh, well.' She closed the case without taking one of the cigarettes herself. She looked at her Zippo lighter for some time while she continued to talk. 'Anyway, you know a lot about the less orthodox branches of science, don't you? Your father – ?'

'I'm afraid I've lost faith in science as anything but a pastime,' Jerry said.

'You were always flippant. You mustn't say things like that, Mr Cornelius. It is technology which will pull us out of our current difficulties.'

'I didn't know we had any.'

'Of course we have. All this glitter simply hides a deeper malaise. You must agree. You're intelligent. This can't last. We must think ahead.'

'I'd rather not think at all.' He got up and looked into the water of the fountain at the multicoloured carp. 'This is where I belong, I'm happy.'

'Happy, Mr Cornelius? How can you be?'

'I don't know, but I am.'

'There's more to life than drugs and sex, Mr Cornelius.'

'There's more than life to drugs and sex. It's better than nothing.'

'You need a goal. You always have. This rejection of your potential is silly. You believe in science as much as I do.'

'What about land?'

'It's abstracts now. It would be ludicrous to continue thinking in old terms about a new situation, don't you agree?'

Jerry became uncomfortable. 'I was thinking of going into the assassination business. You know what a dreamer I am. Would it be too much of a hit and myth operation, do you think?'

'Do you believe in aeroplanes, Mr Cornelius?'

'It depends what you mean by "aeroplanes".' He yearned for the cool gloom of The Pheasantry, to bask in Koutrouboussis's envy.

'A properly organized technology is the only hope for the world unless we are to plunge into total decadence and from decadence into death,' she said. 'If we act now, we can save almost everything of value. Don't you see?' Her circular shades were cocked at an earnest angle. 'If we somehow produce a programme, feed in all the facts, we can get a clear idea of what we must do to prepare for the future. Imagine – the whole future in a single chip.'

For once Jerry refrained from the obvious response. 'I'm only interested in the present.' He sat down close beside her. He put a hand on her knee. 'Give us a kiss.'

She sighed and gave him a quick one. He found that his hand could continue up her shorts unchecked. With a shock his fingers touched her cold cunt. 'Sorry,' he said.

'It doesn't make any difference,' she told him.

He glanced around the courtyard at the flowers. He picked at a tooth. From somewhere overhead there came a bass drone. He smiled without much interest into the sky. 'Bombers,' he said. 'I thought we were going to have a peaceful day.' They were in sight now. A large formation of F111As. 'It's a free country, I suppose.'

'Eloi! Eloi!' Miss Brunner became agitated. She sprang to her feet. 'Peaceful? This enclave of lotus eaters? Don't you realize the world's rotting about your ears? Haven't you got eyes? Can't you smell the corruption? Can't you feel the whole world going out of kilter? Where's your sense? And all you can think of is feeling me up!'

He glanced at her from beneath embarrassed eyebrows. He felt a twinge of self-pity. 'I was only having a bit of fun.'

Some distance to the south, probably over Barnes, the planes began to drop their loads.

She made efficient arrangements to her clothing. She headed for the languid street, still crowded with the festive and the free. 'Fun!'

He was thoroughly demoralized, more by what he had found in her trousers than by what he had done. 'I'm very sorry. It won't happen again.'

'That's all right.' She waved a polyvinyl chloride gauntlet. 'For the present.'

8. The Metamorphosis of Harlequin

For the last three weeks Jerry Cornelius had remained in the roof garden of the empty department store. The roof garden was overgrown and lush; parts of it were almost impassable. Flamingos, ducks, macaws, parakeets and cockatoos inhabited the tangles of rhododendrons, creepers, climbing roses and nasturtiums; yellow mimosa grew adequately close to the various dividing walls of the garden; and, through the ceiling below, several large roots had broken and begun to find the tubs of earth Jerry had removed from the botanical department and placed on the floor so that ultimately the plants would gain purchase here. It was his ambition to bring in increasing supplies of earth so that in time the entire store would become a jungle to which he could then, perhaps, begin to introduce predators and prey, possibly from the zoo of the store's nearby rival.

Jerry had his consolations: a battery-operated stereo record player on which he listened to traditional folk music and laid back C&W, some light reading; he could feed himself from what was left of the Food Hall and from the canned supplies in the roof garden restaurant, where he had also set up his camp bed. The restaurant was more like a conservatory now, for he had been pleased to admit as many plants as would enter. He was never disturbed. He enjoyed the novels of Jane Austin, avoided interpretation, and dreamed of safer days.

Occasionally he would creep from the upper storeys to the bowels of the building and attend to his generators, thus maintaining his freezer and, of greater importance, the central heating. He had turned this to maximum so that his plants would be encouraged to extend their roots towards the distant ground. It was his hope that eventually the remains of Derry and Toms would be preserved in a gigantic shrubbery, impenetrable save by those who, like him, understood the labyrinth. At the top of this mountain of foliage and masonry he would then possess remarkable security. Already a number of peonies were blooming in the soft furnishing department and various vines and ivies, without training, had carpeted the floors and festooned the walls of Hardware and Electrical Goods. He remained armed, but he had lost much of his caution. Aerial warfare was almost a thing of the past, the fashion having changed primarily to tanks and infantry which, ultimately, provided greater satisfaction to those who still enjoyed such exercises. London was no longer regarded as a major objective.

Jerry gathered that most of the battles were won in the world and that conferences were rapidly agreeing territorial boundaries. The Continent of Europe had apparently become a vast conglomeration of tiny city states, primarily based on an agricultural economy, with certain traditional crafts and trades (Bohemian glass, German clocks, French mustard) flourishing: forming the basis of barter between the different communities. Not that war was unknown, but it had become confined to the level of local disputes. Jerry had been unable to see this development as a wholesome one, but he supposed it suited the petit bourgeoisie who constituted, as always, the majority of the survivors. It seemed to him that in some obscure way Miss Brunner had, after all, triumphed, through no fault of her own.

The image of a Britain become a nation of William Morris wood-carvers and Chestertonian beer-swillers drove him deeper into his jungle and caused him to abandon his books. He was only prepared to retreat so far. He was forced to admit, however, that the seventies were proving an intense disappointment to him. He felt bitter about missed opportunities, the caution of his own allies, the sheer funk of his enemies. In the fifties life had been so appalling that he had been forced to flee into the future, perhaps even help create that future, but by the sixties when the future had arrived, he had been content at last to live in the present until, due in his view to a conspiracy amongst those who feared the threat of freedom, the present (and consequently the future)

461

had been betrayed. As a result he had sought the past for consolation, for an adequate mythology to explain the world to him, and here he hid, lost in his art nouveau jungle, his art deco caverns, treading the dangerous quicksands of nostalgia and yearning for times that seemed simpler only because he did not belong to them and which, as they became familiar, seemed even more complex than the world he had loved for its very variety and potential. Thus he fled still further, into a world where vegetation alone flourished and only the most primitive of sentient life chose to exist. He was thinking of giving up time-travel altogether.

Apart from the infrequent fights which would break out amongst the birds, there were very few sounds to disturb him these days as he renounced his camp bed and lay deep in his bushes, his back to moist earth, his earphones almost invariably on his head as he listened to the Pure Prairie League, The Chieftains and, believing that this kept him in touch with the world, Roy Harper. He was inclined not to notice when his batteries had run down and the records were playing sometimes at less than half speed. He was also inclined to fall asleep when the needle stuck in a groove and not wake for two or three days.

He was dimly aware that these long periods of sleeping were increasing but, since he felt no physical effects, he preferred not to worry about them. It was likely that his activities through the past couple of decades had exhausted him more than he knew. For the moment, too, he had even forgotten about his sister, who lay in her padded silk coffin in the freezer, perhaps dreaming of an even more remote past then the one he sought to create for himself.

The summer grew hotter; the jungle grew denser, and then one day, as Jerry slumbered in misty heat in a little tunnel he had made for himself in the foliage, an unread copy of *Union Jack* for 21 September 1923 (*X-ine* or *The Case of the Green Crystals*, A Zenith Story) lying foxed and damp-stained by his limp right hand, the comforting rumble of Centurion Thirteens, Vickers Vijayantas and Humber FV1611 armoured personnel carriers augmented the sultry tranquillity of the day, the hum of bees, the hiccuping of crickets.

The little fleet of armour came to a stop at the signal of a round-shouldered old man in the dress uniform of a major in the Royal Hussars who emerged from the leading Humber, adjusting his busby. A captain, in conventional khaki, pushed up the hatch of the Centurion immediately behind the Humber and ran over the weedy tarmac to receive orders. The major spoke a few words, contemplated the outside of the store which was almost entirely covered by thick ivy, checked the dark green interior of the main hallway, then returned to his personnel carrier. A head wearing a green, gold and purple turban raised itself over the camouflaged metal. A chubby brown face showed a certain amount of astonishment as it caught sight of the department store, which somehow had come to resemble the forgotten ruins of Angkor Wat in Cambodia. Green and gold shoulders followed the face and eventually the whole figure, small and stocky and round, stood on the surface of the vehicle, hands on hips. He was dressed in the impressive uniform of the 30th Deccan Horse, a broad sash around his waist, his sabre and pistol supported on a Sam Browne belt which was oddly functional compared to the rest of the ensemble. The major saluted and lifted a hand to help the splendid Indian to the ground then, together, they entered the forest.

The engines of the tanks and personnel carriers were switched off; silence returned. Slowly the crews began to climb from their machines and, stripped to the waist, smoke cigarettes and chat amongst themselves. They seemed to be a mixed force in a variety of uniforms – English, Scottish, Indian, Trinidadian, Jamaican and Cornish among them. Tinny Heavy Reggae began to sound from at least one turret.

The two officers reached the roof garden three hours later. They were sweating and stained, the collars of their jackets opened, their headgear askew. They searched the restaurant and the restaurant kitchens. The first thing they found was

463

the display freezer with its pale blue contents, the beautiful smiling madonna. The major shook his head. 'About the only thing he ever thought worth preserving. Poor little chap.'

'They were in love,' said the Indian. He tried to push his hand down the side of the coffin to get a tub of Honey and Acacia ice cream below, but failed.

'More than that.' The major sighed. 'She represented everything he thought important. He believed that if he could revive her he could revive the world he had lost.'

'She is dead, then?'

'As good as, old boy.' The major closed the lid of the cabinet. 'We'd better check the garden now. You take the Tudor and I'll take the Spanish. If you don't have any luck, meet me back here.'

They went their ways.

The major found it almost impossible to climb over the tangled branches and roots blocking the entrance to the mock-Moorish splendours of the garden where the fountains were now choked with dark green vegetation, with magnolia, over-sized tulips, peonies, poppies, sunflowers. The heavy scent from the place almost drove him back. He was about to press on when his ear detected a faint sound from his right and he looked towards the gigantic rhododendron mass immediately opposite the restaurant. Two or three flamingos stalked from it, their pink necks wobbling, splashing on broad feet through what remained of the miniature river. But it was not the birds who had made the sound. The major moved towards the rhododendron, almost blinded by the intensity of the purple, scarlet and pink blossoms, the powerful odour of earth and decaying undergrowth. He pushed branches aside and found a low archway. He bent down and peered through the green semi-darkness. He went on his knees and began to crawl until the tunnel opened into a tiny cavern in which lay curled, foetus-like, the body of the man the major had sought over five continents.

The body was dressed in a green and khaki camouflaged

safari suit, there was black Koss earphones on his head and the lead of the earphones was attached to a record deck on which Al Bowlly was singing *What a Little Moonlight Can Do* with painful slowness. On its side, near the player, was a clock, decorated in red, white and blue, and beside it a gesticulating figurine in a traditional white pierrot costume with a black skull-cap, perhaps a contemporary likeness of Charles Debureau himself; near that a copy of a *Fantomas* novelette and a copy of *Le Chat Noir* magazine. The *Union Jack* was open at the beginning of the story. A box below the illustration, showing an open safe, a swirl of vapour and two men apparently confronting one another (one wearing full evening dress) read: *This story very worthily upholds the UNION JACK tradition – the tradition for really well told stories, full of character and action. It is a Zenith-Sexton Blake story, written as only the creator of the Albino knows how. If you want anything better than this you are indeed hard to please.* The major carefully picked the fragile magazine from the earth, rolled it and tucked it into the top pocket of his dark blue tunic. Then he inspected the stiff figure of the man. It was thin. The face was quite long, the lips full, the eyes, though closed, apparently large. The hair was black, long and fine, but appeared to have been dyed white at some time. There was a very close resemblance to the blonde young woman the major had discovered in the freezer. He lifted his head:

'In here, Hythloday. I've found him, poor old chap. Just made it, too, it seems. He's almost gone.'

The major waited, rolling himself a cigarette as he looked down at the curled figure. There came a blundering sound from behind him and eventually a panting Hythloday crawled into view. There was not really room for all three of them. It was obvious that Hythloday at first suspected the major had been forced to defend himself.

'He's not dead, I hope. Was he violent?'

'Oh, no, no.' The major smiled sadly. 'As far as this chap's concerned I'm afraid violence is a thing of the past.'

9. The Death of Harlequin

'Ten bloody years!' Miss Brunner was incongruous in a red and white Malay sarong, her head tied in the kind of blue turban hat popular four decades earlier. Her breath smelled of chloroform from the Victory V throat lozenges she had taken to consuming. In wedge sandals she hobbled across a green, blue and gold Kazhak carpet to the mock-Adam fireplace where old Major Nye stood looking at a collection of photographs in black and silver Mackintosh frames. Major Nye wore the uniform of his first regiment: a pale blue and yellow tunic, dark blue britches with a double yellow stripe, black riding boots with spurs, a sabre, white spiked helmet; the 8th King George's Own Light Cavalry. He had become so frail that it seemed the uniform alone kept him on his feet. He turned, blinking mildly, raising a grey eyebrow, bending his thin good ear towards her. 'Eh?'

'I don't think you realize how very difficult it's been for some of us.' She stared coldly at one of the marble pillars near the tall double door. Ceramic Siamese red and black lions returned her gaze. The whole place was a mixture of oriental styles except for the original architecture, which was Victorian Greek. 'I spent nine months in a Cornish internment camp for a start!'

'Start?'

'Underground bunkers. They put anything undergound that will go underground. They're fond of holes, the Cornish. They're afraid of the sun.'

'Ironical, in their case. They're like the Welsh. Mining you see. They love it. Like the Seven Dwarves. *Heigh ho, heigh ho, it's off to work we go . . .*' He chuckled. '*Dig, dig, dig*. It's made them very rich these days, I gather. Tin, clay, gold and silver even. Oh, they've done it for centuries. Since before the Romans. Two thousand years at least. Give them a pick and shovel and they'll burrow through anything. It's instinctive. You have to admire them.'

She had heard his racial views more than once. She sighed deeply. 'Oh, yes?' She rubbed at her raw bare arm. 'They're also notoriously horrible to the prisoners – including the other Celts.'

'True. You heard that stuff about the flint knives, I suppose and the menhirs?'

'I saw it,' she said. 'I was lucky.'

'Well, they've achieved their object. They don't get many unwanted visitors any more. They've a new arethyor enthroned at Tintagel at last. I got the news this morning.'

'Which one won?'

'Arluth St Aubyn, naturally.' He shrugged and rubbed at his blue-veined nose. 'They can't help themselves. Ancient instincts, you see, as I say. Old habits die hard.'

'It seems you pulled Cornelius out in time again. He owes a lot to you.'

'Someone has to look after him when he goes walk-about.'

Miss Brunner glanced over to the bay windows where her old lover sat, silhouetted against the light, wrapped in a Kashmiri shawl, his eyes vacant and unblinking. 'Oh, Christ,' she said, 'he's dribbling. And he used to be tipped as the Messiah to the Age of Science!' She shook her head in disgust.

'It's his amnesia,' said Major Nye, to excuse Cornelius. 'He never knows where he's going. He just keeps revisiting certain places that have some private meaning for him, some mythological significance. He's much better today. He keeps collapsing into catatonia, especially after one of the wandering spells. It can't be his sister he's looking for now. She's perfectly safe.'

Miss Brunner glared into the vacant face. 'There are no sancutaries any more, Mr Cornelius. There are none in the past, none in the future. I advise you to make the best of the present!'

'Best not to disturb him,' said Major Nye. On frail legs stiffened at the knees by the boots, his spurs rattling a little,

467

he went to stand behind Jerry's wheelchair. 'All right, old son. There, there, old lad.' He patted Jerry's shoulder. Since he had lost his wife and family, Major Nye had found his only fulfilment in taking care of the mindless assassin. 'He never believed in the possibility of sanctuary, you know. Not for years. He disdained the idea. He was born in the modern city, you see.'

'You mean he never needed security? I've known him longer than you, Major, and I can tell you . . .'

'The city was his security, with all its horrors. As the jungle is security to the tiger, you might say. When they began to destroy his city he lost his bearings completely. For a while he evidently thought that the landscape of warfare might be a substitute, but he was wrong. It's strange, isn't it, how the city grew from the town which in turn grew from the encampment formed against the terrors of the wild . . .?'

'I don't know anything about that. I was born in Kent.'

'Exactly. I was born in the country. We can't possibly understand the comforting familiarity of the city to someone like Cornelius. The worse it is, in our terms, the more he feels at one with himself. Even at the end his instinct was to hide in the heart of the city, climbing to the top of a tall building for safety, reintroducing the jungle . . .' Major Nye's voice faded. He smiled tenderly at his charge.

'He's a wild beast. A monster.'

'Indeed. That's why he became such a totem to so many.'

'I always considered his apparent sophistication, his affectation of an interest in science, to be a veneer.' Her voice became more confident as she began to feel she and the major were on common ground at last.

'On the contrary. A creature like Cornelius takes technology for granted. It is real enough to him for it to possess a genuinely mythological significance.'

Miss Brunner tightened her unlikely lips. 'I never denied technology had a purpose . . .' She frowned. 'A usefulness. If handled properly . . .'

'You tried to use it to maintain the old order. Your friend

468

Beesley wanted to turn it against itself, to destroy it altogether. But Cornelius enjoyed it for its own sake. Aesthetically. He had no interest in its moral significance or its utilization. Computers and jets and rockets and lasers and the rest were simply familiar elements of his natural environment. He didn't judge them or question them, any more than you or I would judge or question a tree or a hill. He picked his cars, his weapons, his gadgets, in the same way that he picked his clothes – for their private meanings, for what they looked like. He enjoyed their functions, too, of course, but function was a secondary consideration. There are easier cars to drive than Duesenbergs, easier, faster, cheaper planes to fly than experimental Dorniers. He found speed exhilarating, of course, but again speed wasn't really what he cared about. He preferred airships to jetliners because airships were more romantic, he preferred Mach 3 liners and shock-wave ships because they looked nicer and because they hinted at an ambiguous relationship with space and time – that was where the mystical element came in, as with particle physics. And have you noticed how we still continue to ape the markings of animals in our clothes – particularly our traditional formal clothes? Similarly with technology. He liked the Concorde because it looked most like an eagle. To me it was all completely bewildering, to you it was something that had to be tamed, to him it was normality. He had all the primitive's respect for nature, the same tendency to invest it with meaning and identity, only his Nature was the industrial city, his idea of Paradise was an urban utopia . . .'

'He was a snotty-nosed little back-street nihilist,' she said. 'There's no point in dignifying his attitude.'

'To us he was far more dangerous than any nihilist. He was alien. He came to enjoy the bombing raids because he was interested in what the bombs would do, what sort of pictures they would make, even, as was often the case, when his own safety was threatened. His will to peace was as strong as yours or mine, perhaps stronger, but his methods of obtaining peace were personal. They became personal because we couldn't understand what he was talking about. He was a friendly chap. He allowed us all to use him. But he gradually came to realize that our aims were incompatible. His Utopia was to us an insane technological nightmare.'

'I can't believe this sympathy of yours,' she snapped. She clacked across the carpet to the photographs. They were all there, all his relatives, his acquaintances. 'You're older than me. Your world had nothing at all in common with his.'

'It probably changed just as rapidly. But I suppose it's because I know that I've so little in common with him that I can sympathize.' Major Nye turned the chair slightly so that Jerry could see something of the street below, where the rebuilding work was taking place, where the bunting and the flags were going up. 'Yours is an unfortunate generation, on the whole.'

'I am, I hope, broadminded. But one can take for granted far too much, Major.'

'Not as much as poor Cornelius. He took it all for granted. It ruined him. He wasn't his world's Messiah. He wasn't the Golden Trickster. He was his world's Fool.'

'Is that what he's suffering from?' She became curious, advancing again to the wheelchair, staring coldly into the drooling face. 'Shock?'

'He was shown too much of the past at once. That's a theory, anyway. He hardly knew it existed before.'

'And you continue to support him, you and Una Persson. Even Auchinek, who has no love for him. Why?'

'Perhaps we thought we could maintain our humanity by studying him. In Auchinek's case, at least, and in mine, you could say that we saw him as a model. In an inhospitable world he seemed to be at ease.' Major Nye fingered his moustache. He sucked his lips. He dismissed the notion. 'No. It's too hard for me to define. It might be much simpler than that. I need to give my loyalty to something. It's my training, d'you see. With all his faults, he seemed the best bet. He took his world for granted, just as I had taken mine for granted – not complacently, but with the sense that, drawbacks included, injustices included, it was the best of all possible worlds.'

'To be quite candid,' Miss Brunner began, and then was horrified to see Cornelius looking back at her through sardonic eyes.

'You'll never be that, I'm afraid,' said Cornelius calmly. Then the head dropped. The lips began to drool again.

'He has these flashes,' said Major Nye affectionately.

She clacked towards the door. 'It's disgusting. You're both as senile as one another. You need a nurse to look after the pair of you.'

Before Miss Brunner could reach the doors they opened and a small black and white cat walked in, tail erect, followed by Una Persson who came to a halt when she saw Miss Brunner. Una Persson had her Smith & Wesson .45 in her hand, half-cocked. When she recognized Miss Brunner she smiled and uncocked the pistol, slipping it back into the holster at her belt. She wore the full uniform of a Jodhpur Lancer, for she was currently in the employ of the Maharajah of New Marwar and had come up by train from Brighton only an hour before. 'How nice to see you again. And what a pretty outfit.' Una bowed, the plumes in her turban nodding.

'You've certainly gone all the way, dearie.' Miss Brunner was disgusted. 'Did you bring your harem with you?'

'We're not allowed harems in New Marwar.' Una inched past Miss Brunner and offered Major Nye a broad, open smile. 'Good afternoon, Major. How's the patient?'

'Improving, I'd say.'

Miss Brunner disappeared on angry heels. Una closed the doors. 'It's all arranged,' she said. 'I do pray they won't be disappointed.'

'We can only hope.'

'Hope . . .' mumbled the slumped figure.

'There!' said Major Nye. 'I seem to have offended Miss Brunner. I had no intention . . .'

'I didn't know she was at liberty again.'

'I'd hardly call it liberty. Apparently she plans to found

471

some sort of mission in London, together with Beesley and that daughter of his. They've fallen on hard times, those two.'

'And I didn't realize Beesley was back. Where's he been?'

'He was thrown out of Ohio, I gather. By the Sioux. Then he went to Arizona and was deported by the Navajo. He didn't have much better luck in New Hampshire, where the Elders regarded him, rather ironically, as an atheist. According to our intelligence, and it's always suspect, he spent a while in the West Indies where he managed to build up a small following, but eventually he was sent home on an emigrant ship and landed in Liverpool a month ago. The Chinese authorities sent him to us. So far the only state to offer him a home has been East Wiltshire. But he found out what happens to clergymen in Wiltshire, after their seven-year period of office. Some old custom they've revived.'

'I appreciate this quest for national identity,' she said, 'but it does seem that most traditions were dropped for the good reason that they were revoltingly cruel and stupid.'

'Well, live and let live. Things will probably settle down.' He looked at the red, white and blue French clock on the mantelpiece. It was half-hidden behind the photographs. 'You're about half-an-hour late. I was hoping you'd rescue me sooner.'

'I dropped off to see Mrs Cornelius.'

'I thought she was coming for the festivities.'

'I had something to discuss. She'll be here later.'

'Still going strong, is she?'

'As always. Quite a celebrity in these parts now, and enjoying every minute of it.'

'She's still with Pyat?'

'No. Pyat's working with the Poles now, over in Slough. He sees her from time to time but I think Hira – what's he calling himself?'

'Hythloday.'

'Yes. I might as well call myself Lalla Rookh!' She laughed. 'Anyway, he's still her main boyfriend. It gives him a lot of extra muscle in Croydon, apparently, but the

Maharajah wants him to marry her and she says she's had enough of marriage, though she'd be glad of the status. She could go to Brighton whenever she liked, then.'

'It's even more magnificent, I hear. Lots of gold roofs and pastel walls. Hythloday wouldn't be marrying out of caste, would he?'

'Mrs C is regarded as high caste by virtue of being Jerry's mum. My boss has entertained her to dinner several times and been proud of the honour. She, of course, was in her element. They love her. There isn't a Sikh in Sussex who doesn't. Of course she tends to be hated by a lot of the natives who resent her privileges and think she's socializing above her station or sucking up to the masters, depending on their point of view, but that type of white will bicker among themselves. I get a lot of similar spite, myself, of course.'

Major Nye was amused. 'They think you're a bit of an Uncle Tom, do they?'

'You could put it like that.' She took a step back from Jerry as if she inspected a painting. Her uniform was primarily white and gold with a gold-trimmed scarlet sash. There was an Indian sabre at her belt and her turban was a tall one, wrapped around a spiked metal cap, matching the colours of her uniform and with some thin bands of blue to show her rank. The plumes were also a sign of rank. For Major Nye the uniform somehow emphasized her femininity and made her seem a fraction shorter than usual. 'I wish he'd perk up a bit,' she said beneath her breath. 'They've made so many preparations.'

'Officially we tell them he's been asleep?'

'Oh, certainly. But you know what legends are like. There are an awful lot of people believe that when he wakes up this time an era of peace, prosperity and co-operation between the nations will begin.'

'The British nations, you mean? It was our fault, I suppose, for speaking so highly of him.'

'I don't think it's that. They need a symbol and he's as good as anything. After all, he was a lot of help to many of

473

the independence movements, even before the civil war. Now there's scarcely one of the sixty states that doesn't have some sort of folklore connected with him. Not everything is good, of course, but most of it is. You should hear the stories the Highland anarchists tell. It's astonishing how quickly he's been worked into almost all of Britain's mythologies as well as a good many others throughout the world. As if a gap existed for him to fill. There are Cornelius legends in America, Africa, Asia, Australia, throughout Europe. He's bigger than the Beatles now.'

Major Nye was pleased. He took a brass-plated tin from his tunic. The tin had belonged to his father. It was decorated with a relief bust of Princess Mary flanked by the initials M.M. while the borders contained pictures of stylized arms and ships and the names of various nations – Belgium, Japan, Russia, Monte Negro, Servia and France. In the top border were the words Imperium Britannicum. In the bottom border were the words Christmas 1914. The tin had originally contained a pipe, cigarettes and tobacco and a Christmas card from Princess Mary. Now it contained Major Nye's own tobacco and cigarette papers. He began to roll himself a tiny smoke. 'You don't mind what's happened, then?'

'You think I should be jealous?'

'Miss Brunner certainly is. So's his brother.'

'He was always a better entertainer than I was.' Una shrugged. 'And I was always a better politician. He refused to make something of himself and now the world has made something of him. There's nothing like having a common hero.'

'And I'm not nothing if not common,' said Jerry. He blinked. 'It's a bit bright in here, isn't it?'

They watched him carefully, expecting him to subside.

'What's been going on?' he asked. 'You were talking about me, weren't you?'

Una shook her head chidingly. 'You sneaky little bugger!'

'I didn't really take much in.' He was apologetic. 'Where am I?'

Major Nye seemed to grow younger by the second. He was almost dancing with pleasure. 'Ladbroke Grove, old chap.'

Jerry looked around him at the magnificence of it. 'Must be the posh end,' he said. 'I never knew it very well.'

'This is all new. It was built on the site of that convent. The one they bombed.'

'Blimey!' Jerry shifted in his chair. It rolled slightly and he realized it was on wheels. He cackled at it. 'Was I injured?'

'You could say that. You were catatonic.'

'Black or white? Or both?' Jerry thought he saw a tail disappearing up the chimney. He accepted the information without question. 'It's a family trait. Like the Ushers. Wasn't it?'

'Like the bloody Draculas.' Una Persson's amusement was admiring. 'Pulled through just in time, as usual, haven't you? You've missed all the work and can enjoy all the fun.'

'Oh, good.' He yawned. 'Is this your place, Major? Or is it a new town hall?'

'It's your palace, old son. Built by public subscription. All the British nations, bar one or two, chipped in.'

'So the war's over.' He stood up and the chair shot away across the smooth floor and struck the far wall. He was still a little shaky on his pins. 'Well, it's very kind of them. I didn't think I was that popular.'

Una hid her pleasure behind an expression of mock severity. 'You wouldn't have been, if it wasn't for the fact that, for the past decade, you've done absolutely nothing. You're the stuff heroes are made off, Jerry.'

'Yeah? What's London like, these days?' He walked to the huge bay.

'There's a great deal to be done yet,' said Major Nye. 'Those skyscrapers over there are just the beginning. They'll have high-level moving pavements going between them eventually. And gyrocopters and airships and everything. Just as you visualized it.'

'The City of the Future,' said Jerry breathlessly. 'Is it all for me?'

'And anyone else who chooses to live here.' Una joined him at the windows. 'Otherwise the rest of the world's regressed somewhat, though there aren't many people complaining. This will be your monument, where past and future come together. London's independent now, too, you see. It has no authority over anything but itself. It's a free city, a mercantile, cosmopolitan neutral zone, a symbol.'

'A meeting place for artists, scientists, merchants,' continued Major Nye. '*In Xanadu did Kubla Khan . . .*'

'Cor!' exclaimed Jerry. 'Is it going to have a dome over it, too? A power dome?'

'If that's what you want.'

'I can't just say what I want, surely? Who's the boss?'

'You are, Jerry.' Una Persson's eyes were shining. 'Happy Birthday.'

'I get the whole of London?'

'Why not?'

'Nobody else,' said Major Nye with a small grin, 'wants it, really.'

'Cor!' The shawl fell from his shoulders. He was still in the uniform of the 30th Deccan Horse. 'An O'Bean Utopia!' Major Nye went back to the mantelpiece and got his head dress for him. Jerry put it on as he stared through round, delirious eyes at the golden city of marvels beginning to rise from the ruins. Then he peered in the direction of the demolished Ladbroke Grove Underground Station. 'There seems to be a lot of people coming up the road.'

They stood on either side of him.

'We'd better get you upstairs,' said Una, brushing at his back. 'Onto the balcony.'

'It's only fair. They'll be wanting to see you. You represent the future for them, you see. The wonderful tomorrow.'

'Tomorrow? I don't get it.'

'You will. They're not ready for it yet. Not personally. But it's comforting to be able to see what it will be like if they ever do want it.'

476

Between them they escorted the astonished Cornelius from the room, through the double doors, up a wide staircase and into an even larger hall where the french windows had been opened onto the white marble balcony.

From below came cheers. A large crowd had gathered, clad in the costumes of a hundred nations, in plaids and lace; in kilts and pantaloons and britches and trousers and trews and dhotis; saris, sarongs, of silk and satin, chitons, chardors and cholees, frock-coats of cotton and felt, capes, cloaks and kaftans in moire, astrakhan, corduroy and gaberdine, bowlers, boaters, Buster Brown and pillbox caps, turbans and kaffiyehs, buskins, moccasins, mukluks, wellingtons, chuckars, brogues, slippers, sandals, plimsolls, pumps and trepida in colours more varied and dazzling than the rainbow's. And Jerry saw skins of every shade, African, Asian, Anglo-Saxon, Latin and Teutonic, and the faces of all these representatives of the races were turned to him and, when he waved, they waved back.

'Hi,' said Jerry in some awe, 'fans.'

He saw a small figure break through the crowd and move across the street. 'Miss Brunner?'

Did she turn and present two fingers to him? He could not be sure, for now the procession was passing the palace.

'Bloody hell!' said Jerry. 'What is it? A carnival?'

'It's in your honour,' said Una with great satisfaction. 'They're deputations from every British state.'

'Just like the Jubilee!'

'More or less,' said Una, 'though things have perhaps changed a bit.'

Precedence had been given to the knife-wheeled Celtic chariot driven by a lady in a sky-blue smock who hailed him with her long spear, but she was followed immediately by the ceremonial elephants, festooned in scarlet and gold, jade and silver plumes of ostrich, peacock and bird of paradise, with intricately woven shawls, tassels and jewelled tusk rings, some of them bearing enormous howdahs on their backs – howdahs of bronze and gold or carved from rare woods and set under with mother-of-pearl . . .

'Those belong to my master,' said Una proudly, 'the Maharajah of New Marwar. He's one of the most powerful monarchs in Britain.'

. . . and some of the elephants pulled monstrous carriages, not unlike ornate railway coaches, the windows curtained with green velvet, the metal glowing with brilliant enamels, containing the families of the rulers of Surrey, Sussex and South Dorset. The rulers themselves, maharajahs and rajas in traditional military uniforms similar to those worn by Jerry and Una, rode at the head of their lancers and their riflemen, their splendid infantry, veterans of Dorking, Bognor Regis, Lewes and Hastings, swords raised in salute to the Lord of London. Next came the mandarins of Liverpool and Morecambe, in glinting rickshaws, coaches and sedan chairs, their retainers waving dragons banners, beating gongs and playing pipes as they marched and danced their superb acrobatic steps; the great Captains of Birmingham and Bristol in vast open Cadillacs, sporting the blazing flags of New Trinidad and Old Jamaica, accompanied by masked troops playing drums of every description, by lovely black drum majorettes, by batmen and panthermen, all style and dash. Then came the great clans of Scotland, with wailing bagpipes and rattling drums, plaids bright enough to dim the sun, the green-kilted warriors of Eire and Cymru, the Coal Dancers of the Federation of Miner's Republics, bearing their bowler-hatted Chief Executive on their shoulders; the Lancashire Free State leaders, carrying their own banner, the great red and yellow tapestry with their famous slogan *Wigan Won the War* woven into it; there were more Irish Hussars, and Scottish Mounted Rifles, Australian Light Horse, Canadian Artillery, Welsh Irregulars, Wessex Roughriders, regiments of horse and foot from South Wiltshire, East Kent, North Yorkshire, West Wickham, all carrying flags of their states, some of them wearing uniforms whose origin was thoroughly obscure to Jerry, who knew nothing of recent history; some of the mascots and totems – skulls, pieces of furniture, sheep, dogs, goats, bulls, portraits, items of clothing, children, mummies – were equally mysterious.

There were Briganti, Iceni, Trinovantes, Cantiaci, Catuvel-
launi, Coritani and Cornovii, with red gold bracelets and
bears and braids and burnished shields of brass and bronze,
with glittering M-16s on their backs, with horned helmets,
huge beards and fierce eyes. There were Mercians and
Northumbrians, with blood-red banners and dark helms,
mounted on bucking motorcycles decorated with chrome
and gold and semi-precious stones and, after all seventy-two
British nations had displayed their military strength, there
followed the pipe bands of Surrey and Inverness, the brass
bands of Fazakerly and Bradford, the steel bands of Ashton
and Shepton Mallet, many of the tunes recognizable, many
others hauntingly alien – a great wailing of sitars, saxophones, syrens and serpents, a banging and beating of bongos
and congas and kettledrums and tablas, of gongs and cym-
bals, of xylophones and glockenspiels, the thrumming of
guitars and mandolins, violins, banjos and double-basses,
maraccas, mouth-organs, cowbells, sleigh-bells, tubular
bells, songs and chants and shouts in fifty different dialects,
all of them full of wild, innocent joy, for this was a
celebration of peace of which Cornelius and his London
were the concrete symbols.

'The king! The king!' they cried. 'For he's a jolly good
fellow!' they sang, and 'Auld Lang Syne!'

Jerry was weeping as he waved back. He turned to old
Major Nye who smiled behind his moustache.

'Am I really the king? Or just a play-actor?'

Major Nye shrugged. 'Does it matter? Elfberg or Cornelius. You are their ideal. Wave to them, Your Majesty!'

Una came close, murmuring: 'It's an honorary title, with
very little actual power. But the honour really is
considerable.'

'But what are my duties?'

'To exist. It would be foolish to make a king who had any
concrete responsibilites, particularly after the trouble the
world's been in. It's all titular, though you do have the
whole of London to play with. Anyway, nobody else wanted
the job.'

'Not even Frank?'

'Almost nobody else.'

Jerry continued to wave. 'I don't know about you, Miss Persson, but it's the best offer I've had so far.'

'You've never been one to resist a bit of glamour.'

'It's more the security I like.'

He waved violently at the airships, keel after keel, making their stately way across the sky. 'I wish Catherine could see this. Is she about?'

'She's still sleeping, I'm afraid,' said Major Nye. 'We didn't like to try waking her until you . . .'

'Of course. But King Pierrot must win his Queen Columbine now. It's only right. Catherine would expect it of me. I've never let her down before. Pierrot's been waiting for centuries, hasn't he?'

Major Nye looked baffled. 'I thought you were playing Harlequin?'

'I wasn't suited for the part. I changed. It was quite natural. No danger.'

A shadow fell across the balcony and for a moment an expression of terror appeared in Jerry's eyes. Then it vanished. He turned, arms outstretched. 'Hello, Mum.'

'Cor! Wot a scorcher!' Mrs Cornelius was sweating as only she could sweat, her huge bulk dripping with diamonds and pearls. She sported an ermine-trimmed robe of scarlet silk, a huge feathered hat. 'D'yer like it? I 'ad it run up special for yer corernation. Lovely turn art, innit?'

'Lovely.'

The procession was over. The sound of it began to fade near the top of Ladbroke Grove, heading towards Notting Hill.

Frank stood behind his mother. 'Congratters, old son.' Rage flitted in his eyes. 'Feeling all right now, are we?'

The roar of the crowd below began to rise higher and higher and drowned whatever it was Jerry had been hoping to say.

10. The Mirror; or, Harlequin Everywhere

London, England: the time is Christmas Eve, probably during the nineties, and from the black night sky drop flakes of soft snow, covering roofs and walls, trees and streets, giving to the air a silence, a taste at once damp, fresh and salty; and with the flakes, from the huge darkness, there descends a fluttering, indistinct figure whose feet touch the flat top of a tall, deserted building, the new Derry and Toms. The figure darts for the shadows, even though the roof garden is closed for the season, but the footfalls, which leave light prints on the surface, together with the slap of the snow on the broad rhododenron leaves, disturb the birds there and they move in their sleep. Overhead we hear a distant bass drone, as if a flying machine departs.

Wrapped in a cloak of red velvet trimmed with green moire, the hood covering the head, a black domino mask disguising the features, the figure looks this way and that, then slips towards the exit, leaving more footprints behind it. As the figure moves, the cloak falls back to reveal the vari-coloured costume of Harlequin.

Harlequin flits down the darkened stairs to the emergency doors, takes out a key, unlocks them, pauses, as if drawing breath, then enters a side-street bustling with cheerful life: gas-jets roar over stalls and under stoves, some for light, some for heat: there are braziers, crimson and black, of jacket-potatoes and hot chestnuts; there are pans of pies, apples, toffee, cakes and fried sausages; all for sale, all cheap: fish and chips, barley sugar twists, humbugs, gum-drops, bullseyes. Huge, scarlet faces hang over the wares, shouting, laughing, crying. "Ot codlins. 'Ot codlins!' Father Christmas pads along the narrow space between the stalls, ringing his bells, while his costumed imps caper here and there, handing gifts to any children they meet. 'Plump turkeys! Merry Christmas! Merry Christmas! Best pippins!'

A sweet for a girl, a sprig of mistletoe for a boy. 'Carp! Carp! Merry Christmas!' And the breath streams from their lips, muffled in collars and scarves, to join the boiling mist from the pans and cauldrons which, in turn, meets and melts with the falling snow so that the air immediately above the stall glows like a yellow aurora. 'Roast goose! Salt beef! Merry Christmas! Merry Christmas!' Dogs bark, horses neigh, children scream for the joy of it all.

Harlequin moves quickly into the broader canyon, the renewed Kensington High Street. Here, beneath arcades created by overhead pedestrian galleries climbing, step by step, into the black and white sky, among elegant towers with windows of glittering gold and silver, whose tops are lost high above, between moving sidewalks, packed with shoppers, are the warm lights of more stalls: stalls piled with vegetables, with meats, toys and sweets; stalls burdened with fowl and game, salmon and trout, pine branches, bunches of heather, holly and laurel; and behind the stalls are coffee-houses, where men and women of every nationality – Hindoos, Russians, Chinese, Spaniards, Portuguese, Englishmen, Frenchmen, Genoese, Neapolitans, Venetians, Greeks, Turks, descendants from all the builders of Babel, come to trade in London – seek the warmth alike, joining there in friendly intercourse; chop-houses, where merchants exchange Christmas gifts and clap one another upon the shoulder – 'Merry Christmas!'; pie-shops, whose windows are heaped with beef puddings, steak and kidney pies, treacle tarts, sweating and smoking in great white enamel basins and trays; bazaars and emporia bursting with rich, mouth-watering smells, crammed with customers still upon their Christmas hunt, while from the other side of bright frosted windows, in the public houses, comes the sound of pianos, pianolas, fiddles, harmoniums and accordions.

God rest ye merry gentlemen, let nothing ye dismay . . .

Harlequin passes on, muffled in the cloak, head hidden by the hood, between a little knot of boys and girls gathered round a lanthorn pole, their shadows huge on the snow, to sing:

> Good King Wenceslas looked out
> On the feast of Stephen
> When the snow lay round about
> Deep and crisp and even . . .

Already children stoop to gather the snow in mittened hands, knead it into balls, throw it at one another, laughing, screaming, yelling fit to burst . . .

> Bring me flesh and bring me wine
> Bring me pine-logs hither.
> Thou and I will see him dine
> When we bear them thither.

. . . Omnibuses rattle by, lights ablaze, top rails crackling like so many Christmas stars; carriages, rickshaws, cabs and cars. 'Merry Christmas! Merry Christmas!'

> Page and monarch forth they went,
> Forth they went together.
> Through the rude wind's wild lament,
> And the bitter weather.

A mass of loose snow suddenly tumbles into the street, covering the children who shriek with delight and look up.

> Sire, the night is darker now,
> And the wind blows stronger . . .

A mighty airship moves slowly between the towers, its engines idling to produce the sound of a slow, gigantic heart-beat, while tiny silhouettes look down from the yellow illumination of the observation galleries to catch glimpses of the rich world below.

Fails my heart I know not how,
I can go no longer . . .

The 19.00 is bringing in the last of the Christmas mail, proceeding with such stateliness that snow is able to form on the top of her hull; she resembles a huge Yuletide pie. The bells of St Mary's Kensington ring out from the church in the shadow of the archway formed by two fourth-storey pedestrian roads:

Ding, dong. Ding, dong. Merry Christmas.

Mark my footsteps, good my page,
Tread thou in them boldly . . .

Ding, dong.

And another bell joins in, held in the hand of a fat great-coated figure with a huge white cap nodding on his head, a tray depending from his broad shoulders by cords, a huge grey muffler around his neck. 'Mince pies! Tasty mince pies! Merry Christmas!'

Harlequin dodges the revellers who come round the corner from Church Street dragging two or three of their number on a broad, flat sledge. The sledge is stacked high with wicker baskets, a Christmas tree, balloons and bunting. Up the hill runs Harlequin while the snow grows thicker and thicker and the traffic moves very slowly, hooting, jangling, creaking, squeaking, engines revving, horses snorting. Over-excited dogs bark and snap at Harlequin's heels. Harlequin ignores them. Old ladies pause in their black fur coats to press coins into the hands of bright-cheeked small boys. 'Merry Christmas! Be good to your pa, look after your ma!' And whistling delivery lads ride their big bikes along the pavement, scoring the snow with thin black lines, swerving amiably to avoid dancing Harlequin who is almost at Notting Hill Gate where crystal towers glow green and red, black and gold, blue and silver, overlooking a plaza where a fair is in full swing, with sparking dodgems and dazzling roller coasters, merry-go-rounds and whips, rattling and banging and smashing and crackling; with rhythmic wheezing music of the calliope, with the hot smells of oil and steam and sweet cooking fat, the bawling voices from the megaphones in the hands of the sideshow men. 'Roll up, roll up, roll up! Merry Christmas! 'Ere we are again! Merry Christmas! Ten for a tanner. 'Ave a go, luv. Merry Christmas! Anyfink on the top shelf, George! Merry Christmas!' The fairground is full. Holiday-makers from the world over patronize it, for London is the centre all travellers hope to visit, the only city of its kind, where representatives of hundreds of independent nations meet to trade and to treat and to take advantage of the city's entertainments, to gape at its marvels, for London lives again as the City of the Future, a wonderland to visit but not to make one's home, rich with vice, and art, and cunning; radiant, articulate and wise. There are ships at anchor in the docks – ships from Shanghai, Toronto, Cape Town and Makhnograd, from Manhattan, Cardiff and Rangoon, from Darwin, Singapore and Freetown and a hundred states besides – there are airships at their masts over White City, bearing the flags of still more nations. The world is made up of thousands of such tiny states, most no bigger than Surrey, some no bigger than London which, itself, is independent, maintained by the pragmatism and the sentiment of a million survivors of a half-forgotten Age of Empires.

'Merry Christmas! Merry Christmas!' Down the main street, between the plaza on one side and a court of frozen fountains on the other, comes the huge sleigh with Santa Claus at the reins, drawn by six white ponies in green and black harness, with scarlet plumes on their heads, nostrils flaring, eyes flashing in the light from the huge triple globes on standards at intervals along the concourse, their rays diffracted by the falling snow. The crowd cheers. People pause to look. Harlequin crosses in front of the sleigh, just in time, dodging into the comparative peace of a narrow, north-bound street. Little houses lie on either side now and in the window of each is a splendid Christmas tree alive with candles and bunting. From the doors come the smells of log fires, of roasting goose and capon and turkey and guinea fowl, of puddings on the boil, of beef and ham and sausages and pork pies, pickles and sugar plums, carp and codlins – all enough to tempt the palate of the most jaded libertine – but Harlequin hurries on. 'Merry Christmas!' call the red-cheeked old men as they turn into their gates. 'Merry Christmas!' sing the housewives and older daughters, in aprons and headscarves, opening their doors to their loved ones, their friends and neighbours.

'Merry Christmas!' cries the tall airship pilot, home for the holiday, his kit bag over his shoulder. 'Merry Christmas!' reply the post-man, the baker, the muffin-man.

But Harlequin replies to none of them, running on down the winding snowy street, darting in and out of the shadows cast by the sputtering lamps. Now dark figures leap from a gateway, dressed as knights, a dragon, a Fool, a Saracen:

> And a mumming we will go, will go, and a mumming we
> will go;
> With a bright cockade in all our hats, we'll go with
> gallant show!

It is the mummer's play with *St George and the Dragon*, taking their entertainment from house to house, to anyone who wishes to see it. The Fool blocks Harlequin's path, cap and bells a-jingle:

> 'Alas, alas, my chiefest son is slain!
> What must I do to raise him up again?
> Here he lies before you all,
> I'll presently a doctor call,
> A doctor! A doctor! Are you a doctor, sir?'

Harlequin dodges to one side of the Fool, smiling, waving on down the street. Harlequin comes to a cross-roads between tall buildings. High above lights still burn in

486

windows, illuminated clocks display the time, a board flashes the schedules of the airship and the Super-Concorde flights and black shapes of family flying machines drift across the glare. At the corner, beside a lamp-post, an old man smiles at Harlequin, turning the handle of his plunking barrel-organ. A monkey in a velvet jacket and cap shivers on his shoulder. The man's voice is as old and as steady as Stonehenge. 'A pleasant Yuletide to you, Arlekin.'

Harlequin bows and runs on. In the distance now, at the bottom of the hill, is a glory of twinkling electric bulbs decorating a magnificent building whose front aspect dominates Ladbroke Grove. Of porphyry and jade and marble and lapis lazuli, the building is a palace from a dream, built by a genii for Aladdin. In all this magical city there is nothing more vibrant than the Palace in the Enchanted Dale. It glows so that, from here, it seems the snow avoids it, or is melted before it can settle, yet the white lawns surrounding it deny this and here, too, the water of the fountains is frozen, reflecting all the colours which blaze from the house. The snow has settled on the hedges and the walls, it lies heavy on the shoulders of the statues and the ornamental beasts on pathways and flowerbeds, shrubs and tubs, the populars, cypresses, oaks and elms, all erected on the site of the legendary Convent of the Poor Clares Colettine where so much of Old London's history was made. Set back from the bustle on the hill, the palace seems a zone of tranquillity in all the Christmas merriment – but there is merriment here, too.

Harlequin darts through open gates which are decorated with Christmas wreaths, along paths, over hedges, through clumps of trees, across lawns, to stand at last at the side of the palace and peer through the holly-framed windows of the ball-room where red velvet curtains have been tied back to reveal a magnificent Christmas tree dominating a crowded hall. The dark green pine is trimmed with globes of scarlet and white, bunting of silver and green, a golden star. The hall itself is hung with laurel and holly wreaths, with ivy garlands, with mistletoe, and lit by hundreds of tall candles in crystal chandeliers. The warmth and the light pour into the garden where Harlequin hesitates and studies the guests. It is a masque that Harlequin witnesses, a masque that draws the hidden figure closer as if yearning to join. Harlequin sees all the old familiar characters of the mummer's play, of mime and pantomime, of folklore and traditional tale – Widow Twanky, Polichinelle, Abanazar, The Demon King, Mother Goose, Jack Frost (a genuine albino with crimson eyes), The Green Knight, Scaramouche, a rather lost looking Pierrot, Hern the Hunter with his stag's antlers; a Fool, in motley with bladder, and bells, Saint George, Captain Courageous, Gammer Gurton, Buffalo Bill, Peter Pan, The Babes in the Wood, Cinderella, Britannia, Dick Whittington, and some dressed in a Harlequin costume almost identical to Harlequin's own; Queen Mab, Prince Charming, Robin Hood, Robinson Crusoe, Sleeping Beauty, Puss in Boots, Pantaloon, Goody Two Shoes, Hereward the Wake, Puck, Gog and Magog, Lady Godiva, King Canute, Blue Beard, Dick Turpin, Hengist and Horsa, The Three Wise Men, King Arthur, John Bull, The Fairy Godmother, Cock Robin, Father Neptune, Jack-o'-Lantern, Sweeny Todd, Doctor Faustus, Jenny Wren, The May Queen, Humpty Dumpty, Old King Cole, Sawney Bean, Springheeled Jack, Charlie Peace, Queen Elizabeth, Mr Pickwick, Charley's Aunt, Jack Sheppard, Romeo and Juliet, Doctor Who, Oberon, The Grand Cham, a Dalek, Old Moore, Falstaff, Little Red Riding Hood, Beowulf, Reynard the Fox, St Nicholas, Boadicea, Noah and Nrs Noah, Jack the Giant Killer, Mother Hubbard, Beauty and the Beast, The King of Rats, Yankee Doodle, Nell Gwynn, John Gilpin, Baron Munchhausen, Alice, Sitting Bull, Ali Baba, Little Jack Horner, Asmodeus, Mother Bunch, Sinbad, Dame Trot and her cat; there was a badger, a bull and a bear, a wolf, a cow, a sea-serpent, a dragon, a hare, a cock and an ass, old men dressed as young women, old women dressed as young men, girls dressed as boys, boys dressed as girls, so that another observer might have thought he witnessed some innocent Court of Misrule.

488

Harlequin held back from entering, partly because of the false Harlequin within, partly because in all that company only Columbine was not present. Laughter washed from the hall as a band played a sprightly Lancers and the guests danced in long columns, up and down the ball-room, round and round the tree, clapping and whistling, leaping and pirouetting, fingers on hips, wrists raised, bowing, prancing, arm in arm, hand in hand, shouting with merriment and good humour: the ballroom shook to their feet as figures in elaborate silks and velvets, in laurel, in Lincoln Green, in cloth-of-gold, in brocades, in motley, in animal heads, in scarlet and black moleskin, in hoods, capes, cloaks, tabards, doublets and hose, in leather and lace and living plants and flowers, in painted wood and padded fur and polished metal, masks and powder cosmetics, wigs and false noses, silver – and bronze – and gold-gilding, whooped and giggled and bent their bodies in the ritual of the dance.

The windows rattled, the log fire blazed, the candles flickered, the creatures of folklore, mythology and fable capered and shouted. Harlequin retreated.

'Better the myth of happiness,' Harlequin murmured, 'than the myth of despair.'

Then Harlequin had slipped away, to climb nimbly up a trellis at the side of the palace, swinging on to a balcony and through a window already open. Snow blew into the darkened room as Harlequin closed the window and drew from a sash wound twice about the waist, a traditional wand, crossing rapidly to the white bed in which lay a golden-haired girl dressed in a daffodil-yellow ballet costume – Columbine, already masked, but pale, breathing sluggishly, fast asleep. Harlequin seemed sad, looking down on the girl for long moments, cocking an ear as the music rose from below, hands on hips, indecisive. Then Harlequin skipped a few steps, almost involuntarily running to the door to look out – a wide landing, a marble balcony, the ball below – back again to the bed, taking one of Columbine's cold hands, kissing it as a single tear crept from beneath Harlequin's domino and fell upon the flesh. And where the tear had fallen it appeared that the skin grew warmer and that colour spread along the bare arm to the soft shoulders, the neck, the wonderful features of Columbine.

Then Harlequin kissed Columbine upon her gentle lips, stood up and placed the tip of the wand upon her breast and Columbine opened her eyes. They were blue. They were bright. They were kind.

'Merry Christmas, my own, dear Columbine.'

'Merry Christmas.'

There came a noise from the marble landing beyond the door. Two guests – Britannia and the mock-Harlequin – went by. Harlequin moved to close the door, hearing a little of their conversation and smiling at its familiarity.

'He'll always fall on his feet, it seems – but I think he knows he hasn't really earned the position.' Britannia spoke sharply, trying to adjust an uncomfortable sword and shield carried in one hand so that she might with the other clutch her punch. The shield was decorated with a Union Jack and the motto: *Honi Soit Qui Mal Y Pense*. She supported an elaborately plumed helmet of engraved silver and red horse-hair, a scarlet and gold coat, with epaulettes, and her skirts were made up from the old arms of Britain: lions and harps for the most part.

'He thinks he has,' said quasi-Harlequin peering over the balcony and almost losing his triangular hat, 'that's the worst of it. He's all cocky again, as usual – never seems to realize how much other people protect him.'

'You can't say you've actually protected him, Frank.' Britannia was amused. 'I, on the other hand, did my level best to look after him . . .'

'I've offered him dozens of really good opportunities in the past, Miss Brunner.'

'I suppose that's where we both went wrong. All the opportunities were in the past . . .'

Singing rose from the hall below:

Peace on Earth! How sweet the message!
May its meaning bless each heart,
And today may all dissension
From the souls of men depart.

Britannia accepted the false Harlequin's arm. 'I suppose we'd better join them.' They began to descend the wide staircase.

'Merry Christmas!' cried Major Nye in the armour of St George (he had always felt a strong sentimental enthusiasm for *Where The Rainbow Ends*). 'Merry Christmas, Miss Brunner! Merry Christmas, Frank.' He waved an arm which clashed faintly. 'Food at the buffet. Anything you like. Drinks at the bar. Hot punch. Name your grog!' His pale eyes twinkled. He clanked back into the milling crowd.

'I suppose all this devolution has its virtues, after all,' said Miss Brunner. She dropped her sword. Frank picked it up for her. 'I, of course, was a firm believer in centralization. However, your brother ruined that. We were partners at one time, but there was a division.'

'I remember,' said Frank, 'I got shot!'

'Did you? Poor boy. Now I'm reconciled. I'm a school-teacher these days, did you know? For the Maharajah of Guildford's children actually. Seriously, I'm beginning to think that it was a good idea to slow the pace, absorb things better. There isn't much of the century left. Of course, we still have the moral superiority, don't we?'

Frank turned his masked face so that he could see the buffet. He licked his lips.

'It's a bit mediaeval, I suppose,' continued Miss Brunner nodding agreeably to Bishop Beesley as he went by with Mrs Cornelius in tow. Bishop Beesley had come as Widow Twankey, Mrs C. as Mother Bunch, 'but none the worse for that, by and large.'

'Yeah,' said Frank with a certain relish, 'they're thinking of re-introducing the Black Death next year.'

'This isn't really the season for cynicism, Frank, dear.'

491

She drew him towards the tables. 'Now, what shall we have?'

Frank picked up a plate. 'What about some devilled bones?'

'Spare ribs, aren't they? I suppose its appropriate.' She began to gnaw.

Mr Koutrouboussis arrived at the buffet panting and exhausted. 'Phew! You need a lot of energy for this!' He had come as Aladdin's wicked uncle, Abanazar, with a dark, pointed beard fixed to his chin and heavy robes of green satin sewn with gold astrological symbols, a monstrous turban on his head. He studied the fowls, the cold meats, the blancmanges, the jellies, the flans. 'It all looks so delicious.' He handed a plate to Prinz Lobkowitz who wore an Elizabethan Oberon costume and whose mask glittered with real gems. 'We've met before, I think. Merry Christmas to you.'

'And to you, sir. Our host seems a trifle under the weather.' Prinz Lobkowitz chose some olives.

'Perhaps hosts never can enjoy themselves as much as their guests. There must be so many anxieties. Were you at the last party?'

'During the Peace Talks? An absolute disaster.'

'Doomed to failure, one could argue. A worthy attempt.'

'To maintain the old order. Isn't that what most peace talks are about?' Prinz Lobkowitz smiled. 'It's a natural enough instinct, surely.'

'Ah, you would know better than I about such things.' Abanazar rubbed his hands and picked up a dish of plums.

'It is true,' said Oberon, 'that I have been a politician all my life, and an idealist for most of my career, if the search for perfect compromise can be dignified by the description of "ideal".'

'It is better than anything I ever possessed,' Koutrouboussis told him sadly, spooning at a plum or two, 'save for a passion, once, for a young girl. But she evaded me, though for some time she was mine. Do you understand women, Prinz Lobkowitz?'

'Oh, women, women, there are far too many different ones. You speak of the romantic kind?'

'I am not sure. Romance remains a mystery. I enjoy power, however. Women are said to admire men who enjoy power.'

'They use them often enough, that is true, to further their own romantic dreams. The more a man loves power for its own sake, the less he interferes with their fantasies, while at the same time he is able to indulge them. Such relationships were once quite common, when I was younger. They seem to work excellently. And yet you have never experienced one, with all your ships and oil?'

'Never. I suppose I was too direct. She obeyed me, but only up to a point. She disappointed me. She would not commit herself as much as I had hoped.'

'There you have it. She saw you as committed to your power and therefore thought she would be free, that she need not give too much of herself to you. It was you, Mr Koutrouboussis, who disappointed this young woman.'

The Greek tugged absent-mindedly at his false beard. Parts of it came away in his fingers. A peculiar knowing light burned and faded in his dark eyes. He fumbled in his robes and withdrew a cigarette case, offering it to Lobkowitz, who declined. 'I want her very much.' He said again: 'She evaded me.'

'My friend,' said Prinz Lobkowitz sympathetically, and chewed a pickled walnut.

A large crowd was now approaching the table. Prinz Lobkowitz and Mr Koutrouboussis wandered away.

Sebastian Auchinek arrived with Mitzi Beesley. Sebastian Auchinek was not quite right as The Demon King, though the costume itself was splendid, with a long pointed tail and real horns. He held his pitchfork gingerly, anxious not to hurt any of his fellow guests. Mitzi Beesley was a depraved Peter Pan. 'The English have always needed queens,' he was saying. 'They are useless without them. Queens created the Empire, after all.'

'Half the greatest explorers were – ' began Mitzi.

'I'm not sure that's quite what I meant.'

Mitzi giggled. 'But Mr Cornelius isn't a queen. He's a king. Or is he a king *and* a queen?'

'His trouble is that he's all things to all men – and women too. Perhaps he doesn't know himself. It's probably the secret of his success.'

'He doesn't seem too pleased with that success.' She craned to catch a glimpse of a darting white costume.

'I agree he seems ill.'

'Hello, father,' said Mitzi. 'You make a lovely widow.'

'Thank you, child.' Bishop Beesley was a picture of dignity in his flounces and ribbons, his huge hat, his rouge. He had already been twice mistaken for Mrs Cornelius. He continued his conversation with Colonel Pyat, a Saracen King in golden armour. 'My motives were questioned probably because I was always a trifle unorthodox. I hoped to show people the way – back to decent standards. I did my best to be up to date at all times. I did not reject technology, nor did I turn my back on drugs.'

Mo Collier, as Robin Goodfellow, had been standing at the bishop's elbow. 'I read one of your sermons. It was great. *Cocaine in the Treatment of Sinus Infections*. Remember?'

'Not too easily.'

Mitzi joined the conversation, glad to help her father. 'It was just before *Salvation through Sugar*,' she said. 'The Mars Bar Messiah, they called you.' She became sentimental, recalling former greatness. 'The Orange Fudge Oracle. The Chocolate Cream Cleric. The Hershey Bar Bishop. The Man Who Brought the Tootsie Roll into the Pulpit. The Turkish Delight – '

'There was so much to do,' said the Bishop. 'Some of the details have become a trifle hazy now.'

'Sort of set into the blancmange of the past.' Mo was in a rare philosophic mood. 'Stuck to the sides of the great jelly mould we call Life.'

'The Smarty Saint,' continued Mitzi. She began to pant. His eye had fallen on her.

Dazed, Mitzi dropped back. To escape the dreamy Robin

494

Goodfellow beside him, Bishop Beesley gathered up his skirts and followed her.

Mo was tasting some cream. Dubiously he licked his lips. 'Does it go off?' he asked a nearby Karen von Krupp, who said, without taking her attention from her companion, 'That'll be your epitaph, Mr Collier.'

'. . . but I can't hope to survive for ever in this environment,' Miss Brunner was telling Karen von Krupp, who wore her Beowulf outfit rather well, in spite of her age and frailty. 'All I wanted was to create a little peace and quiet for myself. People kept interfering.'

'*Ja*,' said Karen von Krupp. She was quite drunk. '*Ja, ja, ja*.'

'Simplification had always been my goal. Naturally, I had to synthesise a great deal of information. The world had to be broken into the proper bits in order to produce a programme suitable for processing by a reasonably spohisticated computer . . .'

'*Ja, ja*,' said Karen von Krupp. '*Ja, ja, ja*.'

'You thought she embraced the world.' Professor Hira (as Polichinelle, with peculiar protruberances on chest and back) was no longer calling himself Hythloday. He was talking about Miss Brunner, unaware that she was behind him. Mr Smiles knew; he looked awkward as The Green Knight. They had made him leave his green-painted Shire horse with its blood-red bridle in the stables where, unbeknownst to him, it was fighting with the two lions which had drawn Miss Brunner's chariot as far as the front door. 'She did not! She crushed it, forced it into a little square box; packed it in a hurry, too. Some try to understand the world, while others seek to impose their understanding on it. Unfortunately, Mr Smiles, these latter folk are those least equipped to perform the operation. Like Frankenstein, my dear Mr Smiles, they produce a monster.'

'I'd considered coming as Frankenstein.' Mr Smiles brightened behind his black beard which he had, unsuccessfully, also tried to dye green, 'but I gathered it wasn't suitable. Too modern or something. Or too general? And yet Doctor

Who is here. Is everyone supposed to be part of British folklore tonight? Frankenstein, I should have thought . . .'

'I think so.' The little Brahmin physicist was disappointed in his audience. 'Although I'm Italian, aren't I? Pulcinella? Punch?' He chuckled. 'Or Vice, if we're getting down to basics. We're all part of the same zany Cavalcade, eh?'

'I'm not sure about that. They made me leave my horse outside.'

'Harlequinade, then. Where is Harlequin?' Professor Hira sought about him in the crowd. 'Or what about Masquerade? Or is it a Morality Play? You're the Englishman, Mr Smiles. You tell me what it is we're in!'

Mr Smiles sipped his spiced rum. 'God knows,' he said. 'A bloody madhouse.'

Mrs Cornelius had somehow got hold of part of Old King Cole's costume. She still wore her skirts of green and brown, but she had a crown askew on her head, a white beard hanging around her neck. She spotted Hira and was delighted. 'Oo! There yer are! Where yer bin 'idin', eh?'

Punch blushed.

'I jest bin talkin' ter Robin 'Ood,' she confided to Mr Smiles, putting a hearty arm about her lover, who gasped. 'I arsked 'im where 'is mate wos – you know, ther monk.' She screamed with laughter and her crown threatened to fall off her head altogether. 'As usual I got me pees an' kews mixed up. Where's yer Mate? sez me, Wot mate's that, madam, sez Robin 'Ood, Oh, yer know ther one, I sez – Wot's is name? Then I remembered you know, didn't I? Triar Fuck? sez me. Then Robin 'Ood straightens up like a telegraph pole. Forgive me, madame, 'e sez, but I don't believe as 'ow I 'ave the where-wival!' She flung back her head and just saved her crown as she shook with mirth. 'Get it? See? Robin 'Ood ain't a bloke at all. It's a bloody woman, innit! Ah, har, har, har! They always bloody are in fings like this, ain't they?'

Professor Hira was baffled as usual but he managed to laugh with her through long practice. 'He, he, he. Oh, very good!'

Robin Hood herself strode by, equally baffled, causing Mrs Cornelius another outburst. Lady Sue Sunday had lost Helen Sweet again.

'It's traditional, see,' explained Mrs Cornelius to Professor Hira. The band had begun to play an Irish jig. 'Oo, come on!' She seized her lover and dragged him back towards the tree where most of the guests were dancing again.

Lady Sue found Helen Sweet, as Little Red Riding Hood, talking to Simon Vaizey. The elegant playwright had almost not come, since he wanted to wear his own Pierrot costume, but he had compromised and come as the Fool. '. . . Through dreaming towns I go, The cock crows ere the Christmas morn. The streets are dumb with snow,' he was saying to a rapt Helen. 'I've long since given up any hope of finding *my* Grail, dear. I haven't the brains. Well, God give them wisdom that have it; and those that are fools, let them use their talents.'

'I'd suggest you try using them elsewhere, Mr Vaizey,' said Lady Sue jealously. 'Nice to see you again. I'd heard you were dead.'

'I couldn't miss the party, could I?' Simon Vaizey stole away.

Jerry Cornelius, moving gracefully amongst his guests, bowed his Pierrot bow, elaborate and strange, passed Simon Vaizey and winked, reached his seat of honour. In his black and white Pierrot costume, his make-up, he bore an aura of sadness with him which no amount of capering and smiling could dispel. He sat down with a sigh, long and limp in the marble chair at the farthest end of the hall, just below the musician's gallery, from which dripped bunting, laurel, holly and ivy, so that he was half-hidden by decoration. Above his head the band was playing traditional music – fife, tabor, pipes and the beat of the snare dominated everything while the guests whirled about the tree in a haze of green and gold, scarlet and silver. He was feeling that loneliness most painful when one is amongst friends; and there was more than a touch of his old self-pity. He pursed cherry lips and whistled, against the harmony above, a

Commander Cody and His Lost Planet Airmen song, *I'm down to seeds and stems again blues* . . .

'Merry Christmas, Jerry!'

Flash Gordon found him, brushing aside the bunting, sympathetic and unwelcome as usual. His hot, dog-like eyes were about the only recognizable thing behind his thick make-up, his long golden wig (he had come as Lady Godiva). 'You'd have been much better as Harlequin, Jerry.' Evidently he believed that his friend was sulking. 'Somehow the part doesn't suit Frank.'

'I used to be,' Jerry crossed his billowing legs, 'but Harlequin somehow metamorphosed into Pierrot. It happened in France, I think. Don't ask how. I used to believe I was Captain of my own Fate. Instead I'm just a character in a bloody pantomime.'

'It's not too bloody now, at any rate.' Flash always tried to look on the bright side. 'Everyone's cultivating their own gardens. I didn't tell you about my new strain of peas, did I?'

'I was never much interested in gardening,' Jerry told him, doing his best to be friendly to Flash.

Flash laughed. 'No! You like blowing things up. You and Mo Collier. Blowing things up.'

'Of course,' Jerry continued, 'I'm grateful for what everyone's done.' He reached out to pat a slightly hurt Flash on the heavily sweating right hand. 'But all I wanted was Catherine back. They could have had everything else. There's no point without her. It's all my fucking fault, Flash.'

'You shouldn't feel guilty.' As someone whose main relish in life came from feeling guilty, Flash was unconvincing. 'You shouldn't blame yourself.'

'I'm just pissed off. I've ruined it, as usual. I can go anywhere I like in the city. Do anything I like. See anyone I like. Disguises are easy. Nobody bothers me. But all I want to do is stay home and make love to Catherine.'

'Well,' said Flash speculatively, 'you could always . . .'

Jerry shook his head. 'It's not the same.'

'I'd agree with that!' Flash's eyes grew rounder and hotter with reminiscences. He realized, suddenly, that he was being selfish and did his best to return to more general topics. 'They say that's the trouble with Utopia. You get bored. While there were big countries to fight, or big corporations, or just very powerful people, it was easier to be an individual.' He sighed artificially. 'Now everyone's an individual, eh, Mr C? It's taken a lot of the fun from life, I'll tell you.'

Jerry was surprised to find himself agreeing with Flash. He nodded. 'It's horrible, winning. With everyone on your side. It makes you edgy. And I've run out of things to do.'

'You've done a lot for everyone. I'm grateful. We're all grateful.'

'It's nice of you to say so, Flash.' Jerry looked down as a small black and white cat rubbed its thin body against his leg. He picked it up and stroked its head. It purred. He smiled.

'That's what you need,' said Flash encouragingly. 'A pet. You've cheered up already.'

'I love it.' Jerry spoke in some awe. 'That's what I need. Love.'

'Everybody loves you, Jerry. Well, almost everybody.'

'It's not being loved, Flash, that's difficult to come by. It's loving.'

'You love everyone. Everything.'

'That's my trouble. Oh, I wish I could find a way to wake Catherine up. She was my lodestone. Past, present and future. Reality, if you like – myth, too – of hope, of reconciliation, of peace and freedom.' He had to raise his voice for the music was growing louder and louder, the shouts of the guests noisier and noisier. 'She's my ideal, Flash. Nobody else will do. Have I said all this before?'

Flash came closer, to make himself heard. His breath was warm in Jerry's painted ear. 'Not in so many words. You've been a good brother to her, Jerry, in your own way. You've looked after her, even though she hasn't been able to give you much in return.'

499

'I was willing to destroy the world for her.'

'That's real love all right,' said Flash. 'That's the test, isn't it? Still,' he smiled nervously, 'I'm glad you didn't.'

'I thought I had.'

'Oh, not you, Jerry. Never!'

Jerry put his chin on his fist. Pierrot defeated.

'I'll go and get something to eat. Do you want anything?' Flash moved away, rubbing at the make-up on his face. 'This stuff's going to bring on my blackheads something rotten. See you later, Jerry.'

Gathering his blonde locks about him, Flash sidled for the buffet tables.

Jerry saw Harlequin break from the dancing crowd and run towards him. 'You ought to get a spot of grub down you, Jerry,' said Frank. 'You're looking like a bloody phantom at the feast. Enjoy yourself, boy! What price entropy now, eh?'

'Oh, piss off,' said his brother, and stroked the cat.

Frank seemed unmoved by Jerry's rudeness, perhaps because he was very drunk. His mask was higher at the left than at the right, his hat was too far back on his head. 'You're not sleeping enough, these days, are you?' He staggered and leaned against the back of Jerry's marble chair. 'You ought to try to get a bit more shut-eye. Mind you, you shouldn't need that much, considering all you've had in the past ... On the other hand, sleep isn't cumulative, you know. That's the irony, isn't it? Tiredness, of course, is. You get worse and worse. That's what's wrong with speed. Less and less real, in a sense. You've been pushing yourself beyond the limit. All these new schemes ... these potions you've been cooking up in your lab ...'

'You don't look that well, yourself.'

'I've given too much of myself away, Jerry. It was always my trouble.'

'You've never given anything away in your life. Sold it, more likely. Blood and souls ...'

'Steady on, old son. Noblesse oblige!' Frank burped. 'Pardon.' He was gleeful, evidently sensing that he had got through to his brother. 'I could let you have something to

500

get you moving again. A few mills of – hic – tempodex.' He made a plunging motion towards his arm. 'Back on your old form? No danger!'

'I'm all right here. If you could find a drug to perk Cathy up, that'd be more useful. After all . . .'

'No recriminations! We agreed. Anyway, it's not in my interest, is it?' Harlequin smirked. 'Not with you in your position and me in mine. Now, if you were to give me more power . . .'

'I haven't got any bloody power!'

'Well, influence, then . . .'

'You can't transfer influence, Frank.'

'I dunno. I've been experimenting . . .'

'I wish I'd never bought you that chemistry set when we were kids. It's been nothing but trouble.' Jerry stared moodily over his brother's head. The music had stopped again and the guests were surging towards the buffets and bars, parting like the Red Sea on either side of the tree. 'This is all your fault. Not mine.'

'Oh, come on now. Do me a favour, Jerry. You were the one with the big ideas. It was just carrying on the family business. What's born in the blood is bred in the bone. We're all victims of history.'

'That's why I was trying to get rid of history.' He rose from his throne, now that he could see a clear path ahead, and left his brother standing beside the chair, running a grey hand over the cold stone.

'You want to get yourself a proper job, old son,' called Frank. 'This is no work for a man!'

Jerry ignored him. Already the guests were beginning to move back into the centre of the ball-room. His mother approached, holding a plate on which an entire trifle staggered. ''Ere yer are, Jer' – wanna bit?'

'No thanks, mum.'

'Good fer yer.' Evidently she had been sick down her dress and had cleaned it inexpertly with the beard she now held in her other hand.

Prinz Lobkowitz rescued him. 'What a nice little cat. What's its name?'

'Tom,' said Jerry, 'I think.'

'And the costume! Perfect.' Prinz Lobkowitz quoted knowingly, probably Verlaine.

> 'Ce n'est plus le rêveur lunaire du vieil air –
> Sa gaieté, comme sa chandelle, hélas! est morte,
> Et son spectre aujourd'hui nous hante, mince et clair.
> Et voici que parmi l'effroi d'un long éclair
> D'un linceul.
> Sa pâle blouse à l'air, au vent froid qui l'emporte,
> Ses manches blanches font vaguement par l'espace.
> Avec le bruit d'un vol d'oiseaux de nuit qui passe,
> Des signes fous auxquels personne ne répond.'

'Oh, I wouldn't say that,' said Jerry. He pushed on, the crowd growing denser. Major Nye leaned against a pillar talking to Karen von Krupp, St George in conversation with Beowulf. 'The British, you see, have an ability to shuck off the civilization in an instant and become, for as long as it suits them, wild beasts. It is the secret of their survival – it is what makes great explorers, mountain climbers and killers. They do not belong in Europe. They never belonged in Europe. Their instincts have always led them to more savage parts. It was civilization brought the British down – as civilization crept across the globe like rabies, they were forced to turn on one another and, for a long time, make a savage environment of their own land. You take my meaning?'

'*Ja*,' said Karen von Krupp, '*ja, ja, ja.*'

A great mound of vegetation, Jack-in-the-Green, that had been Herr Marek, the Lapp priest, was confiding in a whisper to Cyril Tome, who was now setting puzzles for children's television and who had come as a somewhat anaemic Hern ('more a Hernia,' as Lady Sue had said to Helen Sweet when they had arrived). 'I've been haunted, you see, for years by the knowledge that I am the slave of a machine existing somewhere underground. It has forced me to simplify my language so that it can communicate with me better. I *could* attack it by using complicated and poetic language, but it takes reprisals, killing or maiming not me but my friends – in railway accidents, planes and car crashes, lift failures, and with electric shocks. I have to think of others, but I must warn them, somehow, too. In order to do this I have resorted to complicated subterfuges . . .'

'Merry Christmas!' Mitzi Beesley raced past, pursued by her grunting father. 'Now,' he breathed, 'now we'll see!' He had his skirts to his knees as he chased her. She disappeared behind the tree.

'The failure of the second half of the twentieth century was to absorb the achievements of the first half,' said Dick Whittington (ex-prime minister M. Hope-Dempsey), 'particularly the rarer malt whiskeys.' He was speaking to Eva Knecht, also a principal boy. She had come as Prince Charming. 'You are drunk,' she said. 'Would you like to tie me up?'

Jerry could see that the party was beginning to lift. Stroking his cat he continued on his way through the throng and reached the wide stairs just as the band began to play Doctor Hook's *Queen of the Silver Dollar*.

It was a beautiful Christmas, thought Jerry. The nicest he had had. Slowly, he mounted the stairs, pausing to look back at his happy guests, at the snow falling outside. It was getting quite late. He looked for Frank in the hall, but the Harlequin costume was nowhere to be seen. He shrugged and continued up the stairs, tripping over his long satin trousers.

He had reached the landing and was on his way to his own apartments when he heard a noise behind Catherine's door. He paused, made to enter, then changed his mind. Almost in panic he began to run along the landing to his own rooms, dashing through the door without bothering to put on the lights, dumped the little cat on his bed, and went to the trunk in his study, rummaging through it rapidly until he found what he wanted. 'Wait here,' he told the cat. It was best to take no chances.

Needle-gun in hand he returned to Catherine's room. 'Who's in there?' He kicked open the door and walked in.

Frank stood at the end of Catherine's bed. He had removed his mask. He had a loaded hypodermic in his hand. He was looking tired and ill, like a sick vulture. 'I don't feel very well,' he said. 'Look. She's woken up.'

Catherine, in contrast, was in the peak of health. Her skin glowed, her eyes were bright, if a little dazed. She and Una Persson were propped on their pillows, in one another's arms. Catherine was entirely naked, her Columbine costume scattered across the floor. Una was naked save for her Harlequin's mask. She did not seem to realize that she was still wearing it.

Frank fell to his knees. Una pulled a smoking S&W .45 from under the bed-clothes. 'I'm sorry, Jerry. I've shot your brother. He was going to . . .'

'That's all right.' Jerry put his needle-gun in his baggy pocket. Joy mounted within him, slowly. 'How long have you been awake, Catherine?'

'Not long. Una woke me.'

'I'm very grateful, Una,' he said, 'for all you've done.'

'Ugh!' groaned Frank from the floor. 'She's two-timing you, Jerry. Ugh! Both of us!'

'I don't think so,' said Jerry, smiling tenderly at both of them. 'Are you?'

'I must be going.' Una Persson's smile was just a fraction late, but it was a good, brave one. 'Leave you two alone.'

'Oh, no,' said Jerry. He sat on the bed beside her, still looking at Catherine. 'Please stay.'

Una stroked her hair. 'I was just saying goodbye.' She looked at her wrist. 'What's the time? My watch has stopped.'

'About midnight, I think.'

'Good. I can catch the last flight out.'

'You're welcome . . .' Jerry said.

'Ugh.' Frank's voice was fainter.

'I'm still a working girl, you know.' Una climbed from the bed and, walking around her victim, began to pull on her own Harlequin costume. 'I'm sorry about the mess.'

Frank groaned. His chest was crimson.

Una tucked her slap-stick into her sash. 'I didn't mean to kill you. It was the shock. You shouldn't have dressed yourself up like that. I thought you were me for a moment. What were you trying to achieve? Imitation isn't art, you know, Frank.'

Unclean blood fell down his chin. 'Merry fucking Christmas,' he said, 'you bitch. Both of you. All of you.' Clutching himself he began to sidle across the floor. 'Oh, fuck. Oh, fuck.'

'He'll be all right, I expect,' said Catherine to reassure Una. She reached out and took Jerry's hand, squeezing it. Jerry sighed. 'He's always making a lot of the things that happen to him.'

Frank reached the door and crawled through it into the light of the landing. 'God help us, one and all.'

Una went over and closed the door. 'You'll want to be alone. I've told her everything you've done for her, Jerry – and all that's happened.' She bent to fluff at his ruff. 'Pierrot wins Columbine, at last. It's taken hundreds of years.'

Jerry could see that Una was close to tears. He stood up and helped her on with her red and green cape. 'Let me know if there's anything I can do.'

'Your work's over,' Una said, 'but mine's not finished yet. Otherwise I'd give you a run for your money. Pierrot couldn't wake her, you see. Only Harlequin has the power to do that. Pierrot has no power – only charm.' She kissed him briskly on the cheek. 'Cheerio, you little bugger.' She paused by the bed and bent to kiss Catherine's lips. 'Merry Christmas, Columbine.'

'Oh,' said Catherine. She looked from her brother to her friend.

Una reached the window, opened it and stepped through. Cold air filled the room. A few flakes of snow settled on the sill. Then she had gone, Harlequin returned to the night,

505

and the window was shut. There came a sound, like the crying of hounds, but it was either made by the guests below or came from the traffic in Ladbroke Grove.

In the ball-room it seemed that the Christmas Party had taken on fresh life as wave upon wave of laughter rose up to them. 'Merry Chrissmas! Merry Chrissmas!' they heard their mother shout. 'Merry fuckin' Chrissmas!'

Then the music started up and the palace shook to their dancing feet.

Jerry pulled off his huge trousers but kept his flowing blouse and his skull-cap on. He knew how much his sister liked it. He got into bed. He touched her vibrant skin. They embraced. They kissed.

From outside, from below in the whiteness of the garden, a light voice was raised for a few seconds in song:

For in you now all virtues do combine –
Sad Pierrot, brave Harlequin and lovely Columbine . . .

There sounded a bass drone, then silence.

Jerry rolled into his sister's soft arms and the two were joined together at last.

'Catherine!'

'Jerry! Jerry!'

A crack of light appeared from the door as it was pushed open and a small black and white cat entered. It jumped to the foot of the bed and began to wash liquid from its paws. It looked up at them and purred.

All in all, thought Jerry, it was going to be a very successful season.

Early Reports

What wonders now I have to pen, sir,
Women turning into men, sir,
For twenty-one long years, or more, sir,
She wore the breeches we are told, sir,
A smart and active handsome groom, sir,
She then got married very soon, sir,
A shipwright's trade she after took, sir,
And of his wife, he made a fool, sir.

The Female Husband, c. 1865

Old England, once upon a time,
  Was prosperous and gaily,
Great changes you shall hear in rhyme,
  That taking place is daily.
A poor man once could keep a pig,
  There was meat for every glutton,
Folks now may eat a parson's wig,
  For they'll get no beef or mutton.

What Shall We Do For Meat! c. 1865

Now the trial is o'er, and the Judge did say
Mistress Starr, you have lost the day,
And five hundred pounds you'll have to pay
  For tricks that are play'd in the Convent.

Funny Doings in the Convent, c. 1865

All the world will mount velocipedes,
  Oh won't there be a show
Of swells out of Belgravia,
  In famous Rotten Row;
Tattersall's they will forsake,
  To go there they have no need,
They will patronize the wheel wright's now

For a famed Velocipede.
The dandy horse Velocipede,
   Like lightning flies, I vow, sir,
It licks the railroad in its speed,
   By fifty miles an hour, sir.
      The Dandy Horse; or, The Wonderful Velocipede,
                        c. 1865

Three men they say on that fatal Friday,
   At four o'clock on that afternoon,
Those villians caused that explosion,
   And hurried those poor creatures to their doom.
They from a truck took a barrel of powder,
   A female, Ann Justice, was there as well,
And in one moment death and disorder
   Around the neighbourhood or Clerkenwell.
           Awful Explosion in Clerkenwell, c. 1865

I am the famous dancer, Harlequin.
I've shown my postures and my grace sublime
In every epoch and in every clime.
Wherever Youth and Beauty gaily meet
I am the dancing pattern of their feet.
                Harlequinade, c. 1865

The myth of the golden past gave way to the myth of the
golden future but, for a short time in the 90s and then the
1960s we enjoyed the myth of the golden present.
              M. Lescoq, *Leavetaking*, c. 1965

Tuning Up (5)

'Who are we today, then?' Miss Brunner leered at Jerry over her pint. 'Che Guevara?'

Jerry hesitated at the door of the Blenheim Arms. The pub had a special extension for the evening. It could stay open until midnight. It was very noisy. It smelled strongly of mild beer. It was packed with celebrants. It was warm. 'Happy New Year,' he said. He closed the door of the local behind him.

'That suit's very light-weight for the weather, isn't it?' His brother Frank took Miss Brunner's lead. 'On our way to Bermuda, are we?'

'I don't feel the cold,' said Jerry. He knew that he looked smart in the suit, even if it was rather thin, and he hadn't bothered to wear an overcoat because he was only popping into the pub from across the road where he was staying with his mother. Gradually, however, he became self-conscious. He approached the bar. They were all in tonight. All facing him. Mr Smiles wiped the froth from his moustache. 'The trousers are a bit baggy, aren't they?'

'They're meant to be baggy.' He felt in a pocket for some money. The pocket seemed the size of a sack.

'Stop taking the piss out of him,' said Catherine. She wore blue denims and a dark green sweater with a picture of Dr Hook and the Medicine Show on the front. 'I think it's very sexy, Jerry.' She opened her shoulder bag, looking for her purse, but Mo Collier was ahead of her. He waved a fiver at the barman. 'Usual?' he asked his friend.

'Why not?' Jerry had forgotten what his usual was. He was attempting to regain lost ground by cultivating an air of insouciance. He looked Miss Brunner up and down: black strapovers, fishnet stockings, skirt just above the knee, square-cut jacket with heavy padded shoulders. Perm. Earrings. 'That's a sweet costume. Are we going as historical figures? Where did you hire it?' He was lame.

She shook her head in genuine disappointment. 'This gear cost a fortune and you know it. You can do better than that.'

But she tugged for a second or two at the back of her jacket and raised his spirits.

Frank said anxiously, looking at his wrist-watch: 'We'll have to drink up. The coach'll be here any minute.' They were all going to Brighton to celebrate New Year's Eve at Mr Smiles's new hotel. He had spent the last ten years in Rhodesia, where he had made a fortune, and was anxious to renew old acquaintanceships. Frank wore a red polo-neck sweater, purple bell-bottoms and a black velvet blazer-style jacket. He held a double gin in one pink hand.

'Still teaching at St Victor's, then, are we?' Jerry asked Miss Brunner. 'Having our way with the tweenies?'

'That's defamation if ever I heard it.' She spoke without much conviction, almost amiably. Even though she had been prosecuted for her sexual activities at the school she had not only managed to get off all the charges but had somehow managed to become headmistress of St Victor's Primary School. Her attempts to re-introduce corporal punishment, though, had not been all that successful. Increasingly the parents of the children were from the upper middle classes – people who had moved into the district as their incomes declined, who sustained their position in the world by selling their houses in Chelsea, South Kensington and Belgravia for large profits and buying cheaper houses in North Kensington, with the result that rents had risen all round, though the authorities tended to be warier of residents who might now be the sons and daughters of rich people, or literate radicals, rather than working-class youths. There were distinct, if superficial, improvements. Black men were hardly ever beaten up in public by the police any more (this distressed the new arrivals) and the police had increasingly come to see their new role as the protectors of Rate Payers from Non-Rate

Payers (those whose rates were included in their rent and paid by the landlord). Street fighting in North Kensington had declined and street music and street theatre had increased, but the police did not discriminate between these activities: all were likely to cause annoyance to the Public (Rate Payers) and were dealt with with equal ferocity. According to the methods favoured by the individual officer, friendly banter would be employed, an attempt to 'jolly' the victims into giving up without a struggle, or outright threats and violence would occur from the start. Miss Brunner approved of the police's new attitude but mourned the days before parents became sophisticated and could now recognize, pursue and pillory the poor paedophile. Not everyone gained from the New Liberalism. Ten years before, hardly anyone had heard of her particular passions, except her little charges and their hopeless parents who had been content to recognize her authority, as they recognized all authority, with a dumb and wholesome fear and, amongst the more spirited, like the Cornelius children, a little primitive and easily handled backmail. As well, the older and more knowing they became, the less interest she took in them. The seventies were increasingly difficult years for Miss Brunner. In her opinion children were growing up far too early.

'I still fink 'e shouldn'ta moved me wivvout arskin',' Mrs Cornelius was complaining. She sat at a little corner table, behind two pints of stout, talking to Colonel Pyat who sipped his vodka and nodded intensely at almost every word. He was dressed in an old fur coat, part of the stock of second-hand clothes at his Elgin Crescent *Glory of St Petersburg Vintage Fur Boutique* which was doing such excellent business, these days; time had given him wealth, a seamed and baggy face, a decadent dalmatian, which wheezed on a leash at his feet. Mrs Cornelius had recently been given accommodation in the basement of a house in Talbot Road and was shortly to be moved to an identical basement in the house in Blenheim Crescent whose second floor she had occupied for so many years. Frank had sold the

511

family flat for a handsome sum to a young doctor and his wife and had told his mother that the council would be bound to find her a new home when they saw the condition of the basement, which was very damp. However, it had not taken her long to get comfy and now she didn't really want to move. She wore a vast ragged coney coat, a present from the colonel. She saw Jerry at the bar and waved him over.

''Ullo, Jer' – yore lookin' very dapper – they put yore dole money up? Har, har, har!' She shook, looking to the others for confirmation of her drollery. 'Her, her, her, ker-ker-ker-ker . . .' She had developed the local cough almost to perfection. Jerry picked up his whisky and swallowed it down. His mother felt in her handbag and produced a tenpenny piece. 'Ker-ker-ker-shu-hu-shove some-ker-ker-ker-money in the juke box, love. 'Ere yer are!'

Reluctantly he came over to take the coin. 'What d'you want to hear?'

'Oh, you know best. One o' yore fav'rites. Wot abart that 'Oo lot?'

'Don't like 'em any more.'

'Rollin' Stones, then.'

'They haven't done anything worth listening to in ages.'

'Chuck Berry!'

'Come on, mum! He's gone completely commercial. Years ago.'

'There must be someone yer like, Jer'. Ya used ter 'ave all these 'eroes.'

'They've all gone off. Or died.' His smile was wistful. 'I haven't got any heroes any more, mum – at least, nobody you can hear on the average juke box. Not these days.'

'Well, give us some Gary Glitter. I like 'im. Or Alvin Stardust. Or the Bay City Rollers. They're like the Beatles, ain't they?'

'Why not?' He pushed his way through the crowd to the glowing juke box. He put the money in and pressed buttons at random. He returned to the bar and gave his mother a thumbs up sign as Paul Simon began to sing something miserable and only barely revived.

'Oh, I like this,' she said, 'it's one of the old ones, innit?'

A plummy voice rose to challenge the music. The Bishop was drunk again. 'We gather today to celebrate the deaths of enemies and to mourn the deaths of our friends . . .'

'Go on, Dennis!' shouted Mrs Cornelius. She was always kind to the old has-been.

''E must be on 'is ninth creme de menthe,' said Mo Collier, grinning at Jerry. Ex-lay preacher and boy scout leader, Dennis Beesley had once run the local sweetshop but had sold it years before. Rumour had it, he had eaten all the profits. He had taken part in many neighbourhood activities, had organized the North Kensington chapter of the Monday Club, been chief representative for the Union Movement, the Empire Loyalists, and until lately, the National Front. He was still regarded by some residents as a political sage, in spite of the mysterious scandal which had led to his being expelled from both the Boy Scout movement and the National Front. His daughter Mitzi, who had looked after him since his wife had run off with a black Methodist preacher from Golborne Road, was also in the pub, being chatted up as usual by half a dozen or so of the lads, though she was showing more interest in the owner of the nearby all-night supermarket, Mr Hira, known as 'The Professor' because of his constant references to his university degree.

Dennis Beesley continued his oration, cheered on by several regulars. '. . . to execrate those whom we hate and to praise those whom we love. From the highest and noblest of motives are brotherhoods such as ours formed so that we may comfort one another, huddling close, turning our backs on the terrifying darkness of Eternity, lifting our quavering voices in hymns of praise to the Great Idea, the Desperate Hope.' He raised green liquid to his full, sticky lips. The red blotches under his cheeks clashed badly with the creme de menthe. He drew a breath. 'My dear friends, let us now kneel to stroke one another's heads, to murmur reassurance, to pretend to divine commitment, to rage, for a short while, against the Unacceptable, to complain of our wrongs, to seek scapegoats for our own shortcomings, to protect the

513

indigenous people of these isles against the encroaching hordes of the Children of Israel, against the Yellow Peril, the Black Invasion, the Asian Tidal Wave, the Red Menace, the Brown Betrayer, the Olive Exploiter and – and . . .' He frowned as he drained his glass.

'And the Great White Whale,' suggested Mr Hira, putting his arm round Mitzi's waist. Mitzi rubbed herself against him. Beesley burped. 'Thank you,' he said. His flesh turned to a shade of green much paler than his drink. He shut his mouth suddenly and rolled urgently towards the lavatories.

'Hurry up,' Frank called after him, 'or you'll miss the coach.'

'Such a shame,' said Miss Brunner. 'They ruined him, unfrocking him like that – or un-knickerbockering him, is it? The elders made far too much of it. He was only after their bulls-eyes.'

'Definitely the post-war answer to Walt Disney,' Major Nye was saying enthusiastically to Catherine. 'I love him. I've enjoyed them all. Ten Thousand and One. The Clock and the Orange. Barry Lindsay. He can do no wrong in my eyes.'

'I've always thought his pictures have everything except a good director,' said Jerry, not for the first time.

'Yes, I know,' said Catherine. 'You've mentioned it before.' She meant no harm, but she crushed him. He drank another whisky.

Mrs Cornelius came flat-footed to the bar. ''Ow old's that Miss Brunner nar? She was a stoodent teacher, wa'n't she, w'en you woz at school? Must be fifteen years, eh? Still at St Victor's, is she?'

'Still there.' Miss Brunner had heard her. 'I'm headmistress now, you know.'

Mrs Cornelius was admiring. 'I've got ter 'and it ter yer.' She winked at Miss Brunner and jerked her thumb towards her son. 'Carn't yer do somefink abart 'is appearance? Ain't yer still got some inflerence over 'im?' 'E used ter be such a smart dresser – all the trendy colours, all bright an' sharp. Nar look at 'im. Looks as if 'e's garn on a bloody safari!

514

Looks like a bleedin' clarn at ther circus wiv them trahsers! Ah, ya, ha, her, her – ker, ker, ker, ker, ker!'

'The world caught up with me,' said Jerry, 'that's all. Anyway, I never liked going with the crowd.'

His mother hugged him and stopped herself coughing. 'There, there! Don't let yer ol' ma git yer dahn. No offence meant, Jer'.'

'None taken, mum.'

'That's the stuff. There's not a lot o' 'arm in yer, Jerry. I'll say that!'

'What you drinking, then?'

''S'all right – ol' money-bags is payin' – 'ave one on the Fur King o' Elgin Crescent! I did okay stayin' wiv 'im, eh?'

'You certainly did.'

'I've never gone short o' beaux,' she said. 'Whatever else 'as 'appened ter me. Men've orlways fancied me. An' I, I've gotter admit, 'ave orlways fancied them.' She shifted on her massive legs. 'Ker-ker-ker.'

'I don't know how you do it, mum,' he said as she shouted for service. 'You'll still be going in a hundred years.'

'Two bloody 'undred!' She winked at him. 'Vodka, port an' lemon an' whatever 'e's 'avin',' she told the barman. She indicated her son.

'Double brandy, please,' said Jerry. He thought he might as well get something out of an evening which had so far been more than a little depressing.

'Is 'at right,' said his mother, 'abart you goin' off all them pop stars yer used ter like?'

'They never fulfilled their promise, did they?'

'An' Georgie Best and Muhammad Ali and them others?'

'Same went for them. They all seemed to let me down at the same time.'

'Funny, reely, wiv Caff takin' up with all that, nar. Wot yer like nowadays?'

'Nothing much. I've lost faith in heroes.'

'Ah, well. Yer orlways did 'ave yer 'ead in the clards. Come darn ter Earf a bit now, eh?'

515

'Looks like it.'

Catherine put her arm through his. 'Don't needle him, Mum. Everybody's picking on him tonight.'

'She wasn't,' said Jerry. 'Not really.'

'Buyin' 'im a bloody drink, wa'n I?' His mother was defensive. 'You wos orlways too protective to'ards 'im, Caff. Let 'im stand on 'is own two feet – 'e's old enough an' ugly enough nar!' But Mrs Cornelius was smiling as she carried the vodka and port back to her table.

Jerry sipped his brandy. He offered the glass to her. 'Want some?'

She nodded and took the drink. 'You coming with us to Brighton?'

'Depends how pissed I get. It's the worst New Year I've ever had. I feel so lonely. I'm really depressed, Cath.'

'That's not hard to see. Whenever you wear the wrong clothes for the weather I can tell. Clothes are a dead give-away, aren't they, to how a person's feeling? If you like we can go back to my flat. I don't particularly want to spend God knows how long in a smoky coach, singing rude songs – besides the roads are almost impassable, apparently. Heaviest snow of the century. We could see the New Year in together.'

'What about your girl friend?'

'She's working. Gone abroad for a few days. She knows about us, anyway.' Catherine squeezed his hand.

He was profoundly grateful. 'Why not?' he said casually.

The door of the pub opened and cold air blew in. There was a glimpse of the frozen street. A bulky figure stood there. He was dressed in a vast dark overcoat, with a black muffler over his face, a fur cap on his head. In the odd light from the pub the tall dog at his side seemed to have red ears and eyes.

'We're off!' cried Frank with delight. 'Off into the country-side. A-hunting we will go. Tantivvy, tantivvy!'

Jerry saw a small black and white cat run from the warmth of the bar into the chill of the street and had an

516

impulse to stop it, but the newcomer was shouting now: 'All aboard what's going aboard!'

Hooters, whistles, rattles clattered and cawed and shrieked as, baying, the party surged out into the old year's last night.

But Harlequin's domination has waned ... In the modern world he is pale and lost, the frustrated Pierrot. Columbine has become a gold digger, Pantaloon is gaga, and the Harlequinade itself which used to be the core of the Pantomime, the mythical world into which all waited for the particular scene to be transformed, is now separated off as a quaint little period piece.

Randall Swinger, *The Rise and Fall of Harlequin*, *Lilliput Magazine*, December 1948

Overcrowding – The Increasing Stress in North Kensington

North Kensington's Golborne Ward is the most severely over-crowded area in all London. Here 40% of the people live at a Housing Density of more than 1½ people a room. Kensington is one of the four London boroughs in which 'signs of increasing stress can be seen through the effects of overcrowding.' These are some of the stock facts to emerge from the Milner Holland report on housing in London.

KENSINGTON POST, 19 March 1965

Mrs C. and Frankie C.

'They say in the paper that we are on the brink of a new Ice Age,' said Colonel Pyat hopefully, casting a gloomy, Slavic eye over his ranks and ranks of old fur coats, evening capes, stoles, cloaks, hats and gloves. Spring had just arrived and with it the normal slackening off of business which always depressed him. He had long-since ceased to believe in the future.

'Stop broodin' yer silly ol' bugger an' 'urry up,' said Mrs Cornelius cheerfully. Her old eyes glittered behind a barricade of cream and powder. 'Ker-ker-ker. We still got ter call fer Frank.' Out of loyalty she wore his latest gift, though the weather was unusually mild. They were on their way to the People's Spring Festival, organized by local community leaders on the Westway Green below the motorway flyover to the west of Portobello Road. Mrs Cornelius was excited. It was to be Jerry's first public appearance with his rock and roll band, The Deep Fix.

'Mind you,' she said as an afterthought, 'these fings orlways start late, if at all. Still, it's up ter us ter be on time, innit!'

'I hate it,' grumbled Pyat. 'Jungle music. Teddy boy noise.'

'Cor! You are art o' touch, incha!' She snapped her fingers and rocked from side to side, wafting lavender water and scented powder. 'Y've gotta be wiv it these days – trendy, far art, too much, rock an' roll!'

She swayed through the door into Elgin Crescent. It was a busy Saturday in the market. Colonel Pyat glanced viciously at the Indians, with their cheap cheesecloth shirts and dresses, who were doing such a roaring trade. There was the usual confusion of locals trying to shop in a hurry while visitors moved slowly and uncertainly along the narrow street between the stalls, wondering why so many people scowled at them. Most of the money they brought to

Portobello Road stayed in the district for the few hours that the antique-dealers and stall-holders remained there. Colonel Pyat followed Mrs Cornelius from the shop, locking the door carefully behind him. He, too, wore an enormous fur coat. The day was miserably bright and sunny.

Together they pushed their way up the Portobello Road, through the trinket-sellers, the street-musicians, the purveyors of craft-goods, the racks of denim and cheesecloth, the mass-produced patches and buttons and belt-buckles, the green grocery stalls, the sellers of Indian metalware, of beads, flutes, drums, posters, army uniforms, handbags and purses, weapons, Victoriana, until they reached Frank's shop, which was currently dealing in stripped pine. Frank waited reluctantly outside, holding a brass candlestick in each hand, part of his old antique stock. 'If I sell 'em for that,' he told a small man in a pork-pie hat, a camera and a black blazer with four metal buttons on the cuff (evidently a German), 'I shan't make any profit, shall I?'

'Fifteen?' said the German.

'Sixteen,' said Frank, 'and that's final.'

'Done,' said the German awkwardly.

'You're so right,' said Frank accepting the money. 'You won't regret it. That stuff appreciates, some of it.'

'Come on, Frankie,' said his mother, pulling at him. 'Yer can't stop dealin' can yer, yer littel cunt?'

He was offended. 'At least someone in this family's making their own living.'

They trekked on until they reached the railway arch and, immediately after it, the motorway arch, where dozens of small stalls were set out selling the accumulated junk of the twentieth century. They skirted the stalls even as their eyes automatically shifted across the wares, rounding the corner to the big patch of grass where a crowd of young bohemians and their children had already gathered outside the graffiti-smeared walls of one of the motorway bays. This bay had a chicken-wire fence strung between its columns and a sign, already much attacked by weather and local children: WESTWAY THEATRE. Within the bay old railway sleepers had been arranged in banks to form seats. On the wall behind the seats were three murals, one by Cawthorn, one by Riches and one by Waterhouse. Somehow the murals had escaped the ravages of the rest of the theatre which had long-ago collapsed as a result of calculated lack of local government support. The Council had been reluctant to allow the project in the first place and had made sure it would not flourish by bringing in an administrator from outside the district and making sure that he had no power, no money and no encouragement. After a while enthusiasm had broken down into a classic series of disputes between a variety of splinter groups and an attempt to produce a free theatre for the district had failed. But, for the first time in over a year, it was to be opened – or had been opened – by the people who had originally started the scheme with their free Saturday concerts featuring Quiver, Brinsley Schwartz, the Pink Fairies, Henry Cow, Mighty Baby, Come to the Edge and Hawkwind, until the police, in support of seven Rate Payers, had managed to put a stop to them – and Jerry and his band were to have their chance at last.

Mrs Cornelius, with the dignity of one who was related to an artiste, Colonel Pyat in tow, Frank in the rear, went through the gates, calling out to her son who sat dreamily on the little stage trying to put a new plug on his amplifier. ''Ere we are, then! Give us a number, lads!'

Mo Collier grinned at her in some shyness. He had plugged in his bass and was plunking at it. No sound came from his own amp. He turned a couple of knobs and a screeching rose and fell. He made another hasty adjustment. ''Ullo, Mrs C. You're a bit early, aincha? We don't start till 'alf-past two.'

'It is now exactly a quarter-to-three,' said Colonel Pyat. He tapped his wristwatch as if it were a barometer.

'Sod,' said Jerry. He looked through the chicken wire at the gathering crowd. Behind it a number of policemen were beginning to line up. He finished with the plug and fitted it into the board. A red light flickered on his amplifier. He was surprised. He took his Rickenbacker electric twelve-string

523

over to the amplifier and pushed the jack-plug lead into the socket. He played a chord. Mo winced. 'We'd better tune up.'

Terry the drummer suddenly came to life behind the kit and played an erratic roll before subsiding again. He looked like the dormouse in Alice in Wonderland. They had all had several tabs of mandrax and had become very stoned to help quell their nerves for their performance. Jerry began to plunk at his many strings, staring vaguely at Mo, who plucked back. Gradually they got their instruments into some kind of uniform tuning. Mo nodded towards the centre of the stage where hardboard had been placed across a gap (there had been two attempts to burn down the theatre during disputes between different radical groups). 'Watch out for the 'ole, man.'

Jerry nodded absent-mindedly. He was visualizing the enthusiasm of his public. He had a glazed, harried look.

'All right, Mick Jagger,' shouted Frank in his poshest voice, 'let's hear you!'

'Ker-ker-ker,' said his mother.

Jerry approached the microphone and began to chant into it. Nothing came through the PA. He staggered back towards the amplifiers. Elsewhere various people were fiddling with other pieces of faulty electrical equipment. Jerry had a word with his friend Trux, who was holding a wire in one hand and scratching his head with a screw-driver.

'Ker-ker-ker.'

People were beginning to file into the theatre now, although the stage was so arranged that the band would play facing the people who sat outside on the grass. Some of the organizers of the event had not yet turned up. There had been a problem involving fresh disputes with a group of Rate Payers; the organizers could be seen on the far side of the green, gesticulating, deep in conversation with a number of middle-aged men and women with arms folded in front of them and expressions of extreme distaste on their faces as they looked first at the crowd and then at the stage. Once or twice a policeman wandered over and talked to a long-haired man in a fairisle pullover or had a word with the thin-lipped Rate Payer.

Jerry went behind the stage into the connecting bay, which served as a dressing room. He was beginning to feel much better. He accepted a joint from a girl whom he remembered vaguely. Her name was Shirley Withers and she had offered him a warm look such as he had not received for a very long time. He felt taller, slimmer, more hand-some. He grinned at her. A promising grin. He began to move with some of his old grace, the guitar resting casually on his hip. He went back on stage and plugged in again. He played a fast twelve-bar progression. He knew he was playing well. He nodded to Mo and Terry and began to jump up and down as he played. Some people were already clapping and cheering.

Mo put a final turn on his A string and inclined his head in a brief bow. Mrs Cornelius, Colonel Pyat and Frank Cornelius sat down in the front row. Jerry did not look at them. He was looking at his Fame.

Unexpectedly, they all started more or less together, going into a fast, standard boogie rhythm. Jerry danced towards the mike. He had never felt so happy. At last he was able to emulate all his earlier heroes. Perhaps he could become a hero himself, only he wouldn't let people down the way the others had. The crowd was his. He stepped up to the mike and opened his mouth.

The crowd roared.

It was the last thing he heard before the floor gave way beneath his feet and he fell into the shallow pit below.

He was far too drugged to feel any real pain, or even much concern, as he lay on his back looking at the dim patch of daylight above, at the broken Rickenbacker on his chest, listening to the waves of laughter and applause from the audience, to Mo's bewildered bass, to Terry's inappro-priately determined drum solo. Then he passed out for a moment or two.

He felt sick and miserable when he woke up. Shirley

525

Withers was in the hole with him. She was trying to lift him upright. He saw his mum peering over the edge.

'You okay, Jer'?'

'I'm fine. I can carry on now.' He knew his chance had disappeared.

'Your guitar's *ruined*,' said Shirley. 'Have you got another?'

He shook his head. He got to his feet, the pieces of smashed wood still hanging around him by the strap. He climbed out of the hole and blinked. The police had closed in on the crowd. A fight had started. Two panda-car constables were already on stage. Frank was talking to them.

'Pigs!' shouted Jerry weakly. He turned to Terry. 'Keep playing. Keep playing.'

'They turned the power off,' said Mo. He sat down crosslegged and buried his face in his hands.

'Don't let them stop your music!' Jerry addressed the confused crowd. 'You've got rights. We've all got rights.'

'No need to make any more trouble, sir,' said one of the constables. 'How's the head?'

'Piss off!' said Jerry. 'It's a plot. Why'd you bloody have to interfere?'

'We've had complaints. I've nothing against this sort of music myself. I like it. Not that you could play any now, could you, old son?' He indicated the broken Rickenbacker. 'So there's not a lot of point in making a fuss.'

'I haven't had a go yet,' said Jerry mournfully.

His mother moved to his defence. 'Lay off the poor little sod – it was 'is turn to do 'is act. 'E's bin waitin' years fer the chancest, an' you 'ave ter go an' spoil it!'

The constable backed away from her. 'We didn't damage the stage, madam.'

'Pigs,' said Mrs Cornelius with some relish. 'Motherfuckers!'

'It's all right, mum,' murmured Jerry.

'I'm on your side entirely,' Frank was saying to the other constable. 'If I had my way I'd ban this sort of thing altogether. I'm a Rate Payer.'

'Put 'em all up against a wall and shoot 'em,' said the constable with relish, then, as one of the organizers approached, 'I'm really sorry about this. We're just doing our duty.'

'Are you sure you're okay now?' said Shirley. Her eyes were worried rather than warm.

'Fine,' said Jerry, 'um . . .'

She anticipated him. 'Got to go now. See you around. Bye, bye.'

'Bye, bye,' said Jerry.

'You were very good,' said Mrs Cornelius. 'Wan'e, kernewl?'

But Colonel Pyat, a huge, frightened hampster, was already on the other side of the barrier and making for home.

'I'm a Trader *and* a Rate Payer,' Frank continued. 'I've lived here all my life. I remember when this was a quiet, decent neighbourhood.'

Mrs Cornelius gurgled sceptically. 'Wot? Oh, yeah. So fuckin' quiet yer couldn't get a bloody taxi ter take yer 'ome. They woz shit scared o' Nottin' Dale. They wouldn't drive yer beyond Pembridge Gardens! An' the coppers used ter patrol in threes. I remember one year they barricaded the Nottin' Dale coppers in their own nick and they couldn't git art till the people let 'em art!' She eyed the constable with fond speculation. 'We woz famous in them days,' she said, 'for bein' fierce. They're all soft nardays – coppers *an'* yumans.'

'Listen,' said the policeman with some heat, 'they wanted to send the SPGs in – then you'd 'ave known what for!'

'Took pity on yer, did they?' said Mrs Cornelius contemptuously. 'Ruddy little squirt.'

'Now, then, madam . . .' He reddened, seeking support. 'Arthur . . .'

With a quick, cunning movement, Mrs Cornelius stuck out her varicosed leg. The constable yelped and fell head-first into the hole. Mrs Cornelius took her son by the arm.

'C'mon – let's go an' 'ave a cup of tea. Yer'll make it yet, Jer' – I know yer will.'

The sleepers and the dope had begun to take effect. Jerry's eyes were watering. As his mum led him off the stage, he burst into tears.

Auchinek

Sebastian Auchinek's expensive white suit thoroughly out-
shone Jerry's cheap one. They sat together, side by side, on
a long, deep tan ottoman, in Auchinek's elegant, sparsely
furnished, Sackville Street office. Big windows admitted
cool sunlight as if it were exclusive to the establishment.
Auchinek was hatless. Jerry wore a broad-brimmed fedora.
'Sam Spade? Right?' said Auchinek pointing at the hat.

'Philip Marlowe,' Jerry told him. '*The Long Goodbye.*'

'Right! Beautiful.' Auchinek returned to his commiserating mood. 'But they're not cheap, are they, Rickenbackers?'
He spoke reverently. '£500?'

'About that,' said Jerry. He had got his guitar from a friend
who had done Sound City's entire stock in 1973, loading
two pantechnicons in half an hour on a Sunday morning in
July.

'And,' said Auchinek smiling, 'of course it wasn't
insured?'

'No.'

'You people!' Auchinek wore a waistcoat of pale blue
leather, its edges trimmed with metal studs, a lilac shirt, a
yellow cravat. Somehow all he seemed to lack was a green
parrot on his shoulder. 'So, Jerry! What can I do you for?'

'I wondered if you could get us some gigs. We did very
well at the Westway, until the accident.'

'Heavy rock?' Auchinek rose sadly and went to his desk.
He looked significantly back over his shoulder as he picked
up a black plastic box which looked as if it had cost much
more than anything in silver. 'Heavy rock? It's not my
scene. Solo singers, yes. Orchestras, yes. Boy and girl singing
acts, yes – soul trios, quartets, quintets, sextets, septets,
octets, yes, yes, yes, yes. Soul, soul, soul, soul – that's your
basic day-to-day demand anywhere in the country or on the
Continent, Las Vegas, you name it. Soul isn't just a popular

fad – it's the genuine commercial music of a decade. Black or white, it makes no diffcrence. Country music, rock and roll groups, reggae – nothing compared to soul. Jerry, you haven't got a bad voice – make it sweeter – get together with some other guys, maybe some gals, and do some harmonies – a good funky bass, a touch of wa-wah, even a taste of fuzz, nobody's objecting to that. It's fine, gives it body, texture – do you know how many records I've produced myself? – you don't have to give up your principles, just alter your angle a little. Mainly it's the songs, see.' He began to sing in a low, lugubrious voice, hunching his shoulders, awkwardly moving his lips. 'Baby, baby, baby, you broke my heart in two – now two hearts beat as one, but they're not having any fun, 'cause both those hearts belong to me! See? Lovely stuff.' He made a cryptic wind-milling motion with his arms. It was on the strength of this motion that Jerry, for the first time in his life, had developed racial prejudice while watching *Top of the Pops*. He had discovered that he hated black people. Then after another week or so of watching similar acts, he decided that he hated white people, too. Now he was hating Jews. He wondered just how much disharmony *Top of the Pops* was responsible for. It was surprising what music could do for the racial situation. However, he was desperate enough to continue trying to reason with Auchinek, his only contact in the commercial music business.

'I can't do it. But we thought of this idea – Music from the Spheres – astronaut music that's come from the stars – it's a good gimmick. We tell the kids it was given to us by space people, see. Like *Chariots of the Gods*, you know.'

'*Gramophones of the Gods*? Jerry, a gimmick's as good as the thing it's promoting. Okay – yes, good gimmick – but did the astronauts send us soul music? Maybe they did. You prove it. If the music isn't soul – if it isn't what people want to hear – it doesn't matter how good a gimmick you've got. It's the Number One Rule, Jerry. I've told you before.'

'But that stuff's just so much Muzak. It's piped music for

supermarkets. People didn't want to hear the Beatles till they heard them, or Hendrix, or The Who.'

'They heard them – they liked it – therefore it must have been what they wanted. My point!'

Jerry accepted the Camel Auchinek offered him. 'But mythology, see? Everyone's into mythology. I was reading this book – *The Mythical History of Britain* – yeah?'

'Fabulous . . .'

'It reckons we're all descended from the Trojans . . .'

'Trojans? I thought we were all descended from Martians. Maybe Trojans was their word for Martian?'

'You're probably right,' said Jerry.

'So what about the Martians?'

'An album – the mythical history of England up to the present day.'

'So?'

'Couldn't you interest someone?'

'Certainly I could interest someone. With my muscle, Jerry, I could interest anyone. Fabulous history of England? – fine – as rock music – the sort you like? – not really – as folk music? – who cares – as soul? Very good! Good orchestrations, nice arrangements, easy swinging rhythm – lovely – but King Arthur? A soul opera of King Arthur? Maybe, maybe. You are thinking of King Arthur? Like Wakeman? That's nice, the Wakeman. Exactly what I'm talking about. But it's been done. Can it be done again? With a new angle? Well, maybe. But Wakeman isn't The Miracles, if you see what I mean. A market, I grant you. A good market. But not a really solid market. Not so safe as soul. So what else were you considering? Let's spell it out, eh? Talk it through. Fine? Trojans? Who's heard of Trojans, these days?'

'We could make it Martians, as you suggested – gods as astronauts, the Bermuda Triangle – something up to date. The same stuff – but more modern . . .'

'Yeah, but that's mythology – the Bermuda Triangle is *science*. You don't want to get them mixed up, Jerry. There's too much confusion already in the world today. Still, not to split atoms, eh? Okay. Martians. Bermuda Triangle, Scifi, right? Far out. Okay, the market's getting big enough to stand it. Super. Fab. So far so good. So we have a Soul Opera about the Bermuda Triangle – '

'Or Jaws Superstar,' said Jerry wildly.

'Sharks? Sure, maybe. Giant sharks. Up-dated Moby Dick, with good music. Why not? We do a film. We all go out to Bermuda for a few weeks. Why not? Sure. Come to me with something on tape, some notes. Good. I'll listen to it. I'll take it down to the country with me. If I like it, I'll sell it. Can I say more?'

'But I need a new guitar first. If you could lend me the bread . . .'

'You still have that Equity card since I got you the film extra work?'

'Yes.'

'Then I can help you earn some money. Una's new show.'

'Playing guitar?'

'They don't need a rock guitarist. Not another one. A good part. The show's about Frankenstein, see, and what it means in moral terms today – beautiful songs.' His hands windmilled over one another.

'But I haven't had any acting experience.'

'You don't need it.'

'And I can't sing songs.'

'You don't have to. You yell. Rock and roll experience is perfect for this part. You scream. You jump up and down. With these teeth in. You get three appearances, maybe more. A night, I mean.'

'Who am I?'

'Who are you? You're the vampire. I should have thought of it before. I apologize. Okay? Want it? The pay's good. Get your name on the programme. A start in a career. Look at "Hair", how many people made it from that! Look at "Jesus Christ Superstar"? And "Godspell"?'

'Oh, blimey,' said Jerry.

'Contacts. You'll have a new guitar in no time. A break. Una'll be delighted.'

'You hate me, don't you?' said Jerry.

'Hate you? What's hate? I disapprove of you, because you're a talented boy who doesn't know what's good for him. You frustrate me, Jerry. You do. You frustrate me very, very much. So what's it to be? The vampire? Or back to busking on a borrowed banjo? Down the garbage chute or up the golden escalator?'

'I'll try the vampire,' said Jerry.

Persson

'You were splendid,' Una Persson leaned over a drowsy Catherine and lit Jerry's cigarette for him. She climbed across their bodies to be on his left. They all lay together in Una's king-size four-poster. It was early afternoon. 'You're a natural actor.' Una was talking about the movie rushes she had seen earlier that day at the studios. The film was her own first starring role (a remake of *Camille*) and by encouraging Jerry (who played Armand's friend) she seemed also to be encouraging herself.

Lying between the two women Jerry was in his element. His emotions were mixed but all pleasant. He felt they were three sisters sharing a delicious conspiracy, that he had two mothers, two concubines, two loyal friends; moreover he became still more cheerful when they ganged up on him, to take the piss out of him, to dress him up, to have their way with him. Perhaps it was their affection for each other which turned him on most, the fact that they were able to relax with him and therefore make him relax in turn. They enjoyed going out together, forming a little exclusive club whose erotic secrets only the three of them would ever know. Depressed, they were able to comfort one another; happy, they were able to infect one another.

'And you're better than Garbo.' It was true. 'Much better. You're a bit like her in looks, but your range is greater.'

Una lay back on her pillows, fingering her breasts as she absorbed his praise.

'You can out-act anyone, Una.' With a luscious sigh Catherine ran her soft hand down her brother's chest and stomach. 'Ah! I don't know how I get the work at all! I can't act for toffee. Still, six weeks in panto's better than nothing. We start rehearsals next month. It's hard to get into the Christmas spirit in September, mind you.' She rubbed her own stomach. It rumbled. 'Cor, I'm starving. Breakfast time.'

'It'll be tea-time soon,' said Una. 'I've been working since six o'clock.'

'I'll get some tea, then,' said Catherine agreeably, running her fingers through tangled blonde hair. 'Did you pick up the tickets from the agent?'

'Three one-way Class 1 berths on the *Alexander Pushkin* sailing next week for New York. We'll have to fly back.'

Catherine put her dirty feet on the white carpet, stood up and took her pale brown Janet Reger negligee from the back of the door. 'It'll be nice to see the old house again. And a good time to go.' Like her brother, she shared with Una an enthusiasm for American Gothic wooden houses.

'Will they let us sleep in the same cabin?' Jerry asked as his sister left. 'Do you think?'

'I've arranged it. They think we're ballet dancers. It's okay.'

'That's the Russians all over. One rule for the ballet dancers and another for everyone else. I wonder what it'll be like.' Jerry's Russophilia was only equalled by his romantic love for the United States. He could think of nothing more marvellous than travelling to one place on a ship belonging to the other. He had often remarked on the strong similarites between the two nations and believed this similarity to be the cause of their rivalry.

Una indicated the print on her wall. It showed the famous 18th century actor John Rich in his role of Harlequin. The caption above the print read *Harlequin Dr Faustus in the Necromancer* and below it was a verse:

Thank you Genteels, these stunning Claps declare,
How Wit corporal is yr. darling Care.
See what it is the crowding Audience draws
While Wilks no more but Faustus gains Applause.

'I told them we were putting on a new production,' Una said, 'but I didn't tell them you were playing Columbine.'

Jerry patted his stomach. With success, he was expanding.

'I'm not sure I'll get into the dress. Can't I be Harlequin or the Pierrot?'

She shook her head. 'It's not your turn.'

He giggled as she took him in her arms.

Nye

'You're Nöel Coward, if you want to be,' Major Nye stiffened his shoulders. 'I can't say fairer than that. You've the figure, now that you've lost a few pounds, the voice, the looks – or can have. What d'you say, old chap?'

It would be Jerry's first real star part in the West End, but he remained reluctant to begin a new commitment. Una would be back from America soon and Catherine would have returned to the provinces. If he took the role it would mean quite probably that they would not be together for several months.

'I don't know an awful lot about the thirties,' he said.

'Twenties, actually, this setting. *Bitter Sweet* with an all male cast. As he'd have liked it himself. You're not worried?'

'Not about that. So it's Brylcreem and six-inch fag holders, eh?'

'That's a bit superficial, old boy, but you've got the mood – it's what the public's desperate for . . .'

Major Nye had become an impressario late in life, with his run of successful nostalgia shows on stage, screen and television. Series like *Clogs* and *Mean Streets*, set during the depression in Northern towns, had shown people that things had been worse then they were now and taken their minds off their current troubles, while musical versions of *King of the Khyber Rifles*, *Christina Alberta's Father*, *A Child of the Jago* and *The Prisoner of Zenda* were all still running in West End and Broadway productions, as well as in touring companies (Catherine was currently playing Rupert of Hentzau in one of these).

'The traditionalists are going to be a bit upset,' Major Nye continued, pausing by a railing and staring out to sea. He had come down to Brighton especially to meet Jerry who was just finishing a run as Harlequin Captain MacHeath in the revived *Harlequin Beggar's Opera* which Jerry had himself suggested to Major Nye after Una Persson had given him the idea. The revived full-blooded pantomime was just one more of the major's successes in England and America. 'But we're used to that by now – and we're doing more for them than anyone else, even if we do take liberties occasionally. Still, it's the literary bods do the complaining, not the public, and it's the public that matters, eh?'

'Every time,' said Jerry. He waved. Elizabeth Nye, the Major's daughter, who had first interested her father in the stage, was running along the promenade to meet them. She was playing Columbine Polly Peacham to Jerry's Harlequin. 'Hello, Jerry. Hello, Daddy. Is lunch still on?'

'If you're interested, my dear.' He looked questioningly at Jerry. 'Spot of lunch, then?'

'Lovely,' said Jerry. 'Have you asked Sebastian about this?'

'No need to bring in agents until the last minute. They only confuse things. I didn't know you were still with him.'

'He's useful,' said Jerry. 'Anyway, I feel sorry for him. His musical interests have taken a turn or two for the worse.'

'He didn't move with the times,' said Major Nye. 'Lived in the present too much, in my view. Couldn't see that the wind was changing. Of course, I never expected anything like this myself. I started, you know, doing modest little music hall evenings with amateur performers. Now we're dragging up every damned traditional entertainment since Garrick's day – and before. We'll find we've got mass audiences for *Noye's Fludde* next season, at this rate.'

'The eighteenth-century satirists thought the Harlequinade was going to be the death of the theatre.' Jerry had pursued his usual research. 'They thought Shakespeare and Jonson were done for – pushed out of business.'

'Nothing ever kills off anything else,' said Major Nye comfortably, pointing his stick at Wheeler's across the road. 'Nothing invented ever dies. Fashions change. But it's always there, waiting to be revived according to the mood of the times. History is retold by every generation, always slightly differently – sometimes very differently. Funny stuff, when you think about it, Time.'

'I've never thought about it,' Jerry said.

A Bundle

Jerry sat in the studio mock-up in his elegant evening dress smoking a sophisticated cigarette, copying his successful Coward role but looking more like a Leslie Howard, sardonic, quizzical, as he turned to the camera and said:

'Once upon a time it meant something to be the owner of a car. It put you above the common herd. Now Rolls-Royce brings back meaning into motoring . . .' The camera pulled away from the close-up in order to show the whole scene '. . . with the mini-Phantom.'

'Cut,' said Adrian Mole, the director. 'There's a phone call for you, love. That was beautiful. All right, lads and lasses, you can go home now. Everything's perfect.'

Jerry climbed from the cramped seat and moved stiffly from the studio. In the office one of the bright, competitive girls who worked there handed him an instrument. 'Hello?'

The voice was indistinct, accented, anxious. Colonel Pyat.

'Your mother, Jerry. She is not at all well. She wants to see you.'

'Is she in hospital? St Charles?'

'No, no. She wouldn't let them take her. Still in Blenheim Crescent. You haven't been to visit her lately and I think she's upset.'

It was more likely that Colonel Pyat disapproved of him, thought Jerry. 'Thanks, Colonel. I'll go and see her right away.'

'I've looked in, but I have the shop to run. I'm all alone, you see.'

'Don't worry. Has the doctor been?'

'I haven't spoken to him, yet. But I think it's serious. She could be – oh, well, you had better look for yourself.'

'Does Frank know?'

'Frank, too, has his business. He's going to try to pop round this evening. Catherine we can't find.'

'She's on tour.' Jerry was surprised by his lack of annoyance, his spontaneous feeling of concern for his mother.

The evening clothes were his own so he did not need to change. He went straight to the car-park where he picked up his real Phantom. He nodded to two young girls who recognized him as he drove into the street. It was surprising how popular he had become since he allowed Auchinek to give him the 'conventional' image. It offered reassurance, of course. He touched the stud to lower his window and threw his Sullivan's cigarette into the street. He looked bitterly at his eyes in the driving mirror. He had always hated reassurance. Reassurance was death.

He reached Shepherd's Bush and headed up Holland Park Avenue, turning eventually into the maze that was now the Ladbroke Grove area, all diversions, and one-way streets, coming at last to Blenheim Crescent. Opposite his mother's basement, which was identical to the one she had temporarily removed to in Talbot Road, was the fortress of the new housing estate, built on the site of the Convent of the Poor Clares and named after the order (Clares Gardens, though no garden was in evidence anywhere). He found a space close to his mother's flat and parked. All the meters had been smashed, though he didn't benefit, however, since he had his resident's parking permit. He still lived in Kensington, in the more exclusive Holland Park area. He locked his car carefully, knowing the habits of the local kids, and descended the makeshift wooden steps of the basement. The wooden door was unlocked. He went in, recognizing the familiar, comforting smell of mildew and stale food.

'Mum?'

A fairly feeble cough came from the back room, where she slept. He made his way through the debris of her living room, with its ancient furniture, its scattered magazines, its unwashed crockery, its dead flowers, and entered the bedroom which smelled of disinfectant, camphor, moth-balls, rose-water, lavender-water, urine, stout and gin, a combination which never failed to fill him with nostalgia.

She lay in the iron-framed bed, beneath several quilts, propped on a variety of dirty cushions and pillows, in full make-up, so that it was impossible to tell from her skin how she was, though her eyes were uncharacteristically dull.

'Hello, Mum. Not too good, I hear.'

Somehow her jowls and her baggy pouches seemed to be one with her disintegrating cosmetics and gave the impression that the face beneath it all was that of a child. She had rarely seemed so pathetic. He drew up a cane-bottomed chair and sat beside the bed. Because it was conventional, he held her hand. She pulled it away with a throaty chuckle. "Oo'd'ya fink I am – Littel bloody Nell?' Her coughing began strongly but quickly grew faint. 'Ker-ker-ker . . .' She reached, unable to speak, for the glass on the bedside table. He handed it to her. She drank. It was neat gin, Jerry guessed, by the smell on her breath as she handed the glass back.

'I've 'ad it, Jer',' she said. 'You know 'ow old I am?'

She had always kept it a secret. He shook his head. She was delighted. 'An' yer never will,' she said. 'Know 'ow old you are, do yer?'

'Of course I do. I was born on 6 August 1946.'

'Thass right. They let orf ther bloody A-bomb ter celebrate. Most people on'y ever got fireworks – an' they 'ad ter be pretty fuckin' posh, an' all!' She eyed his costume. 'Nice. I orlways knew you'd make it, in the end. You an' Caff. Frank's doin' okay, too – but 'e never 'ad much imagination, did 'e? Not like ther rest've us.'

'Yeah,' said Jerry, nodding. He took out his silver cigarette case, offering it to his mother. With some difficulty she removed a cigarette and put it between her lips, drooping as always. Jerry lit it. He lit another for himself. She coughed a little but soon stopped.

'Well,' she said, 'I'm dyin' – it's why I was so keen to see yer. Got yer in'eritance, in I?'

'Oh, come on, Mum, don't be daft.' He tried to smile. 'Besides, you haven't got a penny. It's all gone on wild living.'

'It *as*, too!' She was proud. 'Every bleedin' shillin'. They didn't need no bloody inflation when I was arahnd!' A brief cough and Jerry thought he saw her wipe blood from her lip.

'Shall I go and fetch the doctor?'

'No point.' She tapped the side of the mattress. 'There's a box under me bed. You know – me box. You 'ave it.' She reached into her several layers of cardigan and nightdress and removed a key from her bosom. She pressed it into his hand. 'Open it later. There's yer birth certificate in there an' a few ovver fings, but not much. Yer farver . . .'

He passed her an ash-tray, a souvenir from Brighton, so that she could put her cigarette down while she coughed.

'. . . wanna know abart 'im?'

'I didn't think you knew much.'

'More 'n I've wanted ter tell up ter now. I got a lot of it from me mum and me sister.' She chuckled and the dewlaps shook, threatening to break away and fall on the quilt. 'Bloody funny story. It goes back ter the year dot. I dunno wot 'e'd be – yore great, great grandad, maybe – any'ow 'e was born abart 1870 an' married this, er, Ulrica Brunner. Ker-ker-ker. They 'ad these kids – where is it?' She felt under her pillow and withdrew a sheaf of tiny slips of paper, sorting through them. 'Ah. I've bin workin' it art, see. Yeah, Katrina, Jeremiah an' Franz. Well, Katerina married this Hendrik Persson geezer – a Dane or Dutchman or somefink – but on'y just in time – she woz awready up ther spart – by guess 'oo – '

'Jeremiah,' said Jerry with a sinking feeling. He had come to expect coincidences in life since he had begun to study the history of the Theatre.

'Yeah,' said his mother. Then she realized what he had meant and shook her head. 'Nar! Not 'er bruvver – 'er *dad*.' She winked at him. An ancient owl. 'Give us some o' that Lucozade, love. And put a drop o' gin in it.' He poured some of the yellow liquid into her gin glass. She sipped. 'Ur! Innit

542

'orrible? Well – ker-ker-ker – Katerina 'ad 'er baby an' this Persson feller thort it wuz 'is an' corled it, believe it or not, Jeremiah – in honour of 'er dad, see? Well, Franz marries a cousin corl'd – ' she picked another slip of paper from the shelf – 'Christina Brunner, right? An' they 'ave some kids, one of which is anuvver Cafferine, an' Jeremiah goes ter live wiv 'is married sister an' from wot me mum sez they 'as it away an' a little girl's the result – anuvver Ulrica. Then 'er bruvver goes ter Russia or somewhere an' changes 'is name to Brunner or Bron or maybe Brahn, see. Any'ow 'e meets this Cafferine Brunner later and they gets married, not knowing then that 'e's 'er uncle. They 'ave free kids they corl Frank, Jeremiah an' Cafferine an' 'e goes off again, back ter Russia. Frank marries a Betty Beesley, Jeremiah marries some German bint name o' Krapp, an' Cafferine marries a cousin corled, believe it or not Cornelius Brunner, an' she got one in the oven off 'er bruvver before she trips dahn the aisle. In the meantime Ulrica's grown up an' married anuvver Russian corled – this is funny – Pyat, but, from wot we worked art, she'd 'ad a kid by *er* dad an' it was brought up fer years wivart knowing its mum an' dad till someone tells it – it's registered, see, as Frank Brunner. Eventually Frank Brunner marries Jenny Beesley an' they 'ave two boys an' a girl. The girl does well for 'erself, goin' on ther stage, legit, an marryin' inter the foreign royal fam'ly – Princess Una von Lobkowitz, no less. An' then ther boys marry a Mary Greasby an' a Nelly Vaizey an' settle darn in Tooting or somewhere sarf o' the river, but Jerry's a widower in ther meantime, wiv a fair amarnt o' Krapp money, an' there's two kids – Alfred and Siegfried – 'oo 'ave ter change their name ter Krapp an' go an' live with there fam'ly in Germany, while Jerry comes back ter England an' marries a Greek girl, daughter of ther shippin' millionaire Kootiboosi or somefink. They 'ave free kids – Francesca, Joacaster an' Constant – an' live up Campden 'Ill somewhere. Francesca marries a bloke called Nye an' goes art ter India wiv 'im where she dies in childbirth – one son, Jeremiah. Joacaster marries a cousin, Johannes Cornelius, an' goes art ter Sarf

543

Africa, an' they 'ave a little girl, an' Constant marries a Katerina Persson an' thcy 'ave a little girl an' all, 'oo's up ther stick a monf after 'er first period, if wot I 'eard wos right, with 'er dad's daughter, Honoria – which *might* be me – in fac' I'm pretty sure it is. Well, you know a bit abart yore dad – 'e wos moody – 'e married me, I'll say that, though a good deal older'n me, but corled 'imself by 'is secon' name, Jeremiah, for ther weddin' an' I never woz sure it was legal – 'e scarpered o' course an' fer a long time I thort it woz 'cause o' ther coppers. Anyway, you free come very close tergevver, though yer might not 'ave all been 'is, or any of yer – yer could've bin 'is bruvver-in-law Frank's, 'oo I sor a lot of 'cause 'e – ther one wot married me – was orlways travellin' or lockin' 'isself away – or, I must be honest, *my* dad's, if it woz me real dad or me mum's – the ol' goat. 'E wos a kernewl, too, yer know, in Mexico, it woz, an' ovver places. Any'ow me sister Doris married a bloke corled Dennis Beesley (an' I sor a fair bit o' 'im while she woz doin' war-work) an' me ovver sister, Renie, married yore little mate Mo Collier's dad Alf – nice bloke 'e woz, killed in Germany 1946, somefink ter do wiv ther black market, wannit? Anyway, there woz a lot've ups an' darns rahnd abart that time an' I don't blame meself, though no one'll ever know exactly 'ow oo's related to 'oo – except we're sure as eggs related – we woz orlways a close family. Sammy, 'oo died, was Alf Collier's bruvver, an' they 'ad a Brunner, a Persson an' a Cornelius or two in there some-where, an' all. Well, ther's on'y a few *main* fam'lies in this distric', ain't there? Like over in Nottin' Dale they got abart free clans – 'Arrises, Sullivans and Kellys – it's ther same wiv ther Corneliuses, Cornells an' Carnelians rahnd 'ere – along wiv ther Brunners, Perssons an' Beesleys, though they woz never much compared ter ther Corneliuses 'oo really run these blocks for a 'undred years or more – since the Convent woz built an' there was on'y that an' the Elgin 'ere an 'undred years ago or so. An' they did well for themselves, some of 'em.'

'Where did they come from, Mum?' Jerry asked. 'Ireland?'

There were a lot of Irish moved in here, didn't they – because of the convents?'

'Some finks Ireland – but this area's orlways 'ad a lot o' immigrants in it – Dutch, Italians, German, Swedish, French – it's a common name. English an' all. Wot abart *that* fer a tale o' scandals, then? Incest on top a bloody incest, eh? D'yer believe it?' Her eyes glittered.

'Every word,' he said. 'I'm glad it's cleared up the mystery of my birth.'

She bawled with laughter. 'Yer sarcy sod! Ker-ker-ker.'

'Others did well for themselves, did they?' He frowned. His mother never took him seriously.

'Oh, yers. One got a knight'ood, one opened a department store, anuvver started a rest'rant – gold mines, ships, factories, greengrocers – yer've on'y got ter name it! There wos a doctor or two an' all – an' some of ther girls married inter the English aristocracy. They spread all over, ther Corneliuses!' She gasped and laughed again. 'Like muck! Like a fuckin' plague, eh? Har, har, har, ker-ker-ker-fuck!'

Blood really was coming from her mouth now. Jerry helped her sit upright. Her body shook. Her skin sagged as if she shrank within it. 'Oh, fuckin' 'ell. Oh, fuckin' 'ell, Jerry. 'Ere, did Caff tell yer?' She struggled. Her eyes ran with tears; her make-up smeared. She looked like an eight-year-old. She was full of fear. 'Did she? Don' let 'er 'ave it, Jer'.'

'Have what, mum?' He was distracted, holding her in one arm and trying to reach for the glass of Lucozade with his free hand. 'Eh?'

'Ther baby . . .' Her frame reared in his grasp. 'Yore fuckin' bastard baby.' She began to cough but was too weak. Her body quivered. The fear fled. She grinned. 'Yer got ter larf, incha?'

'Drink this, Mum. I'll go and get the doctor.' He was weeping. He knew she was dying.

She cuddled against his chest, like a baby animal. She sighed. It took him a few moments to realize that she had not breathed in. She grew cold. He kissed her stiff, lacquered

545

hair, the powder of her face, and then he was calm, standing up, pulling the sheet to her chin, kneeling to feel under the bed and pull out the box.

It was too dark to see properly in the bedroom and he did not like to turn on the light. He carried the cheap wooden writing chest into the other room and put it on the table in the window. He looked out, over the top of the area, through railings at the blocks of new flats. He shrugged and used the key to open the box. It folded back into a surface on which one could write, each half of the surface being the lid of a section. He pulled up the top flap, using the little loop of string his mother had nailed there, in place of the original tag. There was a bundle of papers amongst the cuttings of advertisements, beauty treatments, anecdotes his mother had accumulated or inherited from her mother. They stretched back more than a hundred years, to 1865. He took out the bundle and set it aside. He opened the bottom flap. There was a fairly new book there which he had brought while researching his part of a year or two earlier. It was called *Pantomime, A Story in Pictures*, by Mander and Mitchenson, published in 1973. He was puzzled. It was not like his mother to keep any book, let alone this one. Perhaps she had intended to sell it. He turned his attention to the bundle. He was very close to breaking down.

He fingered the papers, secured by rubber bands. He turned to call back into the cold, dark bedroom. 'Don't worry, mum – old Corneliuses never die – they just fade into someone else. There's too bloody many of us, eh?'

He was certain that he had heard her chuckle. He jumped up and went back to look into the bedroom, but she had not moved. She lay dead in her bed.

He returned to the table. He pulled the bands from the bundle. The bands were so old that they perished and fell away beneath his fingers.

He found some photographs, very faded, of himself and Frank and Catherine when they were children. They had been at Brighton and had had their photographs taken in a booth, poking their heads through holes above cut-out figures so that it looked as if they were three Pierrots, with children's faces and adults' bodies, on the pier. Their mother, standing beside them, looked far more innocent than her children, just as she looked now. She had been thinner, then, too. He found a marriage certificate for his mother's wedding. *Honoria Persson married to Jeremiah Cornelius at the Parish Church in the Parish of Tooting in the County of London on 22 July 1944 according to the Rites and Ceremonies of the Established Church after Banns by me, Wilfred H. Houghton, Curate.* At least he seemed legitimate, he thought. He could find no birth certificate for either his mother or the three children, though she had said his would be there. Perhaps she had been thinking of the marriage certificate. He found ticket stubs for his first appearance at the Prince of Wales Theatre as the vampire in *Soul of Frankenstein*, which had run for a week. He found ticket stubs for Catherine's early appearances in the Jupiter Theatre repertory company, where she had met Una Persson and Elizabeth Nye. There was a Royal Premiere programme for *Queen Christina*, the successful follow-up to *Camille*, which his mother had attended in full regalia, outshining anything the Royal Family could produce. There was a programme for *Twelfth Night*, decorated with a Heath Robinson jester and a phrase from the play – *A great while ago the world begun, With hey, ho, the wind and the rain. But that's all one, our play is done, And we'll strive to please you every day* – in which Una Persson had appeared as Viola and he as Sebastian. There were a number of other programmes and tickets, all of them connected with the careers of himself or his sister. There was a film company handout, giving the synopsis of a bad science fiction film in which he had appeared for a few seconds, as an extra, and on this had been scrawled a peculiar doodle, apparently in his own hand. He could remember nothing of it. He held it closer to the light from the window, trying to see if it made any sense at all. As he lifted it, his brother's staring face appeared, grinning at his with comforting malevolence.

547

Jerry got up from the table and went to let Frank in. He opened the door, lifting the handle so that it would not scrape on the floor as it usually did. 'She's dead,' he said.

'Catherine?'

'No, Mum.'

Frank made a small, unpleasant sound and went to check. Jerry again picked up the dirty hand-out:

He screwed it up and let it fall on the floor, then he called goodbye to his sobbing brother and left the basement, climbing aboard his Phantom, on his way to find Catherine. He turned on the stereo. The Beatles were singing *Hello, Goodbye* again. The sky was dark grey. He switched on the windscreen wipers. It was raining heavily. He, too, had begun to cry by the time he reached Greyfriars Bridge, on his way to Blackheath, the bearer of bad news for the mother of his unborn son.

— MICHAEL MOORCOCK
Notting Hill
April 1976

Appendix I

The following is reprinted from *The Nature of the Catastrophe*, London 1971:

The chronology begins with the convenient date of 1900, but there is evidence to support the existence of a Jerry Cornelius even in pre-Christian times (the first significant reference, of course, is the famous one in Virgil!) just as there is evidence to say he did not appear on the scene until much later. We are not here suggesting, for instance, that a child of one year could have been a spy during the South African War. The chronology merely lists well-supported references to Cornelius. It does not propose that they can possibly refer to the same individual!

The Compliers

1900
18 December
Birth of a boy, christened Jeremiah Cornelius, at the Bon Secours convent, Guatemala City. Mother died: father unknown. He lived in the convent until the age of about six when he was transferred to a monastery school some distance from the city. (Letter to David Redd of Haverford West from Sister Maria Eugene of the Bon Secours convent, who died in 1960).

1901
25 January
Boer War double agent known as 'Cornelius' caught and shot by a party of Boers under Commandant Pretorius, about two miles west of Jericho, Transvaal. (Despatch from Pretorius to Kruger.)

1903
9 April

Log of the *SS Maureen Key* reports picking up an English-speaking seaman in Bay of Biscay about noon. Seaman was adrift in small boat and was incoherent. Name: Jerry – possibly Cornell or Carnell, Carmelion or Cornelius. Was handed over to port authorities in Bilbao but disappeared shortly afterwards having stolen a coat and a piece of meat.

14 October

Catholic mission in Djelfa, Algeria, contracts plague of unknown origin and all die. Scrawled on the side of the confessional are letters JE CORNELIU, plainly recently written by the monk who had been acting as Confessor when overcome by the disease. (*Le Monde Catholique*, 30 October.)

1904
24 January

Programme of the Empire Theatre, Leicester Place. The Grand Spectacular Tableau, No 7 on the bill – 'The Treasure Island of Monte Cristo': the part of Edmund Dantes played by Mnsr J. Cornelius. At No 10 on the bill Mdlle Marguerite Corneille, Comedienne.

14 October

The St Petersburg uprising. A list of arrested 'foreign elements' issued by the Okharna (secret police) includes a Jeremiah Cornelius (thought to be a pseudonym). It is unclear whether he was deported or executed. (Burns Collection.)

1905
November

Reports from the Carpathian Mountains in Rumania that a bandit – 'perhaps an Englishman' – called Jeremiah Cornelius has been operating there for more than a year, organizing several bandit gangs into a single force. (Records of Transylvanian Central Police Bureau now at the Austrian War Museum, Vienna.)

1907
16 February
   Reference to a Jerzy Cornelius in list of thirty prisoners tried by military court as Socialist Democrat terrorists, St Petersburg. All found guilty and shot. (Burns Collection.)

8 July
   Rouvenjemi, northern Finland. A gang of criminals thought to be Russian nihilists rob several banks, a post office, several shops and are thought to have escaped by train. One suspect, a Russian Jew calling himself Bronsky, claimed that the leader of the gang was known only by the name of 'Cornelius'. The Russian thought the leader was probably a Swede. (*Dagbladet*, Sweden, 12 July.)

8 October
   'A young man of well-bred appearance, speaking Danish with a French accent, giving the name of Jeremiah Cornelius and his country of origin as Australia, formally accused of indecent assault by Miss Ingeborg Brunner at the 11th Precinct Police Station, Göteborg, last night. So far police have failed to arrest the accused.' (Despatch sent by Thomas Dell to *Sydney Herald*.) The story was not published, although a subsequent cable informed the newspaper that Miss Brunner had dropped the charges. (*Sydney Herald* correspondence files.)

12 November
   The journal of Yüan Shih-k'ai, Commissioner of Trade for the Northern Ports, China, notes the employment of a Captain J. Cornelius, described as 'an American soldier of fortune', to 'help in the training of officers for the Peiyang Army', Tientsin. It appears that Yüan Shih-k'ai's commission was later countermanded, but that an appeal to the Empress Dowager reinstated Cornelius, though his position

with the Peiyang Army became poorly defined. When, in 1909, Yüan was dismissed from office, his American protégé, on leave in Shanghai, disappeared. (*The Journals of Yüan Shih-k'ai*, edited with an introduction by Prof. Michael Lucy Smith, Collett Press, 1942.)

1908
19 February
   Calcutta. Aurobindo Ghose of the extremist Nationalist Party records that Tilak, leader of the party, sent 'a Eurasian called Cornelius with a message' to Congress leader Gokhale, a moderate. Gokhale never replied to the message which, Ghose thought, contained some suggestion of a secret meeting, but Cornelius was later arrested in a waterfront brothel where he had disguised himself as a woman. He was charged with the attempted assassination of Gokhale's close associate, Shastri. 'A meaningless action,' comments Ghose. There is no reference to the result of any trial. (Ghose, *India's Lost Opportunity*, Asia Publishing Co, Bombay, 1932.)

13 April
   Afghanistan. Despatch from Colonel R. C. Gordon commanding 25th Cavalry Frontier Force. Rumours that dissident hill tribes are united under a quasi-religious chief who appears to be of European or Eurasian ancestry and is referred to variously as Elia Khan, Shah Elia or Cornelius. 'A tall man with burning eyes who rides better than any tribesman and who has already cost us some fifty men, including three lieutenants and our Risaldar Major.' Colonel Gordon asked for reinforcements but died with the rest of his post when it was wiped out two days later. (Michelson, 'Lords of the North West Frontier,' *Strand Magazine*, April 1912.)

1909
30 March
   A man known only as 'the English assassin Cornelius' is arrested in Innsbruck after hurling a bomb at the Kronprinz

Frederik of Statz-Pulitzberg whose horse reared in time so that the bomb missed and exploded in the crowd. The assassin later escaped under circumstances which indicated help (or even orders) from someone highly placed in the government. (*Daily Mail*, 2 April.)

17 May

Secret dispatch from Captain Werner von K. (probably Koenig) dated Linz, 17 May, to Ludendorff of the German General Staff, Berlin: 'I am sending to you Herr Cornelius, who has convinced me that he can supply much exact information concerning our good neighbours!' (Records in Berlin Military Museum Document PRS-188.)

1910
29 January

Gustav Krupp writes to his chief ordnance technician Fritz Rausenberger: 'You were quite right to employ the Herr Doktor Cornelius. His efforts have contributed greatly to the speedier development of our new gun. Please convey to him the firm's congratulations.' (Krupp correspondence files.)

1911
22 May

Passenger list of the SS *Hope Dempsey*, leaving Southampton 22 May, bound for Rangoon, via Aden, Karachi, Bombay and Madras, gives a Mr Jeremiah Cornelius (who later disembarked at Port Said).

August

Sir James Keen, an amateur archaeologist exploring ruins in Chad, reports meeting a fellow Englishman in the town of Massakori. 'A tall, youngish chap, very brown, affecting native dress and living, apparently as the sheik's chief lieutenant, with one of the tribes of armoured nomad horsemen. He was civil, but reticent about his origins, offering me only his local name, which I did not catch.

However, I learned the day after he had left that he was regarded by the French as one of the most painful thorns in their sides and that the garrison at Fort-Lamy had orders to shoot him on sight, no matter what the circumstances. I was informed that his name was Gerard Cornelius and that he was a deserter from the Foreign Legion.' (*The Lost Civilizations of Africa*, Harrap, 1913, p. 708.)

2 November

Report of Lieutenant Kurt von Winterfeld, commanding a company of Protectorate Troops stationed temporarily at Makung on the Njong River, Cameroons, states that a European called Cornelius was shot while attempting to steal the steam launch serving the garrison. He had passed himself off as a German trader in order to board the vessel, but von Winterfeld suspected that he was an English spy. His body fell into the water and was not recovered. (*German Imperial Year Book for 1911*.)

1912
7 March

The Bight of Biafra. The *Santa Isabella*, a Portuguese schooner, hailed by a European sailing a dhow. The European gave his name as Cornelius and offered to work his passage to Parades, the ship's home port. In Parades Cornelius was believed to have transferred to the *Manité*, an American barque bound for Charleston via Boston. (Log of the *Santa Isabella*.)

1 June

Captain Simons of the *Manité* records loss of the seaman Cornelius overboard three miles off Nantucket in heavy seas. (Log of the *Manité*.)

13 November

Discovery of a cabin, recently built, on Tower Island, Galapagos, by crew of an Indian fishing boat blown off course and seeking shelter. No sign of cabin's occupant.

Indians frightened, left island as quickly as possible after one of them, a half-caste known as 'Cortez', had taken an empty metal box bearing the lettering 'Asst. Comm. J. Cornelius, Sandakan'. (Journals of Father Estaban, San Lorenzo mission, San Domingo, Ecuador.)

27 November

An English engineer Jeremiah Cornelius offers his services to help in the completion of the Panama Canal but cannot produce satisfactory references. He is not employed. Later, parts of the canal near Cristoban are dynamited. Colombian guerillas are suspected. Manager of the Company hears rumours that Cornelius is working with the Colombians. (Records of the Panama Canal Co.)

1913
5 April

United States troops in Nicaragua attacked by a well-organized band of 'nationalist' terrorists in several areas around Lake Nicaragua. US marines in Granada are wiped out and all arms, including several artillery pieces, stolen. Interrogation of suspects reveals that the terrorists are said to be led by an American, Jerry Cornelius. (Records of US Marine Corps.)

30 October

Peking. The missionary Ulysses Paxton mentions a conversation between himself and Liu Fang of the Methodist Episcopal Church. Referring to the possible conversion of the military leader Feng Yü-hsiang (later to be known as the 'Christian General'), Liu told Paxton that a certain 'Father Cornelius' had been responsible for Feng's interest in Christianity. Neither Paxton nor Liu knew of a missionary of that name in the area, though Liu had heard it said that the so-called 'White Wolf', a remarkably intelligent and powerful bandit leader who had taken to roaming north-central China in the wake of the Second Revolution, was rumoured to be an ex-Catholic missionary called Kang Na Lu ('Acting with High Resolve') or Cornelius. (*Devil against Devil* by Ulysses M. Paxton, Grossett and Dunlap, N.Y. 1916, p. 179.)

1914
Summer

The White Wolf, pursued by Feng's and other armies, is killed in Shensi during a pitched battle between his men and 'government' troops. Feng weeps beside the corpse and repeats the name 'Cornelius' over and over again. 'Later he ordered the body burned, but it had been stolen, presumably by survivors of the White Wolf's band.' (*North China Herald*, 25 August.)

1915
May

Rumours of the White Wolf's reappearance in Kansu. In Kungchang Mission, Father King, an American priest, lends rail fare to a fellow missionary, Father Dempsey, who claims to have been the captive of a bandit gang. Father King notes the initials J. C. on the other priest's bag. Father Dempsey claims that the bag belonged to a fellow missionary, Father Cornelius, who was killed by the bandits. Father Dempsey boarded train for Haichow and Father King comments on his surprising fitness, his apparent youth, his brilliant eyes. (Letter to Father King's sister, Maureen O'Reilly of Brooklyn, 8 June.)

3 August

During the famous Okhotsk Raid (thought to be inspired by Germany), two of the attacking gunboats were sunk before the defender's batteries were put out of action. The commander of a Russian launch heard the name Cornelius shouted several times during this engagement and gathered that this was the name of the officer in charge of the raid. He assumed the name to be German (although Germany continued to deny responsibility for the raid long after the end of the war). Upon the surrender of the garrison, the attackers disembarked, imprisoned all military personnel, and looted the city of most of its food, treasure and arms. The name Cornelius was heard by civilian witnesses who thought it referred to the tall man in elaborate Chinese dress who wore an ivory mask, carried no weapons, and appeared to supervise the pillage of Okhotsk. (*Report of the Official Committee Investigating the Fall of Okhotsk*, St Petersburg. March 1916, pp. 306–9.)

1916
4 February

Sale by Henrik van der Gees of Samarana, Java, of his estates (inc rubber plantations and tin mines) throughout the East Indies. To: Mnr Jeremiah Cornelius, a Dutch banker. The estate was the largest singly held property in the East Indies and was sold for a disclosed sum of eighteen million guilders. (Samarana Land Office records.)

17 August

The Cornelius estate made a public company, the managing director being a Francis Cornelius, believed to be the brother of the purchaser who has returned to Rotterdam. The chairman is given as a Herr Schomberg of Sourabaya. (*Die Gids*, Batavia, 20 August.)

1917
14 July

Parish register for St Saviour's Church, Clapham, records the marriage of Captain Jeremiah Cornelius, RFC, to a Miss Catherine Cornell, respectively of Nos 32 and 34 Clapham Common South. Captain Cornelius was on a forty-eight hour leave and returned to France immediately after the marriage. (Note: There is no record of a Captain Jeremiah Cornelius having served with the Royal Flying Corps.)

1921
6 May

The Interior Department of the USA leases naval oil reserves at Teapot Dome, Wyoming, to the Jeremiah Cornelius Company of Chicago. Various accusations in the press (notably the *Philadelphia Enquirer*) concerning the allegations that the founder of this company is none other than 'German Jerry' Cornelius, a notorious racketeer often considered to be a more dangerous, though less notorious, character than Dion O'Banion, of which he is a known associate. Thomas Redrick of the *Enquirer* disappears, presumed killed. The Cornelius Company continues its activities, although it denies any connection with criminal elements and claims that its president is 'travelling in Europe.' (*American Mercury*, 15 October 1923, p. 38.)

1922
1 March
The Munich Riots of February-March. Arrested as a 'socialist agitator' by the police, a J. Cornelius. Tried 3 March and imprisoned for thirty days before being expelled from Germany on his failure to produce papers proving his citizenship. (Munich Court Records.)

September
Rout of Greeks from Asia Minor by Kemal Pasha greatly facilitated by the tank company commanded by Major Cornelius, a South African soldier of fortune. (*Daily Mail*, 3 October, *The Sin of Pride* by Victor Manning.)

December
During the March on Rome a Geraldo Cornelius prominent in the Fascist take-over of power (for a short time he was editor of *Il Popolo d'Italia*) until assassinated 'almost certainly on Mussolini's orders' in December of the same year. (*Threatened Europe*, J. P. H. Priestley, Gollancz, 1936, p. 107–8.)

1923
July
Lithuanians capture Memel from the French garrison installed by League of Nations. 'The plan was successful almost entirely because of the work of the Dutch adventurer

Cornelius.' (French commander quoted in *Le Figaro*, 12 August.)

1924

21 January

Death of Lenin. A suspicion that he was assassinated on Stalin's orders voiced in the English-language *Exile* (14 February), a White Russian newspaper published in London and aimed at arousing sympathy for the émigré cause. Count Birianof wrote: 'Various Russian expatriates were approached by those who were plainly agents of the Bolsheviks and told that they would be given the opportunity to 'eliminate' the Red leader. It was so plainly the kind of trap we have become used to that all émigré organizations gave orders to their membership to pay no attention to the schemes. However we have reason to believe that a Levantine gentleman, originally of Kiev and familiar in the Whitechapel area as 'Cornelius the Nihilist' made it known that he would be willing to do the deed. Whether 'Comrade' Lenin died of natural causes (a guilty conscience, perhaps?) or whether he was killed, we shall probably never really know. However, if he was killed it was almost certainly by Cornelius acting on the orders of General Secretary Joseph Vissarionovich Dzhugashvili (who prefers to hide behind the name of 'Stalin') – a man with a greater lust for power than even his fanatical master knew! And what has happened to the nihilistic Jew? Dead, himself, by now, if we know anything at all of Bolshevik plots and counterplots.'

1926

27 February

Otto Klein shot on the steps of the Regensburg Opera House. After preliminary investigations, Regensburg police ordered the arrest of a tall, dark slender man of about thirty going by the name of J. (possible Johannes) Cornelius, a known member of the NSDAP. (Mackleworth, *The Return to Barbarism*, Gollancz, 1938, p. 18.)

18 April

Ernst Auchinek tried for the murder of Klein strongly denies that he had been known as Cornelius or that he has any connection with the NSDAP. He was hanged a month later. (Mackleworth, ibid, p. 22.)

1927
22 November

Leon Trotsky records a meeting with 'the man generally known as "Cornelius"' in Siberia, where they were both exiled. 'I was curious to meet this mysterious fellow, of whom I had heard much from Stankovich, in particular. He was undernourished and poorly dressed for the winter, but his eyes were hot enough to melt snow and he seemed singularly self-contained. I met him only for those few short moments before he was led away, but I had the impression that he was almost enjoying his imprisonment.' (Letter to Manfred Schneider, 5 June 1930.)

1928
April

Mount Chingkangshan, between Hunan and Kianri. Mao Tse-tung has retired here after his recent defeat of September 1927. He is joined in the spring by Chu Teh, who brings with him an occidental sympathizer called Cornelius. Mao and Cornelius discuss tactics for several days and Mao is much impressed by the man's knowledge of China, as well as his grasp of Communist theory and its application to the special problems of China. Mao offers Cornelius a position in the army he is planning to reform, but Cornelius disappears that night and there is some suspicion that he may, after all, have been a spy of the Kuomingtang. (H'ang Lean-li, *Two Paths to Freedom*, Routledge, Kegan Paul, London, 1940, p. 807.)

January-December

All Cornelius properties sold up in US and Britain.

1929
November

Wall Street Crash. 'Situation not improved by the sudden pulling out of Cornelius interests from many major companies.' (*Wall Street Journal*, 26 November.)

1931
December

Japanese invasion of Manchuria. British minister in Tokyo telegraphs London: 'Would suggest preparedness re rumours Japanese aided by English fascist associated with Russian émigrés here. Could prove embarrassing for us as basis for potential propaganda. The Englishman is said to be called Gerry Cornelius. Suggest you ascertain origins, etc, and speedily cable any information to here.' (6 December.) The telegram was acknowledged but its contents ignored. (*Imperial Policy in the Far East*, 1909–1939, C. W. Nolan, Samson and Hall, 1950, p. 506.)

1932
12 April

Body of a young man about thirty found in Thames near Hammersmith Bridge. Several stab wounds in the throat. A gold and ormolu striking watch marked *Thos. Tompion, London, 1685* on its inside case and on the inside of its outer case *Jerry Cornelius from his dear friend Southey, Keswick 08*, the only object discovered on the body. The engraving is of little help in identifying the body since it evidently cannot be addressed to so young a man. Records show that no such watch has been reported stolen. No further evidence comes to light and the case is closed for the moment. ('London Keeps Her Mysteries', *Union Jack* magazine, August 1934.)

1934
1 July

Secret message from Himmler to Hitler on morning after extermination of Roehm and SA supporters: *All cleansing*

561

operations successful. Only the Jew-lover Cornelius remains to be tidied away. (Night of Terror, Barry Hughes, Scion Books, 1951, p. 64.)

1935
March
One of the 'freelances' used by Mussolini in the Abyssinian campaigns of March is listed as Cornelius, a Dane. (*The Times*, 29 March.)

10 August
Arab Nationalists meet in Cairo for the third Secret Congress at which Comintern representative is present. Representative used name 'Cornelius'. (Adad, *Arabia Reborn*, Daker, 1962, p. 76.)

1937
18 December
Palestine. Jews and Arabs clash outside Qasr-el-Azak. British special patrol discovers corpses morning of 18 December. Among the bodies are those of two Europeans. One carries a revolver of unusual design and with no maker's name or registration marks. An inscription on the barrel reads 'From Catherine to Jerry'. The other corpse is that of a woman, very like the man in features and colouring. She has a similar gun with the inscription 'From Jerry to Cathy' on the barrel. 'The odd thing was that they seemed to be fighting on opposite sides.' (Report of Lieutenant Robert Gavin, Special Police, Palestine, quoted in Fennel and Harvey's *British Political Policy in the Middle East 1900–1950*, Benson and Bingley, 1958, p. 569.)

1938
14 September
Madrid. 'An offer was made through a Dutchman called Cornelius to supply us with 5,000 Mauser rifles and about a million rounds of ammunition. The Dutchman also offered tanks, planes and so on. We believed that he must be

representing a foreign government but he insisted that he was an independent dealer. He demanded 50,000 dollars (US) for his 'wares' which, of course, at this stage we were unable to raise. We learned later that he had sold the guns to the Falangists and that they had proved to be in a dangerous state of disrepair and caused a number of casualties before being abandoned. We concluded that the Dutchman had unconsciously done us a favour in preferring to deal with our enemies and we drank his health!' (Palero, *The Betrayal of Spain*, Independent Publishing Association pamphlet, 1948, p. 12.)

1939
5 January
Czech Ambassador in Copenhagen writes to his government in a despatch: 'I strongly recommend that you accept Herr Cornelius's terms and ensure speedy delivery of the arms he mentions.' (A. P. Peters, *The Day before Doomsday*, Viking, NY, 1960, p. 56.)

3 March
Ivan Jeczakowski, the Polish industrialist, acting as agent for his government, pays two million American dollars to the Brazilian arms dealer Geraldo Corneille on delivery of fifty British Mk 1 infantry tanks, in Warsaw. (A. P. Peters. ibid, p. 72.)

6 July
Passenger list for the SS *Kao An*, a Panamanian passenger steamer, leaving Southampton, includes a Mr and Mrs J. Cornelius, a Miss Christine Brunner, a Mr S. M. Collier and a Mr Gordon Ogg, all bound for Macao.

22 September
The British tanks sold by Corneille to Poland develop technical faults and are abandoned after one engagement with the German Army near Lodz. 'We placed too much reliance on them. They seemed to fall apart around us,'

reports the colonel in command of the regiment. (A. P. Peters, ibid, p. 106.)

1940
20 August

Assassination of Trotsky, Mexico City, by a Russian using the names of Jacques van den Dreschd of whom Trotsky had written just before his death: 'He claims to be a friend of Cornelius, whom I met briefly in Siberia. At certain times I felt they could almost have been brothers – particularly about the eyes.' (Letter to Marie Reine, August 1940.)

1946
Summer

Nuremberg War Crimes Tribunal. During their trials von Ribbentrop, Goering and Streicher speak repeatedly of a witness who will come forward in their defence. He is referred to sometimes as 'Herr Mann' and sometimes as 'Cornelius'. After being sentenced to death, they claimed that Cornelius has betrayed them. Unsuccessful attempts are made to trace 'Cornelius' but the only person of that name seems to be one of Himmler's astrologers believed to have committed suicide soon after the Fall of Berlin. (*The War Crimes Trials, Nuremberg and Tokyo* by Walter P. Emshwiller, Reilly & Knap, NY, 1949, p. 1003.)

1948
11 February

Assassination of Gandhi. Police seek 'a one-armed man called Cornelius' in connection with the crime. Cornelius believed to be an Eurasian living in Delhi. There is some information suggesting that he was a collaborator with the Japanese in Burma and that he had an Indian wife. All investigations prove fruitless. (Mehda, *What Killed Gandhi?*, Indian Publishing Company, Bombay, 1954, p. 40).

1949
14 March

Jerusalem. Israeli commanders interview a captured Egyptian spy Cornelius. He dies during questioning. (Uncorroborated report in *Freedom*, 12 October: *The Needless Agony* by Sandra McPhail.)

1953
May
   Kenya. 'One of the captured Mau Mau who had almost certainly been involved in the massacre of the Gordon family claimed that they had been led by a white man who had dyed his skin and posed as one of them. This man, said our prisoner, had been directly responsible for the rape of the two younger girls and their subsequent dismemberment. Several stories of this kind were circulating at the time but no evidence ever came to light to confirm or, for that matter, deny the rumours, though one of the Mau Mau leaders came up with the name of Jerome Cornelius, a businessman of Afrikaaner extraction, who had been lost in an aircrash the year previously. If a white man was directing Mau Mau operations in the Muranga district – which seemed to us highly unlikely, to say the least! – he must have made himself scarce soon after our big operation of June and July when the Mau Mau were virtually wiped out for the time being.' (James B. Bayley, *The Darkening Continent*, Union Movement pamphlet, 1956, p. 7.)

1954
3 June
   Angkor Wat, Cambodia. The bodies of five French soldiers discovered in a temple. They had been tortured. The sixth soldier was still barely alive. The torture was evidently the work of Cambodian terrorists calling themselves the Cambodian Liberation Army. Before he died, the sixth man claimed that the terrorists had been led by a European whom they called Cornelius (*Campaignes en Cambodie*, Versins and Henneberg, Gallimard, Paris, 1963, p. 98.)

1955
18 July
   Algeria. French intelligence contacts FLN officer who uses the pseudonym 'Cornelius' and gives information

which leads to the death and capture of nearly twenty important members of the FLN. (Peter B. Saxton, *The Sun is Setting*, Howard Baker, 1969, p. 103.)

30 July

Nicosia, Cyprus. Eight Cypriot terrorists are captured by British troops in the Hotel Athena. Before the captives can be transported to prison a counter-attack takes place and they are rescued. The only survivor of the raid is Corporal John Taylor who says that the raid was led by a masked man whom one of the captives addressed as Cornelius. (*Daily Sketch*, 1 August.)

1956
October

Suez Crisis. 'It was rumoured that Eden had received a report from a Foreign Office man in Cairo called Cornelius. The report advised immediate occupation of the Canal Zone. This report, so it was said, was what finally decided Eden to give the necessary orders.' (Sir Hugh Platt, *The Defence of Suez*, Collins, 1960, p. 17.)

10 November

Budapest. Russian and Hungarian secret police seek an Englishman believed to have taken an active part in the uprising of 23 October. He is sometimes called Cornelius. For a while the police place much importance on his capture and interrogate all imprisoned foreigners as to his whereabouts, but suddenly stop their investigations and no more is heard of him. (Richard Geiss, *They Went to Hungary*, Hodder and Stoughton, 1958, p. 400.)

1958
September

China's Great Leap Forward. European refugees cross from China to Hong Kong. Among them is a Jeremy Cornelius, half Chinese, half English, who disappears before he can be vetted by the authorities. (*Hong Kong Times*, 21 September.)

1960
Spring
   The Ladbroke Grove Murders in London. Within three months eight women disappear. All live in Ladbroke Grove. Two of them are found dismembered in the grounds of a disused monastery in Kensington Park Road, the others are found in Hyde Park. All corpses have the initials J. C. carved on their foreheads and the work is thought to be that of a religious maniac. The last corpse found has the slogan 'J. C. loves C. B.' carved into its back. Moses Collier, a labourer, confesses to the murders but further investigations and questions prove that he is mentally unbalanced and could not have been responsible for any of the murders. The case remains unsolved. (R. W. Eagen, 'The Killer's Mark,' *Weekend*, 4 July 1966.)

1961
Summer
   The war in the Congo. White mercenaries fighting for the Congolese are commanded for a while by a major Jerry Cornelius apparently a Belgian deserter. Later Cornelius disappears, believed killed by UN troops. (Alexander Charnock, *Twilight of Africa*, Hutchinson, 1965, p. 607.)

1962
20 November
   The Cornelius Realty Company of Key West buys large areas of land in Florida at a time when values are relatively low because of the Cuba Crisis. After the crisis is over, the company resells the land at 100 per cent profit and then dissolves. (*Business Month*, January 1963.)

1963
24 November
   Dallas, Texas. Police seek a Jerry Cornelius in connection with the assassination of President Kennedy. It is believed

that he is an associate of Lee Harvey Oswald and a young man known only as 'Shades'. The young man, it is rumoured, was heard boasting in a Houston bar that he was Kennedy's killer, not Oswald. After a fruitless investigation Police conclude that Cornelius and 'Shades' are inventions of Oswald. (*Time*, 11 December.)

1964
Spring
Sudden take-over of various large department stores in London and London suburbs by the Torrent Group of Companies. The Torrent Group is described as a partially owned subsidiary of the Cornelius Development Corporation of Chicago. (*Business Journal*, 15 June.)

1965
Spring
The Deep Fix, a pop group, go to No 1 with *Felt for You, Velvet for Me*. 'There's few would argue that lead guitar Jerry Cornelius is the group's real guv'nor and maybe the best white blues guitarist ever.' (Chris Marlen, *Melody Maker* 19 April.)

30 June
Bomb explodes in Alford Street, Dover, Kent. Several bodies found but none identified. The house was owned by a Mr J. Cornelius, believed to be one of those killed. (*Kentish Times*, 5 July.)

14 August
Thailand. A meeting of Chinese trade representatives with Bangkok businessmen. The intermediary is a 'Mr Cornelius,' a Belgian industrialist. (*Eastern Trading News*, 25 August.)

22 September
Death of a youth in Kilburn, stabbed in broad daylight in High Street. A gang of youths was seen running away from

the scene of the crime. An identification bracelet on the young man's body gave the name Jerry Cornelius. Police asked relatives or friends of the dead man to come forward but so far nobody has done so. (*West London Times*, 29 September.)

1967
12 December
'Police raided a flat in Chepstow Villas, Notting Hill Gate, last night and seized what they described as the biggest ever drug cache to be found on private premises. The occupant of the flat, a Mr Jerrold Cornelius, escaped from custody and has not yet been found. The police wish to interview him in connection with their enquiries. The drug cache included marijuana, hemp, cocaine, heroin and purple hearts as well as methadrine and dexadrine.' (*Guardian*, 13 December.)

15 December
Conference of Black Panther leaders in Kingman, Ohio. Minister for Special Activities is given as Jerry Cornelius – 'something of a mystery man even in Panther circles.' (*Newsweek*, 20 December.)

1968
13 January
The highjacked TWA Boeing 707 which crashed in the sea off Trinidad had a J. Cornelius listed among its passengers. There were no survivors. (*International Herald Tribune*, 15 January.)

17 December
Multiple crash on the M1 motorway near Luton. One of those killed in the Phantom V he was driving (and which was in head-on collision with an articulated truck) is a Jerry Cornelius, described as 'a young fashion designer.' (*Sun*, 18 December.)

(*Note*: Although the compilers have discovered other references to people who might be Cornelius since the last entry above, they have not yet been able to check the authenticity of these references and therefore prefer not to include them as yet.)

Appendix II

'What's the hour?' The black-bearded man wrenched off his gilded helmet and flung it from him, careless of where it fell. 'We need Elric – we know it, and he knows it. That's the truth.'

'Such confidence, gentlemen, is warming to the heart.'

The Stealer of Souls, 1963

'Without Jerry Cornelius we'll never get it. We need him. That's the truth.'

'I'm pleased to hear it.' Jerry's voice was sardonic as he entered the room rather theatrically and closed the door behind him.

The Final Programme, 1968

Appendix III

The captions to chapters in this novel are advertisements and headlines taken from the following source, most of them published 1975–76:

Jane's Weapons Systems, Interavia, Official Detective, Crime Detective, Official UFO, Guns and Ammo, Titbits, Weekend, the Guardian, the Daily Mirror, Horology Magazine.

The first four chapter headings referring to Harlequin are taken from productions staged betwwen 1716 and 1740 by John Rich at Lincoln's Inn Fields and Covent Garden. The fifth is from Charles Dibdin's Covent Garden production, Christmas 1779. These classic pantomimes consisted of a dramatic 'opening,' in which the main characters all wore oversized masks, on a theme usually taken from folklore, Romance or Classical Mythology – and which lasted for the first quarter whereupon, at a moment of tension in the plot, the characters would be transformed magically into members of the Harlequinade, to act out their parts in a fantastic, musical, satirical and symbolic manner and bring the whole entertainment to a satisfactory resolution. There were some 400 pantomimes of this kind staged in the 170 years between Rich's first production and the start of the modern pantomime which began to take its place from the 1870s and had almost completely superseded it by the 1890s.

The Broadsheet quotes at the beginning of the Coda section are almost all taken from John Foreman's excellent two-volume collection of fascimile broadsheets Curiosities of Street Literature (London 1966).

Muzak is a trade name for piped music used in restaurants, supermarkets, bars and other public places.

Stephen Donaldson

The Chronicles of Thomas Covenant, the Unbeliever

'Comparable to Tolkien at his best . . . will certainly find a place on the small list of true classics.' *Washington Post*

'An irresistible epic.' *Chicago Daily News*

'The most original fantasy since *Lord of the Rings* and an outstanding novel to boot.' *Time Out*, London

'Intricate, absorbing, these volumes create a whole new world.' *Sunday Press*, Dublin

The First Chronicles of Thomas Covenant, the Unbeliever

LORD FOUL'S BANE
THE ILLEARTH WAR
THE POWER THAT PRESERVES

The Second Chronicles of Thomas Covenant

THE WOUNDED LAND
THE ONE TREE
WHITE GOLD WIELDER

FONTANA PAPERBACKS

The Winter King's War

The Ring of Allaire
The Sword of Calandra
The Mountains of Channadran

An exciting new fantasy trilogy by
SUSAN DEXTER

To save the land of Calandra from the greed of the evil ice-lord Nímir, Tristan, a mere apprentice, begins a perilous quest where a thousand master magicians have failed . . .

FONTANA PAPERBACKS

Duncan Kyle

'One of the modern masters of the high adventure story.' *Daily Telegraph*

FONTANA PAPERBACKS

Fontana Paperbacks
Fiction

Fontana is a leading paperback publisher of both non-fiction, popular and academic, and fiction. Below are some recent fiction titles.

You can buy Fontana paperbacks at your local bookshop or newsagent. Or you can order them from Fontana Paperbacks, Cash Sales Department, Box 29, Douglas, Isle of Man. Please send a cheque, postal or money order (not currency) worth the purchase price plus 22p per book for postage (maximum postage required is £3.00 for orders within the UK).

NAME (Block letters) _____

ADDRESS _____

_____

_____